PORTRAIT OF A SCOUNDREL

Also by Nathaniel Benchley:

Novels
SIDE STREET
ONE TO GROW ON
SAIL A CROOKED SHIP
THE OFF-ISLANDERS
CATCH A FALLING SPY
A WINTER'S TALE
THE VISITORS
A FIRM WORD OR TWO
THE MONUMENT
WELCOME TO XANADU
THE WAKE OF THE ICARUS
LASSITER'S FOLLY
THE HUNTER'S MOON
PORTRAIT OF A SCOUNDREL

Biography
ROBERT BENCHLEY
HUMPHREY BOGART

Play
THE FROGS OF SPRING

Editor
THE BENCHLEY ROUNDUP

Junior Books
GONE AND BACK
ONLY EARTH AND SKY LAST FOREVER
FELDMAN FIELDMOUSE
BRIGHT CANDLES
BEYOND THE MISTS
A NECESSARY END
KILROY AND THE GULL

Motion Picture
THE GREAT AMERICAN PASTIME

PORTRAIT
OF A
SCOUNDREL

Nathaniel Benchley

DOUBLEDAY & COMPANY, INC.
GARDEN CITY, NEW YORK
1979

ISBN: 0-385-12893-2
Library of Congress Catalog Card Number 78-6361
Copyright © 1979 by Nathaniel Benchley

For Jamie, Virginia, Didi,
and all the other Greenleafs

NOTE

The basic facts of James Greenleaf's life are known, but the details must remain guesswork. The genealogist James Edward Greenleaf, who traced the family from 1574 to 1896, went to some length to obscure the last half of his ancestor's career, mentioning the early successes and then suddenly and inexplicably going into great detail about Greenleaf's Point, in Washington, D.C., on which stood the prison where the conspirators in Lincoln's assassination were hanged, thus leaving the reader with the suspicion that he wanted to fill the space but didn't want to discuss the subject. Various books on the early days in Washington mention Greenleaf, but mostly in the context of his financial and real-estate operations, and no Senate investigating committee yet conceived could unsnarl all the knots and tangles of those wildly manic adventures. The only hint as to what James Greenleaf himself was like comes from the mass of letters, both from and about him, that his brother Daniel kept, and even here (as also in his portrait) he shows two faces—the one he and a few friends saw and the one seen by the rest of the world.

—N.B.

PORTRAIT OF A SCOUNDREL

1

Chester Simmons sat at the desk that occupied one corner of his embalming room and stared glumly out the window at the growing city of Washington. The mid-September sun was hot and the rutted streets were caked and dry, but he knew that with the first autumn rains the city would again become a swamp and the matter of getting from one place to another a long and muddy struggle. He wondered, as he had so often recently, if he'd been wrong to move his business to Washington; he'd come in 1815, at the close of the disastrous war with Britain, when it seemed that the new capital, with its fires and its fevers and its plagues, would be an ideal place for an undertaker, but several others had apparently had the same idea, and after almost thirty years he had very little to show for his theory. What was needed was a good, rousing war, but the Mexican border was the only place where that might erupt, and Mexico was a long way from Washington.

Simmons glanced at the array of jars and bottles on his shelves —they contained such time-tested preservants as oil of lavender, camomile, turpentine, Venice turpentine, vermilion dye (which was for coloring rather than preserving), and assorted powders and spices—and he reflected that the art of embalming had changed very little in the last hundred years. It was said that the French and Italians were experimenting with such things as disinfectant gases, aluminum salts, zinc chloride, and bichloride of mercury, but only time would tell how effective they were, and in the meantime he'd stay with the older and less expensive methods. Simmons was basically conservative, although there were times when he had to admit he yearned for something different. Among its other drawbacks, his business had a depressing monotony about it—a day-to-day sameness with very few variations. When the good Lord made people, Simmons reflected, He neglected to build in any surprises for embalmers.

There was a knock at the door, and he rose and admitted a ragged messenger boy, who handed him a slip of paper and then stood, first on one foot and then the other, sniffling and wiping his nose with the back of his sleeve. The note instructed Simmons to come to the home of James Greenleaf, in the southeastern section of the city near the Anacostia River, and while the name meant nothing to him there was always the possibility of a good fee. He went to a closet and brought out his plug hat and black frock coat.

"Any reply?" the messenger asked in a clogged voice.

"I'll get there as soon as a reply would," said Simmons. "I won't detain you any longer."

The boy didn't move. "This service ain't free, you know," he said.

"I assume they paid you at the other end," said Simmons, buttoning his coat and smoothing the frayed cuffs.

"Well, they didn't," the boy replied.

Simmons's hopes for a good fee began to fade, and he dug in his pocket and produced a coin. "Here," he said, and handed it to the boy, who snatched it and vanished.

Luther, his assistant, was in the stable currying the mule when Simmons came in, and after one glance at Simmons's attire he put down the currycomb and began to harness the mule to the black-tasseled hearse. There was also a wagon, for the unceremonious collection of customers, but Simmons never wore his formal clothes when using the wagon, so Luther correctly assumed the hearse was to be used on this occasion.

"Anyone I'd know?" he asked, as he backed the mule between the shafts.

"James Greenleaf," Simmons replied, checking the hearse to make sure the equipment was all in order. "The name sounds familiar, but I haven't heard it in a long time. I think he was in business, or government, or something like that."

"Makes no difference what they do, we get 'em all in the end," Luther announced. It was his only prop for his ego, and he invoked it whenever a celebrity died. At one point, Simmons had thought of using it as the firm's slogan, but on sober reflection the next morning had discarded the idea. During his occasional, morose spells of drinking he had a tendency to think of ways of improving the business, but none of them ever withstood the test of cold daylight. He closed the back of the hearse and mounted the seat beside Luther.

"To the southeast end," he said. "By the river."

"Greenleaf's Point is down that way," Luther said, giving the reins a snap. "I wonder if there's any connection."

"By God, you're right," said Simmons. "This might be something worthwhile, after all."

Forty-five years before, when the city was being laid out, the area by the Anacostia River had seemed a likely place to build. But then the city expanded to the northwest, and the southeast began to deteriorate, leaving amidst the shacks and shanties a row of six red-brick Federalist houses, built by Greenleaf during the first rush of expansion and known, for reasons that became obscure, as Wheat Row. The houses, which had once been considered models of elegance, had deteriorated over the years until they now looked like smudged woodcuts of their former selves. The bricks were chipped and stained, the paint on the woodwork was cracked and peeling, and here and there tiles had skidded off the roofs and shattered on the ground below. Simmons stopped his hearse in front of the center house, and while Luther tethered the mule, he went to the front door, straightened his lapels and removed his hat, then tapped twice, discreetly, with the silver knocker. He heard footsteps inside and assumed his professionally mournful attitude.

The door opened, and a small, seedy man, wearing wire-rimmed eyeglasses and a rumpled dark suit, stood there. "I'm Dr. Eckman," he announced. "Come in."

Simmons turned and gestured for Luther to bring the carrying bag from the hearse, but Dr. Eckman stopped him. "No need for that," he said, with a gesture toward the adjoining room. "I have already ordered the coffin sealed."

Simmons looked into the dim, high-ceilinged dining room off the entrance hall and saw, in front of the fireplace, a plain wooden coffin with the top nailed in place.

Above the fireplace was the portrait of a man in eighteenth-century costume, with the high collar and full, lace-trimmed neckpiece. He was young, and the warm flesh tones made him look healthy and cheerful, but his face was too full to be really handsome, and the hint of a smile about his eyes and mouth gave him an expression that was more calculating than amused. It was as though he knew a secret that would someday confound the rest of the world. Then, as Simmons continued to look, he seemed to see two faces—or, rather, two expressions—one calculating and almost sly and the other gay and cheerful, like a youth on a holiday outing. He stared, fascinated, and the portrait smiled back at him, as though daring him to guess the secret. He turned to Dr. Eckman.

"Would that be the deceased?" he asked.

Dr. Eckman glanced up. "Yes. It was painted by Gilbert Stuart, some years ago."

"Remarkable," said Simmons. "A very interesting expression. And the flesh tones—one thing about my profession is it teaches one to pay attention to flesh tones. I always say, if you can give your subject the proper flesh tones, you can—"

"Quite so, quite so," said Dr. Eckman. "Should we get on with the business? I ordered the coffin sealed because Mr. Greenleaf died of a"—he lowered his voice—"I hope you'll keep this confidential—he died of an extremely contagious disease." He produced a piece of paper and handed it to Simmons. "The death certificate. If you read it, I feel sure you'll understand."

"The plague?" said Simmons, a note of hope creeping into his voice.

"No, no. Worse than that. Paresis." Simmons looked uncomprehending, and Dr. Eckman went on, "Tertiary syphilis. Throughout his body."

"I've done them time and again," Simmons began. "It's just a matter of—"

"There's a new theory that this syphilis is carried in the air," Dr. Eckman said, quickly. "Dreadfully contagious. Flies have been known to drop dead in the room where a patient is afflicted."

Simmons looked doubtful. "Very well, if you say so," he said. "What do you want me to do with the remains?"

"Bury them as quickly as possible." The doctor produced another paper. "This is the plot in the Congressional Cemetery. The monument should be plain, and the inscription should read

'James Greenleaf, born in Boston June 9, 1765; died in Washington September 17, 1843 Æ 78.'"

Simmons took the papers and made notes on the back. "And to whom am I to send the bill?" he asked.

"Mr. Greenleaf's brother, Daniel, who lives in Quincy, Massachusetts. He is in charge of the entire estate."

"There'll also be a fee for the messenger," Simmons said, as he wrote.

"What messenger?"

"The one you sent to me. I had to pay him twenty-five cents."

"That scoundrel," said the doctor. "I paid him fifty cents when I gave him the message."

Simmons looked up from his writing, and there was a short silence. "I still had to pay him a quarter," he said.

"That is no concern of mine. I have already paid him more than enough."

Simmons shrugged, making a mental note to adjust his fee to cover the cost of the messenger. "As you prefer," he said.

Between them, Simmons and Luther carried the coffin out and put it in the hearse. Estimating the weight of the deceased, Simmons theorized that the terminal illness must have been a ravaging one, because the coffin was so light as to feel practically empty. He could tell, from the odd way the weight seemed to shift, that it was in fact occupied, but he found it hard to imagine that the deceased was the same robust man he'd seen in the portrait. But then, if what the doctor said was true . . . He wondered why he hadn't heard of this particular form of syphilis, because he thought that by now he knew every symptom of passion's uglier penalties. He'd seen them all, but he'd never even heard of one that would kill flies across the room. However, the death certificate seemed to be in order, so it was no concern of his; he took over when the doctors had finished with their experiments.

By the time he reached his establishment, Simmons had decided to take one quick peek into the coffin, to see what this dreadful disease looked like. His professional curiosity was aroused, and the more he thought about it the less he was convinced that Dr. Eckman's warning was entirely warranted. After all, he, Eckman, seemed unworried about having contracted anything, and he must have been a great deal closer to the patient than Simmons intended to be. One look, and then he'd seal the coffin and notify the cemetery.

When the coffin had been placed on the embalming table he dismissed Luther, locked the door, then removed his frock coat and put on an old, stained, leather apron. Next he inspected the coffin nails, found a screwdriver, and pried experimentally at the lid. It raised slightly. He thought a moment, then produced a strip of linen, cut off a piece about eighteen inches long, soaked it in turpentine, and then bound it around his nose and mouth, tying it behind his head. The fumes were strong and oily and made his eyes water, but he felt there was no harm in the extra precaution. Then he set about prying the lid open, and the only sounds were the shrieks of nails and the gasping coughs as he breathed in the turpentine fumes. Finally the top came loose, and he raised it and peered inside.

The cadaver was that of a small, old man, naked except for a dirty shroud that had mostly fallen away. The skin was the color of dark wax and clung tightly to the bones, and a faint stubble of white beard showed along the angular jaw line. There were no visible signs of disease; there was only a long incision in the abdomen, roughly stitched together with black thread, showing where the viscera had been removed. Simmons stared for a long time into the coffin, then took the cloth from his face and began to nail the lid back in place. It's none of my business, he told himself; I don't get paid for identifying people. I get paid for putting them in the ground.

In the house on Wheat Row Dr. Eckman watched the hearse drive off and then mounted the broad staircase to the library on the second floor. Dark blue swags framed the windows, and the color was repeated on the sofas and the fabric chair seats. In one corner, an elderly man was seated at a small Hepplewhite desk, staring at a sheet of paper in front of him while he gnawed at the feathered end of a pen. He looked up as the doctor came into the room, and in his face was a faint echo of the portrait in the dining room. The cheeks were no longer ruddy and the hint of a smile was gone from the eyes, but the facial configuration was the same, and the lips were still full and soft. It was as though the man in the portrait had been kept for many years in a dungeon and had only recently returned to daylight.

"All is well," the doctor said, answering the unspoken question in Greenleaf's face. "He accepted the story without blinking an eye."

Greenleaf nodded and turned his attention to the paper in front of him.

"Are you still working on your obituary?" the doctor asked.

Greenleaf nodded again. "It's harder than I imagined," he said. "I try to make it impersonal, but I find I always seem to be defending myself. The odd thing is that two people can look at the same fact in two entirely different ways. *I* don't think I have anything to fear, but there are others—Webster, for instance . . ." His voice trailed off, and his face took on the blank look of suppressed hatred.

"He died last May," the doctor said. "No need to worry about him any more."

"So he did. I must try to be charitable. I was just using him as an example."

"Perhaps you shouldn't try to be so impersonal," the doctor suggested. "You have your side of the story, so why not tell it?"

"It might sound strange. An obituary written in the first person would have an odd ring to it."

"I didn't mean literally. I meant take the story as you see it and present it all as fact."

"It *is* fact!"

"Then what's troubling you?"

Greenleaf thought for a moment. "I simply want all the doubters to be convinced," he said at last. "I should like my name, once and for all, to be cleared."

"Your name. What good is your name once you're gone?"

"But I'm *not* gone! I want to see it cleared while I'm alive!"

Eckman put his hand on Greenleaf's shoulder. "Dear old friend," he said, "you have taken on an impossible task. Flatly and utterly impossible."

"Why? Are you implying that my—"

"I am simply saying that no two people can agree on what a reputation is. Shakespeare, you may remember, said that the evil that men do lives after them, while the good is oft interred with their bones. But Euripides, some thousand years earlier, said that when good men die, their goodness does not perish, while the bad is buried with their bones. If two men like that cannot agree, then how can you expect to solve the problem?"

"I don't want to solve anything. I simply want to clear my name."

The doctor shrugged. "It's your obituary," he said. "I was simply trying to make it easier."

"Very few men have this chance to set the record straight," Greenleaf replied. "I should like to make the most of it while I can."

"When do you leave for Quincy?"

"I wrote Daniel to expect me, but I left the date unspecified. When I've done everything I can here, I shall go by slow stages to Philadelphia, New York, and Boston, like a departed spirit revisiting the scenes of its—what should I say?"

"Crimes?" suggested the doctor.

"No, and not triumphs, either. Perhaps escapades would be the best word. And, like the spirit, I shall to all intents and purposes be saying farewell to this world. And I can't say I shall be unhappy to go."

"Especially since it's only to Quincy," said the doctor.

"Especially since it's only to Quincy. I keep thinking that one more try—perhaps in a new state, or even a new country—and then I tell myself it isn't worth the bother. I suppose that happens when you pass the threescore and ten: your time is all borrowed from the law of probability." He stopped and looked again at the paper. "But that isn't getting this written. I can't afford the luxury of introspection until I have myself properly buried, and my departure chronicled in the press. After that, I shall have all the time in the world."

Joseph Gales, Jr., coeditor of *The National Intelligencer*, took the envelope from the copy boy, broke the seal, and extracted two closely written sheets of paper. The writing was thin and spidery but the calligraphy was good, with only an occasional tremor to show the writer's advanced years. The lead sentence was cluttered and had apparently been written several times. It read:

> James Greenleaf, son of the late Honorable William Greenleaf, who was Sheriff of Suffolk County (Mass.) during the War of Independence, and nephew of the late John Adams, second President

of the United States, died at his home in this city on Sunday last, in the seventy-ninth year of his life.

Something had been written after the word "nephew" and then heavily blotted out, but by reversing the paper and holding it to the light Gales could discern that the words "by marriage" had been deleted. He continued reading the obituary, trying to make it agree with what he remembered of James Greenleaf, but there were few items that coincided with his memory. There was a certain amount of editorializing, in which a number of un-specified good deeds were alluded to as proof of Greenleaf's honor and probity, but in an obituary—especially of a person who had at one time been prominent—there was a tendency to forgive a little generalization. Survivors were listed as his widow, the former Ann Penn Allen of Allentown, Pennsylvania, and two daughters, Mrs. Mary Livingston of Philadelphia, and Mrs. Margaret Dale of Allentown.

When he had finished reading, Gales got up and went to the files, hoping there to find something that would fill in the gap in the story. He couldn't define it; he just knew there was a lot missing, and when he pulled out the envelope on James Green-leaf he was rewarded with nothing but a few scattered and inconsequential clippings. But the files didn't go back beyond 1800, when the paper was founded, and if Greenleaf was seventy-eight when he died, that meant he was thirty-five in 1800, old enough to have become newsworthy in any number of ways. Gales wished that his brother-in-law and partner, William Winston Seaton, was there; Seaton's memory retained a lot of the lurid material that the paper declined to print, while he, Gales, could remember every stick of type that had gone through the presses but no more. Together they had been reporters and official stenographers in Congress, and when they took over the paper from Samuel Harrison Smith, its founder, they brought with them a knowledge of the inner workings of Washington that was little short of encyclopedic. In fact, for many years they alternated as mayor of the city, one holding the civic job while the other ran the paper, and in spite of their obvious ability to turn out a scandal sheet, what they printed was quiet, staid, and stodgy, with no stories in the entertainment field unless they were newsworthy on other grounds. (The shooting in Ford's Theatre, twenty-two years later, was one example of the news outweighing the milieu.) The *Intelligencer* was known as "the court journal" or "THE Paper," and it had no competition. The only other newspaper in Washington was the *Globe,* which confined itself to the doings of Congress.

Returning to his desk, Gales reread the obituary and decided that what he remembered of Greenleaf probably wouldn't be material the *Intelligencer* would publish anyway, so he indicated that the name of the deceased be set in capital letters, to conform to the paper's style, and marked the story to be set in type. He also made a note to talk to Seaton at the first opportunity.

Two days later Seaton came into the office. He went directly to Gales's desk and, without preamble, said, "How did you know about Greenleaf?"

"A messenger brought the obit," Gales replied. "I'm glad you—"

"When did he bring it?" Seaton asked.

Gales thought back. "It would have been Monday," he said. "Why?"

"Because Greenleaf didn't die until yesterday."

"What do you mean?"

"The Philadelphia stage threw a wheel. He broke his neck."

Gales thought about this. "It must have been another Greenleaf," he said. "The woods are full of them."

"Another James Greenleaf?"

"Why not?" said Gales, in mild irritation. "Is it totally impossible there could be two?"

"I suppose not," Seaton replied after a moment. "Unlikely, perhaps, but not impossible."

2

James Greenleaf was just two months short of his tenth birthday when the local militia clashed with the King's troops at Lexington and Concord. To a ten-year-old the events were confused and meaningless; all he knew was that the adults were excited and had differing ideas as to what would happen next. When, in the evening of April 19, the exhausted grenadier and light infantry companies were ferried back into Boston from Charlestown, rumors and speculation filled the air like summer lightning. There had been a major battle in the back country, with the British forces suffering an overwhelming defeat; there had been a minor skirmish against the locals, all of whom had been killed or captured; John Hancock and Sam Adams were being returned to Boston in chains; Hancock and Adams had escaped to the western part of the state, where they were rounding up the militia for an attack on Boston. Those were the first, wild rumors; it didn't take long for the truth to come out, which was that a supposedly secret foray to capture guns and powder had miscarried, and the troops had run into opposition they hadn't expected. Beyond that, nobody knew a thing.

In the home of William Greenleaf, on Hanover Street in Boston, the atmosphere was one of combined excitement and apprehension. Greenleaf, a druggist, shipper, and merchant of considerable prominence, had since 1772 been a member of the secret "commission of seven," who corresponded with similar commissions in the other colonies on matters concerning the growing resistance to the Crown, and so dangerous was their business that they were in constant dread of discovery. They had signed a pact, swearing never to reveal their purpose or their identities, but they had no way of knowing if or when someone in another colony might betray them. Greenleaf, a tall, thin man with an upturned nose and a cherubic smile, was primarily concerned as to how the recent skirmishes would affect the work of his commission; few people had considered an active break with the Crown at this point, but if the reports were true, and British troops had fired on British farmers, then matters might be moving faster than had been intended.

Greenleaf's wife, Mary, had long ago learned not to worry about the future. A solidly built woman with a small mouth and a bulbous jaw, she had borne him nine girls and six boys, only one of each having died in infancy. With thirteen living offspring, ranging in age from twenty-five to three, Mary Greenleaf was aware that there were other things in the world than politics, and she saved her worrying for the crises that really counted.

Now, on this night when rumors were everywhere, she listened politely while her husband explored the possibilities of the future, but her mind was on the more immediate problems of the nine children who still remained at home. The four eldest daughters were already married with households of their own, but there still remained Sarah, who at eighteen was engaged to Dr. Nathaniel Appleton; William, fifteen, a student at Harvard but living at Hanover Street; and then, in descending order of age, Margaret, fourteen; Daniel, thirteen; John, twelve (who had been blind since the age of ten), James, ten; Rebecca, nine; Robert, seven; and Nancy, three. (The Greenleafs were fertile in the most active sense of the word: James's cousin Israel sired twenty-two offspring, and Israel's daughter Tilly had eighteen.)

"As I see it, we have two alternatives," James's father said, as he tapped the fireplace logs with a poker and sent a shower of sparks up the chimney. "We either stay here, or we move."

There was a short pause; then Mary said, "Move where?"

"Cambridge—Braintree—the Cape—Newbury." There were Greenleafs in all four places.

"But why? I'm sure you have a good reason . . ." The sentence faded away, as her mind tried to sort out the problems involved in moving her family.

"The reason is simple. Boston is a British garrison town."

"I know . . ." Mary didn't want to seem to be arguing, but she couldn't follow his train of thought. There had been British troops in Boston for a long time, and one way or another people had managed to live with them.

"If this becomes a war, we will most likely be treated as enemies. Any Whig, for that matter, will be under suspicion."

"A war?" It was as though she'd never heard the word before. "Who said anything about a war?"

"You never can tell. If these reports are true—" He shrugged his shoulders and turned back to the fire.

From down the street came the clop-clop of a trotting horse, and nobody spoke as the pace slowed to a walk and stopped in front of the door.

"I hope that's William," Greenleaf said. "I'd like to know what they've heard in Cambridge."

In a few moments the door opened and William came in, bringing with him a rush of cool air from outside. It had begun to rain and his hat and cape glistened, while his face glowed with excitement and the exercise of his ride. To young James, William was the epitome of manhood, a shining god who moved in an aura of wisdom and courage.

"What happened?" his father asked. "Do you have any details?"

"We waited for them, but they went the other way," William replied, with a broad smile. "If they'd come back our way, there'd have been a really good fight. We'd have had them trapped." He took off his cape and shook it in front of the fire.

"Perhaps you'd better start at the beginning," Greenleaf said patiently. "And please be more specific in your antecedents. Who, for instance, are 'we'?"

"The students. They came out around noon—"

"And who are 'they'?"

"The British. Earl Percy. He came out with reinforcements and asked the way to Lexington, and at first nobody would tell him. We all stood around like morons, pretending we'd never heard of Lexington, and then that tutor, Isaac Smith, spoke up and told him the way. Said he couldn't tell a lie. So away they went, and we all mustered in the Yard, waiting for them to come back, but instead of coming back through Cambridge they went through Charlestown, so we missed them. By this time we'd been joined by a lot of farmers and militia, so we had a fair-sized force. I wouldn't want to be in Tutor Smith's shoes right now. He's a very unpopular man."

"Do you have any idea what happened at Lexington?"

"They fired on the militia and burned some houses. I hear they went on to Concord, but I don't know what happened there. All I know is they needed reinforcements, and then they all came back in a hurry. We could hear the firing."

There was a short silence. Then his father said, "I think we might be well advised to leave Boston."

James felt a small thrill of excitement. He somehow equated leaving Boston with going out to fight the British, and if William had fought against them, then he wanted to, too. His mind had already translated William's account into a battle, of which William was the hero. He would be the hero in the next battle and would chase the British into the harbor. Through the haze of his reverie, he heard his mother saying, "When do you want to go?"

"As soon as possible. Today is Wednesday; do you think you could be ready by the end of the week?"

"Where will we go?"

"I'll have to find out. Cousin Isaac lives in Cambridge, which is closest, so we'll try there first. Otherwise, Braintree or Newburyport. The Cape is too far, and I hear Nantucket is becoming a haven for Tories."

"I thought they were Quakers."

"That's why the Tories are going there. In case of war they'll probably be neutral."

Mary Greenleaf sighed, and rose. "If we're going to leave so soon, I can't be sitting here like a bump on a log," she said and left the room.

But the following day General Gage closed Boston to all traffic, both coming and going, and the Greenleafs went nowhere. The town was like a gigantic clam, which had snapped shut on a stimulus from outside and was waiting for the danger to pass before opening its valves to test the water around it. People moved cautiously, as though afraid to upset some unidentified balance, the Rebel sympathizers afraid of being jailed and the Loyalists afraid of a massive attack from the surrounding countryside. In the Wednesday skirmish, the grenadier and light infantry companies had lost seventy-three killed, a hundred and seventy-four wounded, and twenty-six missing and pre-

sumed dead, which, considering the fact that they had expected
little or no resistance, showed that someone had misjudged the
mood and firepower of the locals.

Mary Greenleaf suspended her packing, on the theory that
until they knew they were going they might as well live in comfort, and the family settled down to a period of uneasy waiting.
William fretted at his inability to return to college but his
mother was secretly glad, because she preferred having him
where she could keep an eye on him and not gallivanting around
with a lot of wild-eyed Harvard students who might take it into
their heads to do the Lord knew what. She was thankful that
James was too young even to think of bearing arms because, although she wouldn't admit it to herself, James was her favorite
of all her children. By refusing to admit it she didn't have to
define the reason, and the reason was too slippery to bear close
scrutiny. He was a beautiful child, but that was only a surface
attribute; he had a simple and almost devout faith in everything
she did, but that didn't necessarily set him apart from the others;
his worship of his brother William made him somehow vulnera-
ble and in need of protection, but no ten-year-old is self-reliant;
and he had almost died in infancy, but two of her other children
had died and she had built up a shell against that kind of grief.
There was one thing about him that made her nervous, and that
was his conviction that he could do anything he wanted; the idea
of failure never occurred to him, and he would unhesitatingly do
whatever came into his head. She once had found him
perched on a window sill (luckily, on the ground floor) with his
arms spread in an attempt to imitate a seagull, and it had taken
her a half hour of frantic explanation to convince him that the
difference between people and birds was fundamental and
created by God and was not to be tampered with. In sum, her
concern for James was a combination of reasons, and no matter
how hard she tried to maintain an even balance, it was always
James she thought of first and James about whom she worried.
John, with his blindness, was in a wholly different category, because fate had already dealt him a blow and he had survived.

On the first Sunday following the battles (what had originally
been referred to as "random skirmishes" and a "forced march"
had now been upgraded to full battle status) there were only
two or three religious meetings in all of Boston, a town that usu-

ally made the Sabbath loud with the pealing of church bells. At a town meeting, held Sunday morning, a group of selectmen were chosen to call on General Gage and see what arrangements could be made for the departure of those who wanted to leave, and for the next few days negotiations were carried on to determine under what conditions they would be allowed to go. Finally, after a good deal of haggling, it was announced that as of Friday anyone who wanted to leave could do so, taking as much merchandise and personal effects as desired, provided only that all arms and ammunition be left behind and the departing citizens promise not to act in any way against the King's troops. The selectmen would receive the arms and ammunition, which would be held under guard pending further developments.

There were two ways to get to Cambridge: one was to ferry across the Charles River and the other was to go overland south of the Charles, through the narrow neck between Boston and Roxbury, thence across the Muddy River through Brookline and over the Great Bridge and into Cambridge. The latter was the route Earl Percy had taken on the nineteenth, when he came out with reinforcements to Lexington, and it was the route William used in getting to and from college. The ferry trip would have been shorter, but because of all their equipment the Greenleafs were forced to take the overland road, along with most of the other refugees. They left at daybreak on Saturday, and when they got to the sentry post at Roxbury Neck they found a milling crowd of people, and the shrill sounds of hysteria could be heard beneath the over-all noise. Greenleaf sensed without being told what had happened: the town had been sealed off again, and nobody was being allowed either in or out. He sent William ahead to confirm the fact, and William returned with the word that it was indeed true and that nobody knew when the ban might be lifted. Also, nobody knew the reason; the officer in charge would say only that it was General Gage's orders and that nothing—not even food or provisions—would move until further notice. The town was already short of food, with salt pork selling for elevenpence sterling the pound and fresh pork at ninepence, and if the embargo continued for any length of time, the situation would be desperate. The Greenleafs returned to their home in total silence, and when they had unpacked the wagon Greenleaf looked at his wife.

"I can think of only one thing," he said. "Stephen may know the facts and be able to advise us. He's the only person to whom I can turn."

His brother was twenty-one years older than he and was second eldest of the thirteen children of the Reverend Daniel and Elizabeth Greenleaf. Now, at seventy-one, he was senior to seven of his eight surviving siblings and maintained relations with his family that were stronger than any surface political differences. He had recently tried to resign his commission as Sheriff of Suffolk County, but no suitable replacement had been found so he continued in the office, discharging his duties with competence but not aggressiveness. His background made him a Tory, but his instincts told him something new was afoot, and while he couldn't join it, he didn't want to oppose it. He steered the middle course and hoped for the best.

He was in his parlor, which fronted on the Common, when his brother William knocked on the door and entered. From outside came the sounds of the troops drilling, and Stephen gestured for William to close the door.

"Greetings, brother," he said, as William came into the parlor. "I thought you might be gone by now."

"It's not for lack of trying," William replied. "We were too late to get out yesterday, and now we hear the town is closed again."

Stephen nodded. "Sit down. You must be tired."

"I'm not tired," William said, taking a chair. "I'm thoroughly irritated. Do you know the reason behind all this?"

Stephen nodded again and smiled. "The military mind is a strange and wonderful thing," he said. "What with all the bickering and petty jealousy, it's a wonder that battles are ever fought, much less won."

"How does that apply here?"

"Well, General Gage—who is, after all, Governor of the Province—gave permission for a certain number of, uh, patriots to leave the town. Some of them, with complete logic, ferried across the Charles rather than take the long way around, and when Admiral Graves heard about this he was furious, saying that the water was his province and nobody might cross it without orders from him. So General Gage withdrew his permission, and there you are. You, who want to leave, and others, who prefer the shelter of Boston to being exposed to the patriots, must stand around and wait, while the Army and the Navy play their childish little game. Take my advice, William, and whatever you do, don't trust your cause to a military man. I have no idea what the future holds, but if you put your faith in a military man, you are doomed."

"There's small danger of that," William replied. "I should think Dr. Warren would be our most likely leader." As an afterthought, he added. "Wherever it is we're going."

"Not Hancock or Adams?"

William shrugged. "They've made many enemies. Dr. Warren is beloved by everyone."

"Not, you may be sure, by the Loyalists."

"I'm sure not. Where does your family stand in all this? How do the children feel?"

"As you might expect. Elizabeth's husband is a captain in the Royal Navy. Anstice's husband is a merchant and loyal through and through. And Abigail is married to that supreme court judge in South Carolina, who after all owes his appointment to the Crown. I'm not sure about Mary, but all the others are solid Loyalists—or, if you prefer, Tories."

"Including yourself."

"I've lived too long to change, William. If I were to switch my allegiance now, I should feel not like a patriot but a turncoat. I have no choice."

"I suppose you're right. Well"—William put his hands on his knees and stood up—"I must go back to my family, and tell them to be patient a little longer."

"My respects to your lady wife, and love to the children."

"Thank you."

"How's Jamie?"

"Fine. Why?"

"I don't know." Stephen smiled. "There's something about him —he intrigues me. He's a very winning child."

"Of that, he is all too well aware."

"It's more than that. I think you may hear great things from him one day."

"A consummation devoutly to be wished." William held out his hand. "Brother—" He paused; then said, "If I don't see you again . . . may God keep you."

Stephen rose and took his hand. "Let us hope this will be over soon," he said.

"Amen." William jammed his cocked hat onto his head, picked up his gold-headed cane, and left. The sounds of the soldiers were loud as he opened the door, then faded as he closed it behind him.

3

James's memories of the first year of the war were spotty. From Cousin Isaac's home, in Cambridge, he remembered hearing the distant cannonading on June 17 and rumors of a battle going on at Breed's Hill, in Charlestown; he remembered the troops parading on the Cambridge Common, in early July, in honor of the new commander-in-chief of the Continental Army; he remembered the occasional sounds of bombardment as floating batteries and ships known as "Washington's cruisers" sailed down the Charles, lobbed a few shells into Boston, and then returned; and he remembered the stories of hunger, sickness, and misery relayed by escapees from the besieged town.

On October 4 Harvard resumed classes, in Concord, and William was one of the hundred or so students who were boarded in taverns, private houses, and whatever rooms could be found. It was the first time he'd been away from home for any extended period, and his departure was an emotional one. Mary carried on as though he were going into the army, his father offered to escort him part of the way, and Daniel and James begged to be taken along. In the end he went alone, and his mother stood outside and watched him until he was out of sight. When she came back into the house, her eyes and nose were red.

"It isn't as though he'd gone forever," Greenleaf told her, gently. "He'll be home at Christmas time, if not before."

She shook her head. "Every time he leaves, I feel it's the last time," she said.

"Madam, please be rational. There is no possible reason to have such a thought."

"Reason or no, I have it. I can't help it."

Cousin Isaac, who was sitting in a corner, spoke up. "If you ask me, he ought to be in the army. No college can do for a man what the army can, and I ought to know. I fought with this fellow Washington down South in the French and Indian War, and it was the best thing ever happened to me. I was thirty-five years old and good for nothing, and I'd probably have gone on being good for nothing if it wasn't for the army. Made a man out of me overnight."

James tried to visualize cousin Isaac as a worthless thirty-five-year-old, but he couldn't make the picture fit. All he could see was himself and William in the army, marching forth to fight the British.

Mary looked at Cousin Isaac coldly. "William isn't thirty-five," she said. "He's only fifteen."

"All the better. A man's never too young for the army."

Mary started to reply, then turned and left the room.

On the last day of October, two men appeared at the house and asked to see William Greenleaf. James had opened the door, and when he saw their solemn faces and official manner, his first thought was that they were bringing bad news about his brother William. He scurried through the house and into the back yard, where his father was helping Cousin Isaac replace the worn stirrup leathers on an old saddle, and announced the presence of the two men in a breathless jumble of words. His father put down the leather punch, wiped his hands, and followed James into the house, where the two men were in the front hall. Mary had come to greet them and had invited them to sit down, but they remained standing, stern and forbidding, until Greenleaf came in. Then one of them gestured to an adjoining room and the three men went in, closing the door behind them. James and his mother stood in the hall, both of them wanting to eavesdrop but, in Mary's case, afraid of being caught at it. James had no such fear; he tiptoed to the door and put his ear against it, but his mother pulled him away and took him with her into the kitchen.

"We'll know soon enough what it's about," she said. "If it's good news, it'll keep, and if it's bad, we're that much happier not hearing it."

It seemed that the men were there a long time, but finally James heard their voices in the hall, and then the front door opened and closed as his father let them out. In a couple of moments his father appeared in the kitchen, a faint smile on his cherubic face. "Mrs. Greenleaf," he said, "I should like to introduce you to the Sheriff of Suffolk County."

Mary looked at him, uncomprehending. "You mean Stephen?" she asked. "Where is he?"

"I mean me," he replied. "I have just been appointed by the Governor and Council to be Sheriff of all of Suffolk County except Boston, where we presume Stephen is still holding forth."

Mary gasped, then began to laugh, and dropped him a deep curtsey. "I am delighted to meet you, your honor," she said. "Pray sit down and permit me to pour you a cup of tea."

"Thank you. I shall." He took a seat at the kitchen table and looked out the window. "This war does strange things," he said at last. "Who ever could have guessed it would work out this way?"

Mary paused, then said, "I keep hoping it won't be a real war."

"That's all it can be. We've come too far to turn back."

"I suppose you're right." She poured the tea, then glanced at James. "At least Jamie won't be in it," she said. "It will be over and settled long before he's old enough to bear arms."

"You do have other sons," her husband reminded her.

"Of course, but—" Mary found herself groping for words and trying to visualize what James would be like in the army. All she could think of was the time he'd tried to imitate a seagull, and translating that into military terms, she could see him rushing singlehanded at a troop of cavalry or leaping a parapet into an enemy trench. "After all," she ended lamely, "Jamie is practically a baby."

"I am not!" James put in, in his shrill voice. "I can shoot like anyone else!"

His father reached out a hand and rumpled James's hair. "Of course you can," he said. "But if the good Lord is willing, you won't be called upon to do so." His mother left the room while his father blew gently on the tea, sipped it, and then looked again out the window. There was a long silence before he said, "Your Uncle Stephen thinks you're destined to do great things."

"What does 'destined' mean?" James asked.

"That it's your fate—your future. Any man can bear arms, but only a very few are great."

"How does Uncle Stephen know?" said James.

His father shrugged. "He's a wise man and has lived a long time."

"Then why is he a Tory?"

His father took another sip of tea, considering the answer. "He has no choice," he said at last. "But that doesn't mean he isn't wise."

That winter was an unusually severe one, although the people in Cambridge and the surrounding countryside didn't feel it as acutely as those in Boston. There, the food, clothing, and fuel dwindled almost to the vanishing point; the King's stores were not enough to feed the troops, let alone the civilians; and people were finally reduced to tearing down derelict houses for firewood. At first this was done with military precision but later the plundering became general, and no fence, tree, or abandoned house was safe from scavengers. The branches of the trees on the Common were long since gone; they had fed the cooking fires in the late summer and early autumn. To cap all the other miseries, smallpox broke out, but the British command considered this almost a blessing, because they felt it would insure them against attack from the outside. The troops were inoculated, so it was the citizenry who, as usual, suffered the most.

Early in March 1776 rumors began to circulate that Washington was planning an attack on Boston, but before any action occurred, the British abandoned the town. On March 17 the harbor turned white with sails, as twelve thousand troops and loyal citizens boarded ships and moved down Boston Harbor as far as Nantasket Roads, where they hovered for more than a week as though wondering where to go next.

Because of the recent smallpox, Washington would allow only those troops into town who had already had the disease, but he had no control over civilians, and the Greenleaf family loaded their wagon and moved back to Boston the day after the British evacuation. On all sides they saw other families who were doing the same, and their return was like their exodus in reverse, with elation replacing the gloom of the previous year. The mood of the town was one of rejoicing, but the surroundings were bleak and chaotic. Everywhere were military stores abandoned after only a cursory attempt at destruction; shops and warehouses had been broken open and their contents strewn about the street; rugs, blankets, and crockery were intermingled with artillery shells, shattered caissons, and hastily spiked cannons. Skeletal dogs and mangy cats roamed the alleys, scouring the debris for anything edible. The whole town smelled of wood smoke, ashes, and excrement.

The family skirted the eastern edge of the Common, and as they approached Stephen's house, Greenleaf wondered if his brother was still there or if he was one of those who had embarked in the ships that even now could be seen anchored in the lower harbor. He was so preoccupied with Stephen's fate that he didn't notice a group of four horsemen coming down a side street, and he reined in just in time to avoid colliding with them. They wore long capes over their military uniforms, and the shiny metal on their harnesses and sword belts made a faint jingling that contrasted with the creak and groan of their leather equipment. When they had passed, Greenleaf flicked the reins and his horse leaned forward, starting the wagon once more on its way.

"That was General Washington," he said.

"Who?" said Mary. "Which one?"

"The one in the middle. The rest were his staff."

She thought for a moment. "He seemed tall, for a Southerner," she said, then lapsed into silence.

Some of the wealthy Tories had left their women behind to protect their property, while others had fled with their whole families. Their houses stood empty, windows hastily shuttered and doors standing open or swinging in the wind. Here and there the Greenleafs saw evidence of looting and vandalism, and as they wound through the narrow approaches to Hanover Street Mary could contain herself no longer. Looking down at Daniel, who was walking beside the wagon, she said, "Daniel, run on ahead and see if the house is still there. The suspense is more than I can bear."

Daniel and James broke into a run, and they raced down the street with the speed of a cavalry charge. They rounded a corner and saw that their house was still there, tilting slightly out over the street as it always had. It looked at first to be intact, but then they noticed that the front door was open a crack, showing a black interior that seemed as deep as a cave. They approached cautiously, their hearts pounding, and Daniel stood in front of the door and tried to see inside. James peered from behind him, ready to dart away like a rabbit if something should come out, but the house was quiet and empty, and nothing moved. The sour smell of smoke hung in the air. Cautiously, as though stalking a butterfly, Daniel reached out and touched the door, and it opened wider. In total silence the boys went inside, and the room they entered was all but unrecognizable. The ceiling above the fireplace was blackened with smoke, and sticks of half-burned furniture lay scattered about the hearth. The walls were scarred by graffiti carved with a knife or bayonet, and filthy straw covered most of the floor. A pile of straw in one corner was strewn with rags, and a split and rotting boot lay among the debris. The room reeked of urine. The boys stood, stunned and speechless, until they heard the sound of horses outside, and their parents appeared in the doorway. Their mother gasped as though stabbed, and their father silently put his arms around her shoulders. For a few moments nobody spoke, and then their father said, "Well, at least they left us the house."

Mary Greenleaf straightened up and turned back to Sarah, who had started to unload the wagon. "That can wait for a while," she said, as Sarah brought an armful of bedding toward the house. "We'll have to tidy up a bit before we settle in."

On June 21 Harvard returned to Cambridge and then immediately broke for summer recess, allowing William once more to come home. He entertained his family with stories about the winter in Concord and of the ceremony on April 3, when the college awarded an honorary degree to George Washington. The general, who was on the point of leaving for New York, had other things on his mind than a piece of parchment from a New England college, and the whole ceremony, according to William, had an air of superficiality about it that not even the ponderous Latin of the pedagogues could make impressive. Almost as an afterthought, he dropped the information that he had decided to become a doctor and would take up the study of medicine following his graduation a year hence. His mother welcomed the news because it would keep him from being a foot soldier in the army; his father was pleased because to be a real doctor was a cut above being a druggist, who customarily used the same title; and James saw it as one more jewel in William's already incan-

descent crown. He decided that he, too, would be a doctor when
the time came, and he would help William care for the victims
of the next plague. The plague was, if less frequent, as inevitable as the sunrise, and it was a time when doctors seemed to
stand out from lesser mortals, immune to the ravages of the disease. This idea appealed to James, because he could help hu-
manity with no real danger to himself and possibly achieve a degree of greatness. The early Christian martyrs, who died for their
causes, held no appeal for him at all; it was no good to become a
saint or a savior if the recognition was posthumous.

For the moment, however, it was Greenleaf Senior who became the center of attention. Early in July the Continental
Congress, sitting in Philadelphia, had, after considerable wrangling, issued a Declaration of Independence from the British
Crown, and the next step was to have it disseminated throughout
the various newly proclaimed states. A committee of the Massachusetts Council, consisting of John Winthrop, William Phillips,
and Francis Dana, met on July 17 and decided that the Declaration should be read from the balcony of the State House in Boston at 1 P.M. the following Thursday, July 25, by the High
Sheriff of the County of Suffolk—in other words, William Greenleaf. Stephen had, to his own great relief, been removed from
office, but because of his generally amiable conduct he had been
allowed to stay on in his own home, untroubled by even the
most vindictive patriots.

Thus Greenleaf had one week in which to study the document
and practice its delivery. The first time he looked at it he was not
impressed; the signatures seemed to take up more space on the
page than did the text, and he was amused to see the gigantic
size and arrogant flourish with which Hancock had signed his
name. It looks as though John has at last found his métier, he
thought. Two years ago he was a failed merchant, eleven thousand pounds in debt, bereft of credit, and forced to sell his ships,
and now here he is, the boldest of the patriots, pledging his Life,
his Fortune (what fortune?), and his sacred Honor to the cause.
I guess the good Lord has a place for every one of us, and some
of us take longer than others to find it.

Greenleaf knew that the good Lord had not intended him to
be a public speaker. For one thing, his voice didn't carry well,
and for another, he felt he distorted the meaning of words if he

shouted. So he was always trying to balance his voice between a reasonable inflection and enough power to project it, and the result was more pulsating than intelligible. Still, he felt that with a week in which to rehearse, he could achieve an acceptable compromise, and with Mary's coaching he might even be able to bring out the drama and historical importance inherent in the document.

Mary sparkled with enthusiasm for the project. "It will be an honor," she said. "And to make it more lifelike, we can have the children as an audience."

"Will that be absolutely necessary?" he replied.

"Why not? If you are to speak from the balcony of the Town House—"

"It is called the State House now," he reminded her.

"Whatever it is, there will be a big audience. The streets will be full of people—crowds of people—"

Greenleaf closed his eyes. "Very well," he said. "Bring in the children. I might as well get used to it now as later."

The children were gathered in the main room, the walls of which still bore the scars of its occupation by the troops. Some of the furniture had been replaced, but there were not enough chairs for them all and the younger ones sat on the floor. Their father stood behind the long trestle table, holding his lapels and studying the paper in front of him. He looked up at them and said, "'When in the course of human events, it becomes—'"

"Remember to speak up," his wife told him.

"'—necessary for one people,'" he went on, more loudly, "'to dissolve the political bonds which have connected them with another and to assume among the powers of the earth the separate and equal station to which—'"

"I saw Billy Cranch today," Daniel whispered to James, referring to their seven-year-old cousin. "He wants to see you."

"What for?" James whispered back.

"Boys!" their mother said, loudly. "Be still!"

"'—the laws of nature and of nature's God entitle them'"—Greenleaf was beginning to hurry the words—"'a decent respect to the opinions of mankind requires that they should declare the causes which impel them to the separation.'" He paused, taking a breath for the next paragraph.

"Try not to bunch your words together so much," Mary said. "Space them out a little."

"'We hold these truths to be self-evident,'" Greenleaf intoned, as though writing each word as he spoke it, "'that all men are created equal, that they are endowed by their Creator with certain unalienable rights—'"

"What does 'naileable' mean?" James asked.

"Quiet!" Daniel bellowed.

"Daniel, don't shout at your brother," Mary said.

"I still want to know what it means," said James.

"It means you can't take it away," Mary told him. "Now, hush."

Robert got up, and began to tiptoe toward the door.

"'—that among these are life, liberty, and the pursuit of happiness'"—Greenleaf had once more speeded up the pace of his delivery—"'that to secure these rights—'"

"Robert, where are you going?" Mary asked, in a loud whisper.

"Potty," Robert replied.

"'—governments are instituted among men, deriving their just powers from the consent of the governed, that whenever any form of government becomes destructive of these ends—'"

"I can't understand a word you say," Mary cut in. "Please try to read it more slowly."

"'—it—is—the—right—of—the—people—to—alter—or—to—abolish—'"

"That's better, but you are reading them all the same. You should try to get some meaning into the words."

"Was Billy alone?" James asked Daniel.

"No, he was with Johnny."

"John the Quince."

"Boys!" their mother said, sharply, and they subsided.

"'—to alter or to *abolish* it and to institute a *new* government'—do you mean like that?" Greenleaf had started to perspire.

"Much better," his wife replied. "Pray continue."

"'—laying its foundation on *such* principles and organizing its powers in *such* form as to—'"

"My peepee broke," Robert announced from the doorway.

"What do you *mean?*" Mary asked.

"It won't work."

"Perhaps you really didn't have to go."

"I thought I didn't, but then I thought I did, and now it won't work." His eyes filled, and his chin began to pucker.

Mary looked at William, who was leaning against the wall in one corner of the room. "William, you're going to be a doctor," she said. "What do you think ails the child?"

"Nothing," William replied. "Give him three glasses of water and wait a half hour. I think you'll find him perfectly normal."

"Very well. Robert, you sit down and be quiet until Papa is through with his reading"—out of the corner of her eye, Mary saw her husband roll up the document and reach for his hat and cane. "Where are you going?" she asked.

"To the State House," he replied. "I think it might be better if I were to rehearse the reading *in situ*. And, if I am blessed with luck, I shall fall off the balcony and dash my brains out on the pavement." He opened the front door and went into the hot sunlight.

The reading was scheduled for one o'clock on the twenty-fifth, and by noon of that day the area in front of the State House was jammed with people. They were in a festive mood, some of them having primed themselves at the various taverns and public houses in the vicinity and many having brought their whole families, so that the children could later say they had witnessed the historic occasion. Mary Greenleaf and her young had been invited into the State House, but she would have been able to see only her husband's back as he stood on the balcony and would have heard nothing of what he said, so she elected to remain outside, where she could see and hear the entire ceremony. She and the children stood in a doorway on King Street, where they could see the balcony and at the same time have a certain amount of protection from the crowd.

"Billy! Johnny!" James shouted suddenly, and two boys about his age made their way toward him, trying to avoid being trampled by the adults who towered above them. All three were related in a distant sort of way: Billy Cranch's father, whose mother was a Greenleaf, was married to Abigail Adams's sister, thus making the children technically cousins by marriage. John Quincy Adams had just turned nine; Billy Cranch was seven, and James was now eleven, so he wielded the unspoken power of seniority over the other two. His brothers were too far either above or below the age bracket to be a part of the group.

"Last one across King Street is a wormy apple!" James announced, starting to run for the other side of the street.

"Jamie, don't go far!" his mother called, but the three boys had already vanished, darting like chipmunks toward the crowd. They reached the farther side with James first, Billy next, and Johnny last.

"Johnny the Quince is a wormy apple!" James chanted. "We'll have to take the worms out of his hair!" He made as though to grasp Johnny's hair, but Johnny ducked away from him, and he turned instead to Billy. "Daniel said you were looking for me the other day," he said. "What did you want?"

"I forget," replied Billy. "It was something we thought you might know, but now I've forgotten. Do you remember, Johnny?"

"Yes," said Johnny. "It was how cows make other cows."

"You live on a farm," James told him. "You ought to know." He had no idea of the answer, but didn't want to admit it to the younger boys.

"I just can't believe it," Johnny said. "It makes me laugh every time I think of it."

"Well, it's true," said James. "You can take my word for it."

"Then that settles that," said Billy. "Is it the same for people, too?"

"Oh, no," James replied, airily. In a desperate attempt to sound as though he knew what he was talking about, he added, "People, of course, wear hats and are more formal."

"I think I'm going crazy," Johnny said.

"Don't let it worry you," James told him, and then, as people began to make shushing noises and call for quiet, he looked around and realized he couldn't see the State House balcony. On all sides were noisy, laughing adults, and although he tried standing on tiptoe and jumping, he could see nothing but people's backs, and greasy pigtails, and hats. Then two large hands grasped him under the armpits, and he was hoisted onto the shoulders of a man who smelled of beer and tobacco. Two other men did the same for his friends, and the boys seemed to float above the crowd like puffs of milkweed. It was a heady sensation, until James saw the familiar, brown-clad figure of his father appear on the balcony. Then his mouth went dry, and he seemed not to breathe while he waited for his father to speak. Colonel

Thomas Crafts, a member of the Council, made a brief introduction, and then James's father stepped forward, raised the Declaration to eye level, and began to read. The first few sentences were totally inaudible, until further calls for quiet stopped all motion and all sound in the crowd, but even then it sounded as though Greenleaf were talking to a nearby friend and only scattered words or phrases reached the concourse below. Finally someone shouted, "Louder!" and Greenleaf tried to raise his voice, but the words seemed to evaporate in the air, leaving only a misty residue of sound. There were more cries of "Louder!" and "Speak up!" and "We can't hear you!" and finally Greenleaf handed the Declaration to Colonel Crafts and stepped back. In a loud and stentorian voice, Colonel Crafts completed the reading, at the conclusion of which there were three huzzas from the people, and then slowly the assembly dispersed. James thanked the man on whose shoulders he'd been sitting and made his way back to the rest of his family. His mother sounded as though she needed to blow her nose; otherwise she showed no emotion. James felt an ache he couldn't quite explain and wanted to cry.

At supper that night, Mary was unusually talkative. She chattered on about all sorts of trivia, relaying gossip about things that had been found in various Tory houses, about which Tories had gone with the fleet to Halifax and which were thought to have remained behind as spies, and, in short, about everything except the ceremony that afternoon. She scarcely paused for breath, until finally her husband said, "Thank you very much, my dear, but what is done is done. I only hope you weren't ashamed."

"Ashamed?" she replied, her voice rising. "Of what, pray, should I be ashamed? I thought you read it far better than that Colonel Crafts—he sounded like a bull in springtime. Yours was the more intelligent reading, and I was proud of you."

He smiled and picked at his plate. "You're a remarkable woman," he said quietly.

William graduated from Harvard College in the spring of 1777 and began the study of medicine. Although the main action of the war had moved away from Boston, there were repercussions that affected the lives of the students. Food was scarce and textbooks were scarcer—in some cases, they had to be obtained from looted Tory libraries—and then in October the British under General Burgoyne surrendered to General Gates at Saratoga, and the problem arose of what to do with several thousand British prisoners. The first solution was to commandeer the buildings at Harvard, and to this end the students were sent home the end of November. But then the Harvard Corporation got its back up, and alternate housing was finally provided. The troops were quartered in barracks, and Burgoyne and his staff stayed in comparative luxury in Apthorp House, in Cambridge. But it was the end of February of 1778 before the students returned to the Yard, their curriculum more than a little out of joint. William chafed at the inaction and passed his time scouring the back streets of Boston for dead dogs or cats he might dissect.

Then, the following autumn, disaster struck. Because of the shortage of facilities in the barracks, any British prisoner who became seriously ill was transferred to a ship in Boston Harbor, where his disease could run its course without danger of infecting his companions. With the onset of cold weather, sickness became more general, and inevitably conditions aboard the ship were such that no well person would venture on board. A call went out to the medical school, not necessarily for a doctor because matters had gone far beyond a doctor's power to be of help, but for anyone who would volunteer to board the ship and separate the living from the dead and dying, in order to make room for the new arrivals. William was the lone volunteer.

When finally, after two days, he came ashore, he went straight home, burned his clothes, and went to bed and slept for fourteen hours. He awoke with a fever; his eyes were bright and his mouth was dry, and when he tried to stand up, the room tipped toward him and he fell. There followed cramps and nausea, and the fever alternated with chills, and for two weeks he lay in bed and became thinner and smaller, while his skin turned dry and crisp and his eyes sank deeper into his head. His talk tapered off to small noises, and then there was only the sound of his breathing, and at last that stopped. It was November 24, 1778, a little more than two months short of his nineteenth birthday.

James had watched his brother's death as though he himself were having a fever dream. The moment the call went out to the medical school something in the back of his mind had told him that William was doomed, and each succeeding event was simply part of the preordained pattern. He remembered his mother's having said—how long ago? two years? three years?—that whenever William left, she felt it was for the last time, and he reasoned that she, too, had some inner knowledge that his life would be a short one. James was unable to weep; he watched the whole process in stunned silence, hovering behind his mother as she did what small things she could to make William comfortable, and when finally the sheet was pulled over William's face, James left the house and walked down to the waterfront, where he breathed the salt air and wished once again he could fly like a seagull.

4

With William's death, Daniel and James were drawn more closely together. They had always been closer than the three-year gap in their ages would indicate, but now they felt like the only males among the Greenleaf children. Robert was still too young to count, and John, set apart by his blindness, was finding a world of his own in music, so Daniel and James stood alone amidst the girls.

Harvard, like the rest of the country, was disrupted by the war. The average graduating class from 1778 to 1783 was thirty students, as opposed to forty-six for the years 1771 to 1777, and the scarcity of food and textbooks, plus the occasional extended vacations, made mockery of any attempts to establish an orderly educational program. In addition, the discipline under President Samuel Locke had been permissive to the point of being slovenly, and that under the wartime president, Samuel Langdon, very little better, and the students could do pretty much as they pleased. Perhaps symptomatic of all this was the fact that nobody from the college war classes distinguished himself during the war; many of the leaders and movers were Harvard men, but of the wartime graduates not one even approached the rim of distinction. Nathan Hale, Yale's contribution to patriotic legend, was of the class of '73 and technically not a wartime graduate, but no Harvard man of the period came even close to Hale as a celebrity. Had Hale survived, of course, he would most likely have been forgotten.

In this generally haphazard atmosphere, William Greenleaf saw no point in sending either Daniel or James to college; they could be trained for their intended vocations in any number of more practical ways and not waste their time larking around in

Cambridge. He had heard that some students had brought a cow into the Yard, claiming it to be the perquisite of one of the professors, and the resulting confusion had canceled a whole day's classes, and to him this indicated that Harvard was in a moral shambles. With the country fighting for its life, this kind of carrying-on was unforgivable and solid proof of the disintegration of the college. When Greenleaf mentioned this to Mary, one evening after supper, she thought for a few seconds, trying to find a way to demur while appearing to agree.

"You are right, of course," she said. "For Daniel, it would be a waste of time." She picked up her sewing basket and appeared to be looking for something in it. "Where do you expect that Jamie will find the"—she hesitated—"the discipline he needs?"

"What discipline is that?" Greenleaf replied. "He's perfectly well behaved."

"Of course, but"—again she hesitated, looking for a soft word to take the place of a harsh one—"sometimes he's a bit unrestrained—perhaps headstrong, or impulsive, is what I mean—I wonder if college might not teach him to discipline himself."

"Not from what I hear of Harvard. If what you say is true, he needs to be taught a few things at home. I have always thought of him as a shade too self-confident, but none the worse for that."

"Pray don't misunderstand me," Mary said quickly. "I wasn't criticizing him. It's just that he has such chances for greatness that I want him to have all possible help achieving it."

"So, dear lady, do I. Which is precisely why I am not sending him to Harvard."

"Yes, of course."

With the discussion concluded, Greenleaf settled back and cleared his throat. "The very idea," he muttered. "Bringing a cow into the Yard. They should be expelled and sent directly into the army."

Without the formality of a college curriculum, James and Daniel were able to explore areas that might otherwise have been closed to them. Daniel intended to become a pharmacist, for which knowledge of a number of subjects was desirable if not required, and James still harbored a lingering desire to be a doctor, although he knew that a college education was the preferred first step toward medical school. What both brothers did, with their father's approval, was to acquire their education where their interests led them, either reading or attending lectures or talking with men whose opinions they respected. Their father asked only that they be diligent in whatever they did; beyond that, he said, their time was their own.

One person who made an immediate impression on James when he was sixteen was a youth about his age named George Eckman, whom he met one day at a bootmaker's. James had left a pair of boots to be resoled, and when he went into the shop to claim them he saw a short, nearsighted young man stamping about and muttering to himself in German. He watched, fascinated, as the German performed a series of military steps, stamps, and heel clicks, softly cursing the whole time. The cobbler stood by nervously, listening to the *"Eins—zwei—Himmelsakramentverfluchtnochmal—Halt!"* and neither he nor James dared to interrupt what was apparently an elaborate drill routine. Finally the German sat down and extended his legs, and the cobbler tugged off first one boot and then the other. "They must be the wrong boots," the German said. He peered inside one, squinting, and added, "Nowhere do I see the name Eckman. They cannot be mine."

"Pardon me," James put in, "but I think they may be mine. Do you mind if I look?"

"Please do," Eckman replied. "They must belong to someone." To the cobbler he said, "You will please look further. My boots must be here someplace."

"And also a pair for Greenleaf," James said, putting the boots aside. "I left mine to be resoled last week."

The cobbler disappeared into the back of the shop, and James and Eckman looked at each other. Eckman smiled tentatively. "Are you of the family of William Greenleaf?" he asked.

"He is my father," James replied.

"I am honored to meet you." Eckman rose, bowed, and tried to click his heels, but in his stocking feet the effect was somewhat muted, and he laughed. "Please forgive the informality," he said.

"Do you know my father?" James asked.

"By reputation only. *My* father is Hauptmann Manfred von Eckman, aide to Baron von Steuben." Eckman's nearsightedness made him look like a ferret peering through tall grass, but something in his delivery suggested there was an undercurrent of humor beneath his surface formality. James had the feeling he had just lifted a flat stone and seen two beady eyes looking out at him.

The cobbler appeared from behind a curtain. "Gentlemen, I must apologize," he said. "My apprentice was taken in drink yesterday afternoon and fell to hurling boots about the shop. I must ask you to come with me and see if you can identify your own." James and Eckman followed him into the back room, which smelled of oil and new leather and about which were strewn perhaps three dozen boots of various colors, sizes, and age. "Of course I beat him," the cobbler went on, "but that did nothing to restore order here. I'm afraid that may take quite some while."

"It looks like the debris after a battle," Eckman observed, as he started to sort through the pile. "Always they take the boots off the corpses."

"Have you ever been in a battle?" James asked. Eckman was the first German he'd ever met, and he was prepared to believe anything about him.

"No, but my father has," Eckman replied. "I know every detail of every battle in which he ever fought. It surprises me sometimes that I from listening have not developed scars."

By the time they had dredged their way through the pile and had found their boots, they felt as though they'd known each other a year. They left the shop together, stopped at a grog shop for an ale, and agreed to meet for dinner that night. Then James remembered that he and Daniel were supposed to dine together, and he asked if Daniel might come along.

"Natürlich," Eckman replied. "What is your saying—more people, more laughing?"

"The more the merrier," James replied.

"Ja, ja. The more the merrier."

They met in a Charlestown tavern that had originally been called the King's Head, but was now renamed the Minute Man. Daniel, who had inherited his father's lean frame and jovial face, was physically the exact opposite of Eckman, but there was a rapport between them that was the same as James had felt, and it transcended all superficial differences. By the time they had ordered their third round of rum the conversation had skipped most of the usual preambles and had veered inevitably around to women. It was not a subject with which James was familiar, and he was intensely interested.

"It is a peculiar thing about women," Eckman said, as though addressing a class. He sipped his rum, squinted slightly, and went on, "Basically they are the same, and yet every one is different."

There was a short silence, while the Greenleaf brothers waited for him to continue. Daniel listened out of politeness but James, whose head had become fogged by the rum, thought that something deep was being said and tried to fathom it.

"In what way?" he asked, after a moment.

Eckman glanced at him, a hint of a smile in his eyes. "Every way," he replied. Then, to Daniel, "Of course, I have no knowledge about women in this country. Since I am here I have seen very few."

"You have only to look," said Daniel. "There's no scarcity that I have noticed."

"Of females, perhaps. A female is one thing, a woman is another."

James tried to bring his eyes into focus. "I never thought of it that way," he said.

"And a wench is something else again," Daniel said.

"A wench I have not heard of," said Eckman. "Explain to me a wench."

"*Dirne*," said Daniel, who had been studying German.

Eckman grinned. "Ah, yes," he said. "Precisely. In all of Cambridge and all of Boston I have not seen one. I have seen young ladies with bosoms like boys, I have seen *Hausfrauen* with bosoms like—like—*wie sagt man auf englisch 'Satteltaschen'?*"

"Saddlebags," said Daniel.

"Like saddlebags," Eckman went on, "but nowhere, either in Boston or in Cambridge, have I seen a good, *süssliche Dirne*, with something a man could take hold of."

"You haven't been looking in the right places," Daniel replied.

"Where? Tell me one place!"

Daniel glanced at his brother. "Some other time," he said.

James knew no German, but he was aware of the trend of the conversation. "Pray don't worry about me," he said. "I can take care of myself." He found that if he spoke slowly, his words

came out as they should; if he hurried, they tended to slur together.

"Where is this place?" Eckman demanded. "I insist I should
know."

Daniel was embarrassed and shook his head. "I've forgotten,"
he said.

"Ach, what a liar," said Eckman. "He tells me I have not been
looking in the right places, and when I ask him the name of
just one, he says he has forgotten. Either he was lying when he
said he knew several places, or he is lying when he says he has
forgotten. A man does not forget a thing like that. So Herr Greenleaf is a liar."

Daniel took a deep breath. "It is nowhere near here," he said.

"Then the sooner we should get started. Landlord!" Eckman
clapped his hands, and in what seemed to James like no more
than a minute they were out in the street, breathing the cool
night air. A faint mist rose from the river and with it, the smell
of mud flats.

"James, why don't you start on home?" Daniel suggested.
"This will be of no interest to you."

James drew himself upright and tried to assume a judicial air.
"Nonsense," he replied. "Such things are of interest to everyone."

"You don't even know what we're talking about."

"I do indeed. Lead on, Macduff, and damn'd be him that first
cries, 'Hold, enough!'"

"It's 'Lay on,'" said Daniel, quietly.

"Be that as it may. View halloo and tallyho."

Daniel shrugged, and they started off. To James, what followed was a series of dark streets, uneven pavements, and every
now and then a man who would appear out of the blackness and
then vanish. There were voices and singing, but they made no
sense, and his main preoccupation was to keep from becoming
separated from Daniel and Eckman, whose figures he could just
make out ahead. The street seemed to move from side to side,
and once or twice he fell, but someone always helped him up,
and then they were in a lighted room that was warm and
smelled of tobacco smoke, talcum powder, and perspiration.
Then someone was shaking his arm, and he opened his eyes and
saw Eckman standing over him, grinning.

"You like a little fresh air, perhaps?" Eckman said.

James struggled out of the chair where he'd been sleeping, and they went outside. His head was clear, though aching, and his mouth tasted like old leather. He had the feeling of having been stunned. "Where's Daniel?" he asked.

"Daniel will, I expect, join us shortly," Eckman replied, with a smile. "He found an old friend with whom he had much to discuss."

James was pondering this statement and remarking to himself how well Daniel had managed to conceal that part of his life, when down the street came a man who appeared to have every attribute of a pirate, or at the very least a privateer. His black hair was gathered back in a tarred queue, his neckerchief was snarled and knotted and covered with debris, and the tops of his cracked leather boots, turned down below his knees, were stained with blood from his freshly lacerated kneecaps. He looked as though he'd been traveling on all fours for several days, although at the moment he was performing a sort of walking motion as though battling a tidal backwash. A clay pipe was gripped between his blackened teeth. He spotted James and Eckman standing under the doorway lantern and made his way toward them. As he got closer, James could smell the fumes that preceded him and could see a short, gleaming knife at his belt. The sailor stopped in front of Eckman and, weaving slightly, examined him as though he were a rare form of bug. Smoke puffed out of his pipe with each wheezing breath.

"Up kinda late, aintcha, laddie?" he said, at last.

Eckman regarded him coldly. "That is no concern of yours," he replied. James felt his stomach contract at the thought of an impending fight. He had always managed to avoid fights, having been protected by one or another of the members of his family, and he had no idea how to handle himself in combat. His heart began to pound, and he wished he were back inside.

"You sound like a bloody foreigner," the sailor said, moving closer to Eckman. "You're not only up late, you're a long way from home."

To James's horror Eckman reached up, grabbed the sailor's pipe, and snapped it out of his mouth. "Do not smoke that thing in my face when you talk to me," he said, handing it back. "I don't like it."

The sailor's hand whipped to his knife, and James stopped breathing. All motion was frozen for a number of seconds and then, very slowly, the sailor reached out his other hand and took the pipe. He continued to stare down at Eckman, breathing deeply, and Eckman returned his stare.

"Nobody ever done that to me," the sailor said, at last. "Nobody ever done it and lived."

"The smoke got in my eyes," Eckman replied.

There was another silence, and then the sailor said, "What's your name?"

"Why?" Eckman's expression didn't change.

"You're my friend. Anyone does that to me, he dies or he's my friend. You're my friend, so what's your name?"

"I am no friend of yours," said Eckman.

"Yes, you are." The sailor's voice became quieter, and James saw his hand edging toward the knife again.

"Look out, George—" James began, and Eckman ducked just as the knife whistled past where his face had been. Eckman closed and grabbed the sailor around the waist, and James, without thinking, jumped for his knife arm. It was like trying to hold the leg of a bucking horse, and Eckman and James were flailed back and forth while James tried to bite the hand that held the knife, and Eckman kept stabbing a knee into the sailor's groin. The tangle of grunting combatants fell to the ground just as the house door opened, and light flooded out into the street. Then Daniel was among them, beating at the sailor's head with a cane, and the struggle ended when a large, burly figure came out of the house, pushed the younger men aside, then lifted the sailor up by the neckerchief and hit him once along the side of the jaw. A sharp crack, and the sailor's head went limp.

There was silence for a while, as Eckman and the Greenleaf brothers made their way back through the darkened streets. Then Eckman cleared his throat. "It would appear I am in your debt," he said.

"What do you mean?" James asked.

"To you, I owe thanks for probably saving my life."

"I did nothing. I just held on." James was faintly embarrassed, because he'd been holding on for his own life as much as for Eckman's.

"Nevertheless. And to you, Herr Daniel, I owe an apology."

"For what?" said Daniel.

"For saying you were a liar. You knew precisely of what you spoke."

Daniel was quiet for a moment, then said, "Only too glad to oblige, I'm sure."

About a week later, Eckman and James were at the Minute Man together. Daniel was studying, and Eckman had suggested that, since he and James had nothing to do that evening, they meet for a bit of social relaxation. Those were his precise words, but James knew the meaning behind them. He felt faint twinges of panic but couldn't think of an excuse to get out of it, so he agreed. What had been curiosity the first time had now changed to apprehension, and he felt as though he were about to enter into a strange world of trolls and hobgoblins, a world to which Eckman's cold-blooded approach was a mystery. It was an area about which he knew absolutely nothing, and he couldn't view it, as Eckman seemed to, like a trip to the blacksmith's. The one thing he promised himself was that he would stay away from the rum; he would have beer or ale, but nothing else.

They talked on general subjects for a while, and then Eckman said, "I think we should have some female company, *nicht wahr?*"

James swallowed. "I'm perfectly happy here," he said.

"Nonsense. You're just nervous. It is a natural thing, but of no consequence. It will pass."

I wish he'd stop talking like a professor, James thought. It might be easier if he weren't so bloody clinical about everything. Out loud, he said, "I'm not nervous. I simply said I was happy here." He ran his tongue over his lips and forced a smile.

"Quite so," said Eckman. "And I know where you will be happier. Come."

This time James was aware where they were going, which was in the direction of the waterfront. The trip seemed much shorter, and it wasn't long before he saw the familiar lantern over the door and had a quick flash of memory of their fight with the sailor. Then they were inside, and the smells and sounds were familiar, and a plump girl with stringy hair and bad teeth put her arm through his, and before he knew it he was on the way upstairs. Things became blurred after that: he remembered the girl's dropping her dress and getting onto the bed, then he was lying on the bed next to her, and he was looking at the dark beams in the ceiling and waiting for something to happen. Nothing did, and after a few moments the girl raised herself on one elbow and looked at him. He glanced sideways, and all he could see was a breast, the nipple pointing at him like an inflamed fingertip. He looked back at the ceiling.

"Is something wrong?" the girl asked.

"No," he replied, his lips sticking to his dry gums.

"Then what are you waiting for?"

He paused and cleared his throat. "I don't know what happens next."

The girl sighed and fell back on the pillow. "Oh, God," she said.

"If I knew what to do," James said, testily, "I would. This is no fault of mine."

"How old are you?"

"Sixteen."

"I'm sorry." She raised herself again. "You must have led one of them sheltered lives I hear about."

"Actually, this wasn't my idea. My friend and—"

"Hush and lie back. The worst thing you can do is to talk."

"But—"

"I said hush!"

What seemed like a week, but was approximately an hour, later, he met Eckman outside. They walked in silence for a while, and then Eckman said, "Was everything satisfactory?"

James paused, then replied, "I honestly don't know. I have nothing with which to compare it."

Eckman laughed. "Time will take care of that."

James was trying to sort things out in his mind. "I suppose it will," he said at last.

The profession of druggist, which Daniel had elected to pursue, had more ramifications than the simple name implied. It was important for anyone who wanted to survive in business to have a number of outlets and to diversify his talents, so that if one market dried up, there would be others on which to fall back. Doctors took to fabricating their own medicines and marketing them, but since there were comparatively few registered doctors, the apothecaries stepped in and filled the gap, manufacturing and prescribing drugs with carefree abandon. The newspapers were filled with advertisements for surgical instruments and medicines for the prevention and cure of smallpox, diphtheria, measles, consumption, gout, rheumatism, rabies, and syphilis, and the apothecaries' shops stocked such diverse items as medicines, crude drugs, chemicals, spices, wines, liquors, dyestuffs, groceries, tobacco, cosmetics, and a highly popular line of what were called "Ship's Medicine Boxes." Another well-advertised item was Dr. George Stuart's Spirit of Scurvy Grass, and a random sampling of the drugs and nostrums in general use would include aloes, Friends Female Pills, nutgalls, People's Water for the Itch, belladonna, extract of hemlock, cow parsnip, Jesuits' Drops, mercury, ambergris essence, Cephalic Snuff, rhubarb, Bateman's Pectoral Drops, Hill's Cure for the Bite of a Mad Dog, vitriol elixir—in short, something for every ailment or affliction known to man.

So popular was this field that printers, and the publishers of the almanacs that ran the advertisements, decided to open apothecary businesses on the side, and such books as *The Poor Planter's Physician* and Buchan's *Domestic Medicine* were in almost every home. Any code of medical ethics was totally unknown, and there was no limit to the claims that could be made.

In such circumstances it was inevitable that some men became extremely wealthy; those with the most widely advertised claims and the fewest known casualties were bound to sell as much of their product as they could manufacture. Dr. Silvester Gardiner, for example, set up an apothecary shop at the corner of Washington and Winter streets, calling it The Sign of the Unicorn & Mortar and advertising "Galenical & Chymical Medicines" as well as the usual Ship's Medicine Boxes, and so successful was he that he finally branched out and set up similar establishments in Meriden and Hartford, Connecticut. Dr. Zabdiel Boylston, who in 1721 was the first in the area to inoculate against smallpox, had an apothecary shop in Dock Square and was a heavy advertiser in medicinals, cosmetics, crude drugs, and surgeon's instruments, and his success may be gauged from the fact that one of Boston's principal streets was named in his honor. Apothecaries were active in politics and the military, as well as the social and religious life of the community. Dr. John Greenleaf,

James's uncle who died in 1778, had been a member of King's Chapel and a well-known apothecary, and many of the Greenleafs had had at least some training in the business, as a hedge against bad times in the business or shipping worlds.

Thus the move was a logical one for Daniel, but it held little appeal for James. He was aware he would need specialized schooling before he could become a doctor, and his main problem lay in trying to convince his father it would be worthwhile. At first he felt he had plenty of time; the war was going poorly and the country seemed without a future of any sort, with what looked like an even chance of being reabsorbed by Great Britain and made to pay the penalty for revolt, and in such circumstances it was impossible to think of any career that made sense. Then, in October of the year he was sixteen, Cornwallis surrendered at Yorktown; three months after his seventeenth birthday the British recognized the independence of the United States, and in November of that year a preliminary peace settlement was reached in Paris, and the whole world took on a new aspect. The future was bright and challenging, and there was nothing that might not be accomplished if a person set his mind to it. George Eckman declared his intention of going to medical school, and James decided this was the incentive he needed to confront his father. But, knowing his parents as he did, he reasoned it would be best to get his mother's support first and let her carry part of the battle.

When he mentioned it to her, Mary Greenleaf's eyes widened as though he'd struck her, and she said, "Jamie! Do you know what you're saying? Have you forgotten William so soon?"

"Of course I haven't forgotten him," he replied. "That's why I want to be a doctor."

"Why can't you be a druggist, like Daniel? People will call you 'doctor,' but it won't be so dangerous."

"It isn't dangerous, Mama. It's no more dangerous than walking down the street."

"I think what you are really saying is a druggist isn't good enough for you. Your father was trained to be a druggist, you know. Many Greenleafs have been druggists, and druggists are highly respected people."

"I had no such—"

"Or what, pray, is wrong with being a merchant? Greenleafs

have been merchants and shippers for more than a hundred years. Do you know how many wharves in Boston and New-buryport are owned by Greenleafs? How many ships? Do you know how much money your father got for selling that prize brig? Just that one ship? Do you—"

"Mama, I—"

"Let me finish. There are great things in store for you, Jamie, if you will only have the vision and the foresight to take advantage of your opportunities. But you have too much—too much *imagination* to be a doctor; you would be smothered in a field that depends so strongly on rules. You need a field where you can be free."

James had already found that charm could get him what cold reasoning couldn't, and he shifted his approach ever so slightly. "Of course you're right," he said, "but you see I have this urge to help people, which I feel can be satisfied only through medicine. Above everything else, I want to help my fellow man."

This was a new thought to Mary, and she took a moment to adjust to it. Then she said, "You can help your fellow man just as well by being a merchant. You can keep him supplied with the necessities of life, and offhand I can think of no greater help than that."

"I wouldn't know where to start being a merchant."

"I'm sure we can find a place for you. When the new government is set up, there'll be all sorts of opportunities, and I'm sure Mr. Hancock will find something worthy of your talents."

"Why should he be interested in me?" James asked. "I can't even remember what he looks like."

"He is married to a Greenleaf," his mother replied, in a tone that made it sound as though all Greenleafs were one. "I can assure you that Mr. Hancock will not let a relative languish for lack of employment."

James could see his career as a doctor evaporating in front of him, and he wished he'd gone to his father first. "I don't care about employment!" he said, loudly. "I want to *do* something! There's a difference!"

His mother retreated into her prim demeanor, which meant that the discussion was over. "I fail to see it," she said, quietly. "I shall take the matter up with your father, and let you know what we decide."

"Why should *you* decide?" James cried. "Why can't I do what I want?"

"You are barely eighteen," his mother reminded him. "You may feel you're a grown man, but you're not. You're still a young, headstrong boy."

"At eighteen, William was doing what he wanted," said James, and then he heard a voice, which he barely recognized as his own, add, "At eighteen, William was *dead*—how much more grown up can you be than that?"

His mother's jaw tightened and her eyes filled, and as she left the room James knew he had forever destroyed his chances of being a doctor.

5

With the war over, James found there was a strange new atmosphere in Boston. He could scarcely remember the time when there hadn't been war, and the political wrangling and maneuvering that followed the peace brought with it the uneasy feeling that all the fighting had accomplished little or nothing. Liberty had been achieved, but with it had come factionalism, ill will, and chicanery to such a point as to make one almost long for the wartime unity—such as it had been. At least during the war there had been a common enemy; now the enemies seemed to be everywhere.

James could see the effect this had on his father, and it distressed him. William Greenleaf's tenure as sheriff had ended December 14, 1780, when he was succeeded by one Joseph Henderson, and with no official duties to occupy him he was doubly aware of all the niggling and backbiting that went on. For one who had been active in the clandestine work leading up to the war, this was irritating in the extreme, and James wished there were something he could do to put his father at ease. He reasoned that what was needed was something to obliterate everything else, so one night, when his father was more than usually depressed, James decided to test a wild idea.

"Father, may I make a suggestion?" he said.

"Of course," William replied, staring into the fire.

"Do you think a change of scene might be beneficial?"

His father turned his head slowly and looked at him. "A change of what scene?"

"Well—is there anything keeping you in Boston?"

"Only the fact that I've lived here all my life."

"Might that not be a good reason to move?"

William stared at his son, trying to fathom his meaning. "Move? Where?"

"Anywhere. Newbury. The Cape. New Bedford. Anywhere, just to be out of Boston."

"But why be out of Boston?"

"It's changed. It's not the town we knew. I think you're beginning to hate it, and I think now that you're almost sixty you've earned a little time to relax. You can't relax here, so why not go someplace where you can?"

There was a long silence. "I never thought of it."

"Do. I think it would be good for you, and good for Mama, and"—he paused—"good for us all. We do care about you, very much."

William was silent for several minutes. "I'll think about it," he said, at last, and went upstairs to bed.

The subject wasn't mentioned for several days, and then one afternoon William said to James, "Would you come with me and see your Uncle Stephen? I should like to hear his reaction to your idea."

"Of course," said James. "I'd be delighted."

Stephen Greenleaf was still living in his house on Common Street and had recently attained the respectable age of eighty. Age had changed his face but slightly; his jowls were still firm, and his nose only a bit more pointed, and while his eyes were clear, it now took him longer to do and say things, and he gave the impression he was thinking between each sentence. When William mentioned James's idea of moving, Stephen was quiet a few moments, then said, "Why move? You're here."

"I want some peace," William replied. "Boston is becoming too big and too crowded. I thought I might go to New Bedford. It's small, and by the sea, and it's peaceful."

Stephen considered this. "I don't know any New Bedford," he said. "I know Bedford, or Bedford Village, named for old Joe Russell. We called him the Duke of Bedford. I never heard of New Bedford."

"It's the same thing. They found there was already a Bedford in the Commonwealth, so they had to change it."

"The King's troops set fire to Bedford during the rebellion."

"I know, but it's rebuilt. And they're building up the fishing

fleet again. There'll be farming, and shipbuilding, and fishing—
everything I need."

"I thought you wanted peace."

"I do, but I'm a merchant. Peace is no good without prosperity
to go with it. I think New Bedford offers a chance for both."

Stephen shrugged. "I'd give you some advice, except I seem to
remember advising you not to put a military man in charge of
your cause. . . ." His mind drifted off, and then, as though it
had reached the end of an elastic line, it snapped back. "So
you're going to pack up your whole family and take them down
to Bedford."

"Not all of them. The older girls are married, and John will
come, of course, but Daniel is finishing his apprenticeship as a
pharmacist and will set up shop in Boston."

"That seems sensible."

"As a matter of fact, I am informed he wants to marry his
cousin Elizabeth, which would so to speak keep everything in
the family."

"You mean John's girl?"

"Yes. Ever since John died, the business has been ailing, and it
would be an ideal way for Daniel to step in and show what he
can do."

"There are worse ways, that's certain." Stephen looked at
James. "And what about Jamie?"

"About James, we don't know," William replied, turning to his
son. "He wanted to be a doctor, but his mother took strong objection to the idea. Has any new thought occurred?"

"No, sir, not so far," James replied. "I have been exploring a
number of possibilities."

"I think we need have no fear for you," his uncle said. "Whatever you decide to do, you will leave your mark."

"Thank you, sir," said James. "That's kind of you to say."

"I didn't say the mark would be good," Stepehen replied,
cheerfully. "That will be up to you. I simply said you'd leave
your mark."

"Yes, sir. I shall try to make it good."

"I am sure you will."

"And you," William put in. "Do you intend to stay on alone in
this house?"

"This house," said Stephen, "has been my house for so long I

can think of no other. How many years do I have left to me?
Two? Five? Ten at the outside—"

"Nonsense, Stephen, you could live a long—"

"Forgive my saying so, William, but you're taking an imma-
ture view. At a mere sixty, a man thinks that life can go on forever; I remember when I was sixty there was a—well, suffice it to
say the juices are still flowing, and the only things to be avoided
are plague ships and duels. But when you are eighty, there is an
unmistakable slowing down; things no longer react the way they
did, and it doesn't take much imagination to foresee the day
when they won't react at all. I intend to keep on doing precisely
what I have been doing, for as long as I am able. You can seek
your happiness in Bedford; I have no needs that are farther
away than the Common."

"Still, you should have somebody with you. You admit you're
slowing down, and after a while—"

"Abigail will be with me, may God bless her soul."

"Oh?"

"Her husband, that Judge Howard fellow, died in England
last fall. She is coming back to live with me."

"I never knew Judge Howard."

"You wouldn't have. I'm sorry for Abigail because I gather she
was fond of him, but I'd be less than honest if I didn't say I'll be
glad of her company."

"That's understandable." William rose and reached for his
cane, and James rose with him. "I'm sorry you don't share my
enthusiasm for New Bedford," he said. "I had even dared to
think you might like to join us there."

"Leaving aside the fact that there *is* no such place as New
Bedford," said Stephen, "I wouldn't go there if you paid me a
king's ransom. It'll never approach Boston as a seaport—or even
Newbury, when it comes to that—they don't have the facilities
for building decent ships, and their fishing'll never amount to anything because they're too far from the Grand Banks. They don't
have one thing that Boston doesn't have three times over."

"They had a pretty fair whaling industry," William replied.
"Until the war, that is."

"Whaling," Stephen said, with a grimace. "There's more profit
chasing goats than whales. Bedford is just a few farms by the

water, and not very good farms at that. Mark my words—in another fifty years no one will even know where it is."

"In another fifty years I won't care," said William.

"I wouldn't be too sure of that. We Greenleafs are a long-lived lot."

William smiled and held out his hand. "I'll let you know what it's like," he said. "They tell me there's even a post road that connects with Boston."

"I'll be interested to know," Stephen replied, as they shook hands. "But not interested enough to come. I'm where the good Lord intended all civilized men should be, and I don't propose to interfere with His doings."

"So be it," said William, and when he reached the door he stopped and looked around. "We always seem to be saying good-by in this room, don't we?"

"I see nothing remarkable in that," replied Stephen. "It's where I spent most of my time." Turning to James, he said, "Are you also making this hegira into the wilderness?"

"I don't know, sir," James replied. "That will depend on a number of things."

"Well, if you need lodgings in Boston, remember that you have them here."

"Thank you, sir. I shall."

"We're not moving tomorrow," William put in. "This is still only an idea."

"Once you've had the idea, you might as well go," replied Stephen. "The thought and the deed are one and the same."

When they had left he closed the door behind them and returned to his desk. He opened a drawer and produced Abigail's letter, now almost three months old, and tried to calculate her earliest possible arrival. He concluded it could be anywhere from one month to six, and he put the letter away wishing for some reason he couldn't explain that she would hurry.

On May 25, 1784, Daniel married his first cousin Elizabeth, whose father had been a well-known apothecary, bearing the title "Doctor," and a member of King's Chapel. When he died, in 1778, he was buried in a vault under Brattle Street Church and his name was cut in stone on the Brattle Street side of the building. His business, as William suggested, had dwindled after his death, but with Daniel in charge it was hoped that things might take a turn for the better. Elizabeth was a tall, thin girl, John Greenleaf's daughter by his third wife, and she had the ability to enter or leave a room without causing any apparent change in the number of occupants. Her presence made absolutely no mark on whatever might be happening, and unless someone were looking directly at her, there was no clue to her whereabouts. James had never thought of her as anything but a name until Daniel announced his intention of marrying her, and then James's first, instinctive reaction was to compare her with the Charlestown girls with whom he and Daniel and Eckman had had occasional traffic. It was an unfortunate comparison, because it was like matching a mouse against goats, and James concluded there must be more sides to his brother than he had ever dreamed of. At the age of nineteen he still had only the most basic knowledge of such matters, and almost all of it ran contrary to what he had been led to expect.

His main problem, as far as Daniel and Elizabeth were concerned, was in trying to fathom what Daniel saw in her that was worth marrying—leaving aside the possibility that it was her late father's business. Daniel was not the kind who would do that, so the answer must lie somewhere else, either in herself or in Daniel, that was invisible to the casual observer. The first time James dined with the newlyweds he saw she was a practiced hostess, who in spite of (or possibly because of) her periods of apparent invisibility managed to see that the meal was efficiently run. Although there were only the three of them for dinner, the table appeared set for a banquet: a sole in cream sauce for the first course, then grouse with rice, followed by mutton, steamed vegetables, a choice of apple or mince pie or both, and a chocolate cake. The serving girl appeared and disappeared as soundlessly as a moth, with no apparent signal from her mistress, bringing the various wines as needed and clearing away the remains of the previous courses. At one point Daniel remarked on the absence of a soup course, and Elizabeth made a fluttering, apologetic sound that James was unable to decipher. When, after the cheese had been served, she vanished for apparently the last time, Daniel produced a pair of clay pipes, and he and James lit them and smoked quietly while they sipped their port and nibbled at the crumbs of cheese.

"Have you decided on a career?" Daniel asked, after a while.

James blew smoke at the beam over his head. "Have you heard of the new federal law regarding land sales?"

"No."

"The government is putting up lots of six hundred and forty acres apiece, for sale at one dollar per acre. The man who can buy that land in quantity—say, ten or twenty thousand acres—will be worth millions in a very few years. He can't fail."

Daniel considered this. "It needs some money to begin with," he said.

"Six hundred and forty dollars. With one lot as security, you can get long-term loans that will allow you to buy more and that way multiply your holdings until your word alone will be worth a million dollars. It's like coining your own money."

Daniel regarded his brother, whose eyes shone in the candlelight. "If it's as easy as you say, there should be a lot of investors," he said.

"Not everybody knows about it, and not everybody can raise six hundred and forty dollars. It is for those fortunate few who—" There was a knock at the front door, and James stopped and listened to the low voices in the hall. After a few moments, Elizabeth appeared.

"It's Mr. Northrup," she said, to Daniel. "His wife is feeling poorly."

"Tell him to come back tomorrow," Daniel replied. "The shop closes at six."

Elizabeth didn't move, and after a moment Daniel looked at her. "Mr. Northrup is an old and valued customer," she said. "He would never go to anyone except Papa."

There was a moment while Daniel let this sink in, then he rose. "Excuse me," he said to James. "Some people's ailments seem to be more serious than others'."

James sipped his port and stared at the candles, while he explored the possibilities of investing in land. It was the commodity the country had most of, and while it was cheap at the moment, there was bound to come a time when more and more was needed, and then the people who owned it would be the ones to set the price. A dollar now could be ten, twenty, a hundred dollars later on, and a man with large enough holdings would make his fortune fifty times over. It was a tempting thought because the actual work involved was practically nil; all that was required was the knowledge of what land to buy, and on what terms. The more he thought about it, the harder it was to find anything wrong with it.

He was so preoccupied with his thoughts that he didn't realize his cousin-sister-in-law Elizabeth had returned to the room. Then he caught a flicker of movement out of the corner of his eye and saw her standing by the doorway, and he rose quickly to his feet.

"Forgive me," he said. "I didn't see you."

"Pray don't let me disturb you," she replied. "I merely came to see if you wanted anything."

"Not a thing. Won't you sit down?"

She paused, then sank with a rustle of silk into the nearest chair. He resumed his seat and cleared his throat. There was a silence, while she waited for him to say something and he tried to think of something to say. He had never known her very well, so there was nothing in their past he could use as a conversational gambit, and as far as the present was concerned, she was simply someone his elder brother had seen fit to marry. The ties between them were little stronger than cobwebs, incapable of supporting even the flimsiest talk. All he could do, he decided, was treat her as though she were a hostess to whose house he had been invited for the first time.

"That was a delicious dinner," he said. "Every dish a triumph."

She lowered her eyes. "You are very kind."

"Few people are so lucky as to have that expert a cook." Dear God, he thought, pray give me another subject quickly. I know nothing to say about food. "Truly a feast for the gods," he concluded, in desperation.

"Actually, Cook has been having seizures all week," she said. "I had to do most of the cooking."

"*You* did?"

"I supervised. The girls did the work."

"You could find no substitute cook?"

She glanced at the tips of her fingers. "None good enough."

"Well, I must say"—James realized he had almost missed the chance to get off the subject of cooking, so changed quickly back to the cook's health—"What appears to be the cause for these seizures?" he asked.

"Nobody knows. She just falls down. The housemaid thinks she's been bewitched."

He decided to try a small joke. "One would think that, with all the medication so readily at hand, a cure could be found before too long. A pinch of this, a dash of that—sooner or later, something is bound to take hold." He started a light laugh, which faded at the sight of her face.

"Mr. Greenleaf," she said, "an apothecary does not experiment. An apothecary must know. Only the doctors can afford the luxury of guesswork."

"Of course," he said, quickly. "How very stupid of me. I spoke in jest, and out of the depths of ignorance." Please, Daniel, he thought, come back soon. Don't leave me here, digging myself deeper and deeper into the ground. "My field is so far removed from pharmacy that I sometimes forget." She said nothing, waiting for him to explain, and he went on, "Land development is a world all of its own." Still Elizabeth said nothing, and he realized that he could go on all night about the buying and selling of land without making the slightest impression on her. He was going to have to improvise something, and if that was the case, he decided to make the improvisation a good one. "You have heard," he said, "of the brothers Montgolfier?"

She hesitated. "I can't say that I have."

"Two years ago, they startled the world by demonstrating a new contraption called a 'balloon.' It is an immense silken bag which, when filled with hot air, will rise with enough buoyancy to lift a man straight into the sky."

Her eyes widened. "Surely you jest."

"Not in the least. The demonstration was held in Paris, before thousands of witnesses. A whole new era has been born."

"I do declare." She didn't quite believe him, but he said it in such a casual way as to defy rebuttal, and she didn't know where to probe for the truth. However, Elizabeth Greenleaf was not accustomed to being on the defensive. "How will this fit in your career?" she asked.

He made a light gesture of dismissal and smiled. "Any number of ways. Once man can leave the ground, there is nothing he cannot do. Travel across mountains, oceans, deserts—explore the clouds and tap them for rain . . . I can see a whole new branch of natural history, the study of birds in flight. Now man can fly along with the birds and perhaps learn from them the secret of flight—and the clouds—snow can be removed from the clouds before it has a chance to fall—blizzards will be a thing of the past . . . Sleet—chutes can be suspended from balloons, which will catch sleet and channel it into storage bins on the ground—or deep underground caverns—"

"Why store the sleet? What possible use is it?"

"Sleet, madam, is ice, and ice is the essence of refrigeration. Without refrigeration, food rots."

"You still haven't told me the relation to your career."

With elaborate patience, he said, "Have you ever studied the flight of the owl?"

She looked startled, and shook her head.

"If you had, you would know that an owl doesn't fly—he coasts. He coasts on large, feathery wings that make no more sound than two balls of cotton, and that way he can hear his prey while it cannot hear him. When he does hear it, he swoops, snatches it, and is in the air and away, still with no sound. I intend to do just that. In this new field I shall coast about and look for whatever land may offer itself, and when it does, I shall seize it and be off, like the owl, leaving no sound and no trace behind me. Does that answer your question? I don't know how to put it more plainly."

She was trying to frame a reply when Daniel returned to the room, and she seemed almost visibly to fade into the background. James greeted his brother with relief.

"Did you get Mrs. Northrup back on her feet?" he asked.

Daniel sat down heavily and poured himself a glass of port. "As much as anyone will ever be able to," he said. "Her malady is one that blossoms with attention. If she were alone on a desert island, she would be in the peak of health; with an apothecary at her command, she is at death's door."

"How do you treat her?"

Daniel waved his hand. "A dash of this—a pinch of that—anything, so long as it makes her think you're interested. One of most difficult things about this profession is feigning interest where none is warranted. I sometimes think I should have been an actor instead."

James had the good manners not to look at Elizabeth. Instead he rose, knocked out his pipe ashes into the fireplace, and placed the pipe on the mantel. Then he turned to her, bowed, and said, "A delicious dinner, madam. My compliments all around."

She inclined her head. "You must come again," she said. "I am consumed with curiosity about the life of the owl."

Daniel looked from her to James and back again. "What owl?" he asked. "Who has an owl?"

"A manner of speaking only, brother," James replied. "For all practical purposes, it might as well be the owl of Athena. Farewell."

He went out, and Elizabeth looked at the door as it closed behind him.

"Did you have an interesting talk?" Daniel asked, sipping his port.

She continued to look at the door. "I really don't know," she replied, at last. "Did you ever hear of a device called a—a 'balloon'?"

"Does it have to do with pharmacy?"

"No."

"Then I haven't heard of it. What is it supposed to do?"

She paused so long that he looked at her, to see if she'd heard the question.

"I honestly don't know where to begin," she said. "It seems to be something they do in France."

"No good can come of that," said Daniel, quickly. "My advice to you is to forget about it."

Three days later James came around to Daniel's shop, which with his house was on School Street, just off Tremont. It was in a good area, handy to the Common as well as to the business district, while not being too close to some of the more unsavory waterfront hangouts. Sailors in need of repair could find several establishments closer to the wharves, and gentlefolk had no qualms about sauntering through the area at all hours of the day or night. Daniel adjusted his business hours only for his more prominent clients, but there were enough of them to make him conscious of the appearance of his neighborhood. He was intent on bringing the business back to the prestige it once enjoyed, and in the process he found he had to think about the small things as well as the large.

It was late afternoon when James stopped in, and except for Daniel the shop was empty. That is to say, it was empty of people; shelves lined every available inch of wall space, and the shelves were crammed with bottles, jars, tins, and packages. Clusters of dried herbs, roots, and berries hung from the ceiling along with strings of onions, cheeses in net bags, and straw-covered bottles of wine. In one corner was a hogshead of to-bacco and nearby two kegs of whisky, while boxes of various flavored teas were stacked atop one another between the whisky and a large barrel of flour. The place smelled of cinnamon, and wintergreen, and pungent oils, with a faint, musty overlay of age and spiced powder.

"How do you ever find what you want?" James asked, looking around in wonder.

"Most of them are labeled," Daniel replied, "Those that aren't are self-evident." He indicated a coiled and brittle snakeskin in a jar. "Like that. Some people swear by it."

"What for?"

"Shingles. Snip off a little skin, pulverize it, mix it with oils and unguents, and rub it into the troubled spot."

"Whose idea was that?"

"I gather the late Dr. Greenleaf's. I'd never heard of it until some of his old customers started asking for it, and I finally had to send a boy out to find a snake. This is the second one in the last six months."

James looked at the tattered skin and absent-mindedly scratched his ribs. "Very well," he said. "If that's what they like."

"They seem to. What brings you here? Headache? Gout? Neu-ralgia? Nervousness? Night sweats? Burning on passing water? Diarrhea? Nausea and vomiting? St. Vitus's dance? Double vi-sion? Incontinence? I can go on *ad infinitum*."

James laughed. "None of those. I come for nothing more com-plicated than your signature."

"Certainly. Where do I sign? Or, rather, what do I sign?"

"I just bought one of those lots of government land. I'd like you to cosign the note for six hundred and forty dollars."

Daniel looked at him. "Don't you have the cash?"

"I do, but I'd rather not use it if I don't have to. This way, I'll subdivide the land immediately, and you'll have your return by the end of the week. Or, if you prefer, I can let it mature a while, until the value appreciates." He held out a paper, and Daniel took it and examined it.

"What you do with this is your business," Daniel said. "I should think that the longer you held onto land, the more valuable it would become, but if this is only the start, I don't suppose it really matters."

"It is only the start," said James. "I can promise you that. This is what you might call first brick—or stone—in the building of a palace."

"You aim high, don't you?"

"I see no reason not to. If you aim high enough, you can hit the moon."

Daniel reached for a pen just as a door in the rear of the shop opened and a maid put her head in. "Doctor, Cook is having another spell," she announced, in a small voice. "Madam would like you to come quickly."

Daniel made a small noise of impatience, put the pen down, and picked up a couple of bottles. Then, as an afterthought, he opened a drawer and produced a brass cube about two inches square, which had slits on one side and a handle opposite, and dropped this in his pocket.

"What's that?" James asked.

"A bleeder," said Daniel, heading toward the rear door. "When in doubt, take some blood."

He vanished, and James wandered around the shop, inspecting the labels and wondering at the names of the various potions. Some were obvious, but there were others like Jesuits' Drops, or manna, or tincture of golden rod, which gave no clue to their function. All he knew about golden rod was that it was bad for hay fever, so why should anyone try to extract its essence? And what would Jesuits' Drops do? Used in conjunction with tincture of golden rod, would they obviate the necessity of saying "God bless you" when the patient sneezed? The more he thought about it, the more irrational the whole business became, and the more he was convinced Daniel was right when he said that the main thing the patient wanted was attention. Just simple, solicitous care, and after that, the administration of some medication that would produce a sensation of radical physical change. An emetic, or a soporific, or bleeding—anything to show that Things Were Going to Be Different. That, plus a reasonable amount of luck, and any doctor or apothecary was on his way to fame and fortune.

He was so preoccupied with his thoughts that he was startled by the jangling of the bell over the front door, and he looked around to see a thin man in his mid-thirties who looked something like a large wading bird. The man's eyes were a pale, watery blue, and a drop of moisture clung to the end of his reddened nose. James tried to guess why he'd come and decided a cold was the obvious answer.

"Dr. Greenleaf?" the man asked, in a clogged voice.

James hesitated, then nodded. He'd made the correct diagnosis, and prescribing a cure would be no problem. "My name is Greenleaf," he said, truthfully.

The man came closer with a strange, shuffling gait, and James was stunned to see he was opening the front of his trousers. With some difficulty and obvious discomfort he produced a gonad the size of an orange and cradled it in his hands for James to examine. James had the sudden feeling he was looking at an ostrich egg in its nest. "Observe that, if you will," the man said, in an accusing tone. "Getting bigger every day, and feels like I'd been kicked by a horse."

"You may put it away," James said, in what he hoped was a professional voice. "A simple description would have sufficed."

"But what do I do? Keep on like this, and I'll need a sling around my neck to hold it."

Having come this far, James was in no position to retreat. He looked around at the jars and bottles but they were no help, so he said, "How long has this been troubling you?"

"Four, five days now. A week at the most. Feels like a horse kicked me."

"So you said. Did you have any other—ah—ache or swelling?"

"Well, come to think of it, my neck was fair tender, right under the ear. It swelled up for a while there, but nothing like this. This feels like—"

"I know. You were kicked by a horse." James looked at the man's neck and saw that one side was in fact thicker than the other. Then, suddenly, he had the answer. "Did you ever have mumps?" he asked.

"No."

"Well, you have them now."

"What do I do?"

"Go home and lie down."

"What do I do about"—the man had just managed to get his trousers closed and was clearly in pain—"about this bowling ball I'm carrying around? This is no fun, you know. It don't seem like I've laughed in ever so long."

"If I had seen you earlier, it would have been one thing," James said, stalling for time while he tried to think of a medication. "As it is"—his eyes lit on a jar of Friends Female Pills, and he shook a few out into his hand—"try one of these, morning and evening, and"—he searched for something that might be a pain-killer and suddenly remembered the whisky—"a glass of this three times a day, in hot water if you prefer." He found an empty bottle and filled it from the whisky keg. "Is the pain better or worse at night?"

"It's no good at any time, but it's better if I'm not walking around."

"Then stay in bed. Get a cushion to support your—ah—afflicted member, and try not to walk any more than is necessary."

The man took the bottle and the pills and looked at them as though waiting for them to speak. "This is all?" he said at last.

"Try them, and see how they work."

"How much will it cost me?"

James waved an airy hand in dismissal. "Whatever you think it's worth. See how they work first."

The man nodded and shuffled out, and as the bell jangled behind him James let out a long sigh. He thought of what the problem might have been and realized how lucky he was, and his only hope was that the pills he'd handed out were harmless. He reasoned that anything with as general a name as "Friends Female Pills" could not be for any specific complaint, and there-fore it should do no harm for any gender to ingest them. And, since the man was superficially suffering from overdeveloped masculinity, there was one chance in a thousand that a few fe-male pills might restore some sort of balance. At least, there was no harm trying. The back door to the shop opened, and Daniel came in.

"Did we have a customer?" he asked, wiping the brass bleeder with his handkerchief. It consisted of a series of small blades, which retracted into their slots and then sprang out when the catch was released. "I heard the bell a couple of times."

James shrugged. "Nothing important. A man looking for Faneuil Hall . . . Now, if you'll just sign that note, I'll be off."

Two weeks later, the man came back. He walked normally now, although he was crouched forward as though following a scent. "Where is Dr. Greenleaf?" he asked in a low voice.

"I am Dr. Greenleaf," Daniel replied. "What may I do for you?"

"You're not the Dr. Greenleaf who was here before. The one who told me I had the mumps."

"I'm afraid I don't recall the incident," Daniel said. "But I am the only Dr. Greenleaf on the premises."

"I come in here a fortnight ago, all swole up like I'd been kicked in the crouch by a horse. Big as a melon, it was, and sore as a bad tooth. This Dr. Greenleaf said it was mumps and gave me some pills and whisky, and by God you know what happened? You know what *happened?*" He started stabbing at his trousers, trying to get them open.

"You needn't show me," Daniel said, quickly. "I think I know."

"*Here's* what happened!" the man went on, his voice rising as he produced a crinkled fold of scrotal skin. "It *vanished!* Right off the face of the earth! From being the size of a melon it got smaller and smaller, and I thought that Doc Greenleaf was some kind of wizard, and then by damn it kept *on* getting smaller, and now there's no more there than a peanut! Vanished into thin air! If I get hold of that Doc Greenleaf, I'll—"

"Wait a minute," Daniel interrupted. "What happened had nothing to do with the treatment. When a gland becomes diseased, as that did, it has a tendency to atrophy when the disease has passed. There is nothing that can be done about it . . . Incidentally, you can put it away now. I am aware of the problem."

Slowly, the man closed his trousers. "I don't know all them words you used," he said. "All I know is I'm left with only one—"

"And that's all you'll ever need," Daniel said, ushering him to the door. "Just keep that one out of harm's way, and you can lead a perfectly normal life."

The man left, and Daniel closed the door behind him. He thought back on the day he'd left James in the shop, and all he could remember was James's saying something about a man looking for Faneuil Hall. That must have been the man, he thought, but it's a funny way to go looking for Faneuil Hall.

6

James, fascinated by the ease with which land could be bought and sold, elected to remain in Boston when his parents moved to New Bedford, preferring to be close to the bankers, brokers, and merchants with whom he traded. He found that in Boston credit was the rock on which everything else was built; with solid credit a man was welcome everywhere, but if ever his credit was questioned—or even in a position to be questioned—he, for all practical purposes, ceased to exist. James, with several generations of Greenleaf business success behind him, was still required to prove his own solidity before he was accepted. The bankers and businessmen admired him for his common sense and saw him as a rising star in the Boston financial community. In another area he might have been referred to as a young Midas; in Boston it was sufficient to say he was "doing well." His Uncle Stephen shimmered with reflected glory, having prophesied as much for many years, and his cousin Abigail, fresh from England, was admiring though slightly more restrained.

James was living with his Uncle Stephen when, one morning, a messenger arrived at the house on Common Street with a letter bidding him to the Governor's mansion. John Hancock had been governor since 1780, and his summons to James was as unexpected as would have been his personal appearance at Stephen Greenleaf's house. The passions of the war were still glowing, and Hancock and the Tories had as little to do with each other as possible. James tried to think of any business deal that might have brought him to the Governor's attention or any land he might have bought that was desired by the Commonwealth, but no rational reason occurred to him, and he finally asked his Uncle Stephen's opinion.

"With a man like Hancock, it's hard to tell," Stephen said, after pondering the question. "First he blows one way, then he blows the other. I recall back in '71, when he was a respectable shipper, you heard none of this equality nonsense he fell to spouting later. He was bred an aristocrat, and showed it. The governor made him colonel of a company of cadets, and you can be damn sure there was never a peep out of him about equality when *that* commission came through. Only when his business went bad did he take up with the rabble, and that's what saved him. He was a rotten businessman but he could make a fiery speech, and the time was right for men who could make fiery speeches. They had a sort of celebration a year after what they called the 'Boston Massacre'—massacre indeed! a crowd of louts attacked the guards and got what they were asking for—and you'd think from the speech Hancock made, they'd all been babies butchered in their cradles. Called the guards 'Dark and designing knaves, murderers, parricides'—which of them killed his own father, if you don't mind my asking? And as for dark and designing knaves, I took a proclamation from the governor down to Old South, where that mob was planning to dump the East India tea in the Harbor—and Hancock was a part of that, too—and I might as well have been singing to the birds in the trees. The proclamation said in plain English they were unlawfully assembled and it called on them to disperse, and do you know what they did? They booed me! They booed and hissed the Sheriff of Suffolk County! Hissed like snakes!" His voice rose, and cracked, and his daughter Abigail came quickly into the room.

"Gently, Father," she said, in a soothing voice. "Try not to get too excited."

"I'm just giving Jamie a little lesson in history," he replied. "He's been bidden into the presence of the great King Hancock and wants to know what to expect."

"I'm sure he'll find out soon enough," she said, tucking an imaginary blanket around her father's legs. "You and Mr. Hancock were never on the best of terms, anyway."

"That doesn't mean I can't speak the truth about him." Looking at James, his uncle went on, "I can tell you one thing you'll find, and that is his famous egalitarianism was a fad of the moment. Just as in this country—a new aristocracy is going to rise, with your sainted General Washington as its leader. You can no more keep the aristocracy down than you can keep a bubble from rising through mud, and all this freedom and liberty you talk about will be controlled by the few who deserve it. Mark my words and see if I'm not right. The entire war was a waste of effort—of men—of money—" His voice started to rise again, and Abigail took one of his hands in hers.

"Would you like some tea, Father?" she asked. "Perhaps a spot of tea would make you feel better."

He glared at her. "Is one allowed to drink tea these days?" he asked. "I thought they dumped it all in the Harbor."

"You know perfectly well you may have tea," she replied. "What you're talking about happened almost fifteen years ago."

He digested this in silence. "Seems like yesterday," he said and took his hand from hers.

As he walked along the northern border of the Common, James reflected that, even allowing for his uncle's prejudices, Hancock had been lucky to have a cause that diverted attention from his business troubles. Granted the periodic boycotts and embargoes and blockades prior to the war had made life difficult for the shippers, any man in Boston nowadays who inherited a prosperous business and let it go quietly down the drain would be socially and professionally ostracized, whereas here was Hancock, a hero of his country and Governor of the Commonwealth. It took a very special form of luck to be able to achieve such a feat, and it was a kind of luck with which not everybody was blessed. He found he was telling himself not to count on it, but being totally honest, he felt that perhaps he, too, might have been touched by the same magic wand. He would know better when he discovered what lay in store for him at the mansion, but he was aware of the aura of success that hung—almost glowed— about him, and he felt that, whatever the governor wanted, it had to be good.

The first signs of fall were in the air, and the ground was crisp with fallen leaves. Here and there were reminders of the trees that had been pruned for firewood during the siege, but for the most part the Common had regained its natural state, and the elms and oaks and sycamores and maples were changing into their autumn colors as though nothing had ever happened.

Squirrels darted among the fallen leaves, and from overhead came the incongruous cries of a pair of circling herring gulls.

The Hancock mansion, which had been built by John's uncle, was set on a slight rise of land at the top of the Common. It stood back from the road, its grounds laid out in ornamental flower beds and bordered in box, with large stands of fruit and mulberry trees, the latter testimony to Thomas Hancock's brief but intense interest in silkworm culture. The entire grounds were enclosed by a low stone wall, topped by a wooden fence, and the gateposts were also of stone. A paved walk and twelve stone steps, terminating in a wide stone slab, led to the front door, over which was a balcony projecting from a large window on the second floor. The house itself was of heavy stone blocks, with the corners and window openings decorated in Braintree stone, and the tile roof was pierced by three dormer windows on either side and surmounted by a wooden balustrade. It was a sharp change from the flimsy wooden house on Hanover Street, where John had lived until his father's death.

James paused before the oaken front door, adjusted the ruffles at his throat and cuffs, and knocked. He felt at ease, and while he was interested in what was about to happen, he was in no way apprehensive. Hancock was, after all, a relative of sorts; he had married Dorothy Quincy, whose sister was married to a Greenleaf, and this connection, however tenuous, removed some of the awe James might have felt. It was true that not many youths of twenty-two were summoned into the Governor's presence, but it was also true that even fewer were related to him by marriage, so the one tended to cancel out the other and leave him just about where he started.

The door opened, and a servant, either recognizing or expecting him, bowed for him to come in. He entered a long hall, paneled in wood and hung with hunting scenes and pictures of dead game, and immediately to his right was a formal reception room, with bird's-eye maple furniture and rich damask coverings. To the left was a smaller drawing room, the walls of which were covered with crimson paper, and into this room the servant ushered him, then disappeared. Hancock was sitting at the far end, one bandaged foot resting on a T-shaped gout stool and one hand grasping the silver head of a cane. He was in his early fifties and showed the effects of his periodic bouts of illness, but there was still the arrogant jut to his jaw, and his face was as sharp as a hatchet. He studied James for a moment, then said, "Sit down."

"Thank you, sir." James could feel his self-confidence evaporating, and he tried to maintain his poise by sitting gracefully in the chair the Governor had indicated. He somehow got his feet crossed wrong and almost fell.

Hancock continued to study him. "So you're William Greenleaf's boy," he said, at last.

"Yes, sir," James replied. "That is, one of them. I have—"

"I know, I know. But you're the one he seems concerned about."

James could think of nothing to say, so didn't try.

"Your father is a great man," Hancock went on, after a few moments. "One of the great unsung men of this time."

"Yes, sir," James said, wondering where the conversation was going.

"Some of us fought the easy way, by shouting in the streets and making ourselves the targets of the tyrants, and we are the ones whose names will be remembered—for a while, at least." Hancock smiled, as though at a secret joke, then went on, "But your father chose the harder way, and by all odds the more dangerous: he worked behind the scenes, in secret, and yet had he been caught, his fate would have been the same as ours. Or maybe even worse—who knows?"

His eyes lost their focus and he seemed to go off on a tangent of memory, and what remained of James's self-confidence went with him. It occurred to James that, although the war had been over no more than four years, both his Uncle Stephen and John Hancock were immersed in memories that would become stronger but less accurate with the passage of time, and eventually the participants on both sides would be swearing to things that never happened—or happened in a wholly different perspective. He wondered how the history of the time would be written and was glad he was not the one who'd be called on to do it.

Hancock's monologue continued, but there was a new note to it, and James's attention was brought back by the words ". . . and now this Constitution. Everyone thinks he knows what's best for the country, and nobody will give an inch unless he has his way. It's a matter of horse trading, but most of them won't admit it. Well, that's neither here nor there."

"Yes, sir," James said, without thinking.

Hancock looked at him for what seemed like several minutes. "This may sound strange," he said, at last. "Do you think you could be United States consul in Amsterdam?"

James stared at him. "Amsterdam *Holland?*" he asked.

Hancock nodded. "I know of no other."

James swallowed and tried to think of what to say. "But why me?" he finally managed to ask. "I mean"—it came to him that for someone who was overflowing with confidence when he knocked at the door, he was now behaving like a back-country farm boy, twisting blades of grass between his toes. "Of course, I am flattered by the offer," he went on, attempting to regroup his forces, "but it's a subject about which I had not given the slightest thought. I was just wondering—"

"Better not to wonder too deeply," Hancock cut in. "These things sometimes happen in spite of the laws of probability. Amsterdam is the financial capital of Europe—of the world, when it comes to that—and you are a young man interested in finance. Your country will in all probability be needing large sums of money in the near future, and it will be important that our credit in Amsterdam be of the highest order. I am not going to try to tell you your duties, because consular duties cover a multitude of —I was about to say 'sins'—a multitude of fields, and you will not be confined to any one of them. For now, I desire only to know if you feel you can carry out the assignment."

"Yes, of course," James said, feeling his confidence return. "I should be delighted to accept. I was simply surprised, because it was the furthest thing from my thoughts."

"And just as well. If you'd been thinking about it, it would have shown an indecent amount of ambition." There was another silence, while Hancock's eyes took in every detail of James's features, clothing, and demeanor. He was like a painter, studying his subject before picking up a brush. Finally, almost as though talking to himself, he said, "I suppose you are too young to remember the remarks I made on the subject of wealth."

James's mind raced about like a dog hunting a scent, trying to think what Hancock was talking about. Nothing came to him, and he said, "Yes, sir, I presume I must be."

"Remember this," Hancock said, obviously glad of the chance to quote himself. "It will stand you in good stead. I said, 'Despise the glare of wealth. The people who pay greater respect to a wealthy villain than to an honest, upright man in poverty almost deserve to be enslaved.'" He continued to look at James, to see his reaction.

"Oh, that's very good, sir," James said, quickly. "I shall remember that." To himself, he thought of his uncle's scorn for Hancock's so-called egalitarianism, and he wondered if this were an example. To him it didn't seem so much like egalitarianism as shallow thinking, because a rich man, no matter how much of a villain, had more power than a poor man, no matter how honest, and if you wanted power you paid attention to the person who wielded it. But Hancock was getting old, and his thinking on such matters was apt to be slightly fuzzy. James tapped his forehead and smiled. "I shall remember it," he repeated.

"'My tables—meet it is I set it down,'" Hancock quoted, "'that one may smile, and smile, and be a villain.'"

James paused. "I beg your pardon?"

"A better known authority than I," said Hancock. "That comes from *Hamlet*."

James nodded wisely, and changed the subject. "My—ah—post," he said. "When am I expected to assume my duties?"

Hancock looked out the window, at the bright yellow leaves of a maple tree. "This is hardly the time to be setting out to cross the ocean," he said. "The winter gales will be on us all too soon, and then only fools and fishermen venture on the water. I should say that next spring would be in plenty of time. That way, you will be able to have some—how shall I put it?—training in your new profession, you will be able to cross the Atlantic in comparative comfort, and you will be able to take with you the memory of the first codfish of the year."

"The . . ." James leaned forward, as though he had missed something. "Do my duties involve codfish?" he asked.

"No, but I have Saturday-night codfish suppers which, if you will forgive my saying so, are becoming something of an institution. The first codfish and the first salmon, and while the Saturday suppers are more or less come-one-come-all affairs, I am more selective on other days of the week. I shall look forward to entertaining you and your—are you married?"

"No, sir. Not as yet."

"Probably just as well. A bride, no matter how decorative, can be a drawback on one's first diplomatic post."

"How is that, sir?"

"A diversion of attention. You should be free to devote your full time to your duties. Besides"—Hancock cleared his throat—"there are times when it is convenient to be able to, ah, move about without any permanent attachments. Not that I'm advocating philandering, mind you. Let there be no mistake about that. Brother Franklin has taken care of that end of diplomacy all too well."

"Yes, sir. I understand."

"Good. Then I shall send word that you have accepted the post, and stand ready to sail in the spring."

"Thank you, sir." James rose, not sure whether to bow, genuflect, or shake hands.

"Don't thank me, thank your father," Hancock replied, and closed the interview with a wave of his cane.

Stephen Greenleaf was incredulous when James reported the news. "United States *consul?*" he said, as though the word had just been coined. "Did I hear you correctly?"

"You did indeed," James replied, glancing at his fingernails. "Those are the words the Governor used."

Greenleaf opened his mouth two or three times, then shook his head. "I am aware this is a new country," he said. "But to appoint a—a—" He left the sentence unfinished and shook his head again.

"You have always said I could do anything I set my mind to," James said, trying not to sound smug. "Has something made you change your mind?" He was teetering on the rim of impertinence and knew it, but felt he could afford to take the chance.

"I mean nothing against you," his uncle replied. "It is simply that the diplomatic service, as I have known it, is a career and not a—a chance assignment. The eldest son goes into the Navy, the next into the Army, and the third into the Foreign Service. One is born to it, not appointed by some—some helter-skelter politician."

"I make no great defense of the position," James said. "It was as much a surprise to me as it was to you. I'm simply pleased that someone has the confidence in me to offer me the post."

"Oh, I have confidence in you," Stephen said, quickly. "I've been the first to say that all along. I was simply thinking of the system."

"As you said, we are a new country," James replied. "The only way we can learn is through our mistakes."

His uncle was quiet for a moment, then with a faint hint of wonder in his voice said, "You have had the appointment less than an hour, and you are already beginning to talk like a diplomat. There may be some hope for the country, after all."

During that winter James found that his status as an embryonic diplomat broadened his social horizons considerably. The name Greenleaf was as familiar around Boston as that of Adams, Warren, or Mifflin, and his various business transactions had marked him as a young man of promise, but the added *cachet* of being designated consul in Amsterdam gave him that aura that hostesses found attractive, and he was in constant demand. The fact that he was unmarried and personable was simply that much icing on the cake.

New York was, at the time, the provisional capital of the country, but to Bostonians this was a mere technicality, like saying it lay two hundred miles to the southwest. Boston was the cradle of liberty, the center of culture and learning, and, looking at it realistically, the heart and blood of the United States. It therefore followed that a son of Boston should represent the United States overseas and that Boston, by logical sequence of reasoning, should be this country's contact with the rest of the world. Boston could be as international as the next place if it chose, and New York and Philadelphia and Charleston and the rest were all very well as seaports, but there their importance ended. Everything else was Indian country, with all that that implied.

It was in mid-November that James was invited for dinner at the home of Mr. and Mrs. Josiah Bartlett. Bartlett was a shipbuilder of some success, whose yards had turned out ships that were swift enough and sturdy enough to become profitable privateers, and with the postwar expansion of trade, he was eager to share in the transatlantic traffic. The Bartlett winter home was not far from the Hancock mansion; in summer they maintained a country estate on the North Shore, near Salem. Mrs. Bartlett, *née*

Nancy Trikes, was a direct descendant of Sally Newell, who was hanged as a witch in 1692.

The first substantial snow of the year had fallen the night before, and the Common was a solid carpet of white. The lanterns and torches at the entrance to the Bartlett house cast flickering fingers of light into the night, pinpointing the arriving guests as they appeared out of the darkness, their horses steaming in the cold. As James gave his cape to a footman, he reflected how lucky he was to be here instead of on some storm-torn ship in the Atlantic, and he blessed Hancock for giving him the winter in which to prepare for the trip. He hoped the Governor would be among those present, but realized that, if he was coming, he would not be among the early arrivals. He would make his appearance at the last moment, just before the guests were summoned to dinner. As it turned out, he had declined the invitation.

None of the guests was familiar to James, and he was dismayed to hear them talking a variety of languages. He could identify French and German, but there was another guttural tongue that seemed to come from far back in the speaker's throat, and this one he couldn't place. It wasn't until he was introduced to one of the speakers that he realized it was Dutch, and he was only partly relieved to hear that the man spoke passable English. If this was how they talked in the country where he was going, he thought, then he was in for some intense studying before he had even a toehold on the language. Then his host took him aside and began to talk about the shipping business, and he was so relieved to hear straight English that he encouraged what was in fact a long and obvious harangue. He looked forward with dread to the seated part of dinner.

His partner was a tall, blond girl with a round face and large eyes, and the roundness was repeated in her chest and shoulders. She was, James reflected, the epitome of what George Eckman had been referring to when he spoke of a girl with something a man could take hold of, and while she seemed aware of this she did nothing to capitalize on it; she stared demurely at her lap as though she were alone in an empty room. If James had hoped she'd help him with the conversation, he was disappointed, and he decided his only approach was to start off directly.

"Please forgive me," he said, "but people were talking so

loudly I was unable to hear your name. Mine is James Green-leaf."

The round eyes rose and stared into his, and the lashes ringing them were almost white. "Juffrouw Scholten," she replied, with only a faint trace of accent.

"I'm sorry—the first name? Yevro?"

" 'Juffrouw' means 'miss.' My full name is Antonia Cornelia El-bertina Scholten."

"My word. I do have a lot to learn."

" 'Juffrouw Scholten' will suffice."

"No, I mean of the language. If I'm to be posted there, I should know the basic words."

She apparently knew about his position, because she said, "It will help. 'Mevrouw' is for a married woman, and 'mynheer' is a gentleman."

"Thank you. That should get me started."

A suspicion of a smile crossed her face. "Just barely."

He laughed, hoping she had been making a joke, but the smile was gone and her mind had already moved on to something else. He could feel a glow emanating from her that had nothing to do with what she was saying, and it intrigued him that she could be so neutral in conversation and at the same time give off waves like a charcoal brazier. He tried another gambit.

"You speak English very well. Have you been here long?"

"My father does business here." She indicated a florid-faced man across the table, who was keeping up a steady stream of conversation while he peered down the dress of the lady next to him. She, impaled by his gaze like a pinned butterfly, was trying to get the attention of the man on her other side.

"Aha," said James. "And is your mother here, too?"

"My mother is dead."

"I'm very sorry." Pause. "In what kind of—ah—business is your father engaged?"

"The banking business."

"Indeed. And that's what brings him here?"

"He also invests in land."

There was a silence, while James turned this over in his mind. The first course, a fillet of flounder with cream sauce, was served, and the man on the other side of Juffrouw Scholten got her attention long enough for James to finish the dish in silence. The

lady on his left was French and had no interest in either him or
the food; after one taste she put down her fork and assumed a
calculated air of boredom. She replied in French to his one attempt at conversation, then looked around for a compatriot with
whom she could talk. James mentally shrugged and let his mind
drift back to Mynheer Scholten, his banking, and his land. Aside
from the obvious attractions of his daughter, it appeared that the
Scholtens were people he would do well to remember.

The soup course was next, and as the host ladled the portions
out of the massive silver tureen, there was an odd grating sound,
like stones being rattled by surf. It was impossible to tell what
kind of soup it was, and when the footman placed James's plate
in front of him he was no wiser because the liquid was opaque,
like pea soup, and whatever the dish contained was hidden at
the bottom. When, finally, the hostess began, James took a quick
sample and found in his spoon one dripping snail shell, with the
parboiled remains of the mollusk protruding limply from the ap-
erture. He stared at it, returned it to the dish, and scooped up
another, aware of a sudden silence that had descended over the
table. The only sounds were the slow scrape of spoons and then
the tiny plop as the snails fell back, and all conversation ceased.

"This is a special dish for our French guests," the hostess announced, brightly. "In honor of the gallant General Lafayette."

She raised her wine glass, and James glanced at the French
lady on his left, whose face had turned ashen and whose hands
were gripping the tablecloth as though to prevent her from falling. Then he was aware of Antonia Scholten on his right, and he
looked at her and saw she was holding her breath. Their eyes
met and hers began to fill with tears, and he had to look away.
By clenching his teeth he was able to keep from laughing, but
the next time he glanced at Antonia the tears were streaming
down her cheeks, and he had to cover his mouth with his napkin.
A man at the far end of the table averted total chaos by rising
and proposing a toast to Lafayette, then someone else proposed
one to Von Steuben and someone else to William V of Orange-
Nassau, and finally the soup plates were removed and the meal
continued. But a lunatic bond had been forged between James
and Antonia, and thereafter they had only to look at each other
to start laughing.

When he told the story the following day, his Uncle Stephen sighed. "I suppose it's better than frogs," he said.

"I beg your pardon?" said James.

"Back during the Rebellion, a man named Tracy—Nathaniel Tracy—owned that big villa in Cambridge and came originally from Newburyport; a big ship chandler he was, and made a fortune at it—he gave a dinner for some French admiral and his officers—a French squadron came into Boston, back in '78—and by God if he didn't give every one of those Frenchmen a frog in his soup. He'd heard the French were partial to frogs, so he had the swamps of Cambridge scoured until he had enough to serve the whole party. Just boiled them along with the rest of the soup and dished out one to each man. They tell me the French got to laughing so hard they couldn't get the soup down, much less the frogs." He cackled briefly, then looked at James. "It doesn't seem that much has changed, does it?"

"Not in Boston," James replied.

"Perhaps it never will," said Stephen, "and perhaps that's what may save you."

7

James saw Antonia Scholten on several occasions that winter, and for a while the bond of the snail soup served to keep their conversation going. But eventually that became too thin to sustain anything more than a passing reference, and he concentrated on learning as much as he could from her about Holland. He was constantly aware of her physical warmth but he was equally aware that it was hardly a subject of conversation, so he did his best to appear interested in her for intellectual purposes only. Her father, seeing she'd caught the attention of the consul-designate to Amsterdam, did nothing to discourage the association; in fact, he saw to it that James was invited to dinner as often as possible. Mynheer Scholten had brought his daughter to the United States for several reasons, only one of them being the pleasure of her company.

Inevitably, the subject of James's departure for Holland came up. It was early March, and while the snow still clung to the ground, there was nevertheless the hint of change in the air—if not a hint of spring, at least the promise that the worst of the winter had passed. At Scholten's invitation James had come to their Cambridge residence for lunch, and after the meal Antonia excused herself. James had the quick sensation that the whole affair had been prearranged and he was acting a part that had been written for him. After lighting James's pipe and his own, Scholten poured two glasses of brandy and settled by the fire.

"You have never been to Holland?" he asked, by way of preamble.

"No, sir," James replied. "This will be my first time."

"A beautiful country. Of course, in the winter one does feel the cold, but this time of year—when do you plan to go?"

"I have no definite plans as yet," said James. "The Governor simply told me to wait until the winter gales had passed."

"That should be fairly shortly." Scholten took a sip of brandy, then drew on his pipe and let the smoke drift toward the ceiling. "My daughter and I will be leaving next month." He examined the smoke as it dissipated in the air.

"Really?" said James. "She didn't mention it."

"She doesn't know it yet." Scholten smiled. "*Wat een vrouw niet weet, wat haar niet deert.*"

"I beg your pardon?"

"It's an expression we have. Roughly, it means that what a woman doesn't know, won't do her any harm."

James digested this information in silence. "Do you know what ship you're sailing on?" he asked.

Scholten waved his pipe in a vague gesture. "Any one of a number," he said. "Dutch ships sail in all weather."

James felt as though he were being cornered and resented it. "A pity," he said. "It would have been pleasant if we could have sailed together."

Scholten stared at him. "And why can we not?"

"I must take an American-flag ship." He smiled, as though Scholten must understand. "Protocol, you know."

"But that is absurd," Scholten replied. "There are no passenger accommodations on American ships."

"On the contrary. They tell me the accommodations on the *Empress of China* were quite comfortable."

"That ship I have not heard of."

"A converted privateer. Three, four years ago she sailed out to China with a cargo of ginseng root and came back with tea, spices, and the like. Our ships are every bit as—ah—commodious as those of older nations."

Scholten changed the subject. "It seems strange to make a whole cargo out of ginseng root," he said.

"There were other items, but that was the bulk of it."

"Do the Chinese prize it that highly?"

"There seems to have been a slight misunderstanding," James replied. "My brother is an apothecary, and he tells me that the aphrodisiacal properties of ginseng are largely imaginary. The fact that the root looks like a human has led some people to believe that it strengthens the reproductive urge, and apparently, if taken in small quantities, it does have a mildly stimulating effect. But when you overload the market—the *Empress* took about thirty tons of it—not only do you drive the price down, but you demonstrate to one and all the impossibility of ginseng's being a—if you'll excuse the expression—magic wand. If it had done all it was reputed to, the port of Whampoa would have been one large"—he cleared his throat—"bordello."

Scholten laughed. "I must try ginseng sometime," he said. "In very small doses, of course."

"It might be an interesting experiment," said James, remembering how Scholten had peered down his partner's dress the night of the snail soup. To himself, he remarked that ginseng was the last thing Scholten needed, and this led him to wonder about Antonia. Had she inherited some of her father's proclivities and was just waiting for . . . ? No. Impossible. But how could he be sure? Might it be almost in the line of duty, as Hancock had suggested, or might it be a tack that could lead him into trouble before his career had even started? Stop it, Greenleaf, he told himself. Don't let your imagination take control like that. Be reasonable. Still, he wished he hadn't so firmly closed the door on a transatlantic voyage with the Scholtens. Unless he could persuade her father . . . "I can assure you," he said, "that any ship I may take will have full and comfortable accommodations."

"I beg your pardon?" Scholten's mind had been elsewhere, and it took him a few moments to bring it back.

"You need have no fear of sailing on an American ship," James told him. "You will be as comfortable as in your own home."

Scholten gave him a baleful stare. "No ship is comfortable," he replied. "It is simply a matter of the degree of discomfort."

In the end, they took passage in the ship *Pigou,* which had been built in Philadelphia in 1783 and sailed between the West Indies, Philadelphia, Boston, and Amsterdam. On the run to the West Indies she would take dried fish, barrel staves and boards, butter, beans, and cheese, returning with molasses, brown sugar, and coffee. The molasses would be converted into rum in the United States, and the cargo to Amsterdam would consist of coffee, indigo, sugar, and pepper. Amsterdam's contribution to the cycle was Holland gin, which filled the hold on the return to the United States. Like a room after ladies have left, the ship breathed memories of its various cargoes, and James, who had never been to sea before, thought that all ships smelled this way. The Scholtens, who knew better, were grateful for minor blessings.

Their quarters were small and cramped, and it was clear that the captain, Benjamin Loxley, Jr., was unhappy at having Antonia aboard. He gave her the best cabin, but he did so in a way that suggested he was kicking a hole in the bottom of the ship, and they would all drown before sundown. A short, leathery man with pale blue eyes and a perennial white stubble, he seemed always on the borderline between talking to himself and thinking out loud, and small, incoherent sounds issued from him as from a distant swamp. He would not allow the passengers to settle in until all the cargo was loaded and the ship ready to sail, and then he looked at their baggage as though it would be impossible ever to fit it aboard. Finally, and reluctantly, he directed the bosun to have it brought on, and then turned his attention to getting the ship underway.

From Long Wharf, where the *Pigou* was moored, James could see straight up King Street to the State House, and he thought back to the time, twelve years ago, when his father had tried to read the Declaration of Independence from that balcony. He felt a sudden rush of affection, seeing for the first time the agony his father must have suffered, and he now realized why his mother's voice had sounded so clogged and strange. He reflected that although children hear and see everything that happens, they don't always interpret it correctly, which in the long run is probably just as well. If he had felt at the time the way he did now, he would have wept uncontrollably. Even thinking about his parents made his eyes sting, and he turned away from the rail and looked up at the rigging, aware that Antonia was watching him closely.

It was the first week in April, and the sky was bright and clean-looking. He could see the men on the yardarms, shaking out the sails in response to incomprehensible orders from below, and he could hear the slap and rattle as the wind spilled past the loose canvas. The *Pigou* had three masts, and by the time the maneuvering sails were in place, the noise was like one long volley of musket fire. The captain gave monosyllabic orders to the first officer, a Mr. Stoughton; Mr. Stoughton amplified them, in a louder voice, for the bosun; and the bosun bellowed and made shrill squeals on his pipe, which caused the men to leap about like apes. The lines snaked in from the dock, the yardarms swung at right angles to the wind; there was a heavy thump, and the ship lurched slightly to leeward. At first almost imperceptibly, by inches, the dock seemed to move away, then the intervening water widened, and finally they were in the stream, headed down harbor. The houses, spires, and wharves of Boston grew gradually smaller, and when the *Pigou* passed Castle Island, James could see the white-flecked ocean far ahead. He looked astern until the houses blended with the land and the hills flattened out into one long line, and then he turned and faced the ocean and felt the sting of salt spray on his cheeks. The Scholtens had gone below and for this he was grateful, because he didn't feel like talking. His mind was a jumble of many things: of nostalgia at leaving his family, of muted excitement at the prospects that lay before him, and of faint flashes of apprehension as to how he would perform. But he told himself that Hancock must have had confidence or he wouldn't have been chosen, and he should take the approach that, young as he was, he was the man best fitted for the job. This was no place for doubt; he should behave with total self-assurance. A man who represented an infant nation could not afford to cringe. The ship's bow rose slightly, then fell, and his stomach felt suddenly hollow.

With the ship on course and the sails set, the captain turned the watch over to Mr. Stoughton and came to where James was standing at the windward rail, facing the wind with his eyes closed and occasionally wiping the spray from his face.

"When yer puke, puke to loord," the captain said.

James opened his eyes. "I beg your pardon?"

"Yer green, which means yer fixing to puke. Get to the loord rail, so yer don't get it all over yerself and the deck."

James looked uncomprehending. "The what rail?" he asked.

Muttering, the captain took him by the arm and led him across the deck to the leeward rail. "There," he said. "Now the wind'll take it clear."

James swallowed, determined that, no matter what happened, he would not be sick. He could feel the saliva flowing around his back teeth and swallowed again. "Thank you," he said. "I shall remember that, in case I should ever need it."

The captain looked at him for a moment. "Yer first time at sea, I wouldn't doubt."

"As it turns out, it is." Don't cringe, he reminded himself. Take the initiative—appear interested. "Could you tell me something about this ship? It seems like a very—ah—nice one."

The captain continued to look at him. "What do yer want to know?"

"Whatever seems important. If I'm going to be aboard for the next few weeks, I might as well know something about where I am."

"She's a hundred foot long, twenty-eight foot beam, three hundred fifty-nine tons. Built four—no, it's five—years ago, owned by John Field, Jesse Wake, Pattison Hartshorne, et al., all of Philadelphia."

"Who was that last?"

"Et al."

"Before that."

"Pattison Hartshorne."

"An interesting name. What does he do?"

"Merchant."

"Pity. He should be doing something a little more—flamboyant."

"Such as?"

"A wigmaker, perhaps. Wigs by Pattison Hartshorne." James looked forward, through the forest of halyards, sheets, ratlines, and stays, and saw that every line appeared to have a purpose and was neatly affixed to a cleat or belaying pin. "A hundred feet long, eh?" he said, and then noticed, for the first time, the blunt, black breeches of the cannon that pointed outboard along each side. In all, he could count about a dozen, some partly covered with canvas and some wholly exposed, lashed in place by heavy lines that ran through an eyehole on each breech. "What are those for?" he asked.

A smile flickered on the captain's face. "Protection."

"From what? We're not at war, are we?"

The captain's smile broadened into a grin. "Yer never know. Yer heard about the schooner *Maria*, a couple of years back?"

James thought for a moment. "There was something about pirates, wasn't there?"

"That's right. Her and the *Dauphin,* boarded by Barbary pirates, and their crews taken into slavery. We don't aim to have that happen here."

"Well, this is a much bigger ship than a schooner. I shouldn't think there'd be any worry about—"

"Mister, the man who goes to sea and *don't* worry, he's a ring-tailed idiot. *Everything* is worry, from the time yer hoist anchor until yer drop it again. Show me a cheerful skipper, and I'll show yer a man who'll fetch up on a lee shore some night, probably still grinning. Why do yer think we get so drunk when we're in port?"

James hesitated. "I wasn't aware you did."

The captain gave a laugh that sounded like the bark of a large dog. "Yer ain't been around much. I recall one night down in Surinam—eighteen, twenty years ago, it must've been—a dozen or more of us skippers got together with the owners' agents, and we went to a tavern, and godamighty what a night we made of it! There was an artist feller there—name of Greenwood, John Greenwood—and he did a painting of it later on. Showed the whole thing—Ambrose Page puking into Jonas Wanton's pocket, Nick Power giving Godfrey Malbone a dancing lesson, Esek Hopkins laughing at nothing at all, and Greenwood himself going out the door to puke. I don't know how he remembered it, but he had it all there. First time I saw it, I could all but taste that Dutch gin." He closed his eyes and shuddered.

"Dutch?" James said, his interest perking. "Is Surinam in Holland?"

It was a moment before the captain answered. "Yer do have a lot to learn, don't yer?" he said.

"I am not widely traveled," James replied, trying not to sound defensive. "I was born and brought up in Boston, and until now I have had no occasion to leave."

The captain nodded. "Surinam's a Dutch possession, down in the Caribbean. There's those who call it Dutch Guiana."

"Ah, yes," said James. "Of course."

"Yes indeed. If yer ever get down there, stay clear of the Lage Dÿk Kroeg. Or if yer do go, don't tell them yer know me."

"I shall remember," said James. "What does the name mean?"

"The Low Dike Tavern," the captain replied. "And well named it is, too." He peered aloft and then at the sea, then said, "Enough of this; I've wasted too much of the day already," and went below.

James looked around and realized that his feeling of seasickness had gone; his attention had been so taken up by the captain that he'd ceased to think about himself. He glanced at Mr. Stoughton, who was looking at the topsails, and after a moment Stoughton lowered his gaze and their eyes met. They held for several seconds, and James had the distinct impression the first officer was laughing at him. Irritated, he returned the look with an icy stare, and after a while Stoughton shifted his attention to the topsails. James clasped his hands behind his back and strode forward, trying to imagine he was John Paul Jones.

He didn't see the Scholtens at the evening meal, which consisted of vegetable soup and boiled beef, and he wondered if they, as seasoned travelers, had brought along some preserved delicacies to consume in the privacy of their cabins. If they had, it was a distinctly unfriendly gesture not to invite him to share with them, and he wondered why Scholten had been so eager to go on the same ship with him. There were plenty of Dutch ships Scholten could have taken, and the fact that he chose to sail on an American ship had indicated there was a definite purpose behind the move. Now James wasn't so sure, and he was puzzled and upset. He tried to think of anything he could have said that might have given offense, but could come up with nothing. Mr. Stoughton, quietly smiling across the table from him, did nothing to improve his mood, and he answered all of Stoughton's questions as briefly as possible. Finally, dropping all pretense of casual chatter, Stoughton rose and looked into the passageway to make sure they were alone, then sat down and spoke in a low voice.

"I hope you didn't let the captain upset you," he said.

"Why should he have?" James replied.

"He tends to look on the dark side of things."

James shrugged. "From what I gather, the seagoing life is a hard one."

"Yes, but his has been harder than most."

For the first time, James looked directly at Stoughton. "And what, pray, does that mean?" he asked.

"Precisely what I said. If there is a hardship that the sea has to offer, Captain Loxley has known it. He has suffered shipwreck, fire at sea, capture by pirates, and the ravages of hurricanes, typhoons, and ice floes. When he was a youth he was on a ship that was stove by a whale; as a second officer he was thrown overboard by mutineers and survived only because the sharks sated themselves on the captain and first officer, who had preceded him over the rail. That time in Surinam he told you about—he neglected to mention that as he left the tavern he was set upon by native footpads, and was unconscious for a fortnight. He revived only as preparations were being made for his burial. If he sometimes seems to take a pessimistic view of things, please understand it is only because he has seen very little that would cause him to be cheerful."

"Yes," said James quietly. "I understand."

"And none of it has been his fault. His seamanship is flawless and his navigation precise; he is admired by his crews, and his ships are often the best; his only problem is that, if there is trouble anywhere on the oceans, he will find it—or, more precisely, it will find him."

"I can see that is a problem," said James. "What else is left to happen?"

"Don't think of it or it will," Stoughton replied. "On this ship we take everything as it comes and try not to look too far ahead."

"Have you sailed with him long?"

Stoughton hesitated. "Long enough," he said. "Long enough to know my chances of survival are as good with him as with anyone else."

James thought a moment, trying to find the tactful way to say what he was thinking. "Forgive me if this sounds odd," he said, at last, "but you—that is to say—"

"I know," Stoughton cut in. "I don't sound like a seafaring man. Is that what you were going to say?"

"Something like that," said James.

"It's a long story, and not a very interesting one. I went to sea for what I'd planned would be a brief stretch of time, and it stretched out longer than I'd expected. Some day, in my cups in some tavern, I might tell you, and I promise you'll be bored. Until then, just remember Hamlet's words: 'There are more things in heaven and earth, Horatio, than are dreamt of in your philosophy.'"

"Ah, yes," said James, remembering Hancock's having quoted something from the play. He made a mental note to read it at the first opportunity. He also wondered if Stoughton's quoting it meant he had gone to Harvard, but found that hard to believe. Still, his brother William had quoted Shakespeare on occasion, so maybe that was a stamp the college put on a man. He regretted not being a Harvard graduate himself and wondered why his father had not seen fit to send him. If, as he was often told, he was the son with the most promise, then it would have seemed . . . Well, there was no point brooding about it now. He'd show them he could be a success without a college degree. Not only would he be a success, he would be successful beyond the dreams of ordinary men.

When he got back on deck, it took his eyes a few moments to adjust to the darkness. He could hear the rush of water past the sides and feel the rhythmic surge as the ship dipped into the waves, then gradually he became aware of the blackness of the sails silhouetted against the stars and of a figure standing motionless at the port rail. As he approached he saw it was the captain, holding something in front of his face and mouthing garbled curses.

"Good evening," James said pleasantly.

The captain mumbled something and continued with what he was doing.

"Is there something out there?" James asked, thinking the captain's professional eyes might have sighted a sail.

"A lot of damned foolishness is what's out there," the captain replied, making an adjustment to whatever it was he was holding. "The owners insist I use this damned thingumabob, and it's no more damned use than a whiffletree." He took the instrument over to where the helmsman was standing, opened the cover of the binnacle lantern, and peered at the instrument. Then he grunted and closed off the light. "It lies," he said. "By three degrees, it lies in its teeth."

"I don't believe I understand you," James said.

"This is what they call a backstaff," the captain said, holding the instrument up in the darkness. "Backstaff, or Davis quadrant, or whatever. It's supposed to give the height of any object, but for all the good it does, it might as well be a set of false teeth."

"Oh," said James, hoping a fuller explanation would follow.

The captain gestured with the backstaff, which looked like a monstrous praying mantis. "Like right now," he said. "*I* know what my latitude is, but the owners want me to take sights to prove it. The latitude of Boston hasn't changed in thirty thousand years, and we're no further from Boston than yer can spit, but this damned backstaff has me up somewhere off Nova Scotia."

"Aha," said James.

"And when I take a sun line tomorrow—if there *is* any sun—the odds are good it'll have me down off Baltimore. I'd be just as accurate if I was taking sights over a camel."

"How can it be so wrong?" James asked.

The captain paused. "In theory, it's all right," he said, at last. "It's in the practice that trouble comes. In theory, the height of the North Star is the same as yer latitude—give or take a degree, and there's a table for correcting it down fine. Or get the height of the sun or moon and go into the tables and also come up with yer latitude. But the tables are full of errors, and unless the sight's right sharp, yer feeding in another error, and pretty soon there's enough errors to look like yer in the Sahara Desert. And there's no way in God's heaven to tell longitude except by dead reckoning, so if yer going to dead-reckon part of it, yer might as well dead-reckon the whole thing. Any decent seaman can dead-reckon his way around the world, given enough time, but now suddenly the owners want everything fast. Speed, speed, speed is all they think about, and they got some crazy idea it makes more speed to go around peeking through a bundle of sticks like this." He shook the backstaff as though to strangle it. "This thing come out some thirty-five years ago, and I'll be willing to bet there hasn't been a day saved in added speed that whole time. If anything, more ships have run aground, while their captains had their noses stuck into a backstaff trying to find out where they were."

"Doesn't the compass help?" James asked.

"It tells which way yer headed. Which way is north, to be exact. But with the North Star, yer don't need a compass. There's no instrument as good as the signs the good Lord hung out for all to see. But the owners think they know better, so that's the way it has to be. They're going contrary to nature, and they're going to pay for it, but of course they only lose their money. We're the ones who lose our lives." He sighed and headed for the companionway. "We're all doomed in the end, anyway, so there's no real use complaining."

"Where are you going?" James asked.

"To enter this donkey star sight in the log. That way, when the flotsam washes ashore, the owners'll know I did my duty." He dropped down the ladder and out of sight.

James moved over to the helmsman, to see how he steered. The binnacle cover was closed and the compass invisible. Occasional stars could be seen through the rigging, seeming to rock slowly back and forth.

"Which is the North Star?" James asked.

"Off there." The helmsman gestured to port, where the only thing James could make out was the Big Dipper.

"Are you watching it now?" he asked.

"No," the helmsman replied.

"Then how are you steering?"

"By feel."

James thought this over, then strolled to the port rail and studied the clusters of stars that filled the sky. He wondered how far away they were and what lay out beyond them, and he was almost hypnotized by his contemplation of space when he became aware of a presence beside him. He looked around and saw Antonia standing quietly by the rail.

"Good evening," he said. "I trust you had a pleasant dinner."

There was a pause, then she said, "Where?"

"I presume you and your father dined in your cabin."

She laughed. "If you had seen my cabin, you would presume no such thing. There is room for myself and my clothes and no more."

"Oh." He felt vaguely relieved.

"My father and I make it a rule never to eat the first day at sea. That way, we become accustomed to the motion without any danger of embarrassment. We simply lie in our bunks and wait there until we feel ready to emerge."

"Like butterflies from their cocoons," James suggested, mentally picturing her as she emerged from bed. Then he thought of her father doing the same, and the picture vanished.

"I suppose you could say that," Antonia replied. "Did we miss anything at table?"

"We had a rather tasty snail soup," James said, and when she laughed, he went on, "All you really missed was Mr. Stoughton's biographical summary of the captain. It is an incredible story."

"And who is Mr. Stoughton?"

"The first officer. I suspect he has his own story, but at the moment he declines to tell it."

"I imagine anyone who goes to sea has a story of some sort," Antonia said. "It is not a pastime one would take up lightly."

"Why limit it to those who go to sea? Everywhere you look, there are people about whom something could be told." He had been wanting to find out more about her, and considered this a particularly deft way of introducing the subject. He was congratulating himself and framing his approach, when she replied.

"You are absolutely right," she said. "You, for instance. How is it that you, so young, are appointed United States consul in Amsterdam? Forgive me if I sound unladylike, but I cannot help asking."

"I am not exactly a child," James replied, suddenly on the defensive. "I have enjoyed a certain success in the world of finance."

"Do you have relations in high places?"

He cleared his throat. "My father played a part in the Revolution. Or, rather, in the events leading up to it. He was a member of the commission of seven." He waited, knowing the name meant nothing to her, then said, "A secret group. They laid the groundwork for independence."

"Ah, yes. How do you say it—'malcontents'? 'Plotters'?"

"Not exactly. When—"

"'Conspirators'! That is the word. Did they hide in cellars and cover their faces with their capes and slink about at night?"

"Not at all. These were patriots, who—"

"The British thought of them as conspirators. I know, because I used to see the British pamphlets on the subject."

"The British referred to us as rebels."

She shook her head. "These definitions are too subtle for me. Or perhaps it is the language. Every time I think I know the meaning of a word in English, I find it can mean something else when used a different way. I sometimes think it is expressly designed to induce madness."

"I must say, you speak it quite well," James said.

"Speak, perhaps, but I cannot think in it. There are things the words do that defy rational thought."

"I wasn't aware."

"You turn pale with anger; you carry water in a pail. You light a candle, lighten a load, and take cargo to a vessel in a lighter. The candle brightens the room, but could you brighten a load or take cargo in a brighter? Where is the logic to the language? What are the words supposed to mean?" She paused, then said, "Please forgive me. This is none of my affair. It just confuses me when I think about it."

"Perhaps I can lessen the confusion," said a man's voice. "What is the problem?"

Antonia started, and James could see, on the other side of her, the dim figure of the first officer.

"Juffrouw Scholten, may I present Mr. Stoughton?" he said, removing his hat. "Mr. Stoughton, you remember, is our first officer."

"Ah, yes," said Antonia, as Stoughton removed his cap. "How do you do?"

"Possibly you would know better than I," Stoughton replied. "I gather you have been discussing me."

"Only in passing," said James. "Juffrouw Scholten's confusion stems from the vagaries of the English language. She speaks it so well it is hard to believe she isn't a native."

"Indeed," said Stoughton. "I took her for a belle from the North Shore."

"Really, sir," said Antonia. "I thought seafaring men were supposed to talk sensibly."

"We do, we do. When a seafaring man says a thing, there is no mistaking his meaning."

"Amen to that," said James, quietly, but Antonia wasn't listening.

"What a refreshing thought," she said, to Stoughton. "I find it positively exhilarating."

"Any trouble you may have with the language," Stoughton

replied, "is wholly imaginary. You know the precise meaning of every word."

"Not all of them, I assure you."

James cleared his throat. "It's getting a bit chilly up here," he said, to the back of Antonia's head. "Wouldn't you be more comfortable if I took you downstairs?"

Before Antonia could reply, Stoughton said, "At sea, we call it 'below.' The term 'downstairs' applies only to houses and other shore-based structures."

"Forgive me," said James, with a slight bow. "I didn't know."

"A natural mistake," said Stoughton. "And now, would Juffrouw Scholten care to inspect the forward part of the deck? There are areas there that are well sheltered from the wind."

"I should be fascinated," replied Antonia, taking his arm, and they strolled off into the darkness. James watched them go, then went to the companionway and clattered down the ladder to his cabin. The first lesson for a diplomat, he told himself, is how to take everything in your stride. Never let them know you're beaten. Never.

8

Next day the wind, which had been from the northwest, backed around to the west and then south, and the sea rose and fell in long, oily swells. The sky was filmed with a high haze, and by midmorning the sun was discernible only as a bright blur to starboard. The captain, who had been trying to get a sight on it with his backstaff, gave up in disgust.

"No damn point trying to find out where we are," he muttered, putting the instrument in its case and slamming the cover. "This time tomorrow we could be five other places."

James had decided to learn what seamanship he could, in order not to look like a complete fool in front of Antonia, and he asked what the captain meant.

"A figure of speech," the captain replied. "We could be any one of a dozen places—the number don't matter."

"I still don't understand," James said. "We are headed east, are we not?"

"For the moment," said the captain. "But yer see that sky? Yer see what the wind's been doing? And the glass? The glass is dropping like somebody shot it."

"Are those bad signs?" James asked.

The captain grinned. "They are. If yer a mind to do any eating, yer better do it now, because there'll be damn little eating the next couple of days."

James swallowed once, then again. "Would it be wiser to turn back?" He regretted it the moment the words left his mouth, and he tried to soften their stupidity by saying, "I mean—might the ship ride more easily if we were to go with the storm, rather than against it?"

"We'll go where the good Lord blows us," the captain replied.

"Just try to keep our rigging intact and stay afloat and leave the rest to the Lord." He put the backstaff case under one arm and went below.

James remained on deck, wanting to postpone as long as possible his descent to the cramped and stuffy cabin, and he tried to fight the feeling of helplessness the captain had given him. He told himself that this was a common occurrence at sea, that the captain had been sailing through such storms all his life, and that there seemed to be no sign of panic among the crew. When the crew become frightened, he told himself, then is the time to worry; until then, accept whatever happens as part of the day's routine. Gradually, he forced himself to feel better; the flash of seasickness passed, and he even found himself curious as to what the seas might have to offer. He was feeling almost confident when Antonia came on deck. Her hat was held in place by a long silk scarf, which tied under her chin and whipped like two pennants in the wind.

"Good morning," James said. "I trust you slept well." He had decided not to mention the previous evening or, for that matter, Stoughton.

"Very well, thank you," Antonia replied cheerfully.

"From what the captain says, I gather we're in for a spell of bad weather."

"Yes, Mr. Stoughton said the same thing." She looked at him with a faint hint of a smile. "Have you ever been in a storm at sea?"

"Not really. This is my first time on the—uh—ocean."

Her smile broadened. "It causes some people to long for death. The one thing you should remember is that nobody has ever died of seasickness."

"I have no reason to believe I shall be sick." He found that he was salivating again and wanted to spit but obviously couldn't.

"No, of course not. And I'm told that the worse the storm the less likely one is to be sick."

"Oh? Why is that?"

"I'm not quite sure. Mr. Stoughton said it had something to do with terror. If you are absolutely paralyzed with fear, your body just gives up and nothing happens. He said that when going into battle, no one on a Navy ship is ever sick."

"Was he in the Navy?"

"He didn't say. He just made the remark in passing."

James tried to think of a way to denigrate Stoughton, but could come up with nothing that wasn't obvious jealousy. "It's an interesting point, if true," he said.

"I see no reason for him to have invented it." She thought a second, then said, "Of course, there is one moment that no one can know about until it happens—it's something one has to learn for one's self."

"What is that?"

"When a ship goes down. When the seas overwhelm it and smash it to pieces, then what you do is between you and your God. There can be no rehearsing for it, and nobody to tell you what it is like."

He looked at her with curiosity. "You sound as though you enjoyed the idea," he said. "You almost seem to be looking forward to it."

"Not in the least. I'm terrified. But I believe you cannot avoid danger by ignoring it; if you face up to the possibilities, then at least you will never be surprised."

"You are a remarkable person. Are you aware of that?"

"I have led a remarkable life."

"In what way?"

She took one end of her scarf and fluttered it as though it were a fan. "This way and that."

He laughed. "In other words, it is none of my affair."

"It is as much your affair as you care to make it."

He was about to remark that coquetry had its places and the deck of a ship wasn't one, when he saw Stoughton appearing from the forward hatch. To divert her attention he said, "I learned an interesting thing yesterday. Let me show you." Taking her arm he guided her to the stern, and looked over the rail at waves that rose, hissing, behind the ship. "Do you know how they tell the speed of the ship?" he asked.

She looked first at the sea, then at him. "How?"

"They throw a piece of wood over with a rope attached to it, and this rope has knots in it, one knot every forty-seven feet three inches. The number of knots that run out in twenty-eight seconds is the number of nautical miles an hour the ship is traveling."

She thought about this. "Who decided that?" she asked, at last.

"I don't know. It's just the way it works out."

"Why?"

"Because forty-seven feet three inches is to a nautical mile as twenty-eight seconds is to an hour."

"I wonder who measured it. I mean, that's not a piece of knowledge one is born with."

He closed his eyes. "All I know is what the captain told me."

She slipped her arm through his. "Please don't think I am unappreciative. It is a very comforting thing to know."

He suddenly realized that Stoughton had come up behind them, and he said, "Perhaps our first officer can explain it better. Mr. Stoughton, do you know who found that forty-seven feet three inches is to a mile as twenty-eight seconds is to an hour?"

"No idea," Stoughton replied. "I always use forty-eight feet and thirty seconds. It's simpler, and the answer is about the same."

"I see," said James. "Thank you."

The wind continued to back, first to the southeast and then to the east, and the sun vanished behind dark, scudding clouds. It was as though they were sailing into a monstrous blackness, and the sound of the wind in the rigging rose from a moan to a whistle to a thin wail. The seas became streaked with white and foaming crests appeared, and the captain changed course to keep the waves just off the starboard bow, at the same time taking in unnecessary sail. First the royals came in and then the topgallants, and as James watched the men teetering on the yardarms and clawing at the canvas, he wondered what could possibly induce a man to become a sailor. Who would want to live this way, if he had any choice in the matter? There would have to have been some disaster at home, or a flight to avoid prison or hanging, to make a man willing to risk his life high in the careening rigging, with every finger torn and bleeding and his whole body flayed by the wind. He looked at Stoughton, as he directed the men in their various duties; the first officer seemed born of the sea and almost a part of it, and it was hard to believe

what he'd said, that he'd originally intended his seagoing stretch
to be a short one.

Another thing that impressed James was the way the ship appeared to shrink in size. Alongside the wharf, in Boston, she had
seemed a large, solid vessel; now, surrounded by towering seas
that came hissing out of the darkness, the *Pigou* was small and
frail, with no more control over her movements than a chicken in
a whirlwind. The captain continued to take in sail, until only the
jib and the main topsail were left to provide steerage way, and
he ordered all passengers below decks, to remain there until he
gave the word they could emerge. For Antonia and her father
this was an unnecessary order; they had already retired to their
cabins, but James had hoped to be able to stay out in the air,
where his chances of seasickness would be minimized. But the
captain made no exceptions; he fixed James with a steely eye and
motioned him below, and James, feeling qualms at the mere idea
of confinement, went down the ladder and into the foul-smelling
cabin.

From then on, his conception of time vanished. He was in a
small, dark space that rose and fell and swooped and shuddered;
the beams groaned and the timbers creaked; water seemed to be
coming from everywhere, and there were occasional crashes and
thunderings that sounded as though the ship were breaking
apart. He tried to stay in his bunk, but was thrown out so often
that he finally gave up and lay on the deck, wedged in a corner
to prevent his rolling, while he prayed for a death that was
tantalizingly close but which always seemed to elude him. Time
lost all meaning; he simply existed but was incapable of movement, and with nothing to look forward to, he had no desire for
anything except the release that never came. He was, almost literally, reduced to jelly.

He may have slept, or he may have lost consciousness; all he
knew was that the noise and the motion, which had been his entire world, had abated somewhat, and he was freezing cold. He
had taken off his outer clothes before lying down and was clad
only in his underclothes, and now, sprawled on the wet and
slimy deck, he felt a chill that made his shoulders quiver. He
rose unsteadily to his feet, groping for a handhold in the darkness, and finally found the cabin door, which he opened, and
peered out. The faint light from the passageway was enough for

him to find his flint and striker, and he lighted the candle that
was in a gimbaled mount on his bulkhead. Then he closed the
door, surveyed his cabin, and was almost sick again. Gingerly he
stepped out of his underwear, wiped himself off as best he could,
then opened his luggage and brought out some clean clothes. By
the time he was dressed he was shaking all over, and it was then
he remembered he had brought along a flask of rum. He found
it, took a long swallow, and for one fiery instant thought he was
going to pass out. Then the warmth spread through his limbs,
and he began to look forward to survival.

It was a long time before he could make himself presentable
enough to risk meeting Antonia, and it never occurred to him
that she might have had problems similar to his. He visualized
her as being always poised and well groomed, and he felt all the
shabbier for not being able to shave. The ship was still too unstable, and his hands too fluttery, to risk an encounter with a razor,
and he took small comfort in the knowledge that the other men
were probably looking as grubby as he. If he couldn't outdo
Stoughton in seamanship, he felt he should at least try to be im-
maculate in his appearance. But as matters stood, he was helpless; it was a new sensation, and it irritated him.

When he got on deck, the sunlight was dazzling. The seas
were still running high, and their crests rolled over in white
foam, but the sky was clear and the clouds were bright, and the
Pigou was boiling along under her topsails, spanker, and flying
jib. James had expected to see the deck a shambles, but everything was as neat as when they'd left the wharf; the cannons
were lashed and covered, and all lines and halyards were secure
in their places. The deck was glistening wet, and some of the superstructure was crusted with salt, but aside from that, there was
no sign the ship had been through anything worse than a run
down Boston Harbor. The captain was, as usual, standing at the
rail with his backstaff, and when he saw James emerge from the
companionway he lowered the instrument and glared at him.

"I didn't say yer could come topside," he said.

"I'm sorry," James replied. "I rather lost track of things. I
thought you might have given the order while I was asleep."

"Asleep?" said the captain. "Yer was closer to dead than
asleep."

"Was I? How long was I—in my cabin?"

"The weather blew up two days ago. Two days and two nights."

"Oh." James rubbed his stubbly chin and saw with relief that the crew were no better shaved than he. With the captain it was hard to tell, but the other men looked more like pirates than merchant sailors. It didn't occur to him that some of them didn't shave from one landfall to the next.

"There'll be a fire in the galley come noon," the captain said. "A bit of hot food should help."

"Is it permitted for me to stay—ah—topside?" James asked. "I feel a little fresh air would do me good."

"So long as yer don't go over the rail," the captain replied. "I've got enough on my mind without having a man overboard this far at sea."

"How far out are we?"

The captain looked at the sun, then at the backstaff, then at the sun again. "The good Lord alone knows," he said, at last. "It smells like we're south of Cape Sable, but this donkey stick has us on the latitude of St. John's. It depends on where the storm took us."

"What does it smell like south of Cape Sable?"

"Yer can smell the Labrador current. And the cod from the Grand Banks. And a hint of the icebergs farther north. They all add up to one certain smell."

James sniffed the air, but could smell only salt. "I presume it takes a certain amount of experience," he said.

For the second time since James had known him, the captain laughed. "Yer could say that," he replied. Then he looked over James's shoulder and said, "Here they all come. The good weather's brought 'em out of their bunks like snails after a rain."

James turned, and saw Antonia and her father emerging from the companionway. Antonia looked pale and only faintly disheveled; it was clear she had worked on her appearance, and the occasional loose ends could be attributed as much to the wind as to anything else. She looked like a lady trying to maintain her composure behind a runaway horse. Her father, on the other hand, was unmistakably in poor shape. His skin was the color of cheese, mottled by an undergrowth of white beard; his stock was awry and his stockings twisted and wrinkled, and he gathered his overcoat around him as though it were a blanket. James found it hard to believe this was the same, faintly lecherous man he had once seen across the dinner table, and in the small eyes that had shone with concupiscence he could now see only misery, like the aftermath of a heavy bout of drinking. He wondered if Scholten had spent the last two days drinking to stave off seasickness, and concluded that from the way he looked now, the one would have been as bad as the other. What interested him most was his impression that, with all the bonhomie gone, Scholten's face gave off a distinct impression of evil. But then, he reminded himself, *he* probably didn't look like any paragon of virtue either, and it would be unfair to judge a man's character by how he looked after a two-day storm at sea. He strolled toward the Scholtens, and Antonia gave him a bleak smile.

"Good morning," she said.

"Good morning," he replied. "I hope you suffered no ill effects."

Scholten glowered, but Antonia remained cheerful. "No lasting effects," she replied. "A temporary loss of dignity, perhaps; nothing worse."

James laughed, as he thought of himself lying sprawled on the deck of his cabin. "There were times when I thought it might be permanent," he said. "I remembered your remarks about the last moments before a ship goes down."

"So, for that matter, did I." She laughed, and added, "But here we are, and none the worse for wear."

"Speak for yourself," her father growled.

"I've often wondered why a man would make a career out of the sea," James said. "To me, the rewards could never be worth the labor involved."

"*Chacun à son goût,*" Antonia replied, and when James looked blank, she said, "A French expression Mr. Stoughton taught me. It means each to his own taste."

"And very appropriate it is, too," said James. He turned to her father. "I trust your quarters are adequate?"

"As adequate as any," Scholten replied. "Why?"

"I feel responsible for your being on this ship. I promised you that American ships would be satisfactory, and I should hate to think I misled you."

Scholten grunted. "It is not the ship that's at fault, it is the sea.

Speak to the man who runs the sea, and that may accomplish
something."

James bowed. "I shall see what I can do."

He left them and went below, and for a few minutes there was
silence. Then, without looking at his daughter, Scholten said,
"Be careful."

"Of what?"

"Be careful you don't lose him."

"I see no danger of that."

"I do, if you keep rubbing his nose in this Stoughton. A man
can take only so much, and then he rebels."

She made a gesture of impatience. "Forgive me, Papa, but I
know what I am doing."

"I hope so."

"Mr. Stoughton only makes it easier. Without him, there might
have been problems."

"I saw none."

"James has great charm, but things have always been too easy
for him. He needs to be jolted every now and then, to prevent
his becoming overconfident."

"I see nothing wrong with overconfidence."

"Neither do I, but I should like to be able to have my way,
too. If I give in now, I shall have no bargaining point later."

Scholten shook his head. "My father once told me, a woman is
a whole different breed of animal. As different from men as
horses from goats. It has taken me fifty years to come to the realization he was right."

She laughed. "We're not all that different, Papa," she said.
"We're just careful."

"That is hardly the word." He spat toward the rail, with only
moderate success. "I feel a need for gin coming on," he said.
"Fetch me my flask, if you don't mind."

"Yes, Papa. And don't worry about Mr. Stoughton."

"I'll try. With gin, I worry less about everything."

Antonia went below and was emerging from her father's cabin
when she saw Stoughton striding down the passageway. She
stood back in the door to let him pass, but he slowed down,
stopped in front of her, and took off his cap. She noticed he was
clean shaven and smelled, incredibly, of cologne.

"Good morning," he said. "Is there anything I may do for you?"

"No, thank you," Antonia replied, holding up a silver flask. "I came to fetch my father's medicine."

"Is he unwell?" Stoughton didn't move.

"Not really. He simply feels he needs a tonic, after the storm."

"I have an old seaman's tonic, that will do wonders for him. Would you care to try some?"

"This is for my father, not for me."

"But you are bringing it to him." He moved imperceptibly closer.

"Sir, if you will forgive me, my father wants his tonic now. There will be ample time to discuss your medication later on." She started to move, and after a second's hesitation he stood aside and let her pass.

"At your leisure," he said. "I have all the time in the world."

Antonia went to the companionway, and Stoughton watched her go. Then, aware of another presence, he looked back, and saw James standing in the door to his cabin. His face was pale, and his eyes bulged out like those of a bullfrog. Stoughton gave him a friendly wave and a smile and then followed Antonia up on deck.

After the first week at sea the days seemed to melt together, distinguishable one from the other only by the frequent changes in the weather and the gradual worsening of the food. The boiled beef James had had for dinner the first night seemed, in retrospect, like breast of pheasant garnished with larks' tongues; the meat became older, and tougher, and saltier, and finally putrefaction set in, to the point where it was virtually inedible. Some attempts were made to scrape the maggots off before the meat was served, but these were not always successful, and the weevils that flourished in the flour barrels had to be either picked out of the bread one by one or gulped down as quickly as possible. The water turned rancid in the kegs, and the only safe thing to drink was wine or distilled spirits, a diet that made the sunlight blurry and brought on prolonged morning headaches. The ship appeared to make no forward progress at all; even when the wind was blowing, it didn't seem to take them any-where except up the side of one wave and down the side of another, sometimes burying the bow so deep in the next sea that it looked as though they might continue straight down. When the wind was not blowing, the ship simply wallowed in the waves, going nowhere.

The Scholtens, as James had suspected, had taken a few precautions against the deterioration of the food, and Antonia invited him to share with them. Shortly before noon one day, when he was standing at the rail watching some tiny sea birds, she came up beside him and said, "I don't mean to interrupt you, if you're busy."

Startled, he turned and said, "I beg your pardon. I was watching the birds."

She looked out at the sea. "What birds? I don't see any."

"They're gone now. They're as small as sparrows, and they fly just off the surface of the water—almost as though they were skating on it. I don't see how they do it without getting wet."

"Those are Mother Carey's chickens. They're supposed to be the souls of dead sailors."

"I wonder where they come from."

"Do they have to come from anywhere?"

He looked at her to see if she were serious and saw in her face the same expression as the first night they'd met. Suddenly cheerful, he said, "I suppose not. Except the sailors had to come from somewhere, didn't they?"

"Where they came from makes no matter to them now. Now they are free, to skip about the water as they choose."

"In a way, that's a pleasant thought. If only the water had more to offer."

"That's why I'm here. Father asks if you would join him in his cabin."

James paused, trying to think what Scholten might want that couldn't take place on deck, and wondered briefly if it had to do with Antonia. Before he could say anything, she put her hand on his arm.

"Don't be worried," she said. "He simply has something to share with you."

"Ah. In that case—" He followed Antonia to her father's cabin, where she knocked on the door. A voice inside said, "Ja," and she opened the door and stood back to let James enter. He went in, and Scholten beamed and beckoned to him.

"Come in, my dear sir, come in," Scholten said, and, as Antonia started to leave, "Antonia, you too. This may be a matter of life and death." Laughing, he reached into an open valise, which appeared to be overflowing with laundry. "At sea, one can suffer from malnutrition," he went on, as he produced a large jar. "Especially in the matter of fruit. Fruit is an important part of the diet, and I have therefore taken this precaution"—he opened the jar and took a knife from his bunk—"of bringing some along, preserved in brandy. Here." He stabbed a piece of fruit and held it out. James took it with care, because it was soft and soggy, and examined it.

"What is it?" he asked.

"Either apple or peach, I don't remember which. It's the brandy that counts, anyway. Antonia, my dear, would you care for one?"

"No, thank you, Papa," she said. "I'm not hungry right now."

"Hunger be damned. This is for your health. Here." He stabbed another piece of fruit, held it out to her, and she took it as daintily as possible. James tasted his, which turned out to be a peach, literally mushy with brandy. The liquor ran down his chin, and he had to wipe it with the back of his hand.

"Excellent peach," he said. "Delicious."

"Have another," Scholten said, stabbing into the jar. He gave James what had apparently been an apple, then took one for himself. "Nothing like a bit of fresh fruit," he said, drooling slightly. "The sailor's best friend at sea."

All at once James felt better than he had in several days, and he laughed. "I never thought I'd be best friends with an apple," he said. "But I can see where it has its advantages."

"No time to stop now," Scholten replied, holding out the jar. "Pick one for yourself."

In a matter of minutes they'd eaten all the fruit, and then Scholten and James drank the brandy, passing the jar back and forth between them. Scholton offered it to Antonia but she declined, and he shrugged and said, "All the more for us," and took a big swallow.

"Does anybody know any sea chanteys?" James asked, when they had drained the jar. "I understand sailors do a lot of singing."

"They only sing when they're working," Scholten replied. "Like hoisting the sails, or hauling anchor, or things like that."

"Then let's pretend we're working. You sing a song, and I'll hoist the sail."

"Very well." Scholten took the empty jar and beat time with it against the side of his bunk while he sang, "Oh, whiskey is the drink for me, whiskey for my Johnny-O," while James hauled on an imaginary halyard. Then Scholten started another song, involving a dairy maid who was also a contortionist, and Antonia quietly left the cabin. Scholten was singing the third verse of "Roll your leg over the man in the moon," and James was beginning to perspire from hauling on his endless halyard, when there was a thump on the deck above, the sound of running feet, and then the sharp squeal of the bosun's pipe. All at once, people seemed to be running everywhere. James and Scholten stopped, and listened.

"I wonder what's happening," James said.

"We'll never find out down here," Scholten replied, rising unsteadily to his feet. "Follow me."

They went topside and saw that the crew was swarming through the rigging, some setting out more sail while others, on deck, trained the yardarms about as the ship came onto a new course. The captain was supervising the maneuver, relaying his orders through Stoughton and the bosun, then turning to train his spyglass on an object on the horizon.

"Is there some emergency?" Scholten asked, bracing himself against the roll of the ship.

The captain ignored him, continuing to examine the horizon, and only then did James see the small white speck of a sail. "She's coming about," the captain said to the first officer. "Come three points to starboard."

"I demand to know what is happening," Scholten said. "Why are we changing course?"

For the first time, the captain looked at him. "There's a ship out there," he said. "I think she may be wanting to close with us, and I'd just as lief she didn't."

"Why not? Who is it?"

"I don't know, and I don't intend to find out."

"And for what reason? Are we carrying contraband?" The brandy had brought out a belligerent streak in Scholten, and he refused to be put off.

"We are not carrying contraband," the captain said wearily.

"But yer never know who's on the sea or what he may want. The best idea is to stay clear of everyone, specially those who try to come close."

"You're not at war—what are you afraid of?"

"War is a word governments use. There's more fighting goes on without a war than does with one. Now, if yer don't mind, I'm busy." He turned away to talk with the first officer, and James noticed that Stoughton was no longer as relaxed and confident as before; he was tense and unsmiling and seemed almost to anticipate every order the captain gave. James found it hard to believe that the small speck of white in the distance could be a menace, but Stoughton's uneasiness communicated itself to him, and all at once his stomach began to feel queasy. He swallowed and breathed deeply and wished he'd had either more brandy or less fruit. If there was to be a battle he wanted to feel his best, which at the moment he decidedly did not.

What he had not realized was the fact that two ships at sea, even if they are heading straight for each other, may take several hours to meet, and if one ship is trying to avoid the other the maneuvering can last for days. As the afternoon wore on, the distant ship came closer, but the captain of the *Pigou* kept changing course in an attempt to put it astern, and with each change of wind he dodged and feinted and tried to gain a favorable up-wind position. The other ship matched him tack for tack, which if nothing else proved its determination to close with him and made his desire to escape all the stronger. By sunset the ships were eight miles apart, and through his glass the captain could see it was a topsail schooner, light but fast, and probably his equal in any but a heavy sea.

"Is she flying any colors?" Stoughton asked.

"None I can see," the captain replied. "But that proves nothing one way or the other. He's aiming to cut us off tomorrow morning, if we both hold course and speed. So come dark I aim to shorten sail, drop back a bit, then come hard a-starboard and get behind him. That way, when the sun comes up he'll be going one way, and we'll be going the other. That'll give us another day, at least."

"The moon's near full tonight," Stoughton reminded him.

"There's also heavy clouds. We needn't worry about the

moon." Then, as an afterthought, the captain said, "What time's it rise?"

"An hour from now."

The captain dismissed the idea. "The moon'll give us no trouble," he said.

"Still, if there were a break in the clouds—"

"Mr. Stoughton, do yer have a better idea?" the captain said, suddenly angry.

Stoughton paused. "No, sir."

"Then we'll proceed as I said. Stand by to shorten sail in a half hour."

"Aye, sir."

Scholten had long since gone below, but James stayed at the windward rail, where he was out of the way but could still hear what was going on. He was aware of Stoughton's increasing nervousness and wondered if this was a normal reaction, but the captain was more preoccupied than nervous, so this had to be something in Stoughton's own make-up. In the gathering darkness he saw Antonia come on deck, and when she saw him she came and stood next to him.

"What's happening?" she asked. "Why is everyone so excited?"

"Didn't your father tell you?" James replied.

"Papa seemed slightly confused about things. He went right to his cabin and fell asleep."

James told her what he knew, and she received the news in silence. She looked for the other ship, but in the half-light the horizon was smudged as though by smoke, and it was hard to distinguish anything. Members of the crew began to appear on deck and vanish up the ratlines into the rigging, and by the time darkness had fallen, the various stations were manned and ready. First the skysails were furled, and then the royals, and finally the fore and mizzen topgallants. The main topgallant was left in place, so as not to change the ship's silhouette too radically. The change in speed was noticeable right away; the ship still moved through the water, but the sounds of the wake and the bow wave were at a lower key and more leisurely than before, and it seemed almost as though the *Pigou* were coasting. James and Antonia watched in fascination as the men came silently out of the rigging, and a quiet descended over the ship that made peo-

ple instinctively hold their breaths. The only sounds were an occasional creak in the rigging and the surge of waves against the
sides. On the captain's orders, all lights were extinguished and
smoking on deck was forbidden. The night closed in on them
like a giant cape, shutting out the rest of the world. James was
aware of Antonia's hand groping for his; her hand was cold but
he felt warmed by the contact, and he wondered why he had
ever worried about Stoughton.

Around ten o'clock the crew were ordered back into the rigging; the *Pigou* came about on a new tack to starboard, and the
sails that had been taken in were unfurled. The ship heeled
slightly and the speed increased, and as they started off on their
new course, there was a sudden exclamation from Stoughton.

"Damn it to bloody hell!" he said. "Look at the moon!"

They all looked up and saw a faint glow appearing in the sky.
It became brighter and rounder, and a thin line of moonlight appeared on the water ahead of them; it seemed to rush toward
them, then the moon burst forth in full view above, bathing
them all in its cold light, while Stoughton stamped and shouted
imprecations.

"If yer don't mind, Mr. Stoughton," the captain said, sharply,
"yer'll save yer remarks for when they'll do some good. The moon
can't speak English."

Stoughton subsided, and in a few moments the moonlight
dimmed and faded, and they were once again in darkness.

"There's nothing more to do tonight," the captain went on.
"Just keep a sharp lookout, and wait for daylight."

James was awakened by the bosun's pipe and the sounds of
running feet, and when he got on deck it seemed at first to be
nighttime. Then he noticed a faint lightening of the sky high in
the east, but what was startling was that the topsail schooner
was materializing out of the gloom not three miles away. The
captain was looking at it through his glass while his mouth
worked silently, as though chewing a cud.

"What happened?" James asked.

"He outsmarted me," the captain replied, not taking his eye
from the glass. "Either that, or he saw us in that minute the
moon was on us."

"Can you tell who he is?"

"No, but I'll know soon enough. Mr. Stoughton!"

"Sir." Stoughton appeared beside the captain, and while James couldn't see his face, he could tell from his voice that he was tense.

"Clear for action," the captain said to Stoughton. "Have the guns loaded and primed, but don't run 'em out the ports. Leave the ports closed till I give the word."

"Aye." Stoughton disappeared forward, and James could hear him giving orders to the crew. James realized to his amazement that he himself was not nervous; there was a dreamlike quality to what was happening that made him feel like an observer rather than a participant, and he was neither involved enough nor knowledgeable enough to be greatly concerned. The possibility that the ship might be sunk or captured never occurred to him.

Gradually it became lighter, and the details of the approaching schooner emerged. She was not quite so large as *Pigou* but she was fast, and a white wave curled away from her bow. She was well manned, both in the rigging and on deck, and although they were not visible to the unaided eye the captain could make out the muzzles of four deck guns protruding through their ports. He studied the ship for several minutes, then turned to a nearby seaman and said, "Run up the colors. Let's see if she declares herself." In a few moments the American flag fluttered up to the spanker gaff, snapping out straight as the wind caught it, and then there was a silence while all hands watched the other ship. Finally a white ensign could be seen, rising smartly into place. "French," said the captain, and grunted.

Stoughton came back to the quarter-deck. He seemed relaxed and at ease, almost smiling. "The guns are manned and ready, sir," he said. "Should I open the ports?"

"Not till I tell yer to," the captain replied. "I want to see what this weewee mongsoor has in mind." He looked around and saw that Antonia was on deck, standing next to James. "I'll want that young lady below," he said. "I can't be responsible for the passengers if they stay topside."

"And Mr. Greenleaf?" Stoughton asked. "Do you want him below, as well?"

The captain hesitated. "As he chooses," he said. "He won't make much difference one way or the other."

Stoughton went to Antonia and touched his cap. "The captain

presents his compliments, juffrouw," he said, "and asks that you
repair to your cabin."

"Is one allowed to ask why?" Antonia replied, assuming a
faintly regal posture.

"He cannot be responsible if you remain on deck," said
Stoughton. "Until he knows the intentions of this Frenchman, he
must be prepared for anything."

"I thought the French were your allies," Antonia said.

"So they were, but privateers have no respect for alliances. If
you would be so kind as to comply, juffrouw, the captain has
other things to concern him besides his passengers."

"Does that include me?" James asked.

Stoughton glanced at him. "The captain says you are to do as
you choose," he replied.

For an instant James was tempted to go below with Antonia,
but he immediately rejected the idea. "I shall stay here," he announced. "Perhaps I can be of some assistance."

Stoughton gave him a look that was not quite a smile and
bowed. "You are very kind," he said. "He will appreciate your
thoughtfulness. And now, juffrouw, if you would do us the
honor—"

"I shall go below," said Antonia, turning away, "but only because I have not yet broken my fast. I despise the sight of blood
before breakfast."

James watched her go and wondered if her sudden icy formality with Stoughton were a sign something had gone wrong between them. His satisfaction at this thought was tempered by
her parting remark, which snapped in the air like the flags of a
storm signal, warning that she did not like being dictated to. She
had the good breeding always to be respectful to her father, but
where other men were concerned, she clearly had her own ideas
and no hesitation about voicing them.

The French schooner had by now closed to within a mile, and
James could just see the muzzles of the guns and the small
figures of men in the rigging. Slowly the two ships came closer,
and on the *Pigou* there was absolute silence. Then there was a
puff of white smoke from the other ship, and a thud, and then
the splash of a shot across the *Pigou*'s bow. The captain took a
long, bell-mouthed speaking trumpet, aimed it toward the other
ship, and called, "What do yer want?"

Faintly, across the water, came the command: "'Eave to!"

"On whose orders?" the captain replied, and then, as an aside to Stoughton, "He's French, all right. Stand by yer guns." There was a long wait, and the two ships came closer and closer until it seemed to James they were about to collide.

"'Eave to, or we fire!" came more clearly, and the captain directed his trumpet toward Stoughton.

"Run out yer guns!" he called. "Stand by to come about!" There was a rumble and clatter as the guns were run out, then the captain said, "Fire!" and the port side of the ship erupted in flame and smoke. The concussion was such that James could barely hear the order to come about; the *Pigou* swung hard to port, and passed just astern of the schooner; as she was crossing the stern the captain shouted, "Fire starboard!" and the other six guns went off. Shouts and cries could be heard through the explosions, and as the *Pigou* pulled away, a gust of wind blew the smoke off to leeward, and they could see a shambles of tangled rigging and splintered superstructure, with several men thrashing about on the deck. The captain looked back, as the water between the two ships widened. "Thought he'd have it easy, didn't he?" he said.

James's mouth was dry, and he reeked of acid, sooty gunpowder smoke. "If he was a privateer, why did he fly the French flag?" he asked. "That isn't legal, is it?"

The captain grinned. "Out here, anything is legal. And the weewees aren't too particular about the niceties, anyway. If he'd flown no colors we'd have known right off what he was; this way, he figured to get in striking range before we knew." He looked back at the schooner, which was struggling to get underway. "His only problem was he got too close."

9

When James first smelled land, he didn't know what it was. The ship had been moving slowly through a bright, hazy world, with only the nearby water visible in sharp detail, and the primary smell was the salt of the sea, tinged every now and then with a whiff of iodine from seaweed. Once or twice he had caught the oily reek of a fish slick, which the captain explained was caused by a school of fish regurgitating after a feeding frenzy, and then one morning he came on deck and found an entirely new smell, which he could describe to himself only as that of the color green. The captain watched him as he sniffed the air.

"Yer know what that is, don't yer?" the captain said.

"No," James replied. "I can't make it out."

"That, my boy, is land. That is the moors and downs of merry England."

James tested the air again and closed his eyes and could see fields and forests and streams. "How far off is it?" he asked.

"We're still a good piece out," the captain replied. "It's just the wind happens to be right. But it tells me to keep a sharp lookout."

Next morning they skirted the Scilly Isles and headed for Lizard Point, from which to take their departure for the run up the Channel. The wind died down but the waves increased, and the *Pigou* reacted with a motion totally different from that in the open sea. It was a short, squirming motion, somewhat like that of a bucking horse, and although James had long since become immune to seasickness, he found himself uncomfortable in the Channel waters. He was also frustrated, being so close to land and unable to go ashore, and when the wind died completely, leaving them wallowing in the swells, he was almost tempted to jump over the side and swim for it. Here and there they saw other ships becalmed, and at night they could see occasional lights along the Devon coast, and to James those lights symbolized all the warmth and comfort of home. He didn't care that a light might actually be a beacon on a rocky point; in his mind it became a snug living room, and a string of lights were the houses along Boston Common. He wanted to reach out to them and lose himself in the pleasure they represented.

Finally the wind freshened from the west, and the *Pigou* settled down for the final four hundred and fifty miles of the journey. Once through the Strait of Dover she ran more easily and took a northeast course up the low-lying coast of the Netherlands. The land became a thin line, broken by the various deltas and estuaries until it looked more like a series of islands than a coastline and reminded James of the dunes and flatlands of Cape Cod. The North Sea, while not as turbulent as the Channel, had a chop and action all its own, and the air was cloudy with flying spray.

The last night at sea, when they were running almost due north for the West Frisian Islands, the wind abated and the waves lost their force, and it was possible to stand at the rail without being drenched. Virtually the entire ship's company was on deck to watch the sunset, and there was the end-of-the-voyage feeling that makes time slow down and everything take longer. At sea, time is of little importance, but with the approach of the destination a form of impatience sets in, which changes the perspective and puts time in another framework. The whole ship seems to change, as though viewed through a different lens. The sun sank into a bank of low-lying clouds that hung over the British Isles; the first stars appeared, and the captain went through his nightly routine of sighting through the backstaff. James watched him in silence, knowing better than to speak until he had completed a sight.

"How accurate has that been over the course of the voyage?" he asked, when the captain lowered the instrument.

"Well, yer see where we are," the captain replied, after a moment. "We made our landfall right where we expected."

"Indeed we did," said James. "I assume it must have proved worthwhile."

"If I'd believed this osprey's nest, we'd now be coming into

Zanzibar," the captain said. "The only reason I'm keeping a record is to show the Messrs. Field, Wake, Hartshorne, et al., just how wrong it can be." He put the backstaff in its case and stamped below.

Antonia and her father had been standing at the lee rail, and they now came across and joined James. He found it remarkable how after five weeks at sea she managed to keep a certain freshness about her and surround herself with an aura that was peculiarly her own. He didn't know whether it was a God-given quality or something that took a great deal of trouble; all he knew was that she could enter a totally darkened room, and he'd know who it was. Her father, on the other hand, walked in an unmistakable cloud of alcohol fumes, apparently acquired over a long period of time. He came up to James and peered at him for a moment in the semidarkness.

"There's still a bit of fruit left," he said, in a tone of disbelief. "Do you think we ought to allow that?"

"Thank you," James replied. "Later, perhaps. I believe I should stay here for the time being."

"Very well," Scholten replied. "In that case, I'll finish it myself."

He headed for the companionway, and Antonia watched him go, then turned and leaned on the taffrail, watching the wake that bubbled off into the darkening sea. James turned with her, and together they looked at the water.

"I shall be glad when this is over," Antonia said at last.

"Oh?" said James. "Has it been all that unpleasant?"

"No ocean voyage is pleasant, but this one . . . I don't know."

James had been hoping for a compliment of some sort—why, it would have been hard to explain—but now the conversation had taken a different direction, and it irritated him.

"I don't understand," he said. He saw Stoughton hovering nearby, so lowered his voice.

"Well, an ocean voyage is always bad for Papa," Antonia replied. "It sometimes takes him a long time to recover."

"In what way?"

"The way you might expect. He takes his—medications to ward off seasickness, and then when he's on land he has become so accustomed to them, he finds it hard to stop. It can be very tiresome."

"Is there anything I can do?"

"I don't believe there's anything anyone can do."

"Still, I should be glad to be of whatever help I can."

"You're very kind. But you have your work, and we're no part of that."

"But I shall see you, shan't I?"

"I doubt it."

"Why not?"

"We have our separate lives. You will be deep in consular duties, and I"—she paused—"I have a life of my own."

"Are you asking me to believe you spend your life taking care of your father?"

"Of course not."

"Then why can't I see you?"

She looked at him, but by now it was too dark for him to see her expression. "You are inquisitive, aren't you?" she said.

He straightened up. "Not in the least. I'm just confused."

"Does it confuse you that a girl should have a life of her own?"

"You misunderstand me." By now he was completely off balance, looking for a way to say what he meant. "Are you—do you have—are you betrothed?"

She laughed. "Do I appear to be?"

He had the feeling she was playing him like a hooked trout, paying out line one minute and reeling it in the next. "Do you realize," he said, "that you have answered my last three questions with questions of your own?"

"Is that not permitted?"

"Is it impossible to give a direct answer?"

"Why should you ask all the questions? Have you taken on the rank of inquisitor as well as consul?"

"*Damn* it!" he said, as his temper snapped. Then, under control, "Forgive me."

"What was it you wanted to know?"

He'd asked so many unanswered questions that it took him a moment to remember the root of the discussion. "I suppose," he said, slowly, "I most wanted to know why you think we won't see each other again."

"Why does the sun rise in the east? Why does water flow down hill? Why does a dog turn around three times before lying down? I don't know *why;* I simply know these things happen."

"I'm sorry you feel that way. I must have had the wrong impression."

"What impression is that?"

"That . . ." He tried to think how to describe what he'd felt, from her father's insistence that they travel together to her holding his hand that night on deck, and he found it impossible to put into words without sounding conceited. Conceit, he decided, is all right until the props are kicked out from under you, and then all that's left is mortification. "I'm afraid it becomes too involved," he concluded. "Simply say I was wrong."

"I don't say we won't see each other at *all*," she said, as though unwilling to let the subject drop. "There will be balls and dinners and the like, where we are bound to meet again."

The thought gave him little cheer. "Of course," he said. "I suppose that is inevitable."

"You don't sound overjoyed."

"Oh, but I am. I'm awash with bliss."

Her mouth tightened. "Good night, Mr. Greenleaf," she said and left the rail.

He heard her footsteps cross the deck and descend the companionway, and he looked up at the stars and wondered if he would ever learn how to conduct a rational conversation with a woman. He saw that Stoughton had vanished, and he neither knew nor cared how much the first officer had heard.

The captain appeared from below, checked the helmsman's course, and came to where James was standing.

"How was tonight's star sight?" James asked.

"Champeen," the captain replied. "Best of the voyage. Has us just south of Paris, France."

The wind was still west next morning, and under reduced sail the *Pigou* slid through the opening between Den Helder, in North Holland, and the West Frisian Island of Texel, then headed south into the Zuider Zee. In the open sea and with a brisk wind she could make ten knots, but conditions in the Zuider Zee were not conducive to speed. There were tidal flats and sudden shoals, with channels that had to be followed with great care; the haphazard nature of the traffic was such that the possibility of collision was always present; and all combined to reduce the *Pigou* to one third of her best potential. Thus she didn't arrive at the mouth of the river IJ until shortly before sunset, and the captain elected to drop anchor and wait until daylight to make his mooring. With Amsterdam a bare five miles upriver, James was forced to spend another night aboard, staring at the glow that tinged the misty sky above the city. Then gradually the lights went out, and the faint smell of the canals hung in the breeze.

10

The next morning they made their landing, and James's first impression of the city was a jumbled one, of red-brick buildings with elaborate top facades, of cobblestone streets, tile roofs and split chimneys, and of ubiquitous canals that reeked of sewage. There were other smells, too: the smells of baking bread and roasting coffee, and an over-all smell of chocolate, tinged around the edges with fish. He left his baggage aboard the *Pigou*, until he'd had time to register his arrival and make inquiries about living quarters. He bade a formal farewell to Antonia and her father and watched them drive off in a landau that had appeared at the dock simultaneously with the *Pigou*. When the landau vanished down a cobbled street, James felt more alone than any time he could remember.

He found a room in Utrechtsestraat, near the center of the city and also near the Amstel River, one of the two rivers at whose confluence the city was first built. Off Dam Square, named for the dam that blocked the Amstel from the IJ, he discovered a merchants' tavern and, suddenly ravenous with hunger, went inside and ordered food. His knowledge of Dutch was nonexistent, but the proprietor had enough English to understand what he wanted, and he showed James to a table in a corner, placed in front of him a porcelain mug of gin, then hurried off to the kitchen. The gin was warm and sirupy, but it induced a blurry sensation of well-being, and by the time the food arrived James was in a state nearing euphoria. He could still feel the motion of the ship, but he found the apparent tilting of the floor more hilarious than unsettling, and he greeted the food as though it were a long lost friend in spite of the fact that, by even the minimum standards of *haute cuisine*, it was uninspiring. There was a bowl of pea soup which, judged on the basis of size and caloric content, was a meal in itself, and it was accompanied by boiled potatoes, cabbage, and herring and followed by a piece of Gouda cheese the size of a baby's head. Mugs of beer arrived at intervals, and the meal was topped off by coffee and a strange but potent liqueur, and by the time James was able to totter outside into the too-bright sunlight, he was bloated and incoherent. He was sick almost immediately into a large bed of tulips, and felt better.

It developed that his consular duties were less impressive than he'd expected. Hancock had mentioned large loans to be negotiated, and this had led James to picture himself plunging into the banking life of Amsterdam immediately upon his arrival, but if any loans were being considered, it was not through his office, and he found that all he was called on to do was care for those of his compatriots who were either lost or in trouble, with nobody else to whom they could turn. It was a considerable letdown, and it left him wondering how he was going to gain entry into the financial world that was, for his purposes, Amsterdam's main attraction.

He had no doubt he would succeed, but it was going to require some careful planning. Once he had made his entry, the rest would be easy.

Then one day, when he returned to his room from having bailed out an American sailor who'd bitten off a man's nose, he found an envelope under his door. The handwriting was familiar, and with growing excitement he tore it open and saw it was a formal invitation to dinner at the residence of Baron Jan Erasmus van der Hoef Smeet Scholten. It was written in English, and the writing was unmistakably Antonia's, and he pressed the letter to his face and breathed deeply, telling himself that it smelled of her. He dashed off a note of acceptance and then went out to look for a tailor who could fit him for a new wardrobe. It wasn't until much later that he looked at the invitation again and realized that Scholten was a baron. In his excitement he had missed it on the first reading.

Baron Scholten's home was on the Herengracht, the first of the canals that spread in concentric circles from the center of the city. Its name meant Gentleman's Canal; it was followed by the Keizersgracht, or Emperor's Canal; the Prinsengracht, or Prince's Canal; and the Singelgracht, the outermost of the four main circular canals. Other canals, radiating outward like spokes in a wheel, crisscrossed these four, forming a compartmentation of the city as precise as a honeycomb. Because of the nature of this layout, the Herengracht intersected Utrechtsestraat, where James lived, and while the houses were some distance apart he was able to reach the Scholtens' by going to this intersection, and then following the canal to the proper number. Once he learned the system, he was able to find his way anywhere in the city.

The Scholten home was a typical town house of the period. A long corridor, decorated in the neoclassical style with pilasters, overdoors, and ornamental moldings, led to a staircase near the rear, and beyond the staircase was the salon. Doors on both sides of the corridor gave onto adjoining rooms, and James had a glimpse of white marble chimney pieces, painted ceilings with stucco borders, and a seemingly endless variety of classical figures and scrollwork. There were also standing clocks, wall clocks, and mantel clocks, none of which agreed in time but all of which had a similar decorative impact—that of a Louis XVI decorator gone berserk. A skylight, two stories up, cast a faint, unnatural tint on the staircase, making it seem like a part of another building. The salon, in which the guests were gathered, was decorated almost entirely with painted wall hangings, mixing Dutch landscape scenes with designs featuring satyrs, griffons, and nymphs; and the fireplace, over which was an immense gilt-framed mirror, was festooned with marble garlands of fruits, grape leaves, and gorgons. The ceiling was painted with a scene that James, on a quick glance, took to be either the dawn of Creation or the rape of the Sabines—he couldn't be sure which —and he was more interested in Antonia than he was in the ceiling.

She was wearing a long-sleeved, yellow silk dress with an elaborately embroidered underskirt, and when he saw her, something thudded in his chest and he felt his face turn hot. She had been looking at the door as he came through, as though knowing the precise moment he would arrive, and she smiled at him like a conspirator in some elaborate plot. Without waiting for the footman to announce him he went to her, took her hand, and bowed.

"Baroness," he said. "You do me great honor."

"Not in the least," she replied, fluttering a silk fan. "You honor us in coming."

He straightened up, and as their eyes met he said, "To say that this is a surprise would be to state the case mildly. Why didn't you tell me?"

"There is a time for everything. Would you care to meet the other guests?"

"Do they speak English?" he asked, as she turned toward the nearest group.

"I can translate for those who don't," she replied, just as her father, red-faced and slightly glassy-eyed, appeared and greeted James with affection.

"Mynheer de Consul!" he said, gripping James's hand. *"Tot je dienst!"*

"I beg your pardon?" said James.

"That means welcome," Antonia put in, quietly.

"Thank you, thank you," James said. "I am most happy to see you again." He was about to make some reference to their Atlantic crossing, when Antonia took him by the arm and steered him forcibly away.

As far as James was concerned, the introductions were a waste of time. Even with English names, he found trouble fitting them to faces when he met people in a large group, and with the Dutch names it was flatly impossible. The difficulty was compounded by the Dutch pronunciation, which blurred the spelling, and James's memory was a jumble of sounds like Stroople, Winkelhoof, Pleet, Byoomeemer, Vanweefenskeer, and the like. Most of them spoke English, although in some cases so heavily accented as to be almost indistinguishable from the Dutch, and if it hadn't been for Antonia's constant presence, he would have found himself wallowing in a swamp of gibberish.

He was seated at her right at dinner. The first course was a thick vegetable soup, and when it was served she looked at him and smiled.

"Have no fear," she said. "In this soup there is everything *except* snails."

He laughed, then looked about and, finding nobody listening

said in a low voice, "Would you be so kind as to tell me why you kept this from me?"

"What is 'this'?" she asked, sampling her soup.

"Your title."

She paused, then said, "Papa thought it best, in America. He felt a title might cause antagonism."

James thought this over. "On the contrary, I think there is still an ingrained respect for titles," he said. "It takes a long time to shake off."

She shrugged. "He saw no point in taking chances. Besides, our Stadholder is a cousin of King George. A title would only have reminded people."

James remembered a painting he'd seen of Prince William V, clad in the anachronistic armor used in state portraits, and he realized that the bulging eyes and protuberant lips were similar to those of the English king. "Cousin or no, he stayed neutral," he said. "He didn't send troops." James was nearing the end of his knowledge, but the conversation was continuing in spite of him.

"When you think of what Van der Capellen said, it would have been impossible to send troops," Antonia went on. "His speech—"

"Of course, you're right," James said, quickly. "Speaking of speeches, my—"

"'A God-fearing people, brave and courageous'—wasn't that what he called you?"

Is she doing this intentionally? he asked himself and then, out loud, said, "Something along those lines. An amusing thing hap—"

"Forgive me," the man on Antonia's left cut in. "What Van der Capellen said was that the Americans were a 'brave folk who in a calm, courageous, and God-fearing manner are defending the rights granted them as human beings, not by the legislature in England but by God himself.'"

"That's what I said," Antonia replied, with a trace of irritation.

James looked gratefully at the man, who was thin and hawk-like, with eyes that were continually darting about. "Precisely," James said. "Those are the exact words I was looking for."

"Tell me, Mynheer Greenleaf, about the French," the man went on. "Are they a powerful force in your country?"

"Powerful?" James replied. "I shouldn't say so. Why?"

"They are powerful here, and for this country they have not done one half of what they did for yours. Here, they have only become a disruptive element."

James began to feel on safer ground, because he'd learned that the so-called Patriot party in Holland was dominated by the French, to the point where a year ago Prince William had called in Prussian troops to keep the party from taking control of the country. The French had been, and still were, putting great pressure on the Netherlands.

"The French are much closer to you than they are to us," James said. "It is hard to exert influence from three thousand miles away—as our British cousins so recently discovered."

Antonia, who had listened to the conversation in silence, now turned to James. "Mynheer van Vliet is overly preoccupied with the French," she said. "He sees Frenchmen under every bed."

"Better under them than in them," replied Van Vliet, with a louder laugh than the joke was worth. "I was simply interested in how far their influence was felt."

"Not very," said James.

"I understand there is a great deal of land to be bought in your country."

"Land? There is very little else but land."

"And it can be bought for reasonable rates?"

Antonia said something in Dutch, to which Van Vliet replied, and then the next course was served. Antonia looked at the plate of herring and eel as though it contained the crown jewels. "How long it is since I've had a good eel," she said, cutting a piece away from the backbone.

"We have excellent eels in America," said James, defensively. "Some of the best I ever tasted."

"So?" Antonia replied. "I never had any."

"They come up the creeks and rivers in the spring. You can net or spear them by the hundreds."

For the first time, the lady on James's right spoke up. She was short and plump, and her mouth seemed full even when it wasn't. "Where do eels come from?" she asked.

James glanced at her. "Eggs, I presume," he said.

"I mean, from what country? What part of the world?"

"Mevrouw Crommelin is interested in anything international," Antonia put in. "Her husband is a banker."

James digested this information, and mentally filed the name Crommelin for future reference. "You have just asked a fascinating question," he said. "One that has baffled naturalists for centuries. Nobody knows exactly where eels go, and nobody knows from whence they come, except that they come from the ocean. They go up the rivers and creeks, and then they vanish. Every year, the ocean brings forth its crop of eels, and every year they apparently disappear inland. One theory is that they burrow down to underground streams and return to the ocean that way; another has it that they grow legs and walk back; and some of the more radical naturalists theorize that they sprout wings at the source of the mountain streams and glide to their native element."

"Incredible," said Mevrouw Crommelin.

"So it would appear. But unless one of those three theories is correct, we must assume that there is a limitless eel garden somewhere in the depths, which annually spews forth its crop to die in the inland waters, and then regenerates itself without benefit of the—ah—normal procedure. Such a hypothesis is unthinkable."

"Which theory do you prefer?" asked Mevrouw Crommelin.

James stared at the corner of the ceiling for a moment, hoping for inspiration, then said, "Have you ever seen a newt?"

"I believe not," said Mevrouw Crommelin.

"Or a salamander? Or an eft?"

"What is this eft?"

"It's in the same family."

"No."

"They are all small creatures, something like snakes—or eels—except that they have legs. Very small ones, but legs all the same. My theory is that these are newly hatched eels, whose parents have come upstream to spawn and then die, and that they grow temporary legs for their journey back to the sea. You will notice—or would, if you had seen an eft—that almost without exception they are headed toward the nearest body of salt water."

James heard a gagging sound at his left but didn't dare look at Antonia. "It is, admittedly, only a theory," he went on, "but there is solid evidence in its support."

"Most fascinating," said Mevrouw Crommelin.

He was saved further improvisation by the arrival of the main course, which was a roast of pork accompanied by a mash of something indescribable. He tasted it, then glanced at Antonia, who was surreptitiously wiping her eyes. They looked at each other for a long moment, and then she controlled her voice enough to say, "How do you like your *plantenmengeling?*"

"Delicious," James lied. "What is it?"

"This and that. Potatoes—vegetables—red cabbage—all mashed together."

James tasted it again. "Very interesting," he said and cut into his pork.

From Antonia's left, Van Vliet spoke up. "Tell me, mynheer, who will be President of your country?"

"I presume George Washington," James replied.

"In this country we are much impressed by John Adams. He was quite highly regarded when he was here."

"So I understand," said James. "However, he is not universally beloved at home." His mind took off, wondering what would happen if Adams should be elected President and what effect that would have on his, James's, career. Nobody in his family knew George Washington, and a Virginian was not likely to be partial to New Englanders when choosing his Cabinet, but if Adams, a long-time friend of the Greenleafs', were to become President, it might be a different story. And if, as consul in Amsterdam, James could in some way distinguish himself . . .

His reverie was interrupted by Van Vliet, who said, "When do you expect to know?"

"The electoral college doesn't meet until next year—in March, I believe—so we won't know until then."

"It seems a long time to be without a leader."

"We were a long time with the wrong one. Everything takes time."

Van Vliet smiled. "*Verzorgd sprekend,*" he said.

James nodded as though he understood, and had turned to speak to Antonia when Baron Scholten arose at the other end of the table, tapped a glass for silence, and started a toast. It was in Dutch, and James only half listened until he suddenly realized, from the glances cast his way, that the toast was to him. This was confirmed when Scholten launched into the English translation, and he heard himself referred to as ambassador from the new country (a sharp upgrading in rank), one who followed in the footsteps of the esteemed John Adams, and one on whom the

Dutch could rely to cement their friendship with America. Scholten concluded by quoting the Mennonite vicar François Adriaan van der Kemp, who had said, from his pulpit: "In America the sun of salvation has risen, which will also cast its rays upon us if we so wish; only America can teach us how to counter the degeneration of the national character, to curb the corruption of morals, to ward off bribery, to suffocate the seeds of tyranny, and to restore to health our dying freedom. The supreme Being has ordained that America shall be Holland's last preacher of repentance." Everybody rose, cheered, and drank, and then James found himself standing alone, glass in hand, trying to think of a reply.

"Mynheeren, mevrouwen, juffrouwen," he said, and realized he had just exhausted his knowledge of Dutch. "Baron Scholten. Baroness." He bowed to Antonia. "I thank you for your most gracious welcome. I hope that my country can live up to your—how shall I say it?—monumental expectations. We should count ourselves fortunate if we ourselves could merit Vicar van der Kemp's description; to think that we could serve as a model for such a proud and distinguished—nay, great—country as yours is beyond rational belief." Then, warming to his subject, he went on, "However, let me say that we, all of us in the government, and I know not whether the President will be General Washington or my long-time friend John Adams, we will all strive to live up to your expectations, and if by chance the fates should smile on Mr. Adams and on me, we—I—can assure you that the Netherlands will be highest in our country's favor. I drink to William V, I drink to you, and I drink to the everlasting friendship between our countries."

Again everyone rose, and for the benefit of the few who didn't understand English Scholten gave a short précis of James's speech in Dutch. When he concluded there was more applause, and Antonia leaned toward James and whispered, "My father's translation has you as the probable next President."

James laughed and then shrugged, as though such an idea were not impossible.

With that, the ladies retired, and for James the dinner took on an entirely new aspect; he was in a group of bewigged men in formal French costumes, with knee-length frock coats, lace ruffles at their sleeves, and knee breeches; most of them were paunchy and flatulent, and out of the dozen or so in the room only two were familiar to him. There was Scholten, of course, and he had been acquainted with Van Vliet for perhaps an hour, but the rest were total strangers.

Knowing this, Scholten made it a point to include him in the conversation. The Baron had been talking with a large man whose stomach seemed to stop just above his knees, and he turned to James and said, "What arrangements have you made for banking while you're here?"

"I haven't given much thought to the subject," James lied. "Other matters have seemed more important." He would have been hard put to it to explain just what the other matters were, apart from buying a new wardrobe and thinking about Antonia.

"My friend Daniel Crommelin, here, is a most respectable banker," Scholten said, indicating the man with whom he had been talking. "I feel sure he would be happy to handle your affairs."

James and Crommelin glanced at one another, and it occurred to James that the banker looked something like a sleepy frog. He was apparently the husband of the woman who had been on James's right at dinner, and considering the excess frontal weight that both of them carried, James found himself wondering if they had ever had children. Perhaps when they were younger they were leaner, he thought; as matters stand now, conception would have to be a long-distance miracle, like hitting a stick with a feather thrown from twenty paces. He became so fascinated by the thought that he didn't realize Crommelin was talking to him.

". . . at any time that is convenient to you," was all he heard Crommelin say.

"Thank you," he replied. "You are very kind."

"I understand you have considerable land holdings in America," Van Vliet put in.

James looked at him, wondering how the subject of land fitted into banking. "I own a certain amount, yes," he replied.

"We do much business in American land," Crommelin said. "The various colonies—ah, states—seem quite anxious to negotiate bonds with tracts of land as security."

All at once, James's interest perked. "Do you, indeed?" he said. "I didn't realize it could be bought this far away."

"It may be bought anywhere," Crommelin replied. "Your Robert Morris apparently has unlimited land to sell."

James had heard of Morris, who was reputed to have financed the Revolution singlehanded, but had never met him. It was said by some that the truth was the opposite of the legend—that the Revolution had financed Morris rather than the other way around; whatever the facts were, he emerged from the war the richest man in the country. As Superintendent of Finance he created a national commercial bank, issued his own "Morris notes" with which to pay off debts, and seemed able to raise money from nowhere when it was needed. It was for him that John Adams had floated a two-million-dollar loan from private firms in Holland in 1782, and it was he to whom Washington turned for help when the troops mutinied for their back pay. He had his detractors, but this was only natural in view of the power he wielded. He was a man whom James would have liked very much to meet.

"Is he in this country now?" he asked.

"No," said Crommelin. "He has agents who represent him this side of the ocean."

"And does one buy the American land through them?"

"Not necessarily. Some states have their own bonds, which they are offering for sale. There is also a large amount of federal land to be had."

"Most interesting," said James.

It was as though Van Vliet had read his mind. "I know several people who are interested in American land," he said, quietly. "I think they might be willing to invest rather heavily in such a plan."

The idea of having a number of partners in the buying of land did not appeal to James, and he said, "I have no intention of forming a company. If I buy anything, it will be on my own."

"These people do not want to form a company," Van Vliet said. "They are simply interested in the land."

James shrugged. "More power to them."

"They have a great deal of money," Van Vliet persisted.

James stopped for a moment. His plan, if such it could be called, was simple: to buy as much land as possible, using bonds, cosigners, and deeds to other land as security, and to amass enough property so that, when the inevitable rise in values took place, his worth would multiply by geometric progression. And while he had no interest in picking up indiscriminate partners, there was no point in being rude to a possible source of money and even less point in being rude to Van Vliet, who apparently knew some important people. So he said, "Thank you for telling me," and to Crommelin, "Perhaps we should talk business at some other time," and all three men smiled and nodded as though they had just concluded some secret pact.

In the room where the ladies had retired, Antonia reached into the sideboard, produced a large chamber pot with a blue-and-white floral design, and offered it to the guests.

"I believe I will," said Mevrouw Crommelin, rustling her skirts, and when she was comfortably settled she went on, "That young Mynheer Greenleaf is the most fascinating man I've ever met. Where did you find him?"

"In Boston," Antonia replied.

"Are there any more like him in Boston?" asked a buxom blonde with braids that circled her head like a coronet. "Because if there are, I could be tempted to make the trip."

"I didn't see any," Antonia replied. "And let your temptation go no further."

"You misunderstand me," the blonde replied, taking the pot from Mevrouw Crommelin. "It's not a crime to look at the man, is it?"

"The way you look at him, it is," said Antonia. "You have a look that comes straight from the pillow."

"Piffle," said the blonde. "Can I help it if I'm nearsighted?"

"Hurry up with that pot," said a large girl with buck teeth. "I'm about to burst."

"You should be more moderate with the wine," replied the blonde. "That's what does it to you."

"And you be moderate with Mynheer Greenleaf," Antonia said. "That is a friendly warning."

"I hear you." The blonde stood up. "All right, Gretel, it's all yours."

11

James and Antonia were married in the autumn. Looking back on it, he couldn't remember having made a formal proposal of marriage; it was simply assumed that he had—or if he hadn't, that he would—and Antonia and her father proceeded on that assumption. James was mystified but delighted; he had worried, on and off, about how he might broach the subject of marriage without making his usual conversational *gaffe* and spoiling it all, and to find that it had been smoothly and painlessly settled was almost too good to be believed. He decided that it was his guardian angel working for him and that he shouldn't question minor details. His guardian angel had been extremely good to him in the past.

The ceremony took place in the Zuider Kerk, a hundred-and-seventy-year-old church on the Kloveniersburgwal canal. Scholten would have preferred to have his daughter married in the Nieuwe Kerk, a cathedrallike edifice across from the Town Hall, dating from 1385, but it was customarily reserved for the weddings and funerals of princes and national heroes, and to fill it would have required inviting a good proportion of the citizenry of Amsterdam. The Zuider Kerk was smaller and therefore more select. And the guest list was by no means curtailed: the House of Crommelin was invited almost *en masse,* as were the more prominent bankers and merchants; independent men of means like Van Vliet were seated in places of honor, and another special guest was Rutger Jan Schimmelpenninck, a young expert in government affairs and admirer of John Adams. Three years before, at the University of Leiden, he had written his doctoral thesis on Adams's constitution of Massachusetts as a prime example of moderate popular government, and his attendance at the

Greenleaf-Scholten nuptials was virtually a diplomatic necessity. His name, incidentally, was the only Dutch name—aside from Scholten—that James could remember with ease; its very complexity made it memorable and caused his mind to search for a literal translation. His best guess was "shining penny," which he was sure wasn't right. As it turned out, the name was untranslatable.

It was a raw, blustery day in October, and the wind whipped inland from the North Sea and scuffed the surface of the canals, but the weather did not deter Baron Scholten from insisting that the newlyweds ride in his open landau from the church to his home, where the wedding feast was held. A parade of carriages followed, and the Amsterdamers who saw the procession stopped and took off their hats, not knowing what it was all about but not wanting to risk offending some high potentate. With Prussian troops in the country, no one could be sure just who or what was coming next.

James's memory of the feast was blurred, but certain scenes stood out like seashells washed up on a beach. He remembered thinking, in one of the periods of detachment sometimes brought on by liquor, that except for the obvious differences the scene was like that in Breughel's "Peasant Wedding": there was the long table, the musicians playing for the bemused bride, the waiters passing trays of food, the guests either quietly interested in food or loudly interested in drink, and there was even the small child, who came from God knew where but most likely from the kitchen, sitting on the floor and eating whatever it could scavenge. The bride and groom shared the first toast, in a silver cup shaped like a woman holding a bowl over her head. When the woman was inverted, her skirt made a cup, and it and the free-swinging bowl were filled. James then drank first, from the larger of the two, being careful not to spill the other; he then passed it to Antonia, who drained the smaller one, to the cheers of the assembled guests. There followed endless toasts, in Dutch and in English and in a language that, as the evening wore on, sounded something like Helvetian or Moravian, and there was a certain amount of singing, primarily of a song the chorus to which was "*Lang zal zij leven,*" repeated over and over in a growing crescendo. At one point Crommelin tried to drink a liqueur without using his hands, by grasping the rim of the glass with his teeth; this started a contest among several of the male celebrants and resulted in less spillage than might have been imagined. Those who did spill were loudly derided by the others, as though their failure were somehow tied in with a lack of virility, and if on a second or third try they finally managed the trick, they were applauded with almost obscene enthusiasm. James was tempted to try, but he had no more than set his liqueur glass in position when a look from Antonia made him abandon the idea. Her look revealed a quality he'd never seen before: that of a Prussian drillmaster addressing a new recruit. They danced the first dance together, and then disorganization, like incoming fog, became general. James had a quick glimpse of Van Vliet, whose partner had returned to the table, dancing alone as though she were still in his arms; there was also the scene of Schimmelpenninck, his hands full of assorted crockery, making his way across the teeming dance floor without once touching anyone; and there was the unforgettable tableau of Baron Scholten, who had dropped a spoon down the front of Mevrouw Crommelin's dress, trying to retrieve it and somehow getting his hand caught as though in a noose.

How or when he and Antonia finally retired, James was never quite sure. He remembered going upstairs and finding one of the wedding guests sprawled across the bridal bed; he remembered dragging the unconscious man into the corridor; he remembered suddenly finding himself on the floor and realizing he'd tried to take off his trousers without sitting down; and then he remembered falling into a fathomless mattress, while the bed whirled around him. Antonia lurked in the periphery of his memory, but always as a figure either behind or beside him, never saying a word. When he awoke the next morning her wedding dress was hanging in the closet, but she was gone. He found her downstairs, looking as though she'd been up for hours.

"Good morning, Mevrouw Greenleaf," he said, bending toward her.

"Good morning." She presented her left temple to be kissed.

He kissed her, lost his balance, and almost fell. "This floor tilts," he said, looking behind him.

She said nothing.

He groped for a chair and sat down, as his heart went into a sudden flurry and his forehead became damp.

"Would you care to break your fast?" she asked, in a tone that implied it was of no importance to her one way or the other.

"No, thank you." He breathed deeply several times, then said, "Has your father come down?"

Antonia hesitated, then said, "Papa has not come home."

"From where?"

Another pause. "I don't know. He appears to have gone off with some of the guests."

James thought back on what he remembered of the evening. "Well," he said, at last, "unless he got his hand out of her dress, he must have gone home with the Crommelins."

"This is no time for joking."

"I am not joking. He was snared as tight as a rabbit."

A footman knocked, entered, and said something in Dutch to Antonia. She replied, and he vanished.

"What was that about?" James asked.

"He said the maid found a man on the fourth floor."

"Alive?"

"Asleep."

"Did he say who?"

"No. I said to have him wakened."

James reflected a moment. "I hope it's Schimmelpenninck."

"Why?"

"I don't know. It's a good name for sleeping on the floor."

Antonia looked at him. "Are you still drunk?"

"Not in the least. Why?"

"You're not making sense."

It occurred to James that the Dutch were literal-minded, unable to cope with a thought that couldn't be logically dissected, so he changed the subject. "I believe I would like a beer," he said.

Antonia looked at him again, then reached out and tugged the bellpull.

The footman bringing the beer was followed by Van Vliet, who looked as though he had been dragged over the cobblestones. He went to Antonia, bowed low, and said, "Baroness, please accept a thousand apologies. I must have become confused."

"Pray do not mention it," Antonia replied. "May I offer you some food?"

Van Vliet ran his tongue across his lips. "Thank you, no," he replied, and his eyes flicked to James's beer. "However, something moist might . . ." He let the sentence trail off, and Antonia gave the footman the order.

"Do sit down," she said. "My—husband—seems to find that a preferable posture this morning."

"Thank you." Van Vliet sank into a chair, then said, "I should make my apologies to the Baron. Has he awakened?"

"The Baron is not at home at the moment," Antonia replied. "He left—ah—early."

Van Vliet shook his head. "A remarkable man," he said. "A man of great strength."

Antonia smiled thinly and said nothing, and James spoke up. "I wonder what became of Schimmelpenninck," he said.

"Why?" said Van Vliet. "Was something supposed to?"

"Not that I know of. I just remembered him last night, passing among the dancers as though walking in his sleep. He seemed like a man searching for the Grail."

"Unhappily, I missed the dancing," Van Vliet said. "I was overtaken by fatigue."

James stared at him. "I beg your pardon," he said. "You danced like a swan. In fact, you danced alone. I saw you."

Van Vliet was silent, trying to think of something to say. The footman arrived with his beer, and he took it gratefully, murmured, "*Gezondheid,*" and drank. "Be that as it may," he said and was quiet again.

The footman said something to Antonia, and she excused herself and left the room. James drew a deep breath and let it out slowly.

"Was that what one would call a typical Dutch wedding?" he asked.

Van Vliet took another swallow of beer and considered the question. "Perhaps not typical," he replied, finally. "But certainly not unusual."

"May the good Lord preserve me from any more."

"Did I do anything else, except dance alone?"

"I don't believe so. You were quite insistent on buying French land in America, or American land in France, or some such transaction, but I don't remember the details."

Van Vliet leaned forward. "What did I say?"

"I told you, I don't remember the details. But it seemed extremely important at the time."

Van Vliet's eyes darted about the room. "Is there some place where we can talk?"

James looked at him for a moment, then said, "What are we doing now?"

"I mean in private."

"This is as private as—" He stopped, as Antonia returned to the room. Her face was expressionless but he knew she was angry, and he said, "Is anything wrong?"

"Not exactly wrong," she replied, resuming her seat. "Call it irregular. There was a young lady at the door, asking for Mynheer Schimmelpenninck. Why she should think he was still here is beyond me."

"Clearly, he's not where he was expected to be," James said. "I imagine she's tracing him from the last place he was seen."

"It is not as though we were running a public lodginghouse. She might at least have *started* looking somewhere else."

"Perhaps she did. Perhaps she came here as a final act of desperation. Perhaps—"

"Excuse me," Van Vliet broke in. "I think it is time I left. Baroness, again my apologies for—"

"Please don't mention it," she said. "It was a pleasure to have you."

Van Vliet glanced at James over Antonia's head, and James said, "My dear, I believe I'll take a short walk with Adriaan. I think the air might do me good."

"I feel sure of it," she replied. "Everyone else seems to be abroad today; there is no reason for you to be the exception."

"If we should see your father, do you have any message?"

She started to say something, then stopped. "No," she replied. "I presume he knows what he is doing."

"Very well. I shan't be long."

"Pray don't hurry on my account."

James and Van Vliet collected their hats and capes and went outside. The air was cold but the sun was bright and made a harsh contrast with the muted light indoors. They breathed deeply, squinting against the glare, and Van Vliet said, "How does it feel to be married?"

James turned the question over in his mind. "So far, there's not much change," he replied. "It feels about the same."

"Time will cure that." Van Vliet stepped onto the cobbles and turned left along the Herengracht, and James fell in beside him.

"Where are we going?" he asked.

"A splendid place. You will thank me for introducing you."

They turned left and crossed a bridge over the Singel, then came to a square on a street known as the Spui. On one corner was a small, narrow building with a front just large enough for two windows and a door, and on one of the windows was lettered the name Hoppe. The air inside was warm, and redolent of sawdust, beer, and tobacco smoke. They went to a booth at the far end of the room, and a waiter brought them two steins of beer. Van Vliet took a long swallow, then set his stein on the table and belched.

"That's better," he said.

James sampled his beer, and for the first time that day felt as though he might survive. His equilibrium had returned and his head no longer felt as though it were on loose hinges, and he began to wonder what he might buy for Antonia to show his contrition. Her anger was as well deserved as it was obvious, and he wished there were some method of instant atonement. After almost a year of desiring her, he now had her, but in the technical sense only, and in some ways he seemed farther away than he had the night they met. He was mulling the problem when he realized that Van Vliet had started talking, looking not at him but into his beer stein.

". . . must be kept in total confidence," Van Vliet concluded. "That is of the utmost importance. I cannot emphasize it too strongly."

"I understand," James replied. "That goes without saying."

"I don't remember what I said last night, but from your report it was somewhat garbled."

"That is correct. I would be happy if you'd be more specific."

"I cannot be too specific, by the very nature of things. But I can assure you you will have virtually unlimited backing for whatever land you may buy in the western part of your country."

"How far west?"

Van Vliet spread his hands. "Wherever you can buy it. Your country extends, I believe, to the Misspisspipi—the Miss—"

"Mississippi," James said.

"Miss-siss-sippi," Van Vliet repeated, laboriously. "Why do you have such outrageous names? Miss-siss-sippi, Mass-sa-chusetts—they sound like sneezing."

"They're Indian."

"Is there no translation?"

"Mississippi means Big River. That sounds like baby talk. If you want something really hard, I give you Lake Chargoggag-goggmanchaugagoggchaubunagungamaug."

Van Vliet closed his eyes. "Say that again."

James did and added, "It's in Massachusetts."

Van Vliet caught the waiter's eye and signaled for two more beers. "I must come to your country some time," he said. "If I do, will you show me that lake?"

"Gladly," said James, who was feeling a slight glow begin to spread through him. "We might even find an Indian who can give us a translation."

"Tell me about your Indians. Have you ever been scalped?"

"I? Good Lord, no. The Massachu—"

"Have you ever seen anyone scalped?"

"No. We've had no trouble with the Indians for many years. The Massachusetts Indians are—well—under control."

In his disappointment, Van Vliet's voice became smaller. "But you have seen Indians, haven't you?" he asked.

"Of course."

"What did they look like? Were they painted and did they whoop and dance?"

"No. They wore blankets, and they were looking for food."

Their beers arrived, and Van Vliet stared glumly into his stein. "What else do you have in your country?" he said.

"What we have the most of is land."

"About that, I know. And you'll not forget what I told you."

James laughed. "Not likely."

"And remember—total confidence."

"My lips are sealed. Except for this." James laughed again and tilted his head back to let the beer pour down his throat.

He had no idea of what time of day it was when they finally left Hoppe's. The light was still bright, but it had taken on a coppery color, and the shadows seemed more pronounced. They crossed the Spui and walked out beyond the Prinzengracht, and came at last to a hundred-year-old building, on which was a sign that read 'T SWARTE SCHAEP. James studied it for a moment.

"You may think Indian names are outrageous," he said, at last. "What kind of silly name would begin with an apostrophe?"

"It means 'the black sheep,'" Van Vliet replied.

"Then why doesn't it say so?"

"Come inside and you'll see." Van Vliet took him by the arm and steered him into the restaurant, which was crowded and which smelled, although James didn't understand why, better than any restaurant he'd been in so far. Then, when he read the bill of fare, he saw the reason. This was no ordinary Dutch establishment; this featured wines and dishes from France, Italy, Germany, and Portugal, and the list of choices appeared endless. After five months of Dutch cooking he was ready for a change, and his only problem lay in deciding what to order. He finally settled on a *tournedos* with a Burgundy to match and wondered briefly if it might be wise to have a short nap before the food arrived. This decision was made for him by the arrival of two small glasses of gin, which Van Vliet had ordered, and he brought his eyes into focus long enough to grasp the glass and get it to his lips.

His memory of the meal was hazy, but became clearer near the end. They had coffee and liqueurs, and as they were paying the bill, Van Vliet said, "I really ought to shave. If I don't, I'll be arrested as a *lummel*."

"What's a *lummel?*" James asked, feeling his own chin.

"A lout. A low person, who never shaves."

"You look respectable to me."

"That's because your eyes are closed. Come to my house, and then we can go on from there."

They made their way toward the door, and James heard familiar laughter. He was able to see that it came from a table at which were Baron Scholten, the Crommelins, Rutger Schimmelpenninck, and a girl he couldn't place but who looked faintly familiar. Scholten called out and beckoned, and James and Van Vliet went to the table. Chairs were pulled around, and they sat down. The hilarity was such that no single sentence was completed, and the only coherent message was from Scholten to a waiter, ordering another round of drinks. Then he turned to James and gave him a bleary grin.

"Where's your wife?" he asked. "You can't tell me you've had a fight already."

"No, no," James replied quickly. "Of course not. Adriaan and I had business to talk about, and we thought it better to leave the house."

Van Vliet said something in Dutch and Scholten laughed, then turned back to James. "Is she concerned about me?" he asked.

"Uh—no," James replied. "She said she presumed you knew what you were doing."

Scholten laughed again, and Schimmelpenninck leaned forward. The girl, who appeared to have adhered to him, leaned with him. "Was there any message for me?" he asked.

"No," James replied, then he remembered. "I don't know if it was a message or not. Someone was asking for you."

The girl said a few words in Dutch, and Schimmelpenninck shrugged and leaned back. "Thank you," he said to James. The girl kissed him on the ear.

It occurred to James that Scholten would be the one to ask about a present for Antonia. He outlined the problem as clearly as he could above the noise.

"So you have had a fight," Scholten replied.

"No, it's nothing like that. I'd simply like to bring her something to show my—appreciation. To show how highly I regard her." He saw no reason to admit it would be a peace offering.

Scholten tasted his new drink, and his eyes suddenly sparkled. "I know something," he said. "I know something she's wanted ever since she was a little girl."

"What? Tell me, and I'll get it."

"A horse. When she was a very little girl she wanted a pony, but her mother was frightened of horses and wouldn't hear of it. Then when she got older she wanted a real horse, but her mother was still against it. Now her mother is—no longer with us, and there can be no objection." Scholten's eyes puddled over, and he looked upward and said, "God vergeve mij, Anna."

"Then she has it." James pounded his fist on the table, just as Mevrouw Crommelin leaned forward to speak to him.

"Mynheer Greenleaf, will you do me a favor?" she asked, her eyes focused on something just beyond his shoulder.

"Certainly," he replied. "Anything you ask." He felt in a

courtly mood toward all womankind. She reached out her hand and squeezed his as he took it.

"Will you tell my husband what you told me about the eels?" she said. "I have tried very hard to remember it, but when I say it it never makes sense. Please tell him just as you told me."

"The eels?" James said, searching his memory. "What eels?"

"What you told me at dinner, about how they get back to the sea."

James glanced at Crommelin, who was staring at him with a sort of benumbed curiosity. "Oh, yes," he said. "Now I remember. Actually, those were efts."

Crommelin continued to stare.

"But they were eels first, weren't they?" Mevrouw Crommelin persisted. "You told me they were eels."

"Newts, efts, and salamanders all head for the water," James said, as though answering the question. He turned quickly back to Scholten and said, "Perhaps we should go to a stable now. I'd like some time to pick out the proper horse." Behind him he heard the Crommelins talking to each other in Dutch, he in a faintly sarcastic tone and she hysterically on the defensive.

"I have to shave before I do anything," Van Vliet put in, without having been asked. "After that, I'll go wherever you say."

"It takes no time to select a horse," Scholten replied to James. "You look at the teeth, and you look at the hocks, and you thump him a couple of times, and that's all you have to do."

"You told me eels changed into efts!" Mevrouw Crommelin said, her voice rising. "You said so in those exact words!"

"I don't care what the rest of you people do, I'm going to shave," Van Vliet repeated, to nobody in particular.

"I said it was a theory," James told the Crommelins. "I didn't say it was a fact."

"Ha! A theory!" Crommelin shouted, in exultation. "Who cares for theories?"

"I want the best horse in the world," said James to Scholten. "I don't want just any old nag, that you can test by thumping."

"He said it happened!" Mevrouw Crommelin cried. "He said they changed to efts!"

"It'll serve you all right if I *don't* shave," Van Vliet announced. "Then you'll wish you'd listened."

"I can thump a horse six times and tell its whole family history. Six times, that's all I need."

"He told me they changed. He said it right out loud."

"I want the best. I don't care how you tell, I want the best."

Antonia was at her desk, writing letters, when she heard the faint sounds of singing. A nameless, instinctive apprehension began to creep over her, and she rose and went to the window and opened it. The sounds became louder, and the voices more distinct; some men were singing, *"Lang zal zij leven, lang zal zij leven, lang zal zij leven,"* in a continuous chorus, punctuated every now and then with cheers and applause. By now certain of the worst, she put her head out and saw her father leading a dappled gray mare, astride which sat her husband and, behind him, Van Vliet, while a group of cheering Amsterdamers straggled along behind and occasionally joined in the singing. She closed the window, went to her room, and bolted the door.

12

Two days later James and Antonia moved into their own home, a house that Scholten had bought for them on the Herengracht not far from his own. They were supposed to move in immediately following the wedding, but the confusion of that day, and the subsequent complications of returning the horse, made moving of less importance than simply keeping the household from flying apart. There were times when James felt the whole idea of marriage was a ghastly mistake; that he had stepped into a world of turmoil, antagonism, and frustration. Then he remembered the Antonia he had first known and loved and felt that perhaps he wasn't doing as much as he might to make things run smoothly. There seemed to be two Antonias, and he had the suspicion that he was partly responsible when she changed from one to the other. So he turned his efforts toward being as thoughtful and attentive as he could, hoping that might improve matters. He was only moderately successful.

In the first place, he was totally confused by the matter of sex. His puritanical upbringing contrasted so sharply with his brief encounters in the field that he didn't know what was correct and what wasn't. He had the feeling that what might seem normal in one context would be considered depraved in another, and by overthinking a basically nonexistent problem he created a formidable obstacle. He realized that the more he thought about it, the worse it got, but he didn't know how to make the initial move without risking either a rebuff or, worse, laughter. He, who was self-confident to the point of arrogance in the world of finance, was stricken mute and flaccid at the thought of proposing coitus to a lady. It was the proposing that stumped him; he felt sure that once that was done there would be no problem.

Finally, and in desperation, he decided that the most radical move would be the best. Tossing aside all caution and all thoughts of the delicate approach, he went into the bedroom after dinner, removed his trousers and underdrawers, and returned to the salon, where Antonia was sitting with her needlework.

"Last one in bed is a rotten apple," he said.

Antonia turned and looked at him, and her eyes widened slightly. "Had you forgotten that the Roggeveens are coming over this evening?" she said.

"Oh, my God," said James and headed for the door.

"Try again later on," Antonia called after him, but he was gone.

Much later, staring at the darkened ceiling above the bed, he said, "I cannot understand it. It's never happened to me before."

"Perhaps you're tired," she replied.

"Not *that* tired. I mean—I'm not—no matter what—"

"Don't concern yourself about it," Antonia said. Her words were a faint echo from the past, but he couldn't remember where.

"Don't *concern* myself? My dear woman—"

"Perhaps if you didn't think about it, it would be all right."

"Have you any thoughts as to how not to think about it?"

"Put it out of your mind. Think about something else."

He made a noise like escaping steam. "Very easy to say, I'm sure."

"Do you know the expression, 'Thinking too precisely on the event'?"

"No."

"It comes from *Hamlet*. It—"

"Why does everybody have to quote that play to me? It's as though nobody ever had a thought of his own—everybody must always be quoting *Hamlet*! I am weary to death of the sound of the name!"

"I beg your pardon. I was only trying to be helpful." She turned away from him and pulled the covers up around her shoulders.

He continued to stare at the ceiling. "Maybe it's the food," he said, at last.

"Maybe what is the food?" Antonia's voice was muffled by the pillow.

"All this heavy Dutch food I've been eating. It has probably affected my liver."

There was a long pause, then Antonia said, "How does your liver enter into it? You might as well be blaming a bad tooth."

"For your information, my teeth are perfect. They have never given me a moment's trouble."

"Congratulations. I still don't see what your liver has to do with—with—"

"My brother Daniel dispenses liver pills to people with a wide variety of complaints. According to him, the liver is the core of all physiological functions."

"Then perhaps you had better send for your brother Daniel."

He ground his teeth. "I was only using him as an example."

"It occurs to me that you're using some odd examples. If Dutch food was the cause of your problem, then how is it that so many Dutch people have children?"

"They're accustomed to the food! I'm not!"

"Twaddle. Some of the food I ate in America was—"

"We are not talking about you, and we are not talking about the food in America! We are talking about me, and we are talking about me here in Amsterdam!"

"And, if you will forgive me, it is fairly pointless talk. We are doing nothing but beating a dead horse."

"You put things so graciously."

"You know what I mean."

There was a long silence, and finally James said, "Perhaps we should go back to the very beginning. Pretend we have just started dinner, and the host is ladling out our dishes of snail soup. Do you think that might work?" He waited for a reply, but all he heard was Antonia's low, even breathing. Then, like a wave cresting, her breath rippled into a snore, and he turned away and put the pillow over his head.

He awoke in the middle of the night in a state of aching tumescence, but he was so cheered by the condition that he did nothing to relieve it. He lay quietly in the dark, smiling, until it faded, and then he rolled over and went back to sleep. Next morning Antonia was up before him, but he knew now there was no cause for worry—all he had to do was relax. The only thing he didn't think of was how she knew more about the subject than he did. And the first time he did have her—in the middle of one afternoon, when he should have been at his tailor's—his sense of triumph was such that he suddenly felt he could conquer the world. He rose from the bed and began to pick up his clothes, which lay scattered about the floor.

"What time is it?" he asked.

From the bed Antonia had been regarding him as he stooped to retrieve his breeches. "Why?" she replied.

"I wondered if I still had time to see Crommelin today."

"May I ask what made you think of him?"

"I just remembered his suggestion that we meet. He's a valuable man to know."

"I heard the clock strike three a while ago. If I know him, he'll have left the office."

He hesitated, holding his clothes in front of him.

"You won't be able to do anything today you couldn't do just as well tomorrow," she said. "Why not come back to bed?" He was still hesitant, and she said, "Haven't you heard the saying that there's a time and a place for everything?"

He laughed. "Now that you mention it, yes."

"And if a thing is worth doing, it's worth doing well?"

"Oh? Do you have any complaints?"

"None at all. But why stop when you're off to such a splendid start?"

He dropped his clothes and returned to the bed. "I'll send Crommelin a note tomorrow," he said.

That winter was a savage one. The gales from the North Sea blasted across the land, piling freezing spray along the tops of the dikes and tearing limbs off trees already weakened by ice. As opposed to the clean, crisp cold of the New England winters, this cold was damp and clammy and penetrating, and the only good that could be said was that it froze the surface of the canals, making them less malodorous than usual. People skated on the canals and ponds and creeks, but no amount of exercise could entirely neutralize the cold, any more than could the dim and smoky fires that burned indoors. The only answer was to wear heavy clothing, drink hot liquids, and pray for spring. Every now and then James was reminded of Breughel's winter paintings, and he reflected that it was beyond the power of paint and brush to show the moisture in the cold. The Breughel scenes looked bright and almost jolly, as contrasted with the quivering misery of reality.

The first time he entered the Crommelin establishment and saw the freshly sanded floors, the blue Delft tiles around the fireplaces, and the lugubrious portraits of company officers, he had the feeling that this was a solid company, one that could be trusted. The turmoil in France, which had started the previous July with the storming of the Bastille and continued with the removal of the royal family from Versailles, had given a severe jolt to the international financial community. It had, for the time being at least, lessened the French pressure on Holland, and while it was too early to tell its long-range effect, any lessening of confidence in a structure that required confidence as its foundation had to be considered an ominous sign. In an attempt to produce some sort of financial stability, the French ecclesiastical estates were made public property, and the state took over the support of the clergy, but this did nothing to allay the general uneasiness. In fact, being as it was a move born of desperation, it had the opposite effect. Thus American investments seemed for the moment to be sounder than any European—or certainly any French—ones, and James felt sure that the House of Crommelin was where his destiny lay. And with the backing of Van Vliet, there seemed very little he couldn't accomplish. He had decided not to call on Van Vliet's money until it was absolutely necessary; insofar as it was possible, he wanted to be his own master. When the time came, he could either snap up some land for Van Vliet's clients or, better yet, sell them some of his own.

His interview with Crommelin was at first slightly uneasy. Crommelin eyed him with his toadlike stare and motioned him to sit down, then began to shuffle papers as though James weren't there. Finally he coughed, looked up, and said, "Before we begin, tell me about the eels."

James leaned forward. "The—?"

"Eels. Efts. Whatever you told my wife."

"Oh, that. Yes." James paused, trying to think of a quick reply, but the unblinking eyes doomed any attempt at evasion, and he quickly gave up. "That, mynheer, was dinner-party conversation," he said. "No more, no less. I was improvising, to try to stave off total silence."

Crommelin made a sound that started like a cough, but turned out to be a laugh. "Exactly what I thought," he said, taking out a large handkerchief and wiping his lips. "But I must say, you were very persuasive. You had Matilda totally convinced."

"I hope I caused no trouble," James said, remembering the Crommelins' argument in the restaurant.

"No, no. Of course not. I seldom believe more than half of what she tells me." He glanced at the papers in front of him. "I think you probably have a great future as a—what is the word?— Entrepreneur? Promoter? Speculat—"

"I prefer to think of myself as an investor," James put in.

"Exactly."

"Speculator implies the possibility of failure. I should like as far as possible to eliminate that chance."

"Exactly. Now then—would you take coffee? Gin? Brandy?"

"Uh"—James glanced at the clock, which stood like an ornately carved coffin in one corner. If it was accurate, there was still an hour and a quarter until noon. Crommelin saw his look and wheezed.

"Pay that no mind," he said. "In the winter, we forget about clocks. The only way to survive is to do what you want when you want to do it."

"Aha," said James. "In that case, I'd be happy to join you in whatever you propose."

Crommelin went to the door, then returned to his desk, dropped heavily into his chair, and picked up a piece of paper. "Several states are offering bonds," he said. "Rhode Island, North Carolina, South Carolina, and such. Also, there are United States bonds. There are—"

"I am primarily interested in land," James said. "That is where I think the greatest future lies."

"Undoubtedly. But these bonds are secured by land grants, so in buying the bonds you are in effect buying the land. How did you intend to pay for them?"

"In a number of ways. I already own a certain amount of land, secured by notes and other collateral, and this in turn could provide security for—"

"Ah, here we are," Crommelin broke in, as the door opened

and a small, wizened man appeared with a tray and two steaming mugs. He passed the first mug to James, and Crommelin took the other, raised it, said, "*Gezondheid,*" and drank. James tasted his and his eyes, nose, and throat were blasted by the hot, stinging vapor.

"Delicious," he said, putting his mug down. "What is it?"

"An old family recipe. We call it '*duivelstong,*' or devil's tongue."

James took another taste. "And well named, too," he said.

"And now," said Crommelin, rubbing his hands together, "let us proceed to the business at hand. You say you are primarily interested in land."

"Put it this way," James replied. "I am interested in anything that will make money. I believe that American land has more possibility of growth than any other commodity, so that is where my main interest lies."

"And would you consider joining a syndicate?"

James hesitated. "Not at the moment. For now, I would prefer to operate on my own and accumulate as much as I can without the—ah—encumbrance of partners."

"And you will pay—with—?"

"With mortgages, notes, deeds to other property—cash if necessary . . ."

"Cash is seldom necessary," Crommelin said. "We find it tends to clutter up the accounting."

"Good," said James. "That makes it simpler all around."

13

It was in March that Antonia announced she was pregnant. The possibility had been lurking in the back of James's mind, but for some reason he hadn't considered it seriously; he had been so busy in his various deals with Crommelin that the idea of parenthood had slipped into the category of the always possible but hardly probable, like being made ambassador to France or contracting dengue fever. Now, with the birth expected some time in September, he took time out from his business long enough to reflect on the change that was about to come into his life.

Looking at it realistically, he didn't imagine the change would be too radical. There were servants who could take care of whatever was involved in the maintenance and feeding of an infant, and Antonia would be free to devote as much or as little time to it as she chose. To him, the child was still an idea rather than a reality, and when, by extreme concentration, he was able to conceive of its having a gender, he assumed it was masculine—or would be when the time came. But the whole business was so improbable that he found it easier to put it all out of his mind, at least until September.

Antonia was not quite so detached: it seemed to James that she was carrying on as though the child were due the following Thursday. The first thing she did was start accumulating baby clothes, and in fairly short order she had amassed enough, by his estimate, to furnish an entire orphan asylum. Then came the matter of the name, which he considered pointless until the gender had been established, but which Antonia insisted was necessary so that baptism could follow hard on the heels of parturition. Considering the number of names she bore, it was obvious that a great deal of thought had gone into the matter and it was not something to be taken lightly. Every name had to be weighed and compared against a possible alternate, always with due consideration for the importance of various members of the family.

In this respect, James suffered from an *embarras de richesses*. Certain names, such as William, Stephen, Daniel, John, and James, repeated themselves over and over in the Greenleaf family history, and Edmund, who came to America in 1634 and was a cofounder of the town of Newbury, was also a name that echoed through the generations. But such was the brush fire fertility of the Greenleafs, both male and female, that almost any name in the church register could be found not once but several times among their number, plus a few less usual ones like Gooking, Rooksby, Sophronia, Dimmis, Electa, and Keturah. The Bible was well represented by Abel, Rebecca, Shearjushet, Esther, Israel, Ezekiel, Samuel, Judith, and Moses, and there were occasional nods to history and mythology, as in Hannibal and Minerva. In the long run, however, the Greenleafs came down on the side of the Anglo-Saxons, with John and Elizabeth being the names most frequently chosen. James and Antonia could have named their child anything they wanted and have been reasonably sure of finding a Greenleaf ancestor with a name to match.

Finally, after sifting and sorting and pondering, they decided that if it should be a boy, he would be named William Christian James, and if a girl, they'd call her Elizabeth. Antonia agreed to this latter, but she agreed so quickly and almost automatically that James had the feeling she was holding something back and would come up with another choice if the occasion demanded. To him it was immaterial, because he never seriously thought the child would be a girl, and September was a long way off anyway.

Spring came, and the canals thawed, and suddenly the land was ablaze with tulips. There were beds of tulips, fields of tulips, and literally acres of tulips, in colors ranging from white to mottled purple to yellow to red to black to red-white-and-blue, and James wondered if this wild profusion were a leftover from the tulipomania that had seized the country some hundred and fifty years earlier. At that time, the demand for tulips reached such insane proportions that people would pay thousands of florins for a single bulb, and a sailor, who mistakenly ate a tulip under the impression it was an onion, was thrown into jail for several months to contemplate his sins. Such was the national madness that at one point a troop of soldiers was called out to trample a field of less-than-perfect tulips in order that the integrity of one perfect one could be maintained. Speculation in tulips and tulip futures swept the country like the plague, fortunes were made overnight, the prices of goods and commodities rose, and a form of hysterical inflation resulted that lasted for the better part of three years. Then, like the onset of sobriety after a long carousal, came the realization that it was based on nothing more than the root of a flowering plant, and the whole thing fell apart—the Dutch economy with it. Speculators were left with attics, cellars, and barns full of virtually worthless bulbs, and the only people who came away unscarred were those who had sold out at the height of the mania. They had good, solid money to show for it; the others had small, gritty bulbs that were good only for planting.

Looking at the tulips and contemplating the disaster they represented, James congratulated himself that he was dealing in a commodity that was as solid as the earth itself—in fact, it *was* the earth. Land was something that would be forever in demand, and those who had the best land were the ones who would have the power. Others would have to come to them and on whatever terms they chose to set. Something in the back of his mind told him that there was only so much he could do from Holland, that sooner or later he would have to return to America to be on the spot when important land came up for sale, but in the meantime he could continue to deal through Crommelin and build a solid foundation from which to operate. He smiled when he thought of the tulip speculators, and wondered how they could have been so gullible as to have been caught up in the hysteria. He could never imagine a Yankee businessman being so impractical, and he concluded that the harsh realities of New England living probably kept a man's feet on the ground. He could think of no New England phenomenon comparable to the tulipomania—except possibly the Salem witch trials and they were a wholly different matter. It was one thing to be afraid of witches; it was quite another thing to worship a tulip bulb. The Yankees were, clearly, the more levelheaded of the two groups.

Spring gave way to summer, and the heat that hung over the Continent brought with it an almost comatose condition, limiting action to the barest essentials. James's business with Crommelin, requiring as it did no physical exertion, continued unabated throughout the summer months, but Antonia found that as she grew larger, it became harder to move about, and she spent most of her time indoors, sitting in the faint breeze that stirred the curtains and applying cooling compresses to her wrists and forehead. The heat even affected the French, who after their initial burst of violence the previous year settled down to the stultifying task of trying to reorganize the government. Nobody, least of all the French, knew exactly where the country was headed; all that anyone could say for sure was that a change was in the making and that the nobility and the clergy were likely to come out on the short end when it was over.

The sulfurous heat of August lasted into the first week of September, and Antonia was by now so uncomfortable that she could barely move. The fetus, which seemed the size of a large pumpkin and which had been riding high up near her rib cage, moved suddenly lower, until she had to lean backward to maintain her balance. James hovered about her like a nervous hen, helpless to do anything but unwilling to leave her side in case he should be needed. He tried to remember what in Daniel's pharmacopoeia was recommended for situations such as this, and all he could recall was that witch hazel made a soothing poultice. The trouble was that witch hazel came from a North American shrub and was unknown in the Netherlands, so as a second choice he bathed her forehead in gin, on the theory that the alcohol would be better than nothing. She'd been lying back in a chair, her eyes closed, and when he began to sponge her forehead a faint smile appeared on her face.

"Thank you," she said, and then, as the smell of the gin reached her nostrils, the smile faded and she said, "What are you using?" He told her, and after a moment she pushed his hand aside, struggled upright, and tottered out of the room. He heard faint retching noises, and when she returned, some ten minutes later, she was pale and her forehead glistened. "Thank you, anyway," she said, dropping heavily into her chair. "It was good of you to try." She breathed deeply and closed her eyes, and her mouth tightened, then relaxed. "Please don't feel you have to stay," she said.

He hesitated, watching her, and when she said nothing more, he turned and left the room.

He had no idea what time it was when she woke him. All he knew was that the bedroom was dark as a cave, and her unseen hand was clutching his shoulder. "Hnf?" he said, struggling toward consciousness.

"I think you'd best call Mathilde," she said. Her voice was calm and unhurried, but it brought him wide awake, and he swung his feet over the edge of the bed and groped for the candle. He found it, then with some difficulty located the striker, and after three fumbling tries finally got the candle lighted. With one hand between him and the flame, he looked at the bed, and in the flickering glow he could see Antonia, whose eyes were large and whose stomach was monstrous. The bedclothes were tangled around her, and she made a faint attempt to straighten them. "Go ahead," she said. "There's nothing you can do here now."

In his bare feet, and wearing only his nightcap and night shirt, he padded down to the servants' quarters and knocked on the door. He was answered by Mathilde, the senior maid, who sounded as though she'd been awake and waiting for him.

"Mevrouw Greenleaf would like to see you," he said. He heard the thump of Mathilde's heels hitting the floor, the slam and bang of dresser drawers and wardrobe doors, and then Mathilde appeared and hurried past him, her candle leaving a thin trail of smoke down the corridor.

From then on, things became blurred. Nothing much seemed to be happening, but servants darted here and there like field mice during haying, and lights appeared at strategic spots throughout the house. Then, gradually, the lights turned pale and thin as daylight came, but no one thought to put them out. James drifted aimlessly about like a ghost who'd come to haunt the wrong house, barred from the bedroom but unable to think of any place else to go. At one point there was a knock at the front door and he went and answered it, admitting a heavy-set woman with a large satchel and an air of determination, who glanced at him oddly as she entered and who, he assumed as she bustled past him and went upstairs, must be the midwife. He wondered briefly at the look she'd given him, then realized he was still in his nightclothes and bare feet. After one more unsuccessful attempt to get into the bedroom, he sought out a kitchen maid, told her the clothes he wanted and had her bring them to him in the music room, where he finally got dressed.

It seemed that half the day had gone by when, glancing at a clock, he saw that it was seven twenty-three. Incredulous, he went and put his ear to the case to make sure it was running and heard the steady, stately plick-plock of its mechanism. There was a click, and the minute hand jumped to seven twenty-four. He stared at it until it jumped again, then turned and went to a front window and looked out at the Herengracht. It was still early September (September what? the fifth? the sixth?), but some of the elm trees along the canal had started to shed, and the surface of the water was flecked with crinkled leaves, dried by the summer heat. A single swan, its neck like a question mark, moved slowly and with no apparent effort, examining bits of flotsam and every now and then thrusting its head beneath the surface. James wondered what was under water that might be tempting to a swan and concluded it was simply checking every possibility, with no specific food in mind. What floated on the surface was bad enough; what lay beneath was something he didn't care to imagine. After watching the swan for about a half hour, he turned away from the window and looked at the clock. It was seven thirty-one.

A maid appeared and told him his breakfast was ready, and he went into the dining room and picked at the bread and cheese and fruit that had been set before his place. When he first sat down, the meal had looked like a posed arrangement for a still-life painter; as he nibbled at it, the composition began slowly to come apart, almost like a melting snowman. It occurred to him that, if a painter wanted to be truly realistic, he would paint the scene at the end of a meal rather than before it, and he wished he were the one who could do it. It would open up a whole new area in the field of art and would represent a truth that had never been put on canvas before. Just as the end of the meal was the logical sequence to the beginning, so what Antonia was going through now was the logical sequence to mating, and the person who could make that statement on canvas would have revealed . . . His thoughts ground to a slow halt as he realized that, in his distracted frame of mind, he was groping for a truth that was evident to anyone with half a brain, and what he had thought was profound went no deeper than the leaves that perched on the surface of the Herengracht. He shook his head, took a long swallow of coffee, and rose and went back into the front room. The swan had gone, and the leaves floated motionless where it had been.

He sat down and tried to think of some way to make the time pass. He told himself that by this time tomorrow he would be the father of a boy or a girl, and he would look back on the day with wry amusement. Or it might happen even sooner: the child might be born any minute, or possibly within an hour, or certainly by afternoon—after all, it didn't have far to travel, and barring some unnatural— His thoughts were interrupted by the maid, who said, "I beg pardon, mynheer."

"Yes?" He looked around, half expecting her to be holding a baby, but her hands were clasped in front of her and her face was blank.

"The *vroedvrouw* asks do you have any rope?"

"What? Who wants to know?"

"The *vroedvrouw*. The how-you-say 'middle wife.'"

"What in God's name does she want *rope* for?"

"For the Baroness to pull on."

"Pull what?"

"I don't know, mynheer. All I know is she asks for a pulling rope."

James pondered what seemed like a preposterous situation and finally said, "We have no rope I can think of. Ask her if harness would do as well."

The maid disappeared and didn't come back. After a few minutes James heard an odd ripping noise, and he rose and followed the sound until he came to the maid, who was busily tearing a bed sheet into long strips. "And what, pray, is this all about?" he asked.

"The *vroedvrouw* says this will serve," she replied, ripping the last segment. She gathered the strips together and vanished. James listened carefully, but could hear no signs of distress from behind the closed door, and after a few minutes he returned to the front room. The clock showed eight-seventeen.

He must have dozed, because the next thing he knew Baron

Scholten had entered the room. "How is she?" the Baron asked, in a voice too casual to be convincing.

"I have no idea," James replied. "The last time anyone spoke to me it was to ask for rope for her to pull on. You now know as much as I do."

"Ah, yes," Scholten said. "That is supposed to help speed the labor."

"Would you mind telling me how?"

"They tie the ropes to the posts at the foot of the bed, then the woman pulls on them, and the strain is supposed to force the child out. When Antonia was born, her mother used the ropes. She told me later it was like being tied to wild horses."

James closed his eyes. Until now he had felt only numb; now he felt sick.

"How long has she been in labor?" Scholten asked.

"I don't know. Some time in the middle of the night."

"It could be a long time yet. She herself was nineteen hours being born." Scholten started to say something more, when the midwife arrived in the doorway. Her sleeves were rolled up, and there was perspiration on her forehead. She spoke in Dutch to Scholten, and he replied, and there was a brief exchange between them. Then he turned to James. "She says it has stopped," he said.

"What has stopped?"

"The labor."

"What do we do now?" James had the brief, insane notion that the whole pregnancy had been a false alarm.

"We wait until it starts again."

James looked at the midwife. "How long will that be?"

She shrugged and spread her hands. "*Ongekend*," she said.

"There's no way to know," Scholten translated. The midwife said something more, and he went on, "She says we might as well go out and get some air. There's nothing we can do around here."

James hesitated. "Is she sure?"

"Positive." Scholten took him by the arm. "Come with me. I know just what you need."

James tried to pull his arm away. "And I know what I don't need," he said.

"Nonsense," said Scholten. "One beer isn't going to do you any harm."

They went first to Hoppe's and then to 't Swarte Schaep, but James found that the beer only made him sleepy and took away what little interest he might have had in food. He listened to Scholten, who went on at some length about Crommelin and the various land deals that could be made, and his interest was momentarily aroused by the news that one J. J. Angerstein, who was presently living in London, owned a considerable tract of land in upstate New York that could be bought at a good rate if secured by the proper notes. He filed the name Angerstein away for future reference and went back to pretending to listen. He found it impossible to concentrate, because his mind kept returning to the incredible matter of labor stopping once it had got started. It was against everything he'd ever heard, and a cold fear began to gnaw at him that it might be a sign of worse to come. It was not at all unusual for a woman to die in childbirth, but until now the possibility had never occurred to him that it might happen to Antonia, and his fear grew to the point of panic. Finally he could stand it no longer.

"I should go home," he said, rising from the table.

Scholten stopped in the midst of what he was saying and looked at him in surprise. "Why?" he said. "There's nothing happening there."

"How do you know?" James replied, putting a shade too much emphasis on the "you."

"They know where we are. I told them to send for us when it came time."

"Nevertheless, I should be there."

Scholten shrugged and looked around for a waiter.

"I don't mean to take you away," James said. "You may stay as long as you please."

Scholten squinted his eyes slightly. "What do you mean by that?"

"What I said. I have no stomach for business talk, but that should not mean there won't be someone else to listen to you." He realized as the words came out he was sounding spiteful, but it was too late to soften the impact. Scholten rose slowly, and his face turned first pale and then red.

"You imbecile," he said in a low voice. "Do you think I was

talking because I cared what I was saying? Do you think it makes any difference to me what land you buy? For all I care, you could buy the mountains of Norway and jump off them into the sea. I was trying to divert your attention and at the same time keep myself busy, so as not to think what's happening. You may have forgotten it, but she is my daughter, my only daughter, and now the only woman in my life, and if in your monstrous conceit you think you are the only person thinking of her, you are very much mistaken. I tell you now that if anything happens to her, I shall hold you personally responsible." He stopped, breathing heavily, then threw some money on the table and left the restaurant. James followed him.

They walked quickly and in silence for several minutes, with Scholten out in front, then James, almost running, caught up with him, and they both reduced their pace. "I'm sorry," James said. "Believe me, I am mortified."

Scholten looked straight ahead. "I'm sorry, too," he replied. "That was an idiotic remark."

"Not at all. I was stupid not to realize."

"I mean about holding you responsible. That was sheer garbage, spoken out of rage."

"Oh. Well . . ."

"It is a trying time for everyone. Let's say no more."

"Agreed. And thank you."

"My pleasure."

They walked the rest of the way in silence, each immersed in his own thoughts. When they reached the house, James noted without interest that the swan had returned to the Herengracht, and he looked at the house as though it might give him some message. But its brick front remained impassive, and the sun reflected on the upstairs windows gave no hint of what was happening inside. They went in and were greeted by total silence. James ran up the stairs, followed more slowly by Scholten, and at the door to the bedroom he saw the maid who had asked him for the ropes. She put a finger to her lips.

"How is she?" James whispered. "Has it been born?"

The girl shook her head. "She is sleeping now. It started, and then it stopped again."

"Where's the midwife?"

"In with her. She is probably sleeping, too."

Scholten caught up, breathing in deep puffs like a blowing whale, and James reported the news. Scholten and the maid had a brief conversation in Dutch, then Scholten turned away. His voice was hoarse and weary as he said, "Dear God, I didn't think I'd have to go through this again."

They went into the front room and sat down, and out of curiosity James looked at the clock. It showed five minutes past three, and he found it hard to realize that it was still the same day. The morning seemed days, weeks, years ago, something that had happened either in a dream or in another world, and the thought that it was only a matter of hours was more than his senses were willing to accept. He felt his brain growing tight, as though someone were winding a coiled spring inside his skull, and he had to get up from his chair and pace back and forth to relieve the tension. The swan, he noticed, had gone again, and he wondered if there were a time schedule by which it came and went. The clock showed seven minutes past three, and he decided to time the swan's return and see if he could establish a pattern. Anything, to keep that spring from becoming too tight. He knew that if it snapped, he would dive right through the window.

The swan came back at ten minutes to four, stayed for eleven minutes, and by the time darkness fell it had not reappeared. The lights in the nearby houses were reflected on the surface of the canal, quivering patches of luminescence that seemed to have lives of their own. The twilight lasted a long time, but finally it was totally dark, and James groped his way back to his chair. He could just make out Scholten's silent form, and he was aware that the other rooms in the house were being lighted, but by unspoken agreement neither he nor Scholten wanted either light or conversation, and they sat in the darkness like two marble tombstones.

From time to time there were small noises, and once the maid came to ask them if they would like some supper, but there was nothing to indicate that Antonia was anywhere nearer the end of her labor than she'd been many hours before. Once or twice James thought he heard a cry, but he couldn't be sure and it was followed each time by total silence, so he concluded that no particular progress was being made. He decided to go back in his memory as far as he could and retrace the events of his life in chronological order, trying to find a pattern to explain the situation in which he now found himself. He didn't expect a coherent answer, but it was one way to prevent the spring from tightening.

He remembered the events of the Revolution only as isolated scenes, with no continuity and no relation to himself except as an observer. He remembered his confusion about Tories and how they differed from other people, and how a patriot like his father could have a brother who was a Tory, and he was fondly remembering his Uncle Stephen when he was aware that the midwife was standing in the doorway. He rose, half fearing what she would say, and when he saw her silhouetted against the light in the corridor he could see she was holding something.

"*Gefeliciteerd,* mynheer!" she said. "*Een jongen!*"

He heard Scholten's exclamation and a brief flurry of Dutch between him and the midwife, and then Scholten was pumping his hand and saying, "Congratulations! You have a son!"

"How's Antonia?" James asked.

"All right, she says. Considering what she's been through."

"I want to see her."

Another flurry of Dutch, and then Scholten said, "You'll have to wait until they clean up. It won't take long."

The door to the bedroom opened, and a maid hurried out with a pile of bedclothes in her arms. In one hand she was carrying a long kitchen knife, and James stared at it in disbelief.

"May I ask what that knife was used for?" he said.

The midwife said something to Scholten, and he said, "That went under the mattress, to cut the pain. She says it's standard practice."

James looked at the bundle the midwife was holding, but all he could see was a wizened, red face and some wet, dark hair. "Well, well," he said, quietly.

"What are you naming him?" Scholten asked. "Antonia told me, but I seem to have forgotten."

James started to say a name, then his mind went blank, and all he could think of were those they had considered and discarded. Stephen? John? Richard? Robert? Daniel? Simon? No, none of them—

"So have I," he said. "But right now, I don't think it matters."

14

For the next year and a half James concentrated on the acquisition of land. He had no detailed schedule, no particular area of development; his simple aim was to amass as much property as he could and see what happened after that. He reasoned that a man with property had power, and with enough power he wouldn't have to look for action; it would come to him.

In the circumstances, his consular activities were minimal, but every now and then his duties took him to the waterfront. The smells reminded him of home, and there were times when he felt that Amsterdam had no more to offer him, that his real future lay back in the United States. It seemed pointless to buy American land from the Netherlands, but until he got home there was no other choice; with war spreading throughout western Europe (Austria and Prussia were now fighting France, on a front that ran from Switzerland to the Channel), no European investments were worth anything.

On an afternoon in April he was summoned to the magistrate's office, to look into the matter of an American seaman who had been arrested while trying to dismantle the night watchman at a warehouse. It had taken three men to subdue him, and when he was led into James's presence he was so badly cut up that at first James didn't recognize him. But when he spoke, although his words were muffled by his swollen mouth, James realized it was Benjamin Loxley, skipper of the *Pigou*.

"Captain!" he exclaimed, taking Loxley by the arm. "How did you get yourself in this state?"

"Thieves," Loxley muttered. "Thieves and brigands to a man. They're worse than the bloody British."

"But what happened?"

It developed that the *Pigou* had taken aboard a sealed cask in Boston, which the consigner had labeled "flour" but which was in fact opium, a discrepancy that came to light when the cask split on being unloaded. The Dutch authorities didn't mind the opium so much as they did the fact that it was a poppy derivative, a product they coveted to match their tulip monopoly. They impounded the *Pigou's* entire cargo pending further inspection, and Loxley, after brooding about matters over several gins, decided to open the warehouse and reclaim what he considered rightfully his. He would probably have succeeded, had not the watchman's cries brought out the constabulary. Loxley was charged with attempted burglary in the night, violation of government property, grievous bodily assault, resisting arrest, and flagrant public drunkenness, a charge seldom brought on its own but used to tie off a list of other offenses. After hearing the story, James turned to the magistrate.

"Your honor, this is not a case for the civil courts," he said. "This case has international implications."

"I see no reason why," the magistrate replied. "He became a public nuisance on the soil of the Netherlands."

"But American property had been confiscated. He was simply trying to defend his country's goods."

The magistrate shook his head. "That does not alter the facts of the case."

"It does not alter the fact that you have seized American property and that I shall report the matter to John Adams. You may rest assured he will not be pleased."

The magistrate was confused. "John Adams?" he said. "What is his concern?"

"He is the one to whom I make my reports," James replied, stretching the truth almost beyond recognition. "And as Vice President of the United States he will deeply resent this high-handed behavior. I imagine he will take the matter up with the President himself. George Washington did not fight for our independence only to have it nibbled away by foreign officials."

"Still," the magistrate said, "this man behaved in a violent and provocative manner. He—"

"Wouldn't you? Would you not fight to defend your country's honor if you felt it had been besmirched?"

The magistrate spread his hands. "If I felt that—"

"I have the solution," James said before the magistrate could answer. "I believe it is a fair and honorable one for all concerned. If you will drop the charges against this man, then I, as United States consul in Amsterdam, will personally assume responsibility for the ship's cargo . . . except for the opium. That I will leave with you, and I will see to it that every other item in the cargo is delivered as specified in the manifest. Surely nothing could be fairer than that."

"It still does not consider the fact that—"

"Very well, then, I shall make out my report to John Adams. If you insist that this go to higher authority, I have no choice but to accede to your wishes. May I have your name, please?"

The magistrate closed his eyes, and sighed. "Let us not trouble Mr. Adams with this," he said.

"You mean you agree to my proposal?"

"That is correct. The case is closed. Just leave the opium here."

Outside, Loxley pounded James on the back. "Mister Consul, yer a bloody wonder!" he said, enveloping James in a cloud of stale gin fumes. "I thought I was doomed to a Dutch jail for the rest of my days. Come, and we'll have a glass to yer health!"

James hesitated. He had no particular desire for a drink, but he wanted to find out the news from home, so he said, "Just one," and followed where Loxley led. They went over cobbled streets to the waterfront, then through a door in the back of a building and down a flight of steps and into a room so full of smoke that James thought at first it was on fire. Then he could make out people sitting at tables and see the faint glow of candles, and as his eyes became accustomed to the murk, he got the impression that most of the customers had been there for several days. Unseen in a corner, someone was playing a concertina. Loxley found two places at a long table, and they sat down. James had the uncomfortable feeling of being out of place, and knew that everyone in the room was watching him.

"Well!" he said, to Loxley, when their drinks arrived. "What's happening the other side of the ocean?"

"Don't they tell yer nothing here?" Loxley replied, burying his nose in his mug.

"Not a great deal," James replied. "I receive news of the family, but not much else."

"I suppose yer know about the Federal City."

"I understand it's going to be in Virginia. When I left, New York was the capital."

"New York and Philly was both after it, but two years ago they settled on this place along the Potomac. The government's supposed to move in there eight years from now, in 1800, but I'm danged if I know how they'll swing it."

"Why?"

Loxley gave a gurgling laugh, then winced at the pain in his lips. "The land," he said, and put the back of one hand to his mouth.

"What about it?" James asked, suddenly attentive.

"There ain't nobody wants to buy it. The government picked up the land fer nothing, figuring to sell it to investors and build the city with that money, but nobody wants to buy, so the land's just sitting there."

"*The land's just sitting there?*" James said, incredulous. "You mean the land the Federal City will be built on?"

"That's right. Some people bought a lot or two, but fer the most part it's just woods and swampland."

James sat back, trying to comprehend what he'd heard. If it was true, a man with sufficient credit could buy up land that would eventually be worth millions of dollars, but it was nothing that could be done from a distance; whoever bought it would have to be there in person, to make sure what he was getting. And it was a state of affairs that couldn't last much longer, because sooner or later someone was bound to see the opportunity and snatch at it. The fact that it had not already happened was little short of a miracle.

"How are they offering it up?" he asked.

"There's some talk of an auction, but I don't know what will come of it. Mostly, the commissioners just sit around and stare at each other."

"And this is the land on which the government will build?" James still couldn't believe he'd heard correctly.

"Unless the whole thing falls through, it is."

"What are the chances of that?"

"Not much. General Washington's got his heart set on it, and what he wants he usually gets. There's some talk the city's going to be named after him."

Loxley continued to talk, but James was only half listening. His mind was exploring the problems involved in getting home to America in time to take advantage of the sale, and the more he thought about it, the more he concluded it was simply a matter of packing up and leaving. There would be the formality of requesting leave of absence, but since his commission came from the interim government, before Washington had been elected, he wasn't sure he needed even to do that. He would get home as soon as the letter did, so for all practical purposes he had only to inform them once he arrived. The only stumbling block he could foresee was Antonia, and if she wouldn't join him, he could leave her here, either to follow at a later date or to await his eventual return. She might be irritated at his departure, but that couldn't be helped; the one important thing was to get home, and get home quickly.

Her reaction, when he told her, was sharper than he'd expected.

"Have you taken leave of your senses?" she asked.

"Not in the least. This is a chance that comes once in a lifetime."

She picked up the embroidery she'd been working on. "Then you'll do it without me."

"What do you mean?"

"I have no intention of going all the way across the ocean and back just so you may be first in line for some land. I have been in your country once, and you will forgive my saying it is not a cheerful experience. I prefer civilization to life on the frontier."

"You seem to forget it's my home."

"All Americans are provincial. They think they can live nowhere except where they were born. If it's land you want, I'm sure Papa can arrange—"

"This has nothing to do with your father. This is something I intend to do on my own."

She shrugged. "Then all I can say is good luck."

"In other words, you refuse to come with me."

"You're so quick, James. You understand everything immediately."

He hesitated. "I may be gone a long time."

She looked at him sharply and said, "Are you telling me you're not coming back?"

"I didn't say that; I said I may be gone a long time. It all depends on what happens."

"But it is possible you may not come back."

"Anything is possible."

"I think the very least you owe me is candor. Do you intend to come back or not?"

"Let me put it this way: my future, and the future of my business, lies in America. You say you prefer civilization to the frontier, but Holland passed its peak a hundred years ago, and there's no more future here than there is in Egypt. You call it civilization but other people might call it decadence, so it's all in how you look at it."

"I see." Her eyes were shining with rage. "I think you've made it very clear."

"You asked me to be candid."

"And you were. For that, at least, I thank you." The only sound in the room was the slow ticking of the clock, but James could almost hear the thud of a door closing between Antonia and himself.

It was a cold, damp day in May when he left Amsterdam. A fine rain clouded the windows and made the cobbles glisten, and the house was as bleak and silent as a warehouse. Antonia, to whom he had spoken very little, had taken their son, Billy, to her father's house with the obvious intention of avoiding a farewell scene, and with nothing else to do James decided to go down and board the ship. His baggage had been taken to the docks that morning and put aboard the brig *Prudence*, which was scheduled to sail on the afternoon tide, and he reasoned he could put the time to good advantage by getting settled in his cabin.

As he had so often in the last ten days, he let his mind drift back over a conversation he'd had with Van Vliet shortly after his decision to leave. They had met on the street when James was returning from Crommelin's office, and Van Vliet had opened the conversation by saying, "Well! I understand you're on your way!"

"Where did you hear that?" James asked.

"News travels fast. You won't forget about our agreement, will you?"

They had then discussed the agreement, and while Van Vliet

would not be specific, James was sure he was working on behalf of the *émigré* French nobility, who were desperately looking for places to live. He assured Van Vliet he would remember, and then, still nagged by the opening remark, he said, "Would you mind telling me how you knew of my departure?"

Van Vliet hesitated a second, then said, "Rutger Schimmelpenninck told me."

"How did he know?"

Another pause. "I presume the Baroness told him."

"You mean Antonia?"

Van Vliet nodded. "That, of course, is only a guess."

"Does she know him well enough to discuss family matters with him?"

This time there was a long pause. "They have known each other for a long time," Van Vliet said, at last.

James digested this. "I see," he said.

"But as I said, that is only a guess."

"Yes. Of course."

Every time he reviewed the conversation it became clearer there was only one meaning, and when he searched his memory for other items about Schimmelpenninck, they all seemed to fit in. The conclusion was inescapable, and while he tried to resign himself to it, he found it continued to gnaw at him, like a sore that refused to heal. The only answer, if there was one, was to get away as fast as he could.

From his cabin he heard footsteps above, and the creaks and rattles and thumps of a ship being made ready for departure. He decided to go topside and watch them leave, if only for the pleasure of seeing Amsterdam fade away into the rain.

15

The lookout first sighted land on a smoky morning in July, when the *Prudence* was wallowing in the oily swells somewhere to the east of Massachusetts. Long strands of floating kelp had been spotted the day before, so they knew they were approaching the coast, but the heat haze had blurred the horizon to the point where the backstaff was useless, and the latitude as well as the longitude was anybody's guess. The captain studied the thin pencil line ahead, then grunted.

"Could be any damn thing," he said, to the first mate. "Double the lookouts, and get a man in the goddam chains."

One man was sent forward with a lead line to measure the depth of the water, and several others clambered into the rigging. James looked over the side, trying to gauge the depth by eye, but all he could tell was that it didn't look like the water off Boston. It was lighter in color, and there were eddies and currents that indicated the presence of shoals and tidal rips, but beyond that he could tell nothing. He thought how ignominious it would be to run aground at the very end of the voyage and either have to row to the distant shore or perish on a sandbar during the next storm. As usual, he thought, the time after landfall passes more slowly than the rest of the voyage.

Almost simultaneously, a man in the rigging shouted, "Sand bar larboard bow!" and the leadsman sang out, "Six fathoms!" and the captain ordered the helm put hard over, then sprang to the shrouds and peered ahead. James, standing at the rail, could see a thin line of waves breaking the surface of the water, and he held his breath as the bow slowly began to swing to starboard. There was a thunder and rattle of blocks as the sheets were loosened; the leadsman made another cast and reported five and a half fathoms, and then, on his next cast, the *Prudence* had settled on a course away from the land, and he got a reading of seven, then ten, and people began to breathe again. The captain squinted back at the rip, and the dim line of shore beyond it.

"By God if that warn't Nantucket," he said. "Ain't no land in these parts got as many reefs and shoals around her as that bitch." He turned, and looked forward. "And, less'n I'm flat-arse crazy, we should pick up that goddam Chatham bar before too long."

They spent the rest of the day moving slowly up the hook of Cape Cod, helped by a light southwesterly wind that sprang up in the afternoon. They rounded the tip that night, guided by beacon lights from the beach, and then headed northwest for Boston, with the wind fair on the beam. James stayed up into the midwatch, hoping to see the lights of home, but then the wind died and the *Prudence* lost speed, and he realized his time would be better spent in his bunk. He went below, praying that this would be the last night he would ever have to be at sea. The eastward crossing had been enlivened by his courtship of Antonia and the encounter with the other ship; the westbound voyage had been week after week of grinding boredom, with no one to talk to who shared any of his interests and nothing to look forward to except the steady deterioration of the food. What few delicacies he brought with him were used up before the trip was half over, and he was reduced to eating the same maggoty meat and weevil-studded flour as the rest of the ship's company. Compared to this captain, the skipper of the *Pigou* had been a model of courtliness, wit, and erudition; this man's conversation was laced with epithets and invective, aimed more or less at the fates that had condemned him to a life at sea, but open to include anybody or anything within range. Thus a belaying pin became "that sodomiting pin, there"; another ship was "that Christ-bitten brig to starboard"; and his own crew were "you tarry-arsed apes," a sobriquet they had learned to ignore. It may have made him feel better, but it made his conversation nearly meaningless, as well as tedious.

They passed Boston light shortly after sunrise and were moored at Long Wharf while the morning was still cool. Looking up King Street (which was now renamed State Street), James could see the State House and all the familiar buildings, and it seemed as though he had never been away. Everything looked warm and welcoming, and the sounds and smells of Boston were like friendly voices from the past. He arranged to have his baggage delivered to Daniel's house and then, after a perfunctory good-by to the captain and first officer, he set off for Daniel's on foot, walking unsteadily because of his more than two months at sea. The streets dipped and tilted and swooped, but James cared only about the fact that he was home, and would have crawled on his hands and knees had it been necessary.

Daniel and Elizabeth had not changed greatly in the last four years, although Daniel was beginning more and more to resemble his and James's father, with the apple cheeks and the upturned nose, and at the same time Elizabeth's features were becoming more neutral, resembling nobody. There was something behind her eyes that implied she was two places at once, thinking about something wholly different from her surroundings. Daniel's business had prospered to the point where he now had two assistants, and he turned the shop over to them for the day, while he and Elizabeth devoted their time to James. The first thing James wanted was a bath and then a change of clothes, and finally, when his baggage arrived, there was the matter of cleaning and airing the clothes and washing the laundry. Elizabeth saw to that side of it, while James and Daniel brought each other up to date on recent events on both sides of the Atlantic.

"First off," Daniel said, as they settled in the living room and lighted their pipes, "tell me what brings you here. Is this government business or something of your own?"

"It is my own," James replied. "And it may take some little while."

"Oh?"

"Yes. In fact, I may ask you and a few others to countersign some notes, as I expect to be making extensive investments. Incidentally, lest you worry about my worth, I've brought along a balance sheet, showing assets of some hundred and fifty-two thousand dollars."

"With that amount of money, I shouldn't think you'd need cosigners."

"That is just the beginning."

"May I ask what kind of investments you're considering?"

"I want to buy land in and around the Federal City, among other places. I think the growth there will be enormous."

Daniel smiled and looked out the window. "The Federal City," he said. "Wherever it may be."

"What do you mean? I understood it was all decided."

"It is, in a manner of speaking. But Philadelphia still hasn't given up—they're even erecting buildings to house the government—and they had a sale of lots in the Federal City last October that was, to put it mildly, a disappointment. As I remember it some thirty-five lots were sold, for about eight or nine thousand dollars. They've decided to name the city in honor of the President, but he seems to be almost the only person who's interested in it."

James thought about this. For his purposes, the confusion was good because it kept public confidence and therefore prices down, making the land easier to obtain. So long as the project was not abandoned, he was still in time to make considerable money. He wished he had been there last October, when the lots were—he figured quickly—thirty-five lots for, say, nine thousand dollars came to about two hundred and fifty dollars a lot, which was quite reasonable in view of how the value would appreciate. But supposing the project *should* be abandoned—supposing Philadelphia, with buildings already erected, should make an offer that would be impossible to refuse—then what would happen? Obviously, land in and around Philadelphia would go up like a balloon. In either case, Philadelphia was the place to be; it was nearer the federal site, and it was where the men of power and the men who made the decisions were gathered. If he stayed in Boston, he would be almost as far removed from the center of action as if he were still in Amsterdam.

Their talk then veered around to family matters, and here Daniel had a number of items to report. Their parents were enjoying their rustic life in New Bedford, Uncle Stephen was still living in his house beside the Common and being taken care of by his daughter Abigail, and blind John, now living in Quincy, had become proficient at the organ and was learning a number of other musical instruments. James already knew of Rebecca's marriage, three years ago, to Noah Webster, the lawyer and teacher of West Hartford, Connecticut, and he had been made slightly envious by the glowing pictures his sister had painted of her spouse. What he hadn't known, and this was by far the most interesting news of the day, was that their sister Nancy, who at the age of twenty was the youngest of the Greenleaf children, had been seeing a good deal of Billy Cranch, and while as yet there had been no mention of anything serious, it was entirely possible they might be married. Since Billy Cranch's maternal aunt, Abigail Smith, had married John Adams, this would bring Adams more directly into the Greenleaf family, and for James's purposes there could be nothing better. To have the Vice President, and conceivably even the President, of the United States a member of the family would provide leverage of the most powerful sort, the mere existence of which would be invaluable. It would be the kind of power that would not have to be exerted; it would be common knowledge not requiring proof. James felt a spark of excitement and said, "Is there anything we could do to hasten matters?"

"I doubt it," Daniel replied. "Nancy has very strict standards, and she wants to be sure that young Billy matches up."

James was about to argue, then realized he was talking to the wrong person. Nancy was the one he should talk to, if he could do it without sounding impertinent. Changing the subject, he said, "Tell me about Becca. Is her husband really the genius she says he is?"

"Webster? I imagine you could say that. His spelling books and whatnot have made quite a name for him—he was famous by the time he was twenty-six."

"What is your opinion of him?"

Daniel hesitated. "I like him," he said. "I fear he might occasionally become slightly pompous, but I suppose in a man of his accomplishments that can be forgiven. He is, after all, one of the Hartford Wits."

"They seem to have escaped my attention. What are they?"

"Yale men, mostly. They were patriotic writers during the War, and they still turn out an occasional work. I think by now their purpose is more social than anything else."

"I suppose some day I should meet this paragon."

"Becca will be very hurt if you don't. She looks on you as her brother who may some day be President."

"There's small danger of that," James replied, feeling pleased at the idea.

"That reminds me—I forgot to mention earlier that Maggie just gave birth to her sixth child. It's a boy, and she's named it after you. James Greenleaf Dawes."

"How very nice of her. When was he born?"

"About two weeks ago. The tenth of the month."

"I gather, then, that Maggie and Thomas are prospering."

"They are indeed. Thomas is in line for a judgeship."

"I'll have to get a gift for my namesake." He thought of his own son and the gifts he had bought for him, and he felt a stab of sadness at the thought that he might not see the child again. At some time in the future, perhaps, but probably not as a child. He saw that Daniel was studying his face, and he tried to assume a cheerful air. "Well!" he said, "What other news do you have?"

"There's so much to catch up on, it's hard to think. Do you remember George Eckman, our medical student friend?"

"I most certainly do. It was you and he who first got me—"

"Yes, exactly," Daniel cut in quickly, with a glance at the door.

"I remember George, although I must say my memory of that first time is—"

"Quite, quite. He's a doctor now, practicing in Philadelphia. He came by here a few days ago and asked to be remembered to you."

"Did he, now? What brings him here?"

"I believe he's doing some special work at the Medical School. I honestly don't know."

James thought a moment, then said, "It's possible he might be able to give me some hints about living in Philadelphia."

"You intend to *live* there?"

"For a while. I'll be much closer to the center of things there than I would be here."

"Yes, I realize, but to *live* there . . ." Daniel groped for words to express his distaste, but could find none. "I wouldn't tell too many people," he said, at last.

"Why not?"

"I can't say what it would do to your credit here."

"My credit is perfectly sound," James replied, trying not to bristle. "In fact, I intend to expand on it while I'm here. I own a considerable amount of land, on which I can—"

"Please don't misunderstand me. Your credit will always be good as far as I am concerned. But you know perfectly well that in Boston we feel that those people who aren't here don't deserve to be, and for someone actually to *leave*—to go and live someplace else—well—a visit is one thing, but to take up residence implies—I can only call it fiscal irresponsibility."

"You don't believe that, do you?" James tried to sound amused.

"Not about you, no. But there are others, not knowing you the way I do, who might not be so charitable."

"What do you think about Brother Dawes?"

"Thomas? What do you mean, what do I think about him?"

"Would he think the less of me if I lived in Philadelphia?"

"Of course not. But, after all, he's a part of the family."

"Would he be willing to cosign my notes? From what you say, he can well afford it."

"I have already told you *I* would cosign your notes. How many comakers do you want?"

"I have no idea, but on the scale on which I intend to work, I shall need the freedom to operate without restraint. I shall want to be able to buy what I choose when I choose, and with no more complication than signing a piece of paper. I have a solid foundation, but to expand it I shall need credit in all directions."

Daniel looked at him for a moment. "And you really believe you can make it work?"

"I know I can. I already have. I can show you my balance sheet for the years 1789 to 1792, listing all my transactions both in this country and with Crommelin Brothers in Amsterdam, and showing a net value of $152,020.21. This is simply the beginning, and with the proper backing I can multiply that many times over. There is no reason I couldn't be one of the wealthiest men in the country."

Daniel continued to look at him. "Next to whom?" he asked.

"Probably next to Robert Morris. I meant in general; when I said, 'One of the wealthiest,' I wasn't thinking of any specific people." After a pause, he added, "Except, of course, myself."

Daniel was briefly quiet and then said, "I have the feeling that Becca underestimated you when she said you might be President. From what you tell me, that would be just a step along the way."

James laughed. "Who knows?" he said. "Nothing is impossible." In his mind he already had Nancy married to Billy Cranch; he saw Adams, who was probably next in line to be President, taking a familial interest in the Greenleafs; and he saw himself, a multimillionaire, the obvious man to be Secretary of the Treasury, from which it would be a logical progression to the presidency—if he wanted it. Secretary of the Treasury might be a more appropriate office for his talents, and he could leave the political wrangling that went with the presidency to someone who enjoyed that sort of thing. He recalled how his Uncle Stephen had long ago predicted great things for him, and he concluded that Uncle Stephen must be clairvoyant to an unusual degree. He determined that, before he saw anyone else in the family, he could call on the old gentleman, and see if he could find out more precisely what the future held in store.

Stephen Greenleaf, now eighty-eight years old, had shrunk in the time that James had been away. His skin had the translucent blue of that of a newly hatched bird, and the veins at his temples were as prominent as the bones beneath. His body was becoming brittle, but his eyes were bright and his thoughts seemed to dart about like water spiders. He was sitting in the same chair as when James had last seen him, with Abigail hovering in the background. She had become if anything more shadowy and tended to her father's various needs in silence. The room smelled of dust, and old age, and distant cooking.

"Jamie!" the old man exclaimed, when James was ushered into the room. "It's good to see you!"

"Thank you, uncle," James replied, taking the clawlike hand in his own. "It's good to see you, too."

"I don't know what you've been doing, but whatever it is, it agrees with you. Something about you smells of success."

This was precisely what James had come to hear, and he smiled and said, "Thank you," again. "I must say, you are looking fit yourself," he added.

"Oh, nothing's going to kill me yet. Not that they haven't tried, mind you. Sam Adams and his Sons of Liberty strung me up on a pole once, and it did me no harm. Of course, it was an effigy, but the thought was still there. A lot of rabble if ever I saw 'em." Then his thoughts zipped off in another direction, and he said, "Tell me what you've been doing."

"Well," James began, "as you know, I married Antonia Scholten, who turned out to be a Baroness, and we have—"

"Never heard of her," his uncle cut in. "Where's she come from?"

"Amsterdam. As a matter of fact—"

"We call that York now. Or New York. Amsterdam was the Dutch name."

"No, this is the real one. I mean—"

"How's the war coming?"

"You mean the French?"

"I mean everybody. The French are just part of it."

"Well—the last I heard, the Austrians and Prussians had the upper hand. Lafayette's army seems to have suffered some reverses."

Stephen cackled. "I could've told you that a long time ago. Young snippet thinks he knows everything—he'll get his comeuppance, you mark my words."

"So it would seem. Actually, things are fairly confused, and—"

"All wars are confused. Braddock's boys never knew which way to shoot. French and Indians behind every tree, only nobody could see 'em. Nothing but confusion from start to finish."

"I suppose that's right. But in Amsterdam we heard—"

"It's York, I tell you. New York. They gave up the Dutch name a hundred years ago."

"I mean Amsterdam, Holland."

"What's that got to do with it?"

"That's where I've been."

"Since when?"

"The last four years."

"Doing what?"

"I was—I am—United States consul in Amsterdam."

Silence. "Why didn't somebody tell me?"

Abigail leaned forward. "We did tell you, Father," she said, gently. "You must have forgotten."

Greenleaf blinked. "I guess I must've. So damn many things on my mind it's hard to keep 'em all straight. I tell you one thing, my boy, if ever they offer you the job of Sheriff of Suffolk, you turn 'em down. Tell 'em you'll do anything but that. It's a damn thankless job, and one that'll bring you nothing but headaches. Do you understand?"

"Yes, sir," said James. "I understand." He saw Abigail looking at him over her father's shoulder, and he rose. "If you'll excuse me, I'll be going now," he said. "I have a number of other calls to make."

"Don't let me detain you. Do you plan to call on William?"

"Uh—you mean my father?"

"My brother William. I don't know what he is to you."

"Yes, I'll see him, but not today. He and Mother are living in New Bedford now, and—"

"It's Bedford, not New Bedford. Named after Joe Russell. We called him Duke of Bedford, but he wasn't."

"Ah, yes. Well, I probably won't see them today, but I plan to visit them in the near future. Do you have a message?"

"For whom?"

"My father. William."

"William's not your father, he's my brother. Do you have a brother William?"

"I did—two of them. One died when he was a baby, before I was born, and the other died during the War."

"Which war?"

"The War of Independence."

"Damn strange I never heard of it. I talked with him just the other day—said he was going down to Bedford to live."

James glanced at Abigail, whose look told him there was no point continuing the conversation. "I'll give him your regards," he said.

"I'd be obliged."

"It's good to have seen you, Uncle Stephen."

"Always glad to see you. If I'm not here, I'll be down at the Town House."

"Good." James went out, closing the door softly behind him, and as he stepped into the hot sunlight it was as though he had just awakened. He wondered vaguely what the Town House was, then recalled that it was the original name for the State House, before the War. Well, he thought, so much for finding out about my future.

George Eckman was at Daniel's when James returned. Physically, he was much the same as when James had first known him, with his pointed face and nearsighted eyes giving the impression he was peering into a high wind; the main difference was that he had lost his German accent and now talked like a transplanted Bostonian. He greeted James warmly, and after a few perfunctory reminiscences he said, "Brother Daniel tells me you're coming to live on the banks of the skulking creek."

"I beg your pardon?" James replied.

"The Schuylkill. In other words, Philadelphia."

"Oh. Yes. It seems like a sensible move. Are you practicing there now?"

Eckman hesitated. "I practice wherever I can," he said. "At the moment, I'm engaged in what you might call further study."

"On what subject?"

"It's too complicated to go into right now. Some day, it may all be simpler."

"I see."

"No, you don't, but it makes no difference. When do you plan to go South?"

"First I must find a place to live. I thought you might be able to advise me."

"Better than that, I'll go with you. That is, provided you're not leaving immediately. I still have a few weeks' work to do here."

"So, for that matter, do I." James glanced at Daniel. "If my brother approves, I should like to complete a number of business transactions before leaving for the skulking creek."

"By all means," Daniel said, quietly. "Please consider the house your own."

"Speaking of houses," Eckman put in, "what was the name of that one you took us to in Charlestown?"

"I'm sure it's no longer there," Daniel replied. "In any case, I've forgotten the name."

"Wasn't it the Jolly Roger?" Eckman persisted. "I seem to remember a—"

"I don't believe it had a name," James said. "All I remember was the lantern over the—"

"Gentlemen, if you don't mind," Daniel cut in, "this is hardly the place for such a discussion."

Eckman looked at him in surprise. "Why not? It was you who took us there."

"I hardly need remind you I wasn't married. And if Eliz—"

"What possible difference does that make?" Eckman looked first at Daniel, then at James. "Can you tell me what your brother is talking about?" he asked.

"I think so," James replied. "In Boston, we have rather strict rules about such things."

"So do we in Philadelphia, but that doesn't mean we obey them. Rules are there so you can say you have them."

"Be that as it may," said Daniel, "I had just as soon such matters were not discussed within Elizabeth's hearing."

"Where is Elizabeth? Is she hidden someplace in the room?"

"I can never be sure. At any moment she may"—he stopped, and listened, then went on—"I spoke to Brother Dawes today, James, and he said he would be happy to oblige you in any financial matters."

"Thank you," said James. "That's very kind."

Eckman shook his head. "I have been in this country fifteen years, and I still do not understand"—he stopped as the door opened and Elizabeth entered.

"Mr. Greenleaf," she said, addressing Daniel, "may I speak to you for a moment?"

"Of course, my dear," he replied. "Excuse me, gentlemen, will you?"

When the door had closed, Eckman looked at James. "Are you free this evening?" he asked.

"I am free almost any evening you care to name," James replied.

"Would you be interested in a bit of research?"

"Social or professional?"

"I think one might call it social. Professional only as a last resort."

"That sounds perfectly splendid."

Eckman bowed and smiled. "My faith in Bostonians has been restored," he said.

That night, as they were walking back over the bridge to Boston, James breathed the warm, fragrant air and said, "It's strange, the different courses people's lives take."

"What brought on that observation?" Eckman asked.

"I was just remembering the nights we used to go to Charlestown. You had decided to become a doctor, and I wanted to be one, too—I wanted to save the world, and wipe out disease, and become a hero. Now you're a doctor, and I'm a—well, call it landowner, speculator—and here we are coming back from Charlestown again, as though nothing had changed."

"I can tell you one thing," Eckman replied, "and that is the quickest way to lose your idealism is to become a doctor. You may think you're going to save the world, but you soon find you're lucky if you can save your trousers. I should have become a druggist like your brother, and then I'd be rich."

"Being rich doesn't help," said James. "It's what you do with your money that counts."

"And what do you intend to do with it?"

James was quiet, while he pondered the answer. "That's the terrible thing," he said, at last. "I don't know. I just want to get it first, and then I'll decide what to do with it."

"Probably a sensible decision," replied Eckman. "There's no point making plans to spend money you haven't got."

"There's one thing I do know, though," James added. "If ever you need money for anything—research, instruments, whatever— I want you to come to me. I don't ever want you to think you have to do without, just because you don't have the money."

"That's very kind of you," said Eckman. "I shall remember that."

"See to it that you do."

James and Eckman left Boston the first week in October, when the summer heat had passed and the leaves were beginning to turn. They had decided to make a detour to Hartford, to see Rebecca and Noah Webster, and after some consideration elected to take the stage on the Boston Post Road as far as the Connecticut River, then change to another stage for the trip inland. It would have been shorter to go to Sturbridge and then down to Hartford, but the roads were little better than log-covered trails, the country was hilly, and the forests gave ideal cover for the thieves who preyed on individual travelers. The shore road was longer, but it offered fewer chances for ambush.

The back country had always been hazardous, in the early days because of Indians and later because of the assorted brigands, outlaws, and fugitives from justice who either preferred or were forced to sustain themselves on what they could hunt, forage, or steal. The frontier attracted a number of types, not all of whom could or wanted to make an honest living, and there was little to keep them from doing as they pleased. When, in 1787, the desperate farmers under Daniel Shays gathered in Springfield to try to block the court from seizing their lands, the militia dispersed them, arrested some, and drove the others into hiding. Their grievances were allayed by the incoming legislature and most of them returned to their homes, but some developed a taste for life in the wilderness and reveled in the challenge of sustaining themselves at the expense of others. Many were war veterans who felt, and not without reason, that they had been ill-used by the government for which they'd fought, and a few were simple malcontents, who felt that the world had been against them from the start and who were out to wreak whatever revenge they could.

Among these latter was a man named Hosmer Barlow, who had been a failure at everything until he took up robbery, and his success in that field was such that his name became known throughout Massachusetts, Rhode Island, and Connecticut, and he was given the ultimate accolade of becoming a generic term. To be "barlowed" was to be robbed naked and beaten and to consider oneself lucky to have survived. Barlow operated behind a cloth mask in which eyeholes had been cut, so none of his victims ever saw his features. Those who could remember his eyes testified that they resembled those of a fish.

The stagecoach was crowded between Boston and Providence, and James and Eckman were wedged in among four other passengers, one of whom was drunk and another of whom was a woman, who held in her arms an infant that regurgitated almost constantly throughout the forty-five-mile trip. Conversation was all but impossible, because the drunk assumed that every word spoken was directed at him and required an answer, and the sounds that issued from him were no more illuminating than those coming from the infant. James would gladly have sat on the roof of the coach, but it was piled high with baggage, and the only seat, next to the driver, had been taken by an experienced traveler before the others got aboard. All James could do was stare at Eckman in mute agony and dream of the time when he would have his own coach to take him wherever he wanted to go. One of the many advantages of wealth, he concluded, was that it separated men from cattle when traveling any distance. He almost longed to be back on the *Prudence*, where at least the air was clean.

In Providence they took on a new team and driver, and when, early next morning, they started south, they were delighted to find that they had the coach to themselves. They put their feet up and relaxed, determined to make the most of their privacy before the next stop. Eckman produced a flask and, on the pretext that it was needed to ward off the morning chill, they each had a swallow of rum. All at once the trip began to look like an expedition with unlimited possibilities.

As they rattled along the shores of Narragansett Bay, inhaling the clean, salty air that came off the water, Eckman took another tot of rum, replaced the flask, and looked out the window. "I've been thinking about your brother," he said.

"What about him?" James replied, wishing Eckman hadn't put the flask away so quickly. "From what I could tell, he's made a great success."

"Materially, yes. Do you think he and his wife are happy?"

"Of course. Why shouldn't they be?"

"I sense a feeling of desperation there. I think they need a child."

"Well"—James spread his hands—"the good Lord alone can take care of that."

"Not without help."

"What do you mean?"

"I doubt that Daniel's wife is aware of the—ah—essentials of conception."

"That's absurd."

"I don't think so. In my business a man learns many things, and by now I can spot a virgin at twenty paces. I'll be willing to wager she has a hymen made of flint, and has no intention of changing it."

James thought about this. "Poor Daniel," he said, at last.

"Poor Daniel, indeed. Although, when you think of that child yesterday, he may not be missing as much as he thinks."

"In what way?"

"There was something wrong with it."

"Just travel sickness, wasn't it?"

"I don't know."

"You're a doctor. If you don't know, who does?"

"The trouble is that medicine is still mostly superstition, and superstition isn't scientific."

"What kind of superstition?"

"I could give you a hundred examples: to cure birthmarks, rub them with the hand of a corpse; to lower a fever, swallow a spider with syrup; to cure diphtheria, gargle with the fluid from cow manure; to prevent baldness, pour rum on the top of the head; for warts—"

"I know a better use for rum than that," James put in.

"Excuse me." Eckman produced the flask, handed it to James, and went on, "These are folk superstitions, but they don't differ a great deal from those of the so-called professionals. For just one example, take bleeding."

"What about bleeding?" James asked, returning the flask and wiping his lips with his fingers.

"Bleeding is the one panacea physicians agree upon—if a patient is ill, it means he has bad blood, so drain some of it off; if that doesn't help, then drain off some more; and so on—working on that theory, they could bleed a man to death and still not cure what ailed him."

"Then what do you suggest?"

"I suggest that bleeding does more harm than good."

"Have you said this to any of your colleagues?"

"I have indeed. That's why I've been in Boston, trying to find proof of my theory."

"And did you?"

Eckman was quiet for a moment, then shook his head. "Doctors are an unimaginative lot," he said. "They suspect anyone with new ideas."

"They can't force you to use bleeding, can they?"

"Of course not, but they can damage your reputation. They can whisper that Eckman is a mad German, who refuses to bleed patients because his mother was raped by a vampire. They're like a group of old women, cackling over their cambric tea and confecting rumors about the parson's daughter." He was about to say more when the coach jolted, slowed, then rattled into a courtyard, and stopped. The driver jumped down and peered in at them.

"Rest stop, gentlemen," he said and vanished.

"It might be a good idea to refill my flask," Eckman said, reaching for the door handle. "One can never tell when there may be an emergency."

The only other patron at the inn was a small man with what looked like a battered sea chest, who was evidently waiting for the stage. But he seemed reluctant to leave the shelter of the taproom, and he eyed James and Eckman in silence for a few moments before speaking. Then he drained his tankard, gave it to the landlord for a refill, and said, "Excuse me, are you gentlemen going southward?"

"For a while," Eckman replied.

"How far?"

"Sayebrook. Then we change for the inland stage to Hart-ford."

"Are you armed?"

Eckman looked at him with interest. "No," he replied. "Should we be?"

"Killingworth is not far from Sayebrook," the man said, as though that explained everything.

"And?" said Eckman.

"The caves of Killingworth are full of thieves and footpads," the man intoned. "People have vanished without a trace, and screams are heard at night."

James studied the man's face and came to the conclusion he was either drunk or crazy, or both. His eyes were inflamed and shiny, and when he wasn't talking he chewed on the inside of one cheek. His hands were continually in motion, even when holding his tankard, and he gave the over-all impression of being as unstable as a firefly. Suddenly he reached inside his coat and produced a pistol, and James and Eckman dove for cover. "Whenever I go near Killingworth, I go prepared for anything," the man said. "I do not intend to be one of those people who is never heard of again." Then his manner changed, and he said, "Would you gentlemen join me in a stirrup cup before we depart?"

Luckily the driver appeared at that moment, and they all went out to the coach, James and Eckman dusting themselves off from the effects of their sudden dive under the furniture. The man sat facing them, the butt of his pistol making a noticeable lump under his coat. As they started up, he looked out the window and said, "This would be a mighty handsome country, if only the devil would leave it alone."

There was a pause, then Eckman said, "Do you mean the country in general or just this part of it?"

"Both," the man replied. "The devil is everywhere, but most especially right around here. When they drove the devil out of Salem, he took up residence in Connecticut."

"I think it only fair to tell you," Eckman said, indicating James, "that this gentleman's sister lives in Connecticut."

"Nothing personal," the man said. "It was a simple statement of fact."

"It had a personal sound to it," Eckman persisted. "I think you should apologize."

James glanced at Eckman, who he realized was trying to bait the man into an argument. The last thing James wanted was to quarrel with an armed lunatic, but Eckman seemed intent on pursuing the matter. "I really don't think—" James began, to nobody in particular.

"I have just told you, sir, that I intended nothing personal," the man said. "There is nothing I can add."

"Supposing I said your sister lived in the devil's country," Eckman went on. "How would that sound to you?"

"I have no sister," said the man.

"Then your mother. Supposing I said your mother came from Salem."

"As it happens, she did."

"Was she a witch?"

The man's hand moved toward his pistol, and James leaned forward. "Excuse me," he said. "The doctor is not trying to be rude; his interest is purely of a professional nature."

The man glanced at him, then back at Eckman. "You are a doctor?" he asked.

"That is correct."

"Do you know a cure for warts?"

"Several. Where are they?"

"Ah—I can't very well show you now."

"Can you spit on them?"

"Not easily. It's only one."

"Then rub a grain of barley on it and feed the barley to a chicken."

"I don't have chickens."

"Then rub a halved potato on it and bury the potato afterward."

"How hard should I rub it?"

Eckman, who had been sitting back with his eyes closed, now opened them and looked at the man. "Just hard enough," he said.

"All right. I'll try."

"That'll be one dollar."

"How do I know it will work?"

"Sir, are you questioning my professional integrity?"

"No, but—"

"Then you owe me one dollar." Eckman held out his hand.

The man hesitated, then reached inside his coat, and for a moment James was afraid he was going to draw the pistol. But instead he produced a small drawstring pouch, picked out a coin, and handed it to Eckman. "It had better work," he said.

"It will." Eckman dropped the coin in his waistcoat pocket, folded his arms, and settled back in the seat and closed his eyes.

The man got off at the next stop, and when he was out of hearing James looked at Eckman and said, "Why did you try to provoke him like that?"

Eckman shrugged and smiled. "It was just a way to pass the time. I like to see how people react."

"Suppose he'd shot you."

"No danger of that. The ones who make the gestures are never the ones who act. Besides, I could have taken his pistol long before he got it cocked."

"Do you often pass the time this way?"

"On long trips, there's little else to do. A man has to take his entertainment where he can find it."

Late in the afternoon their coach was ferried across the Connecticut River, and then stopped for the night at the Black Horse Tavern in Sayebrook. After dinner they sat in the taproom, drinking hot rum to ease the ache in their bones, and they were on their third round when the door opened and a man came in. At first there was nothing remarkable about him, but as he took off his cloak and approached their table it became apparent that he was more than a little bowlegged and had arms too long for the rest of his body. He didn't come to their table, but sat instead at the one next to it, and when the candlelight struck his face they could see that he was so walleyed it was hard to tell in which direction he was looking. One of his eyes seemed to look at James while the other regarded the barmaid, and it wasn't until he asked for a gin that James knew which eye was the primary one. The girl brought him his drink and he took it in silence, a silence that suddenly seemed to echo throughout the room. James and Eckman had been speculating about Daniel and Elizabeth's marriage, but they felt they couldn't continue without whispering, so remained silent. It seemed a long time before the man spoke, but it was probably less than a minute.

"You from this part of the country?" he asked.

James looked at him, trying to decide which eye had been talking, and to be on the safe side he said, "We just arrived this afternoon." He was afraid that Eckman might start playing games again, so to keep control of the conversation he added, "We came down from Boston, and tomorrow we'll take the stage across to Hartford."

"Hartford, eh?" the man said. "What takes you there?"

"My sister lives there. She's married to Noah Webster. You may have heard of him."

"I can't say that I have."

The eyes seemed to be dividing their attention both sides of James, and when he heard Eckman start to speak, he hurried on, "Actually, we're just stopping there for a brief visit. Our final destination is Philadelphia."

"Is it, now? Are you with the government?"

"Not exactly. But I'm planning to buy land in the Federal City, and I assume the government will eventually be building on it."

"That's very interesting. I've always wondered how you go about buying land."

"There's no secret to it. You either pay cash or you put up security of some sort."

The man considered this. "But you have to be able to command hard cash," he said, finally. "You don't just write on pieces of paper."

"Of course not. But once you get started, the paper is as good as cash."

"And you just carry these papers around with you?"

"That depends." James was aware that Eckman was sliding lower in his chair, and he decided the conversation had served its purpose. "When a man has developed a reputation, he doesn't require any proof. I must say, in that respect I've been most fortunate." The rum had made him feel expansive, but at the same time the man's naïveté was such that he was slightly boring, and James wanted to drop the whole matter. Turning to Eckman, he said, "Well, Doctor! Should we gather our strength for tomorrow's journey?"

"That seems like as good an idea as any," Eckman replied, straightening up. "I have a feeling we may need it."

James laughed and clapped him on the shoulder. They paid the barmaid, said good-night to the walleyed man, and retired upstairs to their room. It was small, with a low ceiling, and the large double bed barely left room for a washstand and their overnight luggage. The only other large item was the chamber pot, under the bed, which looked big enough to accommodate a small seal.

Eckman was silent as he removed his boots and breeches, and finally, when he was down to his underwear, he said, "Do you know what we're going to do?"

"I presume we're going to sleep," James replied.

"I mean tomorrow. We're going to leave our luggage with the landlord, we're going to hire two horses, and we're going back across the river and up the east bank to Hartford."

"Whatever are you talking about?"

"Exactly what I said. You just gave that man down there enough information to tempt an honest man to rob the stage, and I very much doubt that he was honest."

"Oh, come now. Just because he looked a bit odd doesn't mean—"

"Come now indeed. I was watching his eyes—or whichever one I could see—and if ever I saw eyes that were alight with cupidity, they were it. Or they were they. I still can't make your language work right. But I can tell you one thing, and that is I am not riding on that stage tomorrow."

"But what could he want? I told him I didn't carry cash."

"But you also told him you were backed by people who have a great deal of cash. You made yourself a perfect target to be taken prisoner and held for ransom."

"Doctor, I think you're an alarmist."

"Think what you like. I told you how I am going to Hartford; you can go how you please."

James's expansive mood had faded, and he was irritated that Eckman thought he'd been indiscreet. Trying to regain a semblance of the upper hand, he said, "I shall be glad to do whatever makes you feel the safest. Far be it from me to impress *my* will on anyone."

"*Pferdedreck*," said Eckman, and put on his nightshirt.

They arrived in Hartford late the following afternoon. James had gone along with Eckman's precautions, even to the extent of buying a pistol, although he knew that in an emergency it would be totally useless. Under Eckman's instruction he learned how to load and prime it, but the matter of drawing it from beneath his coat, then cocking, aiming, and firing it—not to mention hitting anything with it—involved such complications as to render the whole operation futile. He'd had no experience with firearms and had smelled powder only once, during the brief engagement on the *Pigou,* but Eckman insisted that the mere fact that he carried the pistol might be a deterrent to any highwayman. "So long as you don't shoot me," Eckman concluded, "it is preferable that you should be armed."

In the nearly five years since James had seen his sister, Rebecca had changed from a fluttery girl into a mature woman. She had their mother's features, with the straight nose and a prominent chin, but unlike her mother she wore her hair in curled bangs over her forehead, thereby shortening her face and reducing the equine look that characterized Mary Greenleaf. Her delight at seeing James made her eyes glitter with tears, and she greeted Eckman almost as though he were a member of the family. Eckman, who with James had stopped at a nearby tavern for an end-of-the-journey drink, was courtly in the extreme, clicking his heels and bowing over Rebecca's hand as though being presented to royalty.

There was no question, however, as to who was the royalty when Rebecca introduced James to her husband. She dropped a small curtsey, and with a tone almost of awe said, "Dr. Webster, may I present my brother James," and James found himself looking at a solidly built man with a square face, prominent eyebrows, and a jutting jaw, whose blue eyes were looking directly into his own, appraising him rather than greeting him and showing only a guarded cordiality.

"I am honored, sir," said James, and then, to break the hold of the searching eyes, he glanced at Eckman and said, "May I present my friend Dr. Eckman, formerly of Düsseldorf and Boston and presently of Philadelphia."

Webster's eyes took in Eckman, who clicked his heels and made a formal bow, and he said, "Welcome, Doctor. Is your field letters, or law?"

"I am a doctor of medicine," Eckman replied.

"Oh," said Webster, his tone implying pity. Then he turned back to James. "Becca tells me she expects great things from you," he said.

James tried to dismiss the matter, but Webster was looking for a detailed answer. "It's too complicated to go into right now," James said. "The day's ride has jumbled my thoughts."

"You could have taken the stage, you know," Webster said. "What made you decide to ride?"

"Ah—a number of things," said James.

"We were advised not to take the stage," Eckman put in.

"Oh? By whom?"

"A man we met in Sayebrook. He led us to believe the stage might be held up."

"Nonsense. So long as you stay clear of Killingworth, you're in no danger. It's more dangerous to ride the way you did than to take the stage."

Rebecca had left the room, and she now returned with a two-year-old girl, dressed as though for a party, whom she ushered forward. "Emily, say hello to Uncle James," she said.

The girl balked and said nothing, and James knelt down and held out his hands. Her eyes reminded him of his son's, and for a moment he felt he was reaching out to Billy. She moved toward him reluctantly.

"This is Emily Scholten Webster," Rebecca said. "We thought your dear wife would like to have her family name passed on with ours."

James stood up. "How extremely thoughtful of you," he said, and patted Emily on the head. "I shall tell her the next time I write."

"Won't she be joining you here?"

"I rather doubt it. Billy's too young to make the crossing."

There was a brief, uncomfortable pause, then Rebecca said, "Let me show you to your rooms. I feel sure you'll want to freshen up before supper."

Conversation at the supper table was, on the surface, easy and jovial, but there was an undercurrent of tension caused by everyone's trying so hard to be relaxed. When, at the conclusion of the meal, Rebecca excused herself, Webster brought out the port decanter and three pipes, and as he settled back under a cloud of smoke it was clear that an inquisition was about to begin.

"Now," he said, to James, "tell me about these plans of yours. If I am to believe my wife, you will shortly be running the country."

James laughed. "I don't know where she got that idea. I have no intention of going into government; my field is, purely and simply, the acquisition of land."

"How?"

"Any number of ways. Notes, loans, mortgages, bonds—the main principle is to acquire land when it is cheap and sell when it's expensive."

"No cash?"

"As little as possible. Paper is just as good and much easier to come by."

Webster puffed on his pipe. "I hope you'll forgive my saying it doesn't make sense."

"What doesn't?"

"To get something without putting money in and then expect to get money out of it. That is something the alchemists tried for centuries to do and always failed."

"It really is simple," said James, trying not to sound patronizing. "For instance, I intend to buy as much land as I can in the Federal City. That property is bound to appreciate in value, so what I get now will be worth five times as much later on. If you know your multiplication table—and I assume you do—there's no mystery to it at all."

"I understand Robert Morris is interested in Federal City land," Webster said.

"Is he, now?" said James. "In what way?"

"That's all I know, except that Morris is king of all land dealers. Two years ago he bought a million acres in western New York, and last year he bought four million. He made so much money during the War he can buy just about anything he wants —in fact, he even makes his own money."

"Well, well." James blew a trail of smoke at the ceiling. "Where is he living these days, do you know?"

"I presume in Philadelphia. He's given his house to the President for the time being, but I don't imagine he's gone too far away."

"Do you know him?"

"No. During the War the soldiers seldom met the financiers. We did the fighting and they made the money. Morris turned a pretty penny by withholding shipments of flour until the prices rose—I suppose *you* would call that good business, but to those of us who needed the flour it was close to piracy."

Eckman, who had been quietly refilling his glass from the decanter, now spoke up. "They tell me, Dr. Webster, that you are one of the famous Hartford Wits," he said.

Webster gave him an appraising glance. "That is correct."

"Could you tell me the definition of a 'wit'? There are some words in your language that mean a number of different things." His German accent had unaccountably returned, and he seemed to be having some trouble talking.

"It depends on how the word is used," Webster replied. "In one sense, the wit is the mind, the powers of thinking and reasoning."

"Then you Hartford Wits are men who can think and reason?"

"Well—yes and no. I mean yes, but that isn't the genesis of the name"—Webster was in the uncomfortable position of trying to define the indefinable—"I mean, the name is—"

"Is it that you are witty? Does not the word 'wit' imply cleverness, or humor?"

"To a certain extent, yes. But—"

"Are you then jesters? Do you make *epigrammatische* remarks?"

James realized that Eckman was playing his game again, and he decided not to interfere. He was, in fact, fascinated to see how far it could go before Webster realized what was happening.

"Originally, the Hartford Wits wrote poems and satires," Webster said. "They were mostly politically oriented, and they—"

"I have found that political satires are very heavy-handed," Eckman cut in. "The satirist becomes so carried away by his own wit—yes, there it is: wit—that he goes on and on until the reader falls asleep."

"Oh, I don't know about that," said Webster. "Trumbull's *M'Fingal* and Barlow's *Anarchiad* are both considered—"

"Can you make an *epigrammatische* remark? Can you say

something so stunningly *witzig* that I will topple from my chair in astonishment?"

Webster cleared his throat. "It would be diffcult, on the spur of the moment, to—"

"Yet you are known as a wit, are you not? I mean, a member of the Hartford Wits must of necessity be a wit himself."

"I suppose, if you want to be literal about it, yes."

"I see no other way to be than literal. I am seeking a definition of the word 'wit,' and the figurative, or nebulous, approach is worthless."

Webster stared at him for a few seconds. "It seems to me, Doctor," he said, slowly, "that for someone who claims difficulty with the English language, you know a great many intricate words."

Eckman leaned forward. "I beg your pardon? What kind of words?"

"Intricate. Involved. Obscure. Complicated."

"I have had to learn many in the study of medicine. Sometimes some of the simpler ones escape me."

He got out of that one, James thought; now I hope he's smart enough to leave it alone. "Speaking of medicine—" he began, but Eckman was already talking.

"Perhaps you should change your name," Eckman said. "Perhaps you should be known as the Hartford Thinkers."

"I doubt that would be very popular," Webster replied.

"But because you call yourself 'wits' you are popular?"

Webster ground his teeth. "In a sense, yes."

"*Gott in Himmel.*" Eckman looked at James. "To me it simply sounds conceited," he said.

"Not really." James could almost literally hear the steam of Webster's rage, and he knew the game had to be ended. "It's all a matter of the subtleties of certain words, and they often don't translate. During Antonia's confinement the medical terms were completely beyond me, and for all I knew, she could just as easily have been expiring of the plague as having a baby."

"The symptoms are nothing alike," Eckman said, flatly. "In the plague the buboes appear in the armpits and groin, the vomit is—"

"That was a figure of speech," James cut in. "I was simply trying to say that some things don't translate."

"Then you should have said it, instead of going off into an elaborate medical simile. You sound as though you're studying to be one of the Hartford Wits."

There was a silence of perhaps three seconds, then Webster stood up. "I hope you gentlemen will excuse me," he said. "It has been a long day, and I must be up betimes tomorrow."

"I think we would all benefit from some sleep," James said, also rising. "Are you coming, Doctor?"

"I suppose I might as well," Eckman replied. "If the entertainment is over for the evening, I see no choice but bed."

The next morning, after a frosty farewell from Webster, they saddled their horses and headed south. They rode in silence for a long while, and finally James said, "Did you find it absolutely necessary to bait Brother Webster that way?"

"He was pompous and aggressive," Eckman replied. "He was being condescending about your affairs, so I felt he deserved to be taken down a peg." After a moment's thought he added, "His wife is pregnant, and that always makes a man truculent."

"Becca is pregnant? How do you know?"

"By the eyes. A woman's eyes show her condition long before her figure gives her away."

James was silent. A deep, dragging sadness came over him, and he was reliving the long day of Billy's birth when from somewhere ahead came the sound of a low moan, followed by a shriek. Startled, he and Eckman looked into the surrounding trees, but they could see nothing, and they had almost concluded they'd been mistaken when the noise was repeated, louder, but this time it seemed to be coming from everywhere. The horses skittered and shied, and James felt a prickling along his spine as the air was suddenly split with a dismal wailing, interspersed with howls and cries of anguish. They were nearing the town of Moodus, and Eckman spurred his horse and galloped ahead, shouting at James to follow him. James fumbled for his pistol, dropped it trying to cock it, and dismounted to retrieve it, with which his horse bolted into the woods. He stood in the clearing, trembling so that his pistol vibrated like a pennant in a gale and trying to make himself heard above the hellish din as he called to Eckman for help. Slowly the noises subsided, and James's hoarse and plaintive cry of "George!" sounded suddenly loud in the silence. Ashamed, he tried to compose himself, knowing that sooner or later Eckman would return, and not wanting to be bleating like a lost calf when he did.

A few minutes later there was the squeak and jangle of harness ahead, and Eckman appeared, riding his own horse and leading James's by the bridle. He was quiet and thoughtful as he handed over the reins.

"What was it?" James asked. "It sounded like a massacre."

"I don't know what it was," Eckman replied. "It just stopped."

"Did you see anyone?" James's self-confidence had returned, and he mounted as casually as a cavalry officer.

"Most everyone had bolted their doors," Eckman said. "I caught one man running for home, and he was babbling something about demons, but that was all I could get. There must be an explanation, but I don't know what it is."

"Didn't that crazy man mention something about shrieks in the woods?" James asked, as they started slowly forward. "Although I had the impression he was talking about Killingworth."

Eckman shrugged. "I guess he was talking about this whole part of the country."

As they rode through Moodus, they were aware of people peeking out at them from behind shuttered windows. But nobody came forth, and when they had left the town behind James felt as though they'd left some terrible danger and were emerging as though from the den of a Cyclops. Trying to read it as an omen, he thought of the whole trip to see Webster as a foray into disaster, from which they were only now returning to safety. This approach did something to lighten the gloom that still hung over him, but it was not as convincing as he could have wished.

"Perhaps it was an underground stream," Eckman said, after a few minutes' thought. "Water rushing into or through a cave might make noises like that."

"I prefer to think of it as an act of God," James replied. "I think we were being told to stay clear of Brother Webster."

Eckman gave a dry laugh. "You sound like some of the doctors I know," he said.

They returned their horses to the livery stable in Sayebrook and went to the Black Horse Tavern for the night. When they entered, the landlord looked at them and smiled. "Well, here come the lucky ones!" he said. "Did somebody tell you not to take the Hartford stage yesterday?"

"No," Eckman replied. "Why?"

"It got barlowed between Essex and Deep River. One man was beat so bad they fear he might die."

"You see?" James said to Eckman. "I told you it was an act of God."

Eckman started to reply, but James's remark was such a thundering *non sequitur* that there was no logical answer. He finally said, "If you want to look at it that way, I suppose that's your privilege."

"There is no other way," said James with finality. "One should always look on the bright side."

17

James's first impression of Philadelphia was that it was flatter and more expansive than Boston. Bounded by the Schuylkill and Delaware rivers, it had nonetheless plenty of breathing room, and wide streets such as Market and Broad that made Boston's twisting streets look like alleys. Boston seemed to be crouched on its hill overlooking the Harbor; Philadephia was more like a delta town, or even Amsterdam. The floating bridges across the Schuylkill reinforced this impression, which would have been a pleasant one had not Antonia become so much a part of his memory of that city. But after even a few hours in Philadelphia it was clear that it was neither Amsterdam nor any other delta municipality; it was Philadelphia, which in Greek meant "brotherly love," and the residents made sure that newcomers were aware of the fact. The brotherly love, however, applied only within one's particular social stratum; class distinctions were sharply defined and rigidly maintained.

With Eckman's help, James found a room on Market Street near Seventh, which had the double advantage of being located more or less in the center of things, as well as being close to Eckman's own residence. It was also, for what it might be worth, near the house where Jefferson wrote the Declaration of Independence, which appealed to James in a perverse way because of his memory of his father's struggle to read that document to the crowd in Boston. For a reason he would have been hard put to explain, he felt this gave him a tenuous link with his father, whom he had seen too seldom in recent years.

His first order of business, he reasoned, was to meet Robert Morris. If what Webster said was true, and Morris was interested in buying Federal City land, then he'd rather have Morris as a partner than as a competitor, and a personal meeting was obviously essential to such a project. He thought perhaps John Adams might arrange an introduction, but Adams was in one of his periodic sulks on his farm in Quincy (formerly North Braintree) and was not expected back in Philadelphia for at least another month. James set out to develop other contacts and to lay the groundwork for his master coup.

At the same time he decided to learn as much as he could about Morris, on the sensible theory that the more he knew, the better he'd be able to maneuver when they met, and here he ran into a certain amount of confusion. Everybody knew *about* Robert Morris, but not so many *knew* him, and even among those who could lay claim to close acquaintanceship there were wildly disparate opinions. Morris was a devoted patriot, Morris was a consummate rogue; Morris had supplied the Army during the War, Morris had enriched himself at the expense of the Army during the War—there seemed to be two sides to whatever he did, and the choice of sides depended on the point of view. Among the undisputed facts were that he was born in Liverpool in 1734 and came to this country at the age of thirteen to join his father in Oxford, Maryland, where Morris Senior was the representative of a Liverpool shipping firm. He grew up in commerce, and at the outbreak of the Revolution he was a member of the Pennsylvania Assembly and also the Secret Committee and the Committee of Secret Correspondence, which latter two developed into the Department of Commerce and the Department of State, respectively. But he also remained a businessman, and with his partner Thomas Willing he traded in tobacco, flour, and other necessities which, because he was also in charge of naval affairs, he was able to ship in vessels already paid for by Congress. When, in 1781, the troops mutinied for lack of money, Morris was made Superintendent of Finance; he created a national commercial bank and raised money by loans, personal credit, and by any other means available. He distributed "Morris notes," for which he himself was responsible, along with the bank notes, and for a while managed to stave off total financial chaos. He enlisted Gouverneur Morris (no relation), a former member of Congress from New York, as his assistant, and eventually sent him to France to manage his affairs in that country. In 1789, by now a senator from Pennsylvania, he embarked in land speculation with William Maclay, the other senator from the state, and developed a tactic known as "dodging," which consisted of selling, in Europe, American land that had not yet been bought. Gouverneur, in France, registered his nervous disapproval, but to no avail. In 1790 Morris bought a million acres in western New York, and next year sold it through his agents in London for a profit of sixty thousand dollars; he then bought four million acres and sold all but a half million to a group of Dutch capitalists. With deals like that going through, a little dodging here and there was small potatoes indeed.

In the shipping field, Morris's most elaborate gamble was his co-ownership of the *Empress of China,* a refitted and rechristened privateer with which he and some New York financiers decided to open up the China trade for the United States. The ship sailed in February of 1784, loaded with thirty tons of ginseng as its main cargo, the theory being that the supposed aphrodisiac properties of ginseng would make it more valuable than gold, and it arrived in Whampoa at a time when ten times as much ginseng was being imported than ever before. The price of ginseng was roughly equivalent to that of rice, and the fact that the ship carried a mixed cargo was all that saved the voyage from total disaster. When, in August of 1785, the *Empress of China* returned to the United States loaded with the usual tea, silks, chinaware, and spices, Morris was able to recover only 30 per cent of his original sixty-thousand-dollar investment. The New York investors, with less to fall back on, went out of business, but Morris shrugged it off and went on to other projects.

But the item that caught James's interest above everything else was the manner in which Morris's father had died. It was an event so bizarre and unsettling in its implications that it must have had a strong effect on the young man. Morris Senior had planned a dinner party aboard a recently arrived ship, and the night before the party he dreamed he would be killed by the saluting cannon. It was so vivid that he asked the captain to dispense with the salute as the party left the ship; the captain said the crew would be unhappy if they didn't get their tot of grog for saluting, but would wait until the boat signaled it was well away before they fired. An exuberant lady guest in the boat waved her handkerchief; it was mistaken for the signal, and the wadding from the cannon hit Morris in the arm and broke the bone, and he died of blood poisoning. James was accustomed to hearing about pointless deaths (that of his brother William, during the War, was a prime example), but never had heard of one that had been so clearly foretold or in which fate had so doggedly played a part. It must, he reasoned, have left a residue of superstition in the Morris family, to be played upon if the occasion should demand. At any rate, it was something to be remembered.

In November Adams returned to Philadelphia for the congressional session, and James decided that a social call on his putative relation-by-marriage could do no harm. When the government first moved to Philadelphia, Adams and his wife had lived at Bush Hill, outside the city, then moved into town, but the Philadelphia climate didn't agree with Abigail and she finally went back to Quincy, leaving her husband to fend for himself in bachelor's quarters near the State House. It was to these rooms that James sent a note requesting a meeting, and he shortly received an answer setting an appointment for the following day.

He was shocked at his first view of the Vice President. Although only fifty-seven, Adams looked a good thirty years older; all his teeth had been pulled and his face was caved in and puckered; he was wigless, bald, and wrinkled; his eyes were red-rimmed and his nose had taken on the curve of a parrot's beak; his hands trembled as he first shook James's hand and then rubbed his own chin as though testing a recent shave.

"Come in, come in," he said. Then, after a dry cough, he added, "You will be William's son, I presume."

"Yes, sir," James replied, trying to strike the proper balance between respect and self-assurance.

"And how is your honored father?" Adams motioned to a chair, and James sat down.

"Well, thank you, sir. He and my mother are living in New Bedford now."

"An odd place, that." Adams' mind seemed to drift away for a moment, then he said, "And what may I do for you? I fear that most of the positions in the government have already been filled."

"Oh, that's not what I was thinking of," James said, quickly.

"As a matter of fact, I am already in the government. I was—I am—the United States consul in Amsterdam."

There was a pause, then Adams said, "What brings you here?"

"You mean to see you? Actually, it was just—"

"I mean in this country. Were you recalled?"

"No, no. There is some business to be attended to that I couldn't very well do from the other side."

Adams nodded, but made no comment.

"In all honesty, this is a personal visit to you," James went on. "I understand that my sister Nancy and your nephew Billy Cranch have been—ah—walking out, I believe the expression is."

Adams received the news without visible reaction. "Nobody bothers to tell me these things," he said.

"It was my brother Daniel who told me. I thought that perhaps, since you have been in Quincy more recently than I, you might have some more recent news on the romance."

"All I know about Billy is that he's working at being a lawyer," Adams said. "What he does in his spare time is no concern of mine."

"Yes, of course." James swallowed, wondering how to get into the real reason for his visit. Without help from Adams it was hard to sound casual, and by now he had just about run out of conversational gambits. "Otherwise, things go well in Quincy?" he said.

"As well as you might expect. We had a lamb come down with mumps, and Abigail had to rub its throat with goose grease every day."

James laughed. "Life on a farm must have its trials."

"That's as may be; I'd five times sooner be on a farm than tending this pack of hyenas in the Senate. Timber wolves would be a blessing after"—the rest of the sentence was lost in a fit of coughing.

Sensing that he'd better get to the point soon or miss it completely, James said, "Oh—speaking of the government, I understand the President is using Robert Morris's house. Is that correct?"

His eyes watering slightly, Adams said in a strangled voice, "That is correct. One-ninety Market Street."

"Then where is Morris living, do you know?"

"Next door, in the old Galloway house."

"Is he accessible?"

"That would depend on what you want him for. If you're aiming to get to the General through him, don't bother."

"They are friends, aren't they?"

"Indeed they are. But there's been so much talk about his using that friendship that he's a mite sensitive on the subject." Adams's mouth pinched in a parody of a smile. "That's why he moved next door."

"Well, my interest is in another direction. I thought perhaps I might take Morris into partnership."

Adams looked at him with new interest. "Partnership in what?"

"Land. I've acquired a great deal of land in various sections of the country, and it occurred to me that he and I might more profitably pool our resources than be in the position of bidding against one another."

Adams regarded him for several moments, then said, "You shoot high, don't you?"

James laughed. "As high as possible. I see no reason to aim for mediocrity."

"No, of course not. Well—" Adams rubbed one trembling hand across his chin—"all I can say is I wish you luck."

James had hoped for considerably more—at the very least a note of introduction—but Adams seemed to have finished with the subject, so to keep the conversation alive James said, "I don't know if you're aware of how highly you are esteemed in the Netherlands. The mere fact that I was a compatriot of yours, not to mention coming from the same state, opened doors to me that would otherwise have been barred. The Dutch were hoping you would be our first President." As a quiet afterthought he added, "The Dutch among others."

Adams was like a cat that had been stroked. "Ah, the Dutch," he said. "A strange people. When I first arrived there I was most impressed by their industry, their art, and what I then thought was a total lack of avarice. Then, after I'd been there awhile, I realized that they were rabid idolators at the shrine of Mammon, that the prosperity and virtuousness were a total illusion, and that they were sunk in ease, devoted to the pursuits of gain, divided among themselves, and seemingly afraid of everything. It sometimes takes a while to see all sides of a picture."

James thought of the Dutch he knew and thought that Adams's description, while strong, was probably not wholly inaccurate. "If they admired me the way they do you," he said, "I shouldn't worry about their occasional drawbacks."

Adams gave a small grunt that was intended as a laugh. "Occasional drawbacks, indeed," he said. "Although I must say, if they were allowed to vote over here, I would consider them all splendid fellows." He thought for a moment, then added, "And they have been very generous with their loans and their support during the War. Without them, our cause might very well have perished."

"Yes, indeed." James could add nothing to the subject, and before he could think of another, Adams had risen and was extending his hand. "Pray give my respects to your father when next you write," he said.

"Thank you, sir, I shall." They shook hands, and as James headed for the door he said, "It was most kind of you to give me of your time." He was furiously trying to bring Morris into the conversation once more, and he was so intent on his own thoughts that he almost missed Adams's next remark.

"Incidentally, have you met John Nicholson?" Adams said.

"I don't believe so," James replied. "Who is he?"

"He's Morris's partner."

It took James a moment to understand what he'd heard. "His I beg your pardon?" he said. "His partner in what?"

"In land. I imagine, if you were thinking of joining up with Morris, he would be a man you ought to know."

James was so stunned he couldn't think. "Who is he?" he asked. "Where did he come from?" In all the talk about Morris, the name of Nicholson had never come up. The only partner had been Maclay, but that had been two years ago.

"He was formerly comptroller general of Pennsylvania. Morris and he have just formed an association of some sort."

"Where would I find him?" Actually, James wanted nothing to do with Nicholson; it was Morris he wanted, but he imagined he should know as much as he could about this suddenly added starter.

"He lives here in the city—I don't know exactly where—and I imagine the most likely place to find him would be at the Merchants' Coffee House, or some such place."

"I see. Well—thank you again for your time . . ." He could think of nothing more to say, so tried to make his exit as graceful as possible. "It has been most enjoyable," he concluded, and left.

On a cold, bleak day in November, James was sitting by the fire in his apartment and making an itemized list of his various property holdings, when there came a knock at the door. He rose carefully, so as not to disturb the papers, and opened the door and was confronted by a tall man in his forties, with a long jaw, a short forehead, and graying hair trimmed in bangs. He had a frontal paunch that matched his jaw and somehow gave the impression of a rearing horse. His eyes were without humor or expression. "Mr. Greenleaf?" he said.

"Your servant," James replied, cautiously.

"John Nicholson."

"Oh," said James, opening the door wider and standing aside. "Pray come in." His mind was racing ahead, guessing that Adams was somehow responsible for the visit, but not knowing what to expect next.

"Thank you." Nicholson stepped inside, and when James offered to take his greatcoat, he declined, saying, "I bring a message from Mr. Robert Morris. He would be most honored if you would call on him at his residence in the Galloway house tomorrow afternoon."

Stripped of its formal *politesse*, the message was a summons, and in a flash of perception James knew that if he started off a partnership as the subservient member, he would never be able to hold his own. He would be like Nicholson (whom he immediately disliked), an errand boy, with no authority whatsoever. "Please thank Mr. Morris," he said, and then, indicating the paper-cluttered desk, "but as you can see, I am inundated with work at the moment. Tell him I should be honored to meet him on, say, Thursday next, and whatever time and place he desires."

"I shall tell him," Nicholson said, coldly, leaving the implication that the message might or might not be acceptable.

"Thank you. And my sincere apologies for not being more—" he was going to say "tractable," but changed it instead to "available."

Nicholson bowed. "I feel sure Mr. Morris will understand."

Nicholson left, and when the door had closed behind him

James smiled, then started to laugh, and the laughter finally took control of him and he had to sit down, making little braying noises and weeping, until the papers on his desk were flecked with moisture. Then he took out a large, lace-trimmed handkerchief, wiped his eyes and blew his nose, and poured himself a glass of port.

A note from Morris the following day confirmed the appointment for Thursday afternoon, but instead of being at the Galloway house it was to be at The Hills, Morris's country estate which he had built in 1773, on an eighty-acre tract of land he owned on the east bank of the Schuylkill. Morris had, apparently, a passion for houses, and the more ornate the better. His house at 190 Market Street, presently on loan to the President and Mrs. Washington, had housed among other dignitaries British General William Howe, Benedict Arnold, and John Holker, the French consul, and when Morris took title in 1785 he redesigned it to handle everything up to and including state banquets, with formal and informal dining rooms, two drawing rooms, a stable accommodating twelve horses, and servants' quarters that could shelter a brigade. As though this weren't enough, he commissioned Pierre L'Enfant to design him a truly impressive mansion, made of brick and imported marble and occupying the square bounded by Seventh, Eighth, Chestnut, and Walnut streets. Construction was stopped in 1791, after Morris had sunk an estimated million dollars into the still uncompleted project. The Galloway house, to which he had originally invited James, had belonged to a Loyalist named Joseph Galloway, from whom it had been confiscated during the War, and while it was not in a class with The Hills, it was by no means shabby. It was, in fact, larger than the house at 190 Market Street and better situated, in that it was on the corner of Market and Sixth. The fact that Morris had changed the invitation and had bidden James to The Hills indicated that he knew precisely why James had declined the first time, and was prepared to meet the challenge.

James, in turn, was determined not to be impressed. Had the weather been better he would have rented a landau, but as it was, he retained a coach-and-four, with a liveried footman, to take him the six or so miles up the river to Morris's estate. As he rode up the long driveway to the house, he had to admit that Morris had done well. The main house was a two-story edifice with chimneys at all four corners and verandas on two sides; there were also two farmhouses, a gardener's cottage, and assorted barns, stables, and sheds to shelter the horses, cows, and sheep. In addition there were hothouses, in which oranges and pineapples were being cultivated, and what was reputed to be the first private icehouse in the country. James wondered why Morris would ever need any other place than this, and concluded he must have a compulsive desire to display his wealth. So much the better, he thought; I know exactly where it can be used.

He was ushered into the drawing room by a silent servant who took his hat and greatcoat, and for a moment he thought he was alone. He shot his sleeves and rearranged the lace at his throat and cuffs, and then saw, silhouetted against the far windows, a large, bulky figure rising from a chair. Morris came slowly forward to greet him, and James saw a heavy-set man in his late fifties with a clear though somewhat florid complexion and wispy gray hair that hung around his ears. His bulk did not appear to be the result of age; he looked like someone who had always been solidly built and who only recently had begun to soften around the edges. He was dressed in plain broadcloth, with no attempt at ostentation, and James regretted having gone out of his way to appear elegant. Morris took his hand in a firm grip.

"So good of you to come," he said.

"I am honored," James replied. "I regret the pressure of business prevented my coming sooner."

Morris waved a hand as though to dispense with any more unnecessary talk and ushered James into the adjoining library. He offered him a choice of wines or spirits, but James, who knew that of all times this was the one he had to remain alert, declined. Morris put the decanters to one side and motioned James to a chair. They sat.

All right, James thought. This was his idea; I'm going to let him make the first move. But Morris was studying him, as though trying to form an impression before speaking, so in order to break the silence James said, "This is a pleasant little farm you have here. Does it yield much of a harvest?"

"Enough," Morris replied.

James looked out the window, where the carefully tended lawn sloped away to the river. Even the brown grass of November looked lush and testified to the work that had gone into the grounds. "You have much better soil than we do in New England," James observed. "Our land is so rocky it's hard to cultivate."

Morris cleared his throat. "Speaking of land," he said, "I understand you have an interest in acquiring land on a—uh—speculative basis."

"I deal in land, yes," James replied. "Quite a bit of it."

"Where?"

"All through the eastern seaboard. Maine—Georgia—New York —my family even owns land on Cape Cod and Nantucket. I have the original deeds, signed by the Indian chief. Altogether I suppose I own several million acres, although I haven't counted it recently. Crommelin Brothers, in Amsterdam, have done a good deal of the purchasing."

"Ah, yes, Crommelin. I know them well."

That's right, James thought. I imagine you would. "I also have another—," he started, then stopped.

"Yes?" said Morris.

"Nothing. It's beside the point."

"Does it have to do with land?"

"In a sense. But it would be of no interest to you."

"Perhaps I should be the judge of that." Morris smiled a tight and mirthless smile.

"Actually it's confidential," James said. "I can tell you only that I have been promised unlimited backing, in exchange for— certain land purchases."

"Unlimited?" said Morris, his eyebrows rising.

"That was the word that was used." To himself, James wondered how Van Vliet's backers were faring, since the latest news from France was that the monarchy had been abolished and a republic declared, but lacking any definite word James assumed his agreement was still in force. And it was nice bait to dangle in front of Morris, no matter how it worked out in the end.

"Is this—ah—foreign money?" Morris asked.

"My agent is on the Continent," James replied. "Beyond that, I cannot say."

It was Morris's turn to look out the window. "That is a very heady proposition," he said, at last.

James tried to make it sound as though it were not at all unusual. "By certain standards, I suppose it is," he said.

"And do I understand you are interested in buying land in the Federal City?"

"If I'm offered the proper terms."

Morris sat back in his chair, picked up a quill pen, and touched the tip of the feather to his nose. "Do you think that perhaps two men, or three, working in partnership, might be able to get better terms than one man working alone?"

"It honestly hadn't occurred to me," James replied, trying to remain impassive. "Now that you mention it, I suppose such a thing is possible. Although"—he let the sentence trail off, as though an objection had suddenly occurred to him.

"Although what?" Morris prompted.

"Although on second thought I'm not so sure. If it were known that a large—what would you call it? company? combine? syndicate?—were interested in the land, the prices might be higher than if it were being bought by individuals. A partnership is a good idea in theory, but perhaps the business should be transacted as though by single members, to avoid giving the impression of—should we say—excessive wealth."

This time, Morris's smile was warmer. "An excellent point," he said. "After all, one doesn't want to part with any more money than is absolutely necessary, does one?"

"Never," said James, also smiling. "In Boston, we call that bad business."

"In Philadelphia, we call it bad manners." Morris put his hands on his knees and rose. "Well—should we have a spot of something to take off the chill?"

"I can see absolutely nothing against it."

Morris poured two brandies, and as they held their glasses James said, "Do you know when this federal land will go up for sale?"

"Not exactly. Some time next year, I imagine."

"Well, then"—James raised his glass—"to the silent partnership."

"To the silent partnership," Morris said, cheerfully, and they drank.

When James had left, Nicholson came down from the upstairs sitting room. "What did you think of Master Jemmy?" he asked, pouring himself a brandy.

"I think we have made a definite *coup*," Morris replied. "I think we have found ourselves a nice, fat pigeon."

18

Through Morris, James learned that the auction of the Federal City land would take place at the same time as the laying of the cornerstone for the Capitol, in September 1793. This gave him the summer in which to broaden his base, and with help from his friends and relatives in Boston he floated loans and mortgages and expanded his holdings until he felt he could meet any financial demands that might be made on him. It occurred to him that, considering the scale on which he intended to operate, it might be better to work behind the scenes rather than do his buying at a public auction; he could attend the auction, to make sure that nobody bought any important land, but his actual buying could be done later, when there would be no competitive bidding. To accomplish this, he needed a note to the commissioners in charge of the building of the city, and there could be nobody whose note would carry more weight than the President himself. This, naturally, required an introduction to the President, but he felt that in the circumstances Morris would be only too happy to oblige.

Then, in mid-August, yellow fever broke out on the Philadelphia waterfront. It spread like an oil fire through the ships and wharves and grogshops and brothels, and within a week was reaching out into the city. Street traffic thinned and then ceased; those people who could leave the city did, while others remained indoors, and the only moving things outdoors were occasional pedestrians, who darted about with their faces covered, and the slower, plodding horses hauling carts in which the dead were piled like fence posts. The drivers of the carts were blacks, who were thought to be immune to the fever, and they went about their tasks as slowly and impersonally as did the horses. The cry,

"Bring out your dead!" echoed through the still city to the ac-
companiment of the rumble of the carts.

James was in his apartment, chafing at the necessity for stay-
ing inside, when there came a knock at the door and he opened
it and discovered Eckman, leaning against the jamb as though he
were about to collapse. He gave a wan smile and said, "Help."

"Come in!" said James, reaching out to catch him. "What's the
matter?"

"Nothing that twelve hours' sleep wouldn't cure," Eckman
replied, moving slowly into the room. He sank into a chair and
added, "But lacking that, I'll settle for some whisky."

"Of course." James closed the door and brought out a decanter, and as he poured a glass he said, "For a minute I thought
you might have contracted the plague."

Eckman shook his head. "I haven't time," he said. "I've been
watching people die for the last week and trying to discover
what it is that kills them. 'Yellow fever' are simply words that
describe the symptoms, but they don't tell anything about the
disease."

"It's in the air, isn't it?" James asked, handing Eckman his
drink and pouring one for himself.

"So are a lot of other things in the air. Spraying vinegar about
isn't going to do any good, or camphor either, for that matter.
Burning gunpowder will only set your house afire. None of these
cures is any better than the one I gave that man for warts."

"Then what do you believe causes it?"

"I don't know. I've been talking to these poor people, trying to
find out anything they have in common, or have done in common, but by now they can't think. By now they only want to die,
and usually they do." A mosquito whined around his head, and
he watched it for a moment, then shot out a hand and caught it,
and rubbed it between his fingers. "Was there ever yellow fever
in Boston?" he asked.

"I don't think so," James replied. "Why?"

"There may be a clue there. It strikes some cities often, others
never. It seems scarce in the North, prevalent in the South. Yet
the President, who is after all a Southerner, has no concern for
the disease whatsoever. He treats it as though it doesn't exist."

"I should like to get to see him," James said. "But I haven't
thought this would be the proper time."

"As far as the fever is concerned, it's as good a time as any other. He's set September tenth as the date he moves to Mount Vernon, and nothing is going to make him move one minute before that. I think he feels that if he were to leave sooner, the people would panic."

"How many would know if he just slipped away?"

"He can't. He must advertise in the papers, requesting 'all persons having accounts upon the household of the President of the United States' to settle up before he leaves. He has no more secrecy than a fife-and-drum corps."

"Incidentally, did you ever find out what those noises were, the ones we heard in Moodus?"

"No. I've asked everybody who might have been there, and the most I can discover is it's a local phenomenon. Some, naturally, ascribe it to evil spirits, others try to think of a natural explanation, but nobody has yet come up with a satisfactory answer. It's no more explainable than yellow fever."

James looked out the window, at the deserted street. Far away, at the end of the block, a man rounded the corner and, holding a cloth over his face, came toward the house. In the silence of the city his footsteps sounded loud, and then suddenly he changed direction and scurried to the far side of the street, and James heard other footsteps, coming from the opposite direction. He peered out and saw another man, with a sponge over his nose and mouth, begin an identical zigzag pattern with the first, and he watched in amazement as the two, slowly approaching one another, maneuvered to try to get the upwind position. It was like a mad parody of the mating dance of the whooping crane, and finally, when they had reached an impasse, both men stopped, eyed each other for a moment, then broke and ran for opposite sides of the street and continued on their way, and once again the street was silent.

"This fever not only kills people," James observed, turning from the window, "it also makes them act like idiots."

There was no reply, and he looked and saw that Eckman had fallen into a deep, exhausted sleep, sprawled in his chair as though he had dropped there from a great height.

His interview with Washington was brief, formal, and to the point. The President was taller than James had imagined, and his unbending posture added a few apparent inches to his actual height; he was by no means jovial, but at the same time not unfriendly, and James's over-all impression was that he was talking with a statue that had somehow been endowed with the gift of limited speech. He outlined his plan for large-scale buying and development, and the President listened without comment, occasionally nodding to indicate he understood a point without committing himself either for or against it. Finally, when James had said everything he could think of, he stopped, and there was a brief silence. Then Washington rose and went to a desk at the far end of the room, and for a few minutes the only sounds were the scratching of his quill on paper and the hollow ticking of a clock in the hall. Then the President sanded the letter, folded it, and brought it to James.

"That will introduce you to the district commissioners," he said. "I believe it should suffice."

"Thank you, sir," James replied, taking the letter. "I am most humbly grateful."

"We may dispense with the humility," Washington replied, making the "we" sound almost regal. "What is needed here is determination, and courage. A man with those qualities can do his country a great service."

"Yes, sir," said James. "I am aware." He hesitated, not knowing whether to back out of the room or just to turn and walk away. Washington solved the problem by escorting him to the door.

"If you are interested in land," Washington said, as a servant handed James his hat, "I happen to own some thirty thousand acres on the Ohio and Kanawha rivers. It is frontier land now, but in a few years I imagine it will be worth a considerable amount of money."

"That's very interesting," James replied. "At the moment, my main interest is in the Federal City, but I shall certainly remember what you've told me."

Washington nodded; the door was opened and James left. On the street, he unfolded the letter and saw that Washington had referred to him as a man "of good repute" who "has been represented to me"—apparently by Morris—"as a gentleman of large property and having the command of much money in this country and in Europe" and concluded: "If you can find it consistent with your duty to the public to attach Mr. Greenleaf, he will be a valuable acquisition." James read the letter again; it hedged a few points by making them hearsay instead of Washington's own opinion, but taken in sum it was a tremendous boost and would be sure to get him whatever he wanted from the commissioners. He refolded the letter, put it in his pocket, and stepped off briskly down Market Street. For him, the fever held no terror; he felt that the President's letter was an aegis that would protect him from all harm, and he now walked among the privileged few for whom destiny had special favors in store.

He had experienced a jolt earlier in the year when he received a letter from Antonia containing two items of news. One, which was not unexpected, was her request for a divorce, to be accomplished in whatever state could handle the matter most expeditiously. The other, which had him immediately counting on his fingers, was her announcement of the birth, the previous October, of Marie Josephine Wilhelmine Matilda. As far as the timing was concerned the child could have been his, but he wondered how much it had to do with Antonia's refusal to accompany him, and whether he had in fact been the father. Schimmelpenninck's name crossed his mind like a shooting star, then faded. It was immaterial, but it shook his confidence that so much could have been going on without his knowledge. His present letter from Washington went a long way toward re-establishing his self-esteem. Antonia's divorce, he decided, could wait until he felt like giving it to her.

The Capitol cornerstone laying and land auction in the Federal City were set for September 18, and the Order of the Free and Accepted Masons (of which Washington was a member) had been given the honor of organizing the ceremony. This included a parade from the site of the President's house to the site of the Capitol, the dedication and laying of the cornerstone, a barbecue and general celebration, and, finally, the auction of lots in the phantom city. The line of march was carefully planned so as not to be anticlimactic: the lead marchers were the surveying department of the city of Washington, followed by the mayor and corporation of Georgetown, the Virginia Artillery, the commissioners of the city and their attendants, stonecutters and mechanics, fifth-degree Masons, Bibles on ornamental cushions, deacons with staffs of office, stewards with wands, third-degree Masons, wardens with truncheons, secretaries with tools of office, paymasters with their regalia, treasurers with their jewels, a band of musicians, Lodge Number Twenty-two of Alexandria, and carriers of corn, wine, and oil with which to anoint the cornerstone. Finally, bringing up the rear, was the Grand Master of the Order *pro tem*, the President of the United States, followed at a discreet distance by the Grand Sword Bearer. It bore more than a passing resemblance to a coronation parade or that for the opening of Parliament.

It was a clear day, with just a hint of fall in the air, when the marchers assembled at the partly dug foundation that was to be the President's House. It was, basically, little more than a clearing in a forest; trees were on all sides, and the rough road that had been hewn in the general direction of the Capitol was spiked with stumps and cluttered with fallen timber and leaves. After a certain amount of shouting and confusion, the parade formed into an approximation of the line of march, and with a blast from the band they started off. They lurched along over the uneven ground, dodging surveyors' stakes and piles of random underbrush, and had covered little more than a mile when the city surveying department, in the van, came to the banks of Goose Creek, which had been grandly renamed the Tiber but over which no bridge had yet been built. The band music dwindled into spasmodic toots and then ceased, as the celebrants broke ranks and gathered along the creek, trying to decide how best to cross. Someone pointed out that farther upstream were rocks that could serve as steppingstones for the more nimble-footed, and some in fact did manage to cross this way, but the specter of the President of the United States, not to mention any lesser official, losing his footing and flipping into the creek was enough to spur a search for an alternate method. Finally a fallen log was found, and one by one the dignitaries, balancing their truncheons, wands, and jewels, crossed to the other side. Nobody drew a breath as the President, as calmly as though he were entering a carriage, walked along the log and joined the rest; the parade reformed, the band blared, and they were off again.

The cornerstone for what would be the north wing of the Capitol stood in solitary splendor atop a hill, and nearby was a fire pit over which a five-hundred-pound ox was being roasted. By prearranged plan the marchers formed themselves on both sides of the stone, making a lane down which the President could walk. One of the officials handed him a silver plaque, engraved with appropriately verbose sentiments, and with icy dignity he strode to the stone and laid the plaque on top, while off to one side the cannon of the Virginia Militia banged out a salute. A gaggle of Masons then anointed the stone with corn, wine, and oil; the Grand Master delivered a florid and largely unintelligible oration, and the cannon thumped a few more times for good measure. The crowd then adjourned to a booth, where the barbecued ox was being served, and the formal part of the dedication was closed.

There still remained the auctioning of the land, which as far as President Washington was concerned was the most important business of the day. The main problem, which made the auction necessary, was that Congress had authorized him to build the capital but had not appropriated any money with which to do it, the result being that he had had to beg local landowners to give half their property to the government, with the expectation of realizing a great deal of money with the increase in value of their remaining property. The cash necessary to build the city was to be raised by selling the government land, but such was the inefficiency and general apathy that very little was sold, and the whole project seemed about to founder out of sheer inertia. To make matters worse, Philadelphia was still actively trying to become the nation's permanent capital and was building edifices far superior to anything the Federal City could probably produce, and there was a strong body of opinion that maintained it would be cheaper and better in the long run to let Philadelphia have its way. Thus President Washington, for whom the new city had tentatively been named, was fighting a last-ditch battle as grim and as desperate as any he had fought during the War.

James had followed along with the parade and had watched the proceedings in a bemused way, wondering if this was indeed a project in which he wanted to invest. The auctioneer mounted the podium and began his chant, and then one by one the lots were offered up to total silence. James could see Washington leaning forward and looking around for bidders, but few hands were raised and no important transactions took place until one elegant-looking gentleman bid on a lot near the President's

House. It was awarded to him almost immediately, and as he gave his chit to the auctioneer there was scattered applause.

"Thank you, Colonel Burr," the auctioneer said. "And may you enjoy your land."

But for the rest there was silence until finally, out of sheer desperation, the President bought four lots on the East Branch of the Potomac. If he had hoped this might start the ball rolling he was disappointed; no further lots were sold, and an attempt to extend the auction for another day resulted only in his offering to buy four more lots at the opposite end of the city, an offer that was received as the empty gesture it in fact was.

As though the failure of the auction weren't enough, those few who had previously bought land were delinquent in their payments, and the flow of cash into the putative city's coffers was a flat zero. The time was now ripe for James and Morris to step in.

James went first, taking his letter from Washington to the commissioners, and emerged from the meeting with an eminently satisfactory deal: he bought three thousand city lots for $66.50 each, payment to be made over a period of seven years, and during that time he guaranteed to build ten houses a year. In addition, he agreed to lend the commissioners $2,200 a month at 6 per cent interest so that they might have some operating money, and the $11,088 thus realized in interest could be applied against the over-all purchase price of $199,500. That price, breaking down as it did to $28,500 a year, was nothing compared with some of his other deals.

A short while later Morris went to the commissioners and also bought three thousand lots, but when they found out he was a partner of James's they changed the rules, exactly as James had feared they might. They canceled James's agreement and instead sold the two partners six thousand at $80 apiece, making a total purchase of $480,000, and then, hoping to make it easier for the land to be resold, they stipulated that buyers could secure title even before they had paid for the lots. This clause, which had not been very carefully thought through, had within it the seeds of total chaos.

James was upset when Morris recounted what had happened. "Was it absolutely necessary to tell them we were partners?" he said.

"They asked me point-blank," Morris replied. "There wasn't much else I could say."

"You might have said"—James paused, trying to think of an alternative.

"I couldn't deny it," Morris said. "It's not the kind of thing you can keep secret."

"I suppose not. Still, there are ways of getting around the truth without actually lying."

"I've yet to find one. To tell a lie that's sure to be found out is just plain stupid. Something you can get away with is one thing, but something that's doomed to failure is quite another."

"True." James was quiet for a moment, then brightened. "I guess there's only one answer—buy up so much land that we have a monopoly, and then we can ask what we want for it."

"Now that," said Morris, "is the kind of thinking I like to hear."

"By the way, has the President mentioned his land to you?"

"What land?"

"Out on the Ohio and the something-or-other rivers."

"Oh, that, yes. He bought it in 1770. It's way off in western Virginia, on the Ohio River."

"Might it be worth our while? I have the feeling he'd like to sell it to us."

"He would indeed. The trouble is it's still too deep in Indian country to attract many settlers, and at the same time it's close enough to civilization so that the taxes are going up. It's a poor situation no matter how you look at it. If he mentions it again, look thoughtful and say you'll have to talk to me."

"Thank you. I shall remember that."

"Now. What are your prospects in the matter of ready cash?"

"I can raise some. Why?"

"How much can you raise?"

"I don't know. My brother Daniel can always produce money in Boston, either on his own credit or on my Amsterdam notes, but I couldn't give you the figures in dollars and cents. Is this an immediate need?"

"No, no. It was more in the line of a general question than anything else."

"I know one thing we can do. We can organize a company—or society, or whatever—to attract investors to our Federal City property. I can buy another thousand or so lots, and with that we can advertise for subscribers and make it attractive enough to bring in a good deal of money. Capitalize it at, say, $500,000, sell shares at $500 each, and offer up two hundred house lots at $300 apiece. If all goes well, a $500 share should treble itself in fifteen years, which will be a nice inducement."

"Why should people subscribe to this if they didn't buy from the government?"

"This is a business proposition, and the government is known to be unbusinesslike. From its inception it has lost money, and when by accident it does come into some, it fritters it away before it can be put to any good purpose."

Morris was quiet, wheezing slightly. "I remember when I was in the government," he said, "we would float a foreign loan, and before it could reach these shores it would be called for by creditors on the Continent. In '82, France lent us 6 million livres, and John Adams got $2 million from private firms in Holland, and precious little of it ever saw this side of the Atlantic."

"That's exactly what I mean," said James.

"This wasn't the government's fault so much as the fact that the capital just wasn't there. We were doing things that required money, and we were doing them on faith instead. Sometimes I wonder how we ever survived."

"The way I intend to do it, it will be run on a businesslike basis, with a prospectus advertised in the newspapers for all to see, and there is no reason why we shouldn't attract investors like bears to a honey tree."

"Well, go ahead and draw up your prospectus. I'll be interested to see what it looks like."

"I promise you, it will look like pure gold."

"It has occurred to me," Morris said, "now that our partnership is no longer secret, we ought to have a portmanteau name, which will cover all our operations."

"Do you have any ideas?"

"Something all-inclusive, like—well, like the North American Land Company. That has a nice, solid sound to it and doesn't really pin us down."

James said the name to himself a few times and nodded. "That's good," he said, at last. "And it gives us all the land north of the equator to operate in."

Morris laughed. "Who knows?" he said. "We may need it."

James also laughed, and rose. "I shall be off," he said, "to write my prospectus. Do you mind if I list myself as secretary of the society?"

"Pray do," Morris replied.

"I shall also be a subscriber, but it will look more businesslike if we have a secretary."

"So long as it attracts investors, you may list yourself as Catherine of Russia. One title is the same as any other, as far as I am concerned."

For some reason this struck James as inordinately funny, and he was still laughing as the servant opened the front door to let him out. Nicholson was on the steps, his hand raised toward the knocker, and he stood back to let James pass.

"Ah, there!" James said, jovially. "Another partner in the North American Land Company. How fares it, Brother Nicholson?"

Nicholson was struck incoherent with surprise; he muttered a few words about its being a pleasant day, then watched as James, not waiting for an answer, strode down Market Street. When Nicholson got inside and the servant had taken his hat and cloak, he looked at Morris for an explanation. "What is Master Jemmy so ebullient about?" he said.

"This and that," Morris replied. "He is riding, I believe the expression is, the crest of the wave."

"For any particular reason?"

Morris shrugged. "He thinks we may shortly have a monopoly on all the federal land."

"Did you tell him about your London bank?"

"I saw no reason to go into that."

"Might he be able to produce cash?"

"He said he could raise some, but he was vague about the amount. I'm sure he has it; he's just being coy until he knows a little more."

"And how much is it you need?"

"God knows. The failure of that bank cost me £124,000 sterling, but there are European creditors hounding me for considerably more than that. Gouverneur keeps writing nervous little notes urging me to be cautious, but as I see it, this is the last time in the world for caution. This is the time when we must plunge ahead and be bold."

"Do you have any ideas?"

"Master Jemmy's plan may bring in something, but I can't count on it. I hear there are about a million acres to be had out along the banks of the Susquehanna, and if we could get them at a reasonable price, we could build a town and start developing the area, and that would bring in a handsome profit."

"And how would we get them?"

"My credit is still good. I may be pressed in some areas, but people still remember the War, and I can raise any amount of money I want. If I can get it from Master Jemmy, so much the better; otherwise, I can fall back on my well-known financial wizardry." He wheezed and smiled. "Just remember—what worked well once will always work better a second time."

"I hope you're right," said Nicholson.

"Don't worry," Morris replied. "If I didn't know what I was doing, we'd all still be subjects of the Crown."

Nicholson opened his mouth to say something, then thought better of it. "Of course," he said. "I keep forgetting that."

"See that you remember it," Morris said. "You'll sleep a lot better that way."

19

By early December 1793 the yellow fever had started to taper off in Philadelphia, and although people began to return to the city, the government, to be on the safe side, met in Germantown, six miles to the northwest. Very slowly life came back to normal, as more and more people found that the diminishing chances of contracting the fever were preferable to the squalor of refugee existence in the country.

On January 15, 1794, James ran a newspaper advertisement for the land-development society he had discussed with Morris. It was headed ESTIMATED STATEMENT, COLUMBIAN SOCIETY, FOR THE PURPOSE OF RAISING AND INVESTING A CAPITAL IN LOTS AND BUILD-INGS and went on to describe "what subscribers may reasonably expect." Capitalized at $500,000, it would be divided into a thousand shares of $500 each, one share equaling one vote, the subscribers to pay one tenth of their subscription annually. Application would be made to the governor of the state of Maryland for a fifteen-year incorporation; at the end of fifteen years the Society would be liquidated and any excess property sold at auction. James Greenleaf would call a meeting of the subscribers as soon as the subscription was filled, and he would agree to provide two hundred house lots, to be sold at $300 per lot. (These were the same lots he had bought for $80 apiece.) Eighteen houses would be built the first year, eighteen the second, thirty-six the third, and so on, presuming that a certain number of houses were sold and leased each year. After fifteen years, one $500 share could be expected to bring $1,431.48.

"How did you arrive at that figure?" Morris asked, when James showed him the prospectus.

"Mathematics," James replied.

"I am aware of that. But what factors did you use?"

"Well"—James cleared his throat and assumed an offhand air—"that's just the way it worked out. Normal annual growth should be anywhere from .15 to .25 per cent, so I averaged it out and took .19. I realize that isn't the mean, but it looks better than .2. So .19 times 15 is 2.862, and that times 500 comes out to $1,431.48. I originally told you it should treble itself, and this is very nearly that. If I'd put it an even $1,500 in the prospectus, it would have looked as though I'd rigged it."

"As opposed to what you actually did," said Morris.

"That is correct. This represents a conservative estimate."

"What's the significance of the name?"

"I called it the Columbian Society because it's in the District of Columbia. Besides, it has a good sound to it. I didn't want anything too presumptuous."

Morris put the prospectus on the table. "It will be interesting to see how it works out," he said.

"I don't see how it can fail."

"I have been looking over the various papers and deeds, and it appears that we, as a syndicate, now own approximately one third of what will some day be the city of Washington. I think we are now in a position to do as we choose."

"We still have to put up the buildings," James reminded him. "I have plans for six down at the point, on Twenty-second Street."

"And I'm putting up seven on Nineteenth Street," Morris replied. "At the moment, we can meet this year's obligations on our notes, but I think we should start looking ahead and planning for next year."

"Next year we should be even better off than we are now."

"Possibly. But I'm going to buy a large tract of land on the Susquehanna and start a town there—incidentally, what do you think of 'Asylum' as a name for a town?"

James considered this, then said, "I don't know. It has one or two rather unfortunate connotations, don't you think?"

"But it also means a shelter, a haven. I think 'Asylum on the Susquehanna' has a nice sound to it. I'm having Brother Nicholson arrange to buy the land." Morris had been writing on a piece of scratch paper, and he looked up and said, "I've just been working out those figures you gave me, and mine don't agree with yours."

"Oh?" said James, surprised. "In what way?"

"You said .19 times 15 is 2.862, and the way I figure it it comes out to 2.85. And 2.85 times 500 is $1,425, not $1,431.48."

"I told you the figures were approximate," James said.

"Yes, but 2.85 is not even approximately 2.862. Dealing in percentages, that could be a large difference."

Once more, James cleared his throat. "Actually, what I did was work backward," he said. "I took the final figure, $1,431.48, as a reasonable guess, divided that by 15 and got $95.432, and then divided that by 500 and got 0.190864, or .19 in round numbers. It all comes out more or less the same. And, when you come to think of it, an annual growth rate of .19 is nothing if not conservative."

Morris stared at the figures some more, then crumpled the paper. "Let us hope the general public thinks so," he said.

"I care nothing about the general public," James replied. "I care only about that part that has the money." Then, pausing only to draw a breath, he changed the subject. "I need larger quarters," he said. "I need a house to live in, rather than a miserable suite of rooms."

"You said you were building six houses," Morris replied. "Why not live in one of them?"

"Those are for income. Besides, I don't want anything new. I want a house with character—with a reputation—like this one, or the one the President is living in."

"I'm afraid they're both spoken for," Morris said.

"Obviously. I meant something similar in style, and in feeling. Something more appropriate to my position."

Morris toyed with the end of his pen. "I shall bear it in mind," he said. "By the way, I assume you know William Cranch, the Boston lawyer."

"Know him?" said James. "I've known him since we were children. He and my sister Nancy are engaged to be married."

"I thought he might be a good person to have as our business agent in Washington. His connection with the Vice President can certainly do us no harm."

James was delighted. "I think that's a perfectly splendid idea," he said. "Have you asked him yet?"

"I have put out feelers. I have reason to believe he may be amenable."

"What a really splendid idea," James said again. "I don't know why I didn't think of it long ago."

"No one person can have all the ideas," said Morris mildly. "That is what partnerships are for."

The Morris-Nicholson-Greenleaf syndicate met the deadline for the first installment on their loans, and they satisfied the further conditions by starting construction on thirteen houses. But the advertisements for the Columbian Society attracted a disappointing number of subscribers, and the projected meeting, to be held when the subscriptions were filled, never took place. One problem was that the syndicate, owning as much of the city as it did, had set the prices so high that would-be buyers lost interest and retired to the sidelines to wait until the prices came down to a more realistic level. Morris and Nicholson bought their million acres on the Susquehanna and founded the town of Asylum, but the returns on that were of a long-term nature and nothing that could be counted on for ready cash. The only project, in fact, that did well in the first half of 1794 were a wharf and warehouse in the Federal City run by Tobias Lear, formerly Washington's secretary, and Tristram Dalton, a Newburyport shipper, whom James had set up in business. These did such booming business that Dalton decided to leave Newburyport and take up residence in the Federal City. He and Cranch, who had accepted Morris's offer as business agent, loaded their worldly possessions aboard a ship in Boston and set out for Washington.

It was midsummer, and a heavy, oppressive heat hung like a tent over Philadelphia. James had tried without success to find a house in the country—not that they didn't exist, but their owners had no intention of selling—and his only respite from the city was the occasional business visit he made to Morris at The Hills. Morris was concerned at the lack of buyers for their land, but James argued that once their building project got well underway, there would be something concrete to attract investors, and there was no need to worry. James was, in fact, euphoric about the prospects and could not understand Morris's continuing concern about ready cash. The answer, he felt, was to buy as much property as was humanly possible, and the cash would take care of itself. In this Morris agreed, but every now and then he would ask James about his anonymous backer on the Continent, which indicated that his confidence was not as solidly based as was James's.

James's reliance on Van Vliet was by now tempered with caution, because of the total shambles in France. The King, and then Marie Antoinette, had been executed, and suddenly everybody started executing everybody else, in what was most accurately described as the Reign of Terror. It was said there literally was blood flowing in the gutters of the Place de la Révolution, and people who one day thought they were in charge quite often found themselves the next day in a tumbril headed for the guillotine. In the circumstances Van Vliet's *émigrés* were lucky to be out of the country, but how much money they could command was an open question. James could only assume they had taken all their valuables with them and could still make good their offer. When Morris asked him if he had written to his backer, he replied that he had, which was the truth, and added that everything was going well, which was not.

One afternoon in July, when James had returned from The Hills and was glumly contemplating the prospect of a week in the city, he entered his building just as Eckman was coming out.

"There you are," Eckman said. "I've been looking all over for you."

"I have been visiting with the mighty," James replied.

"What was the name of the ship that Cranch and Dalton took to Washington?"

"I don't remember."

"Could it have been the *Susan Bostwick?*"

"Come to think of it, yes. Why?"

"She was lost the day before yesterday."

"My God! How? Where?" James's first thought was that now Nancy would not marry Billy Cranch.

"Coming up the Chesapeake. She caught fire and burned to the waterline."

"Were there any survivors?"

"Yes. They're being taken to Washington, but there are no medical facilities there. A call is out for doctors."

"Are you going?"

"Naturally. I thought you might like to come."

"Like to? It's nothing less than my duty."

They covered the hundred and twenty-plus miles in under two days, changing horses often and riding as far into the night as they dared. When they reached Washington they went to the warehouse on the Potomac, where they found Lear wandering around as though he'd been struck by lightning. At first he seemed not to recognize them, and then he smiled.

"I'm glad you came," he said.

"Where are they?" James and Eckman asked, almost in unison.

"Where are what?"

"Cranch and Dalton," James said, as Eckman asked, "Did they survive? Are they burned?"

It took Lear a moment to sort out the questions. "Oh, they're all right," he said. "Of course, they lost everything."

James felt himself go limp with relief. "If that's all that happened, they're lucky," he said. "Where are they?"

"Off looking for a place to stay, I presume."

"Where are the other survivors?" Eckman asked. "I understand there's a need for doctors."

"Yes. They're in a shelter up on G Street."

Eckman left, and James looked at Lear for a few moments. "Are you all right?" he asked, at last.

"Yes, of course," Lear replied, not looking at him.

"I don't believe you," said James. "What's wrong?"

Lear took a deep breath. "It really is nothing," he said. "But when I heard of the fire, I assumed our partnership would be dissolved."

"Why should you assume that?"

"Because without Mr. Dalton I wouldn't be able to run the business by myself. And even now I don't know—"

"Listen to me," James broke in. "You already know enough to run the business by yourself. Whether Dalton stays with us or not—and I assume he will, because he has no place else to go—this is your business, and you are in charge." Quickly, he added, "And I shall remain a partner, to share with you the bad as well as the good."

Lear's face twisted into a smile. "It's good to hear you say that, sir," he said. "May God bless you."

Is this, James thought, the man who was behind our President

for eight years? Is this the genius who straightened out his affairs
and brought order out of chaos? If it is, then he must have un-
dergone some radical change, because this man is afraid of his
own shadow. Then it occurred to him that, as Washington's secretary and virtual member of the family, Lear had lived in a co-
coon of security, and this was the first time he had been out in
the world on his own. Like a bird kept too long in the nest, he
had not yet learned to fly and was, to continue the simile,
deathly afraid of heights. All he needed was a little experience
and he would be all right. To himself, James observed that a
nervous partner was worse than none at all, but he felt sure that
before too long Lear would be contributing more than his share.
If he didn't, he would be dropped.

He found Cranch, still wearing the clothes in which he'd
swum from the burning ship, standing in a dusty clearing and
staring in a benumbed way at a row of construction workers'
tents. Without seeing his face, James could tell from Cranch's
posture that he was appalled at what he saw and was seriously
considering a return to Boston. He didn't move; he just stared,
but the stare was more eloquent than if his thoughts had been
printed in a speech balloon over his head. James approached
quietly, until he was within a few yards, and then spoke.

"Waiting for Father to read the Declaration?" he said.

Cranch jumped and turned, and when he saw James his face
became incandescent and they fell on each other's necks. When
the exclamations of greeting were over, James took him by the
arm and said, "You are coming with me."

"Gladly," Cranch replied. "Anywhere." He was younger than
James and had a face that looked almost boyish. Glancing at
him, James wondered why Nancy had taken so long to make up
her mind. "Just out of curiosity," Cranch said, "where is there *to*
go?"

"Back to Philadelphia," James replied. "There's no fit place for
you here."

"But this is where I'm supposed to be. Mr. Morris said I was—"

"Forget what Mr. Morris said. You need new clothes, you
need a place to live, and you need time to get established. You'll
never do any of those things here."

"In the first place, I have no money. Everything I own was
burned in the fire."

"Believe me, money is the least of your worries. I have all the money you'll ever need, and a bit more beyond that. Until you can find a place of your own you will stay with me—I regret the quarters are not luxurious, but that will be taken care of shortly —and I shall see that you are clothed and fed. Now, stop quibbling and come with me. I shall hire a carriage, so we may return to Philadelphia in style."

Cranch was silent, as they headed back toward the river. Finally, almost as though talking to himself, he said, "It begins to look as though I were marrying into the right branch of the family."

James laughed. "Did you ever doubt it?"

"Not really. But I can't say I expected this kind of luck."

"This, my lad, is only the beginning. Just wait for a year or so, and then you will see something."

20

In the second half of 1794 money became tighter, and, as is often
the case, those with debts felt the pinch first. Using his connec-
tions in Holland, James tried to float a loan for himself and for
the Federal City, but no such loan was possible without deeds in
fee for the property, and James could produce deeds for no more
than $1,200,000 worth. In the end the Dutch lent him only one
tenth of that amount, which was used up almost immediately. In
his attempts to make the deal attractive, he offered the city lots
to the Dutch without improvement clauses, and he made the city
and the syndicate jointly responsible for the loan. But the Dutch
were having troubles of their own and were not in the mood for
any large real-estate speculation. With the French Army threatening invasion, the financial situation in Holland was, to say the
very least, shaky, and the basic Dutch conservatism called for a
waiting policy on all fronts. James also wrote to Van Vliet, saying he had a line on some splendid property if the money could
be forthcoming immediately, and while this was warping the
truth to a certain degree, he felt he would have no trouble
finding land in the event Van Vliet produced the money and
wanted proof of purchase. The cash was the main thing; with
enough of that, everything else would fall into place.

Then, the first week in September, he received a note bidding
him to call on the Vice President in his quarters. He hadn't seen
Adams since the first interview, and hard as he tried he couldn't
think of a reason for the summons. He felt that it had to be
something good; he had done nothing to merit censure, and all
he could think of was that he was going to be offered some post
in the government, possibly even Secretary of the Treasury. Hamilton had had the position for five years, and it was possible

that, with Jefferson's retirement from public affairs, Hamilton might be moving up to State, leaving room for James to come in. When he remembered the way his appointment to Amsterdam had fallen on him out of the sky, this was not a wholly illogical premise.

Adams was more or less as he had last seen him, wheezing and muttering and discontented, with his mind apparently on several things at once. He gestured James to a chair and said, "Billy tells me you were most kind to him after his catastrophe."

"I was happy to be able to do it," James replied. "After all, he's as good as a member of the family."

"This really isn't in my province," Adams said, changing the subject and coming immediately to the point, "but matters in our State Department are so confused that Mr. Randolph has asked if I would have an—ah—informal talk with you, to straighten out a few items that puzzle him."

"Of course," said James, sensing an ominous turn in the conversation. "Whatever he'd like to know."

"You were appointed during the time John Jay was Secretary of Foreign Affairs, am I correct?"

"Yes, sir," James replied. "Under the Confederation."

"Yes. Jefferson wondered about that. He said it didn't make sense."

"John Hancock told me—" James started to protest, but Adams held up a hand.

"Water under the bridge," he said. "Water under the bridge. What Mr. Randolph would like to know is whether or not you intend to return to Amsterdam."

The question was so unexpected that James had to grope for an answer. "To be honest, I hadn't thought about it," he said. "So many other things have come up—" he didn't want to say a flat "No," but the idea of returning to Amsterdam was in the circumstances inconceivable.

"Mr. Randolph felt that, rather than leave the post completely vacant, it might be wise to appoint a vice consul, to—should we say—take up the slack."

"I think that's a good idea," James said, relieved. "I think he should do it."

"He already has. A gentleman by the name of Sylvanus Bourne has been appointed to take your place."

Well, thought James, so much for becoming Secretary of the Treasury. In order to maintain as much dignity as he could, he said, "An excellent choice. As a matter of fact, he's a relative of mine. I'm sure he'll do quite well."

"Yes." Adams's tone of voice implied that it wouldn't be hard to do as well as James had, if not a great deal better.

James rose. "Would the Secretary want a letter of resignation from me?" he asked.

"I don't believe that will be necessary. Positions established under the Confederation were by their very nature temporary."

"I see. Well—" James hesitated, waiting to be dismissed.

"I understand you and Morris have been buying up land like demented persons," Adams said.

"Yes, sir," James replied, smiling. "We feel it's our public duty to help the Federal City off to a strong start."

"What an unusual way of looking at it. I congratulate you."

"Thank you, sir . . . Incidentally, do you plan to attend the wedding?"

"It depends on when and where they have it. Much as I should like to, I cannot leave the Senate while it's in session."

"Of course." James had been hoping to use the wedding to cement his relationship with the Vice President, but realized it was a somewhat premature idea. In order to close the interview on a cheerful note, he said, "The very least they could do would be to hold it at your convenience. You will, after all, be the guest of honor."

"The bride is always the guest of honor," Adams replied and then, with a thin smile, added, "And I would make a perfectly hideous bride."

By the end of the year it was clear that, if the syndicate were to raise any money at all, its members would have to sell their land in large portions instead of individual lots. The small buyers simply were not attracted, and the only answer was to unload a certain amount of it on people who, like themselves, were interested in large-scale operations. The first buyer was a General Walter Stewart, a Philadelphia friend of Morris's, and he bought a portion of James's property on the northwest corner of Pennsylvania Avenue and Nineteenth Street. Then, on February 23 the following year, an Englishman named Thomas Law bought

$133,000 worth of property from the syndicate. Law was thirty-seven, the son of a bishop in the Church of England, and had spent the last eighteen years in India. With a fortune of some $250,000 he had learned to be a good administrator, and he was prudent enough to get a mortgage on the syndicate property that had been conveyed in fee simple to it, in such a way that he was not an unsecured creditor. Then, sensing that there might be more for sale in the near future, he bided his time and awaited developments.

All in all, the year 1795 was an important one for the syndicate in general, and for James in particular. It started off on a sad note, with the news of the death of his Uncle Stephen, in Boston, at the age of ninety-one. On reflection, James realized that Stephen's life had been not only a remarkably full but also a remarkably lucky one. Few Tories had been allowed to remain in the country unmolested, and it was a sign of the Bostonians' respect for Stephen Greenleaf that he had lived out his life in comparative peace, like an aging bear holed up in its den and asking only to be left alone.

Nancy and Billy set the date of their wedding at April 6, and then, to James's complete astonishment and delight, his blind brother, John, announced that he and Lucy Cranch would be married on April 4. Lucy had for some little time been tending to John's various needs, and it was clear that the wedding was a logical step, but for James, the fact that the ties with the Cranch family and thereby with John Adams were now doubled was almost too good to be believed. He wondered if Adams had known about it at their recent meeting, but decided it had probably been as much of a surprise to the Vice President as it had to him. This, surely, would mean that Adams would attend the weddings, and since John's blindness required they be held in Boston, it was not inconceivable that Adams and James might travel north together. The whole idea left James in a rosy state of anticipation, sure that no matter what happened it was bound to be good.

As it turned out, Adams did not attend the weddings, and Billy Cranch and James and Eckman shared a stagecoach for the long, dull, bone-jarring trip. Billy had invited Eckman who, after a moment's thought, had allowed he might just be able to spare the time away from his practice, adding that there was some research he had to do in Boston that would justify the trip. By this time James knew Eckman well enough to sense there was something more behind his words than he was saying, but he also knew better than to ask. Whatever it was would be revealed if and when Eckman felt like revealing it, and not before.

James had been aware that he had many relatives, but he hadn't realized just how many until he saw them assembled for John and Lucy's wedding. They came from Boston and Quincy and Newburyport and Hartford and points in between and beyond; they came singly and in pairs and in droves; they came in a wide variety of ages, and they came with surnames—aside from Greenleaf—such as Ingraham, Webster, Burgess, and Milton, as well as Appleton, Robertson, Eliot, and Dawes. Among the family Christian names the only one that seemed to be missing was Gooking, who was born in 1721 and died in infancy. Had Gooking survived, James was sure he would have been there, too.

His meeting with Noah Webster was neither friendly nor hostile; both men were correct and slightly formal, and for a while no mention was made of James and Eckman's visit to Hartford. Then, more or less for lack of anything else to say, Webster said, "And how is your doctor friend faring in Philadelphia?"

"I believe he's doing nicely," James replied. "At any rate, he was kept quite busy during the plague."

"Yes, I imagine he would have reveled in that," said Webster.

"You can ask him in person the day after tomorrow. Billy has invited him to the wedding."

Webster's face lost all expression. "How perfectly delightful," he said.

James spotted his brother Daniel among the relatives, which reminded him that he wanted to ask Daniel about the possibility of raising money in Boston. "Excuse me," he said to Webster. "I have some business that requires attention."

Webster bowed, and James made his way across the room to Daniel. Daniel was hesitant as to how much money could be raised, since a number of people in Boston already held James's notes, but he said he would look into the matter, and James veered off in search of his parents.

Nancy and Billy's wedding was like the second day of a carnival, with the same nucleus in attendance and the differences only in the peripheral guests. Eckman arrived, escorting a young lady James had never seen before; she was attractive and neatly dressed and lively, but there was something about her that struck a faintly discordant note, like one cracked bell in a carillon, and it was a while before James realized it was simply the fact that everything about her was one degree too much; her eyes were too bright, her bodice cut an inch too low, the bows on her shoes too pink not to clash with her orange bodice, and the flower in her cap too obviously artificial. Eckman introduced her as "Miss Evans, my fiancée," and looked directly into James's eyes as he said it, as though challenging him to question the statement. James, remembering Eckman's remark about doing research in Boston, bowed to Miss Evans and presented his congratulations to Eckman. She curtseyed, and smiled, and James found himself remembering some of the expeditions he and Eckman had made to Charlestown.

"And when is the happy event to take place?" he asked.

Before Miss Evans could reply, Eckman said, "No definite date has been set. It will depend on my research."

"Of course," said James. And then, to Miss Evans, "I feel sure you will find the life of a doctor's wife an interesting one."

"So he tells me," she replied, with a laugh. "All femurs and tibias, and the like."

"She's just started learning the terms," Eckman explained. "Her progress has been slow, but sure."

"A good foundation is always the best," said James. "May I get you some punch, Miss Evans?"

"Delighted," she replied. "Provided you and the doctor will join me."

James went to the punch bowl and filled three glasses, and when he returned he saw that Miss Evans had managed to corner Noah Webster, while Eckman stood by and watched with thinly concealed delight.

"I do believe that language is more important than anything else," she was saying. "As I said to the doctor only yesterday, you may know all about anatomy, but without language, what benefit is your knowledge to others? Without words, we're like the beasts in the field."

"Indeed," said Webster, whose only lane of escape had been blocked by James's arrival.

"Speaking of beasts," Eckman said, to Webster, "perhaps you can tell us what those noises are, that frighten the people of Moodus."

"Nobody knows," replied Webster. "They're a phenomenon of nature."

"I had a cousin who was a phenomenon of nature," Miss Evans announced. "He was born with six toes on one foot and six fingers on the opposite hand. There were those who said it was the work of the devil, but my aunt was a God-fearing woman who would never have let the devil come near her. My uncle had enough difficulty, as it was."

"And then there was always Anne Boleyn," said Eckman.

"She was beheaded," said James. "What else?"

"She had an extra finger on one hand," Eckman replied. "She also had three breasts."

Miss Evans looked at Eckman in astonishment. "You never told me that," she said.

"The subject never came up," said Eckman.

Turning back to Webster, Miss Evans said, "Mr. Greenleaf has said the life of a doctor's wife is an interesting one, but until now I had never realized how interesting. Tell me"—she leaned forward and a thin trickle of punch dripped from her glass onto Webster's ruffled neckpiece—"do wits lead interesting lives?"

"Do—?" At first Webster didn't understand the question, then he glanced at Eckman, from whom the coaching must have come. "At times we do, and at times we don't," he replied. "It depends on the company in which we find ourselves. And now, if you will excuse me—" He shouldered his way past James and headed for the adjoining room. Miss Evans watched him go.

"I always thought that wits were supposed to be funny," she said.

"Some are, some aren't," Eckman replied. Then, to James, "I hope we didn't cause any serious ruptures in the family fabric."

"Pray don't give it a thought," said James. "I'm only sorry more people weren't listening."

"We can try it again," Miss Evans suggested. "You tell everybody to be quiet, while I ask him about Anne Boleyn."

"I think perhaps not," replied James. "I think that might be asking too much of our luck."

"It was only a suggestion." Miss Evans drained her glass and said, "For some reason, that punch makes me thirsty. The more I have of it, the more I want."

"It's the fruit juice," said Eckman. "It always induces thirst. Perhaps I should take you home and give you a long drink of water."

"What an odd suggestion," she replied and, putting her hand on his arm, allowed him to escort her from the room. As she went James heard her saying, "Just imagine—three breasts! I mean, what good . . ." The rest was lost in the noise of the other guests.

When James returned to Philadelphia, Morris had various items of news for him. The first was that, unless they could raise money almost immediately, they would be unable to meet the second payment on their loans on the Federal City. Morris had sold his share of Asylum to Nicholson but this hadn't produced enough to make a dent in the debt, and, although he had his eye on some property that the North American Land Company might buy, it probably wouldn't produce enough quick money to meet the deadline. James was unperturbed. His new ties with the Cranch and Adams families had given him a feeling of unlimited power, and the matter of meeting one deadline seemed unimportant when there were so many other deals to be considered.

"My feeling is we should buy it," he said. "What is it, and how much?"

"It is six million acres," Morris replied. "In Pennsylvania, Virginia, the Carolinas, Kentucky, and Georgia. It will give us a sizable monopoly in the area."

"By all means buy it," said James. "My brother Daniel is raising money in Boston, and I should be hearing from my man on the Continent fairly soon. This is certainly not the time to be timid."

"I hope your so-called man on the Continent is not in Holland," Morris said.

"Why?" said James. "Supposing he were?"

"The latest word is that the French have overrun that country. They captured the Dutch fleet when it was icebound last winter, and now they've sent the Army in to take over. They're setting up something called the Batavian Republic, modeled on their own government, with the Patriot party in charge."

James thought about this, wondering what it would do to his holdings. The notes and deeds held by Crommelin were mostly for land in the United States and therefore not likely to be touched by the French, but Van Vliet's status would now be murkier than ever. It would all depend on whether he had been able to escape.

"Did anyone get away?" he asked.

"William V fled to England," Morris replied. "I imagine there were others."

"I don't believe I have anything to worry about," James said. "My property is in good hands."

"That's nice to hear. Speaking of property, do you know Lansdowne, John Penn's estate on the Schuylkill?"

"I don't believe so. Is it near yours?"

"It's on the west bank, about four miles out. I have seen it only from a distance, but it looks quite impressive."

"Is it for sale?"

"I believe so. The old man died last week, and I understand his widow wants to sell. It might be worth looking into."

"Splendid. I shall make enquiries today." James rubbed his hands together. "I have a feeling this is going to be an excellent year," he said. "Do you know Aaron Burr?"

"Yes. Why?"

"I've seen him only once, at that misbegotten auction, but I hear he's interested in buying land in upstate New York. I might be able to interest him in joint ownership, and that would increase the size of the holding."

"I suppose anything is possible."

"Might you arrange an introduction?"

"The Senate is about to recess for the summer. I'll try to do it before he goes home."

"Thank you. I like to make the most of every opportunity."

Morris looked at him, and smiled. "The ebullience of youth," he said. "I must say, I envy you."

That afternoon James wrote a note to John Penn's widow, expressing his condolence and at the same time indicating interest in seeing the house should it in fact be for sale. He sent it off by messenger, and then did what research he could about the property. It appeared that Penn, a grandson of William Penn and twice Lieutenant Governor of the Province of Pennsylvania, bought a hundred and forty-two acres from Dr. William Smith in 1773 and on the property built a summer house that was declared by some to be the most ornate of its kind in the area, if not the country. (The idea that he might own a house even grander than Morris's made James tingle with anticipation.) John Penn's wife was Ann Allen, the daughter of William Allen, who had been Chief Justice of the Province before the War, and her brother, James Allen, was the founder of Allentown, Pennsylvania. *His* daughter, Ann Penn Allen, was thereby the Penns' niece and considered the most likely to inherit the property after Mrs. Penn's death if it should not be sold. James felt that, if it should come to a contest between himself and Miss Allen as to who got the house, he would make her an offer of such dazzling proportions that she would be unable to refuse. In his mind, the estate was already his.

The next day a note arrived from, of all people, Ann Penn Allen herself, saying that her aunt was seeing nobody but that she would be happy to show Mr. Greenleaf the property at any time that was convenient to him. James replied, and an appointment was made, and two days later he was on the Market Street ferry, crossing to the west bank of the river. For this trip he had a simple carriage, less elaborate than the one in which he had first ridden to meet Morris, but nevertheless several notches above going by horseback.

Lansdowne stood on a rise overlooking the river, and when James saw it the first word that came to his mind was "palatial." It had a two-story portico, with columns and a balcony, and James was reminded of the drawings of what the President's House, in Washington, would be like when completed. It was not only palatial; it bespoke solidity, and power, and opulence, and the surrounding lawns and trees and gardens gave the estate an almost Arcadian look, like the neoclassical wall paintings in Dutch houses. It needed only nymphs and fauns and satyrs to make the scene complete, and James was making his plans for occupancy before he had even seen the inside.

He was admitted by a servant, and in a few moments a small figure in black came noiselessly down the stairs. He bowed, and she curtseyed and said, "Welcome to Lansdowne, Mr. Greenleaf.

I am sorry you cannot see it under more cheerful circumstances."
Her face was round, and her hair was parted in the middle, and
James found that in spite of her mourning clothes there was
something fresh and colorful about her. She was, he guessed, in
her early twenties, and with no difficulty at all he could picture
her in other, flimsier clothes, frolicking like a nymph about the
lawn. Her eyes were large and brown, and she looked directly at
him as she spoke. Luckily, he told himself, she could not read his
thoughts.

"I thank you for receiving me," he said, in his most formal
manner. "I only hope I am not intruding on your mourning."

"Not in the least. My aunt is in seclusion, and I welcome the
sight of a human face."

For some insane reason James had hoped she would add,
"Particularly a face like yours," and he tried to tell himself the
implication was there. It wasn't, but he nevertheless made small
preening motions.

"Would you care to look through the house?" Miss Allen
asked. "I presume you have some idea of what you want."

James was about to say he needed to see no more, but in order
to prolong the interview he said, "You are most kind. From what
I've seen so far, it fits my requirements perfectly. But then, I suppose it would be good to know the rest."

She took him through the house, and as he went from drawing
room to ballroom to dining room to library to sleeping quarters,
James examined the furniture and the draperies and the paintings, and it occurred to him that, for the first time, he would
have a house in which he could hang a portrait of himself. There
was a portrait of the late John Penn over the mantelpiece in the
living room, and James could imagine his own likeness hanging
in that very spot. It would give the room a whole new character,
and he resolved to seek out the best portraitist he could find and
make an appointment.

When, finally, there was nothing more to see, Miss Allen took
him to the front door. "I am afraid it has a slightly gloomy air at
the moment," she said. "Under other circumstances it is really
quite cheerful."

"Believe me, it is perfect," James replied. "To whom should I
speak regarding the purchase?"

"You may speak to me," she said, with the trace of a smile. "And I will relay the message to my aunt."

"Then you may tell your aunt to set her price, and I will pay it. It is as uncomplicated as that."

Again she smiled, and James could see the little girl just beneath the surface. "Thank you, sir," she said. "I shall relay the message."

James got into his carriage, and as it headed down the drive toward the river he remembered that he had done nothing about starting divorce proceedings against Antonia. He made a mental note to consult a lawyer as soon as he got back, and see where the matter could most expeditiously be handled.

When he asked Morris the name of the best available portrait artist, the answer was unhesitating. "Gilbert Stuart," said Morris. "He's just back from England, where I hear they consider him another Gainsborough. He recently finished a portrait of the President, and already people are queuing up for copies. If you can get him to take you, he's the best."

"What do you mean, 'if'?" said James. "I haven't heard of the painter yet who was immune to money."

"True," said Morris. "But you may find you have to wait."

As it turned out, James did have to wait, but not for long. When at the end of about ten days he went to Stuart's studio, he found the painter sorting through stacks of stretched canvas, trying to bring some order into the cluttered room. In one corner, on an easel, was a head-and-shoulders likeness of the President and below it the sketched-in beginning of a copy, while along the walls were other portraits in various stages of completion. Stuart was forty years old, with a sharp, lean face, a large nose, and a small mouth that nevertheless showed traces of humor. James had worn his best blue-green velvet jacket, with a high collar and a full, lace neckpiece, and he felt ill at ease in the informality of the studio. To make conversation, he indicated the portrait of Washington and said, "That is an excellent likeness. Looks just the way he did last time I saw him."

Stuart grunted and put a freshly primed piece of canvas on the easel.

"I understand you are making copies," James went on. "I should count it a favor if I might have one."

"I'll put you down, but I won't guarantee delivery," Stuart replied. "There are thirty-one ahead of you, and I'm not sure I can paint it that many times, even with assistants. In the first place, I don't like it."

"Why not?" said James, taking the seat Stuart had indicated. "I think it's first rate."

"There's something wrong with it. I couldn't get him to relax, and it shows. He was the most difficult subject I ever painted." Stuart began mixing paint on his palette. "I finally said to him, 'Sir, just for the moment let us forget that you are the President of the United States and I am Stuart the painter,' and he replied, 'There is no possible way to forget that I am the President of the United States and you are Stuart the painter.' With an attitude like that, how could I do a good portrait?"

James glanced at the painting again. "It does seem slightly impersonal," he admitted.

"Impersonal is the kindest word I would use for it. And now I am commissioned to make thirty-one—thirty-two copies. I may very well cut my wrists first." He adjusted James's jacket, gave it a small tug to straighten the creases, and stood back. "All right, sir. If you would turn to your right, then look back at me, and relax. That's fine."

James had eight sittings, and as the likeness grew, so also did a small, nagging doubt grow in his mind. He did not doubt Stuart's ability to create an accurate portrait, but the more he looked at his own, the more he saw that something seemed to be wrong. The eyes, for instance: the left eye in no way resembled the right, and looking at them separately he seemed to have two totally different expressions. One was relaxed and pleasant, and the other was not at all pleasant. It seemed more cunning, even crafty. And yet the face was smiling and the overall impression agreeable. It was only when the parts were taken separately that they seemed to clash. When he mentioned this to Stuart, the painter shrugged.

"No two sides of any face are alike," he said. "In all the hundreds of faces I've painted, I can remember very few with perfect bilateral symmetry. In fact, those faces that *are* symmetrical tend to be dull and uninteresting. It's the way the good Lord made us, and it's not for me to change it. I only show it as I see it, not as it should be."

"Yes," said James, after a moment's thought. "There really isn't much we can do about it, is there?"

"Not one thing," said Stuart. "The only answer is to make the best of it."

21

Between them, James and Aaron Burr bought a large tract of
land in upstate New York from J. J. Angerstein, of London,
whom Scholten had mentioned five years earlier. The total price
was £24,000, of which they paid one half and gave their joint
bond to pay the remaining £12,000 by July of 1796. James then
mortgaged the property, first to one P. Livingston and then to
John Brown, and shortly thereafter sold 210,000 acres to a combine of Henry Newman, Thomas Dawes, Jr. (his sister Margaret's husband, who was a lawyer), his cousin Thomas Greenleaf, and his brother Daniel. The price was $200,000, to be paid
over four years with interest that would finally make it total
$230,000. He also borrowed £5,000 from Daniel, using his so-
called Amsterdam fund as security.

When he was in Boston, James had a long meeting with Daniel, in an attempt to set up some kind of system whereby his running expenses and various debts could be handled on a so-to-
speak day-to-day basis and not be allowed to accrue to a point
where the creditors became overanxious. "The problem is a simple one," James told his brother. "I am perhaps the third richest
man in the country, but my holdings are so diverse and so
widely scattered that they are not always convertible into ready
cash. What I need is someone, such as yourself, who will absorb
the petty expenses, in return for deeds to the properties commensurate with your expenditures. If I had to worry my head
about minor accounts, I would never have time for the important
business."

"I can oblige you up to a point," Daniel replied. "But my
funds are by no means unlimited. I cannot guarantee you the
moon."

"I don't intend that you do," said James. "But there must be others who will cosign a note every now and then."

"With what as security?"

"My Amsterdam fund, for one thing. That in itself is enough to guarantee any loan I might possibly need to make. In addition, there is this land in upstate New York, not to mention our holdings in the Federal City—believe me, security is the last thing you have to worry about."

"I believe you, but I must have concrete facts when I approach other people."

"Naturally. And you may tell them what I have just told you. If they need further proof, send them to me directly. Or look for other comakers—you are really doing these people a favor, you know. It is not everyone who has a chance to join in an enterprise that has a guaranteed future such as this. And, all other arguments aside, consider the fact that we have the backing of the Vice President of the United States, a man who in fact may very well become our next President. A person would be insane not to want to join."

"Is Mr. Adams involved in this?"

"For all practical purposes. He's a member of the family and therefore virtually a partner, and the last time I saw him he congratulated us on what we were doing in the Federal City. I don't know how much more backing you could ask for than that. And the President himself has offered to sell us some of his land—he made the offer to me personally—which I think is fair proof we are not some fly-by-night organization."

"Did you buy it?"

"As a matter of fact, we didn't. We felt it was too much of a risk. So if anyone asks you about our probity, you can say we turned down an offer from George Washington because it didn't meet our standards."

"What was the matter with it?"

"It's in Indian country, and the taxes are more than the land is worth."

"Why are the taxes so high?"

"Let us not become bogged down in a discussion of land values," James said. "Take my word for it, it was not worth the risk."

Daniel was quiet for a moment, then said, "I imagine Henry

Newman would cosign a note. And Brother Dawes. Cousin Thomas—yes, I suppose I could oblige you there."

"As I said, you are not only obliging me, you are doing yourselves a favor. Every dollar you invest now—and you may look on this as an investment—will be worth ten dollars five years from now."

"Will our notes appreciate with the value of the land?"

James cleared his throat. "That will depend on the terms of the loan. On an ordinary loan probably not, but the accrued interest will not be insignificant."

Daniel nodded. "Very well, then," he said. "I imagine this will be as sensible a course as any other."

"Splendid!" James said and slapped him on the knee. "Believe me, you'll not regret this."

When James had left, Elizabeth made one of her soundless entrances into the room, giving the impression she had been there all along. Daniel watched her as she puttered about, doing small, aimless things to the furniture by way of killing time before she spoke. Elizabeth never said anything suddenly; she would circle the subject in silence, like a wolf inspecting a trap, and appear to consider it from every angle before committing herself to speak. It was a pattern that had grown up in the last few years, and he theorized that if she had children to care for, she wouldn't find time so heavy on her hands. Now, as she slowly circled the room, he guessed what was on her mind and decided to help her bring it out.

"James seems to be doing quite well in business," he said. "From what he says, he's the third richest man in the country."

"Then why does he want to borrow money from you?"

"I'm not exactly lending him money . . . well, yes, I suppose in a way I am. But it is simply to allow him to concentrate on the large matters, while I take care of the small. It is more than one man can handle by himself."

Elizabeth was silent as she picked a bit of candle wax from a wall sconce. "I shall never forget him telling me about the McGoogle brothers and their hot-air balloon," she said. "He had me believing such things exist."

"They do. A balloon is a very real thing."

"But even if they didn't exist, he had me believing in them."

"But since they do exist, I don't understand your point."

"My point is that James is a very persuasive talker."

"Madam, if you are trying to imply that my own brother has lied to me, I think you had better reconsider your words."

"I am implying nothing. I am simply observing."

"Then I suggest you do your observing in some area where you are better acquainted with the facts."

"Have you any suggestions?"

The first answer that came to mind was a cruel one, and he left it unsaid. In trying to think of another he found that he was stammering, and he finally mumbled, "Anything—needlework—cooking—anything at all." To cover his confusion he turned and picked a clay pipe from the mantel, and when he turned back Elizabeth had vanished.

James and Mrs. Penn had no trouble coming to terms about the sale of Lansdowne, and in early July he prepared to move in. He had hoped, with complete lack of logic, that Miss Allen would still be there when he went out to supervise the moving, but she and her aunt had long since gone, leaving the house hollow and silent. James's footsteps echoed on the bare floors as he entered, carrying the Stuart portrait in both hands, and set it on the hook from which had hung the likeness of John Penn. Although the paint was dry, the picture still gave off a faint hint of linseed oil, and Stuart had instructed him to be extremely careful of it for the next six months, until it could be varnished. He straightened it as carefully as though it were a newborn infant, then stepped back to inspect the result. He was still troubled by the apparent two sides of his character, but when he consulted a mirror he found that Stuart had been as accurate as paint would allow and that was the way he looked. In fact, Stuart had heightened the flesh tones to give him an almost unnaturally healthy glow. All in all, he felt he couldn't complain, and if there were times when he looked the slightest bit crafty, then so be it. There was no question the portrait made him look successful, which was all that mattered.

He was still contemplating the picture when one of the moving men came in, bearing an envelope. "Begging your pardon, sir," he said, "we found this in the front hall. It looks to be addressed to you."

James recognized the handwriting as Ann Allen's, and he

opened the envelope so hastily he almost tore the letter in half.
It was a brief note, which read: "Dear Mr. Greenleaf: This will
wish you happiness in this house, which was built with great expectations. May you be the one to fulfill them. Most respectfully,
Ann Penn Allen." He reread the note, trying to find more in it
than was there, but the mere fact that she had written it was an
encouraging sign. He folded it carefully and put it in his inside
pocket, realizing as he did that the house had not been the best
of luck for its builder. Penn, a Loyalist, had fled to England during the War and rented it to William Bingham until his return in
1792, which gave him exactly three years to live in the house
until he died. Now it was up to James, the second owner, to realize its potential, and he was moving into it at a time when his career was about to blaze like a comet. Everything up to now had
been preamble; now was the time of fulfillment, and Lansdowne
would be the symbol of his success.

Morris, the next time James saw him, was not quite so san-
guine. "Have you heard from the Federal City commissioners
about our notes?" he asked.

"Not recently," James replied. "They said they would take
legal action if the notes weren't paid when they came due, but
that was last May and I've heard nothing since. I told them at
the time they might have to wait a bit, and nobody seemed too
perturbed."

"Well, the President is," said Morris. "He appears to be more
than a little upset."

"How do you know? Has he spoken to you?"

"Not directly. But he wrote Randolph and told him to tell me"
—he fished through a pile of papers and produced a letter from
which he read—"'in strong and earnest terms' that the most serious damage would be done to the federal building projects 'if
the deficiency, or part thereof, due on (our) contract, is not
paid.'"

"That is probably true," James replied. "But does he say how
he expects us to pay them without money?"

"No. But he adds that 'one can scarcely forbear thinking that
these acts are part of a premeditated system to embarrass the executive government.' In other words, he thinks we are deliberately withholding payment."

"That is patently absurd," said James. "And I trust you will tell him so."

"I shall," said Morris, "at the first opportunity. How much good it will do, is quite another matter."

As it turned out, the federal commissioners were more perturbed than James had thought. They took back a thousand city lots they had deeded to him as part of the collateral for the Dutch loan and were forced to turn to the banks for credit, where they owed $20,000. The image of James and Morris as benevolent patrons of the city began to fade, and in September the President wrote directly to Morris, urging him to pay up lest hundreds of people be thrown out of work. He added there were ugly rumors to the effect that he and James and Nicholson had gone into the deal for speculative purposes only, giving an impression he was sure Morris would wish to correct. Morris replied that he would gladly have paid the notes on the spot, but that a variety of James's harebrained schemes had tied up their ready cash and he was powerless.

James, operating on the theory that the more land they owned the more money they would be able to borrow, bought a hundred acres in New York, and two million acres in the southwest part of the country. Also, to repay his brother Daniel and his brother-in-law Thomas Dawes for the approximately $250,000 they had put up at various times, he transferred to them his deeds to the Amsterdam properties—without, however, producing the papers, which he said were unavailable at the moment. In all, he was able to show that he had made good on $110,845.89 of the notes countersigned by Daniel and $14,133.33 of the $17,500 indorsed by Thomas Greenleaf. Such was the general good will toward him that Daniel and Dawes had no hesitation in cosigning with him a note for $16,000 to Mrs. Elizabeth Russell, widow of Thomas Russell from whom James had borrowed £7,000 a year earlier.

There was less good will among his Boston creditors, whom Daniel had not been able to pay in full, and the mere fact that James had to call a meeting of them, asking for more time, was enough to destroy his name in that city. Some wanted him arrested on the spot, but the majority were content with token payments and the promise that the balance would be forthcoming shortly. The Bostonians were Daniel's problem; Thomas

Dawes, who was by now a judge, became a roving trouble-shooter, going to New York and Philadelphia and wherever necessary to bring some semblance of order into an increasingly jumbled situation. Looking for a root cause of the problem, he could only conclude that it was James's unbounded optimism, mixed with heavy doses of *naïveté*, that led him to make absurd business arrangements. When Dawes, with Thomas Greenleaf and Samuel Dexter as joint trouble-shooters, arrived in Philadelphia late in December of 1796, James had made the usual call for time to his creditors, who had given him only until the end of the year before they would seize his property and put it up for sale. Morris was, for the moment, out of the picture; he had been thrown from his horse after a ten-week visit to the Federal City and had holed up in his home on Market Street, hoping the trouble would blow away.

On December 29, on the rim of the deadline set by the creditors, Dawes was able to report good news to Daniel. His letter said, in part:

The day is broke and the Sun is shining on James's affairs. On the very last night depended his fate . . . The Creditors had several meetings; a Committee of the first characters in the city examined his debts, credit, and Estate, and reported last night such Facts as induced the Creditors to express unanimously that James had enough to pay, leaving a Residuum of two million Dollars. Yet strange to tell, this immense property had been placed by himself out of his power to answer emergencies, and so near had he come to losing it that an immense proportion of it was actually advertized . . . in the papers of this week *for sale;* . . . This is now stopped in mid career and the Creditors are unanimous in praise of James's accounts and his statements and of his fairness in coming forward and displaying the Truth, tho his imprudence in having so committed his property to the power & caprice of others is unjustifiable & without example.

One of the problems was the status of the so-called Angerstein notes, representing the land James and Burr had bought and James had subsequently mortgaged and then sold; not all the mortgage payments were up to date, and bits of land were slipping away for lack of title verification and lack of security. James stoutly maintained that everything was in order and that only a little time would be required to straighten matters out, and he wrote long letters to Daniel explaining everything in such minute detail as to be virtually unreadable. His tone throughout was one of calm, tinged with regret that he was misunderstood by so many people, and assuring one and all that everything would work out well in the end. His greatest regret, he said, was the damage that had been done to his reputation in Boston, and the grief and embarrassment this had caused those dearest to him.

On January 1, 1797, Dawes, who with Dexter and Thomas Greenleaf had been struggling with James's tangled affairs, wrote to Daniel from Philadelphia, expressing guarded optimism and concluding: "Upon the whole it would be Ingratitude to complain To Day, tho' it is impossible to forget the Despair of yesterday. Trust in God!"

Noah Webster, however, was neither so forgiving nor so hopeful. On January 5 he wrote to Daniel:

> The intelligence we have lately received respecting the pecuniary situation . . . is extremely distressing. Becca is quite overcome with anxiety for all that are in trouble, but especially for her aged parents . . . How happy should I have been to have undeceived you all, in respect to JG, two years ago! But my tongue was tied. Such were the prejudices of the family in his favor, that to *tell the truth* would have blasted my reputation with the family. I knew his baseness years ago, & thanks to my good fortune, I quarrelled myself out of his clutches. Had it not been for the dearest connection, I should not have borne his insolence, but he or I must have fallen a victim to my *just* indignation two or three years ago. Nothing short of terrible disasters would convince you all of his want of principle . . . I have known for three years that J was in the path of ruin—converting, with astonishing zeal & folly, good property into bad—I knew he was wantonly & deliberately feeding a long train of *whores & rogues*. But I could not believe till lately, that he would rob his innocent friends for that purpose—It is too much—I drop the subject.

Daniel went over the letter several times, wondering what the specifics were beneath Webster's generalities, and wondering also why Webster had waited so long to discharge his venom. The excuse that it would have put him in bad with the family was a weak one and made his whole tirade sound like an afterthought, born of some recent grievance. It seemed to Daniel that Webster was afflicted with crystal-clear hindsight, distorted by a rage of unknown origin. He put the letter in a pigeonhole in his desk, where it joined a growing stack of letters from and about James.

Three weeks later, he received a letter from James that dealt with the business of the moment, and ended:

> Could you, my Brother, witness the agitation of my mind you would not doubt my love for you & my determination to guard you from ultimate Injury, even tho' I count by it my own destruction— The unremitting Labour of mind and Body to which I am subjected is daily rendering Life more unpleasant to me and if I know myself nothing binds me to it, but the wish to heal the wounds I have occasioned and the dread of inflicting new ones . . . Farewell my dear Daniel, continue in the assurance of my devoting every faculty of my mind & employing every resource to extricate you from the difficulties I have certainly not intentionally occasioned you— My love as usual and believe me etc.

Daniel produced Webster's letter from the pigeonhole and, placing it next to James's, compared the two. Nowhere in James's could he find a hint of a man who would "rob innocent friends" or wantonly "feed a long train of whores & rogues," and this strengthened his earlier feeling about Webster. The more he thought of it, the more he realized that the idea of a man "wantonly & deliberately feeding a long train of whores & rogues" was an impossible one, conceived out of pure malice. It conjured up a picture of James, with apron, ladle, and soup tureen, catering to a noisy line of bawds, pimps, slatterns, and footpads, who sang rowdy songs and reviled him with low talk while he filled their bowls. The picture was so ludicrous that he laughed out loud, and as he was refolding the letters he realized Elizabeth was in the room.

"I am happy you find something that amuses you," she said. "Might I share it?"

"In truth, it isn't all that amusing," he replied.

"But you were laughing."

"There are many different kinds of laughter."

"I should be happy to settle on any kind. It seems a long time since I last laughed."

Daniel took a deep breath and let it out slowly. "Is something troubling you?" he asked.

"Nothing new. Is it wrong to want to laugh?"

"Madam, there are times when laughter is appropriate and times when it is not."

"But you were laughing just now."

"It was not funny. I was laughing at the idiocy of a figure of speech."

"I would you could teach me to laugh at things that are not funny. My day would be considerably brighter."

"Then laugh. Laugh at anything."

"Should I laugh when the butcher reminds me about his bill? Should I laugh when the dressmaker says she has not been paid since the first of the year? Should I laugh when—"

"Very well, very well, you may tell those people they'll be paid. I am simply short of cash at the moment, because of—because of—"

"Because of James?"

"If you insist, yes. But it is only a temporary shortage. He assures me that money will be forthcoming shortly. Besides, my credit is still good. There is no reason why—"

He was interrupted by sudden laughter from Elizabeth. It started quietly, almost like a suppressed cough, then rose to a whinny and finally a shriek, and she threw her hands in the air and laughed at the ceiling until her face turned red. Daniel watched, stunned, as she tottered from the room, and he could hear her laughter echoing through the house and becoming fainter as she climbed the stairs.

22

Antonia was just returning home when James's letter arrived. She had dined, the night before, with Rutger Schimmelpenninck, and as usual one thing had led to another until she found herself spending the night with him. Now, feeling slightly gritty in last night's clothes and tender in the frontal area of her pelvis, she took the letter from the postal delivery man, dismissed him before he could make his usual observation about the weather, and let herself into the house. She was greeted by Billy, now officially known as Willi, who had been watching for her in the window. From upstairs came the sounds of five-year-old Marie berating her nurse.

"Where have you been, Mama?" Willi asked in Dutch.

"Out for dinner," Antonia replied, opening the letter and starting to read.

"You must have had a lot to eat," Willi observed. "Was it good?"

"Very nice," Antonia replied. "Now be quiet and let Mama read her letter."

"Who is it from?"

"Nobody you know."

MADAM [the letter read]: This will advise you that I have this day instituted Divorce proceedings, as you requested. Upon investigation I have found that the State of Rhode Island is the most expeditious in these matters, and I am therefore, and for the nonce, considering myself a Resident of that State. You will be advised when the matter is brought to a conclusion, and will, I trust, understand when I say that at the moment my financial situation will not permit me to provide you with any money in the settlement. It is my dearest wish that I should be able to contribute to the support & upbringing of our Son, but such is my financial embarrassment that I am daily in fear of a visit from the Sheriff. My only comfort, where Billy is concerned, is the knowledge that you have ample Funds of your own with which to provide for him. Trusting, Madam, that this finds you well, I am yours etc.

Antonia looked at the date of the letter, which was January 7, and saw that it had taken slightly over three months to arrive. He had not said how long the divorce would take, but it was a good bet it would not yet have been achieved. The probable grounds, although he had not specified that either, would be desertion, in which case the final decree might take as long as a year, but she was in no mood to wait and see; what she was going to do, she would do immediately, before anybody else had the same idea. Without waiting to wash or change, she ordered the coachman to have the carriage made ready.

"Where are you going now, Mama?" Willi asked, as she put the letter in her reticule.

"Important business," she replied. "Why don't you go play with your soldiers?"

"They broke," said Willi.

"Then play with something else." Willi drifted upstairs, and she went outside to wait for the carriage.

Mynheer Walraven, her attorney, was engaged with a client when Antonia arrived, but when the office boy informed him of her presence, he shunted the client into another room and went out to greet Antonia.

"This is an unexpected pleasure, Baroness," he said. "Would you care to step inside?" She swept into his office and took a chair, and he closed the door gently and said, "How may I be of service to you?"

"You may prepare an arrest," she replied.

Walraven waited a moment, then said, "Of?"

"Of all my husband's property held by Crommelin and the others."

"I see." Walraven sat at his desk and took out a sheet of paper. "Now, the basic facts. Your full name—"

"Antonia Cornelia Elbertina Scholten."

"Occupation?"

She hesitated. "Housewife."

"Married to—"

"James Greenleaf."

"A resident of—"

"North America."

Walraven's pen made scratching noises as, with Antonia supplying the details, he wrote: ". . . does by my subscribed messenger *Arrest* Under their rule and management by Daniel Crommelin & Sons, also by Pieter Godefroy, Rutger Jan Schimmelpenninck, Jan van Loon jr., Robert Daniel Crommelin and Anthony Mylius, all cash, stocks, goods, certificates and legal documents, under instructions of the U.S.A., acts (certificates) in the bank of the U.S., or other funds, proof of property of inherited estates in N. America and also of landed property, acts and credits as owned, arriving of direct or indirect concerning aforementioned James Greenleaf," and so on, until all the legal frills of the lien had been completed.

"Very well," Walraven said, at last. "I shall have the clerk prepare copies, and if you would care to return tomorrow you may inspect the final draft before I give it to Tellingen to deliver."

"Who is Tellingen?" she asked.

"He is the official messenger. He is the one who technically performs the arrest."

"Can't he do it today? I would like this to be registered as soon as possible."

"Unhappily, no. It will take some time to prepare the copies. But I can assure you, the matter of a day or so will make no difference."

When, the following day, she arrived at Walraven's office, she found him less brisk than usual. The papers were in front of him, all neatly copied, but instead of giving them to her, he looked up at a corner of the ceiling, then folded his hands. "An interesting thing happened last evening," he said.

"Oh?" said Antonia, sensing trouble.

"Yes. I dined with my attorney friend Lieblink, and in the course of conversation it came out that last week—precisely one week ago, to be exact—he served an identical arrest to yours on Crommelin, at the behest of one John Julius Angerstein, of London. It would appear that your husband has several people who are anxious to—ah—arrest his holdings."

Antonia's jaw tightened. "And what does that do to my claim?" she said. "Shouldn't the wife have precedence?"

"Essentially, it does nothing to your claim," Walraven replied. "It just means there is one more person to share in the proceeds."

"But it will diminish the amount that I get."

"Inevitably. But when there are many creditors, no one person may expect it all. If you had filed suit a week before this Angerstein, it would still have been the same. And there may well be others; Lieblink tells me that Crommelin themselves have been instructed by a Mr. Daniel Ludlow, of New York, to institute an arrest. Who knows—in the end there may be more plaintiffs than there is property."

Antonia considered this for a few moments, then said, "So long as he himself doesn't get anything, I don't really care what else happens."

"I can assure you, Baroness," Walraven said, "that you need not concern yourself in that regard."

When James had posted his letter to Antonia, he walked through the snow to Morris's house in a strangely euphoric mood. The meeting of his creditors had exonerated him of any wrongdoing, and he felt as though a load had been lifted from him, leaving him free to operate as he saw fit. He had passed through a period of trial and had emerged vindicated—or nearly so—and now all that remained were minor details, such as Nicholson's attacking him in the newspapers. For reasons best known to himself, Nicholson had seen fit to warn the public that James's holdings were of cloudy title and dubious authenticity, to which James had replied with attacks of his own, advising people not to buy any of Nicholson's holdings without first consulting him, James, to make sure their titles were clear. It was all irritating, but of no great moment, and nothing that could affect him in the long run. There was still his Amsterdam fund, and beyond that the unlimited financing that Van Vliet had promised, and between them he was assured of all the operating capital he needed. The main thing was not to let the control get out of his hands; the creditors' report had blamed him for entrusting his money to others, and it was a mistake he did not intend to repeat. He and he alone would be in charge of his destiny, and in that way he could never fail.

He found Morris in a gloomy mood, having recovered physically from his fall from the horse but still mentally bruised and depressed. He looked up as James was ushered into the room and made a low grunt in place of a greeting. "You," he said.

"Whom did you expect?" James replied. "Marie Antoinette?"

"I am past expecting anything except trouble. I have a horrible feeling that history is about to repeat itself."

"In what way?"

"If you and Nicholson don't stop attacking one another in the press, you'll destroy the whole syndicate. I don't care what you do to each other, but I don't want to be ruined because you two are having a public tiff."

"He started it. I reserve the right to defend myself against any attacks on my integrity. You get him to stop, and I shall be glad to."

"It is not only nonsense, it's dangerous. You both ought to know better."

"That is as may be, but I fail to see how history is repeating itself. What did you mean by that?"

Morris leaned back. "People," he said. "Taken as individuals, they can be estimable, but taken as a mob, they have no more brains than sheep. I have spent the better part of my life doing things for people, and twice I have had to barricade myself against the vengeance of the mob. By now I have learned to tell the signs, and I can see it happening again."

"When did you have to barricade yourself?" James asked.

"The first time was during the War, back in '79. There was some rioting because of the price of flour, and finally a few of us had to hole up in Jim Wilson's house, on Third Street. We—"

"Who is 'us'?" James interrupted.

"Merchants, importers. Conservatives. We were hounded by a rabble of perhaps two hundred people, who'd come equipped with, among other things, two cannon, and we turned Jim Wilson's house into a fort. Captain Campbell opened a window to shout at the mob, and he was shot dead. I thought we were done for until Joe Reed arrived with troops and scattered the rioters." He paused, as though sorting through his memory, then said, "The other time, in '83, I didn't have to barricade myself; I had to leave town. The troops mutinied for their back pay and surrounded the State House, and all of Congress plus Gouverneur and I—I was Superintendent of Finance at the time—headed for

Princeton and Trenton until things quieted down. I don't know what would have happened if we'd stayed, but it wouldn't have been pleasant. Those troops were in an ugly mood."

"And what do you think is going to happen now?"

"Creditors. Unless we can find some means of satisfying our creditors, they're going to be onto us like any other mob."

"I really wouldn't worry about that. I just had a meeting of my creditors, and they were quite understanding. They admitted they were puzzled by a few minor matters, but all in all they were very encouraging."

Morris gave him a sour look. "That is not the way I heard it," he said.

"I presume you must have been listening to Nicholson. Well, let me tell you—"

Morris held up a pudgy hand. "Softly, sweet prince," he said. "Do not embroil me in your feud with Nicholson. I have enough on my mind as it is."

James stopped, controlling his temper with effort. Searching for a way to make his point, he remembered the story of Morris's father's dream that foretold his death, and he wondered if this might be the chance to put it to use. Whatever happened, it could do no harm. Pretending to change the subject, he said, "Do you believe in dreams?"

Morris looked at him with interest. "What do you mean?"

"Do you believe dreams can foretell the future?"

"Not as a general rule. Why?"

"I had a dream the other night, and it is as clear as though it were happening now. You were riding along Pennsylvania Avenue, and then suddenly your horse threw you and you landed in a swamp. It must have been quicksand because you began to sink, and you called out to Nicholson and me for help. Nicholson jumped in and clutched you around the neck—only your head was showing by now—and then he began to sink with you, and you were both going under when I threw you a rope, which you took in your teeth, and I pulled you out. Nicholson sank, and big bubbles came out of the quicksand. I can still see them—bubbles as big as apples."

Morris was silent for a while. "Very interesting," he said, at last. "What do you make of it?"

"It is obvious what it means. The only question is whether you believe it an accurate forecast."

"Did you ever hear about my father's dream?"

"I can't say that I did." James was casual to the point of disinterest.

"He had a dream that forecast his death in minute detail, and it all came true a day later."

"How remarkable."

"But he was a man of great psychic powers. I don't believe there are many men who could match him in that respect."

James shrugged. "That is certainly one way to look at it. On the other hand"—he left the sentence hanging.

"Take your dream, for instance. The meaning is clear, but how do you propose to save me? How is it that your dream might be realized?"

James thought for a moment, then suddenly saw a chance for escape. His partnership with Morris and Nicholson was slowly beginning to dissolve, and it was just possible he might get clear before the whole business fell apart. "I could save you," he said, carefully, "by selling you my interest in the syndicate. I will accept your paper, so there need be no cash transfer, and you will have the entire operation to run as you see fit. I don't believe you can ask for a better bargain than that."

Morris was quiet for a long time, staring into James's eyes. James returned the stare, knowing that to look away would be to lose. Finally, in a voice so low as to be almost inaudible, Morris said,

"Agreed."

James could scarcely conceal his delight. Once he got Morris's paper, he would have a hold on him much more binding than any partnership, and one that he could use to his own best interests. "I shall have the agreement drawn up this afternoon," he said, and as he walked to the door he knew that his faith in himself would be fully justified. He now had the upper hand, and nothing could stop him.

In Boston, Daniel sorted through the latest letters from and about James, trying to find a pattern that might give some slight hint to his brother's—and thereby his—future. By now he had so committed himself to James's affairs that his own were inextricably intertwined with them, and he had the feeling that unless something good happened to James in the near future, he, Daniel, would be forced to sell his business and move elsewhere. He had cosigned so many notes and tied up so much of his negotiable worth, as well as his credit, that he was powerless, and he knew that others like Newman and Dawes and several Greenleafs were in the same position. The latest letter from Dawes, dated March 3, told of mounting discontent at James's failure to produce the Amsterdam papers, which he was constantly using as collateral but always keeping in his own possession. The letter ended on a note of total disenchantment and despair.

Daniel looked at the next letter, which was written by James some three weeks later, and from it deduced that Dawes had stated his disappointment directly to James, because the letter said, in part:

> Have had one from Mr. Dawes which I believe was written for the express purpose of driving me to madness and desperation . . . I shall be writing if required to make a general assignment of all my pledged and unpledged property for the use of my Creditors, and . . . will give all the Amsterdam contracts and an order for about 14,000 pounds in State Certificates . . . in a word I will do *everything*, provided I can procure the complete exoneration of my Indorsers in Boston, but without that I will consent to nothing, as I am too well convinced from the bitter experience of the past few Months that the more I part with power the less money have I to expect for myself and my friends. I remain unalterably etc.

But Dawes had more on his mind than driving James to madness and desperation, because on April 19 he wrote Daniel a letter from Worcester, containing forty dollars and saying:

> Please deliver to my beloved Peg the enclosed money I collected unexpectedly from an Insurgent whose cause I pled years ago. She may want it, as we are now poor and as I did not leave her as well shod as usual.
>
> As to James's affairs, his notes have sold for Five Cents in the Dollar at Philadelphia. Fifty years would not retrieve him. Are we to lie down & die without making one more struggle for Security?

The material about James had grown to a point where it no longer fit in a pigeonhole, and Daniel kept it in a large envelope, with newspaper items interspersed between the letters in as close to chronological order as he could manage. The clippings arrived at irregular intervals, depending more on chance than anything else, and thus it wasn't until April that Daniel learned of the so-called newspaper war between James and Nicholson and then, later, Morris and Nicholson combined. The exchange, most of which took place in the Washington *Gazette*, grew more and more vituperative, and finally, on April 22, James wrote an open letter to Morris and Nicholson, saying,

> I may confidently retort your aspersions and menaces with contempt and defiance . . . I have been despoiled of my property, but my integrity, and that peace of mind, which is the inseparable concomitant of integrity, you can never destroy.

Daniel filed the clipping in its proper place, wishing as he did that James would stop being quite so shrill about his integrity. A feeling of gloom settled over him, brought on by his inability to find one spark of hope in the whole situation. James and all those around him seemed to be sailing into a monstrous void, like the ancient mariners' picture of falling off the edge of the world, while James stood on the poop deck and loudly proclaimed his integrity. It was a picture that would have been comical if its implications weren't so disastrous, and Daniel was therefore unable to understand the next letter to him from James, written April 29. It discussed various business matters, and concluded:

> My property is so implicated in every quarter that I can come at the use of no immediate means at any sacrifice.—But I am expecting relief & as soon as I receive it, will impart it to you. My love to all Friends—

What possible relief can he be expecting? Daniel wondered. Where, in all this morass of phantom papers and vanishing assets and clamoring creditors, was there one small item on which he could base any hope? *He* could find none, and if James could, then he owed it to the others to be more specific. He, Daniel, now had his own creditors to worry about, and he would like to be able to give them something more than broad generalities about the future.

James's cause for hope had come at a time when, with increasing frequency, he had found himself toying with the idea of suicide. After less than two years' ownership he had been forced to sell Lansdowne, which was snapped up by William Bingham, its former tenant, for a mere $39,050. The only thing he salvaged was the Stuart portrait, which he took with him to his other, less ornate, house on Front Street in Philadelphia. In March he had applied to the state legislature for an act of insolvency, which, if granted, would prevent his being imprisoned for his debts, but the length of time it took the legislature to act on such a plea, and the number of people who might protest it, made it unlikely that he could expect any immediate relief from that quarter. Then, thanks to some investigative work by Billy Cranch, he found out that of the six million acres Morris bought for the North American Land Company in 1795, two and a third million acres were worthless pine barrens in the Georgia swampland. With Morris and Nicholson's paper up for public sale, its value would be destroyed if the public became aware of this worthless land, and James realized that he now had a handy club to hold over the heads of his former partners. He wasn't sure yet how he would use it, but in his desperation he was willing to do anything.

Then one day he received a visit from a stranger, who gave his name as Loder and said he had important business to discuss. James, who was becoming increasingly nervous about creditors, had instructed the servants not to admit anyone who would not state his business at the door, and when the butler reported that Loder would speak to nobody but the master, James ordered him sent away. The butler withdrew and reappeared in a minute.

"He says he comes from Mynheer van Vliet, sir," he reported. "He says you will understand."

James smiled. "Send him in," he said.

Loder was a short man, with an air of thinking of something other than the business at hand. His words seemed almost like afterthoughts, while his mind took in his surroundings and registered them for some unknown purpose. He sat in the chair James offered, and after looking around to make sure the door was closed he said, "Mynheer van Vliet sends greetings."

"Thank you," said James. "And mine to him."

"He says he understands you have bought the land he requested."

James hesitated. "I did not say precisely that. I said I knew where they *could* be bought."

Loder looked out the window, as though expecting something to appear. "But you do not have deed to it?"

"Let me put it this way," James said. "Have you brought the payment with you?"

"Some."

"How much?"

"That will depend on the land."

"Van Vliet said he was prepared to offer unlimited funds."

"That is as may be. I do not have unlimited funds on my person."

"How much do you have?"

"I repeat, that will depend on the land."

James thought for a moment. "Do you have enough to pay for two million acres? To be precise, two and one third million?"

For the first time, Loder's expression changed. His eyes widened slightly, and he said, "For how much?"

"Two million dollars."

Loder, who had become tense, relaxed. "Impossible."

"Then how much do you have?"

"At one dollar an acre?"

James, sensing he had the advantage, said, "I repeat, how much do you have?"

"Five hundred thousand dollars."

James shrugged, as though the conversation were ended.

"Given time, I could produce more." Loder was clearly anxious.

"In that event, leave what you have as security with me, and we will have a further discussion later." There was a long pause, and James said, "Those are the only terms I will consider. Van Vliet talks of unlimited funds, and then produces a paltry half million; you may tell him he is fortunate I will talk to you at all."

Loder reached into his jacket and produced a bundle of papers, which he handed to James. As James was examining them, Loder said, "They are secured by the Bank of New Orleans. They are completely valid."

James put them in his desk drawer. "When you find an equal amount, we will arrange for a transfer of land titles." He had no idea what titles, but he had a feeling that the Georgia pine barrens could very well enter into the transaction. With the pressure he could now exert on Morris and Nicholson, he could operate pretty much as he chose.

James's next letter to Daniel was written May 16, and after discussing the transfer of some land in Vermont to Daniel's account, he wrote:

My soul shudders when I contemplate the Evils I have innocently inflicted on you and others who have lent your names for my aid and support, and I should fall a victim to the heart-rending reflections I am incessantly tormented with, did I not feel the fullest conviction that an entire reparation, at a time not far distant, will be made you . . . I shall seal up the Amsterdam papers & place them out of my own reach since it seems to be required of me— I shall place them however out of the reach of any other person, until by cooperating with me, they are made to produce the fullest effect they are capable of . . . By the most unlooked-for good fortune I have obtained a further large security from M.&N. and have so much increased my power over them, that they must be forced to render me justice or submit to a yoke that will bear them on to destruction.—The difficulties I have still to go through with, before I can repair all the Injuries I have occasioned, and reestablish even the shadow of my past good fortune I am aware will be very great; yet still I should feel confident of being able to surmount difficulties of even greater magnitude could I but carry along with me the *suffrages* instead of the *execrations* of injured friends, and establish the general & *just* Belief that I have been misled by *error of calculation* or *weakness of intellect* & not (as I am accused of) *by badness of heart* . . .

I shall soon make some remittances for the general family benefit— They may be at first small but will, I trust, go on increasing—at all events, those who look up to me for happiness cannot be left destitute, even tho' *I* should be totally swept away— Farewell, my dear Daniel, give my love to every individual of the family particularly to your Betsey & Sister Dawes whose kind & affecting letter I have this moment received & will soon answer. Believe me your unalterable & affectionate friend & brother

Near the end of July Daniel received a letter from James that was barely legible, apparently written by a demented person in a spasm of rage and frustration. It castigated his creditors and one-time friends and gave the appearance of being the final curse of a dying man. Although it did not say so, it came from the Prune Street jail.

23

What happened was that James's creditors became tired of waiting. All the talk of the Amsterdam fund and the Angerstein land and the Federal City lots produced nothing in the line of ready cash, and no amount of juggling of the books could cover it up. Every source of credit had dried up, and the liabilities seemed only to multiply. Finally, in desperation, James withdrew from Tobias Lear's dock and warehouse in Washington, and he sold his share in the Washington Brewery, which he had only recently established in partnership with one Dr. C. Coningham, an English physician. Lear, blaming James for his failure in business, was taken back into Washington's household, but James had no womb to which to return.

On July 10, 1797, a sheriff's officer appeared at his door. It was a moment he had dreamed of and dreaded; he had even, in periods of panic, bolted the door against all strangers, and now that the time had come, it seemed faintly unreal. The officer was a thin man, with frayed cuffs; one of his stockings was wrinkled, and there was a worn spot on the front of his tricorn hat where his thumb and fingers gripped it. He removed the hat and stepped inside, and said, "Are you Mr. James Greenleaf?" James nodded numbly, aware of a ringing in his ears, and the officer handed him a paper and said, "Will you come with me, sir?"

James took the paper and, without looking at it, said, "May I pack my belongings?"

"Necessities only," the man replied. "You won't be needing frills."

James's memory of the rest of the day came in flashes, each scene more unreal than the last. There was their approach to the Walnut Street prison, with its domed cupola, its rows of barred windows, and the long flight of steps leading to the front door; there was the overpowering stench of sweat and filth the moment they stepped inside; the walk down dim corridors that rang with their footsteps and the groans and shouts and cries of half-seen prisoners; and finally there was the scene in the annex, known as the Prune Street jail, where he was booked and then locked in a room with several other men. The Prune Street jail, being for debtors only, had what might facetiously be called a better class of prisoners, but the absence of felons, thieves, and cutthroats was a negative advantage only, and one that was almost unnoticeable at first glance. Those who could afford it had private rooms, but newcomers and the destitute were thrown together in an atmosphere that differed very little from the Walnut Street side of the prison.

For ten days James lay almost in a coma, and then he pulled himself together and began to see what could be done to improve his condition. By promising to pay an outrageous sum, he managed to secure a room to himself, and by borrowing paper from one man, a pen from another, and ink from a third, he was able to write a letter to Daniel. He found that his mind was so distorted that he could think of nothing but the various people who, he felt, were responsible for his being there, and he also found that his handwriting was affected to the point where the letter was blotted and blurred and virtually illegible. Something in the back of his mind told him it was a pointless exercise, but he sent it off anyway, if for no other reason than that it was action of a sort, instead of stagnation. Stagnation, he knew, would be his greatest enemy, because it would strangle any attempts to get free. He thought briefly of writing to John Adams a plea for executive clemency—certainly Adams, now President of the United States, could not afford to have a member of the family languish in jail—but then he decided to wait until his handwriting improved and his mind was a little clearer. Nothing would be gained by writing gibberish.

Meanwhile, Dawes and Daniel and the others were trying to make some kind of sense out of his affairs and to convert whatever assets they could find into cash. Even Webster's aid was enlisted, and from him came the first ominous note about the overseas holdings.

He reported that one of James's creditors had just returned

from England, where he had attached some of James's goods that had been shipped to Hamburg and had received his money as a result. Apparently other creditors were doing the same, and the suspicion began to grow that the Amsterdam notes might also have been attached. Nothing official had been heard, but the notes were no more invulnerable to attachment than any other asset, and until something definite came through they would have to be considered of questionable value. Webster further reported that the Angerstein land was so heavily mortgaged that it was all but useless and that "the active capital of our country is taken by the French and English—it is not to be had." He wished James would sign the land over to "a man of capital" but said that James was "so much alarmed for fear some persons will *speculate* on his property, that he will let you all go to ruin."

Among those who were the most anxious about the Amsterdam notes was John Appleton, James's sister Priscilla's husband, to whom James had sold his share in the Washington Brewery and whose security, like Daniel's and the others', was dependent on James's holdings. On September 2 Appleton wrote to Daniel, pleading for assurance that he might realize something and pointing out that his losses through James's other deals had brought him to the rim of disaster. If the Amsterdam holdings fell through, he said, he could foresee "nothing before me but the absolute ruin of myself & Family, and I find my fortitude is not sufficient for me." Before Daniel could compose a coherent reply, the word came from Dawes via Webster that the Amsterdam property had been attached.

There were few details except that it had apparently occurred early in the year, and the main question was whether or not it was before or after the title had been transferred to Dawes. But even that could not alter the fact that for present purposes the property was worthless, and James's ready assets were virtually zero. An auction on September 1 had disposed of $60,000 worth of his notes, which in the circumstances was barely worth the trouble. To make matters worse, Philadelphia was in a financial panic; a hundred and fifty businesses had failed, and scores of businessmen went to jail; in Boston the banks had become careful to the point of paranoia, and even people with solid credit were suspect until they had proved their reliability.

Then, as though all this weren't enough, yellow fever broke out

again in Philadelphia. Like a fire in a peat bog it had smoldered
unseen for four years, and the memory of the previous outbreak
sent people pouring from the city like lemmings. They scattered
throughout the countryside while those less fortunate remained
behind and performed the standard prophylactic rituals—burning gunpowder, breathing camphor fumes, and dodging one another in the streets. The dead carts started their rounds and community graves were dug to take the victims.

By the end of September James had recovered his composure
enough to write a coherent letter: he reported to Daniel the grim
conditions surrounding him and concluded:

> I am beyond measure grieved by what is said & thought with
> regard to the Amsterdam Funds, but neither Mr. Dawes's vile
> abuse, nor Mr. Dexter's sage opinions will induce me to change ei-
> ther my sentiment or determination on that subject— If I live I will
> in some way or other be shortly exonerated from Debt and go per-
> sonally and defend that property for those to whom it belongs, for I
> best can defend it— Otherwise this property may be ravaged and
> devastated by the Boston Creditors in their own way, but while I
> have life my duty to them, to you, and to *myself* forbids it . . .
> Oblige me by handing the enclosed note for $50 to our unhappy
> father—it has fallen to me from the clouds & tho' wanting to my
> miseries I will not trust myself with it— Believe me, my dear
> Brother, most affectionately . . .

Inevitably the fever spread to the prison, where conditions
went from bad to unspeakable. Guards refused to touch the sick
and were reluctant to remove the dead, until finally other prisoners, from the Walnut Street side, were forced by whips to perform the necessary cleanup. James, in his own room, was spared
some of the more loathsome details; then he contracted the fever
and lay for two weeks in a state hovering between life and
death. The only good news he received was that his divorce from
Antonia had been approved, but in his condition this seemed so
trivial as to be hardly worth mentioning. His one hope for the future was that his petition for release under the act of insolvency
would be granted; he knew that as long as he remained in prison
he could look forward to nothing better than survival. This hope
was blasted near the end of November on the technicality of his
having used Rhode Island as his residence for the purpose of the
divorce. He wrote Daniel that

some of my personal Enemies, finding nothing to allege against me
on the score of rectitude of conduct, have retained several of the
most eminent Counsel to contest my rights to the benefits of the Insolvent Laws as a Citizen of Pennsylvania, by reason of my having
within two years availed myself of the rights of Citizenship in another State— And as the circumstance of proving myself a Citizen
of this State would have impaired if not invalidated the decree of
Divorce obtained in Rhode Island, I have no alternative but to
remain in Confinement until 10 Jan., which will complete six
months of Imprisonment & entitle me to enlargement as a Citizen
of any other State in the Union.

His ease of mind would not have been helped had he known
that Webster, in a letter written December 24 to Daniel, had
said of him:

His misfortunes have done him little good, as he attributes them *all*
to other people, when in fact his plans must have failed, had every
man he dealt with been honest.—They were all fundamentally
wrong.—If he has not learnt this, his distresses have failed of the
only good that could arise from them—that of *teaching him wisdom*.

On the other hand, he might have taken some thin comfort
from the fact that Morris's premonition about the future had
come true: Morris and Nicholson had barricaded themselves in
The Hills, which they had renamed "Castle Defiance," and were
busy holding off an army of creditors, attorneys, sheriff's
officers, and constables, some of whom were threatening to break
into the house by force and others vowing to shoot either Morris
or Nicholson should he appear in a window. Nicholson escaped
one night and fled to his family, but the siege continued, with
Morris and his gardener holding off the enemy who ringed them
on all sides. As the nights grew colder the besiegers built
bonfires on the lawn to keep themselves warm, and the gardener
conducted scouting expeditions to plot their positions and report
the existence of any potential ambush sites. All that was lacking
was field artillery to make it a standard military operation, and
Morris saw himself as a combination of Horatius at the bridge
and Leonidas at Thermopylae. "God help us," he said, at one
point, "for men will not."

The fever had abated, as it always did, with the advent of cold
weather, and January of 1798 found James trying in every way

he could to hasten his release. But the six months had not passed
before he could apply for a hearing, and an attempt to raise
money "by mortgaging my future services" fell flat, leaving him
faced with the possibility of being returned to the public cell. As
he wrote to Daniel,

> until I am liberated no engagement I could make would be valid
> . . . indeed so totally destitute is my present situation that I have
> not wherewith to pay my prison board . . . Toward the close of
> this month I have a hearing on my petition to the court if my
> health will permit—and as soon as I am liberated and have done
> some indispensable acts of justice to myself and others I shall quit
> this cursed country with a determination never more to return to it.
> Yr always affectionate brother—

Billy Cranch, who had now taken up residence in Washington,
was appointed overseer of what remained of James's estate. (He
was also, thanks to his uncle John Adams, subsequently made a
member of the Federal Commission and a judge of the United
States Circuit Court.) He was probably the one best equipped to
handle the thankless job, because during the years of litigation
that were to follow, he maintained a loyalty to James that out-
lasted even Daniel's once limitless patience. When Daniel, in a
letter to Cranch, referred wearily to some of James's security as
"mere moonshine," Cranch fired back a reply that was a model
of the legal mind at work. Dated January 28, 1798, it said, in
part:

> You ask whether they are "like some other of JG's security, *mere
> moonshine.*" You will pardon me if I ask whether you mean that JG
> has given you *mere moonshine* as bona fide security, knowing it to
> be but moonshine, with an intention to deceive you, and in what
> instances has he done this? You charge him with having *often* and
> *grossly* deceived you. The word *grossly* implies *intentionally.* Pray
> inform me whether I am so to understand it—and in what instances,
> and with what Circumstances such Deception was used. . . . Be-
> lieve me I regret the circumstances which have caused your misfor-
> tune, and I acknowledge the right of "misery to complain." But, my
> dear Brother, can not that Right be exercised without criminating a
> Brother, who has been dear to the heart of every one of us—in
> whose prosperity we have rejoiced, in whose Benevolence we have
> felt a pride, and in whose many virtues we have often exulted? The
> calumnies of Webster have been noticed by me only with silent

Contempt, because of the malicious pleasure which always accompanied his recital of any story which could tend to injure JG . . . and I could not trust my indignation with the power of Utterance without hazarding the peace of the family . . . Bro. James has petitioned the Court for his discharge under the Insolvent Act of Pennsylvania and the 26th of Feb is appointed to hear objections . . . I sincerely wish that no objection be made . . . Nancy joins me in the most affectionate remembrance—

James's poor health, which he had feared might prevent his attending the hearing, received a tremendous boost ten days before the scheduled date, when he learned that Morris had been booked in the Prune Street jail and consigned to the public cell. Apparently Morris had staved off the besiegers until February 15, when a sheriff's officer managed to get into the house and serve him with an arrest, and the next day he made the same long trip James had made seven months earlier. The effect on James's morale was electric; he had felt that he'd been singled out for punishment while the others went free, and to know that Morris was just beginning the nightmare was the next best thing to his own release. There was no word about Nicholson, but if Morris was jailed, then Nicholson could not be far behind, and this was an even more cheerful thought than the first. James had always felt that Nicholson was scheming against him and that somehow things might have worked out if he and Morris had been able to handle the business by themselves. As it turned out, Nicholson was also sent to jail, where he died in 1800, and Morris was not freed until August of 1801. Compared to them, James was lucky.

At his hearing, his friend Dexter was appointed attorney for the Boston creditors, while three of the more upstanding Philadelphia creditors were made trustees to receive assignment of his property, with Cranch in over-all charge. Almost immediately came word from Crommelin that the Amsterdam properties had been arrested before their assignment to Dawes and Daniel, thereby nullifying that transaction, and in all probability there would be very little residue once the various actions were settled. James was technically a free man, but the debris of his business continued to fall around him, like ashes from a volcano. He was literally without a roof over his head, and he turned to his friend Eckman for shelter until he could begin to reassemble his thoughts. Eckman took him in and lent him the money to buy new clothes, so he was able to burn those in which he had spent the last seven months.

A week after his release he was staring out the window at the slushy streets when he saw a familiar figure approaching the building. At first he couldn't identify it, but then as it came closer he saw it was Loder, Van Vliet's agent, and in a minute or so there was a knock at the front door. He heard voices, and then Loder was ushered into the room.

"How did you know where to find me?" James asked.

"Mr. Notley Young told me," Loder replied. "I believe he is one of your trustees."

James nodded. He'd forgotten that his freedom was from imprisonment only; his trustees were required to know his whereabouts at all times.

Loder glanced at the door, then sat down. There was nothing offhand about him this time; he spoke in a low voice, and his tone was urgent. "I have the money you requested," he said.

James closed his eyes for a moment, then said, "I fear you are too late."

"What do you mean?"

"I have no property. Everything has been taken from me."

"But this land was—"

"That land was part of my holdings. What once belonged to me has been assigned to my trustees, and if you wish anything, you must apply to them, like all my other creditors. I am afraid you may have a rather long wait."

There was a silence. "Do you know the importance of this land?" Loder said, at last.

"I was not told in so many words, but I assume it was for refugees. *Émigrés,* I believe the word is. If that is the case, I'm sorry."

There was another silence, then Loder said, "Very well. If you no longer have the land, you no longer have it."

"A very sensible way of looking at it. I congratulate you."

"I presume you still have the deposit."

This time it was James who paused. "I told you," he said slowly, "I have no property. Everything has been taken from me, and by that I mean everything."

Loder's face turned white, and his eyes bulged. "But that wasn't yours!" he said. "That was a deposit only!"

"Call it what you will, it went with everything else."

"It can't have! That's thievery!"

"This is a harsh world, Mr. Loder. When disaster strikes, it cares little what name it goes under. One man's thievery is another man's salvation and a third man's drop in the bucket. In the long run, it all ends up the same place."

"But"—Loder was breathing deeply, trying to find words.

"If you wish, I shall be happy to give you my note for it," James said. "You may present that to my trustees, who will list you among my other creditors. Should I do that?" He reached for a piece of paper, but before he could write anything Loder leaped from his chair and flung out of the room, and in a moment James heard the slam of the front door. There was silence for a few moments, and then Eckman appeared.

"Trouble?" Eckman asked.

James smiled thinly. "No more than usual."

"May I come in?"

"By all means. It will be a welcome relief."

Eckman entered and sat in the chair that was still warm from Loder. "What would you think of moving to Washington?" he asked.

"I had thought more of leaving the country," James replied. "There is no future for me here."

"I think the future lies in Washington."

"And your practice?"

Eckman waved a hand in dismissal. "Wherever a doctor goes, he can find patients. A doctor is simply a frustrated bystander, watching nature take its course. People feel better if he's in attendance, but for all the good he does, he might as well dance around the sickbed, clapping his hands and singing sea chanteys. I feel like a thief every time I accept a fee."

"Would it be any different in Washington?"

"It would be a change of scene. People here are becoming familiar with my beliefs and are turning to the more flamboyant witch doctors. I wish them all good health and long lives."

James looked out the window, wondering what it would be like to leave a civilized city and take up residence in the muddy shambles that was Washington. It would be a long time before it became a real city, and two years before the government was scheduled to move there, but perhaps that would be his best plan—to escape the opprobrium that surrounded him in Philadelphia and Boston and, with everyone else who was going to the capital, make a fresh start in new surroundings. There was a chance that some property might still be left him there, and once his debts were settled he could look forward to acquiring more land. There was always a chance to gain a foothold in the growing community. Looking at it that way, it was the only choice that made sense.

"When do you intend to leave?" he asked.

"As soon as the weather improves," Eckman replied. "This is no time to travel, but come spring we could make the trip with ease."

"Very well. We've come this far together; I see no point in going separate ways now."

Eckman smiled. "This may be the best decision you've made so far."

"I hope so," said James. "I fervently hope that you're right."

One other event occurred that brought him a glimmer of hope. He received a letter from Ann Allen—almost a letter of condolence—saying how distressed she'd been to hear of his ill fortune and wondering if perhaps there weren't a jinx of some sort on Lansdowne, which destroyed its owners before they could fully enjoy it. She hoped things would be better for him in the future, and if there was anything she or her family could do to be of assistance, she wanted him to call on them. She closed by saying she could always remember his kindness to her aunt in her time of bereavement (my *kindness?* he thought; I was just intent on getting the house), and she wished she might in some way be able to repay it. She remained his faithful and obedient so on and so on.

James read and reread the letter until he virtually had it memorized, trying to fathom the reason behind it. It would have been one thing to have written it to an old friend, but to write it to a man she had met exactly once was highly unusual, and so out of the pattern of accepted ladylike behavior that some compelling force must have driven her to do it. The only such force he could imagine was himself. Recent events had pulverized his self-esteem to such a degree that he found it hard to believe he was attractive to anyone, but he could think of no other reason for the letter, and he clutched at it and magnified it until in his own mind it had become a proposal of marriage. He immediately sent off a reply, not exactly accepting this imagined proposal but indicating warm personal sentiments and saying that he would inform her as soon as he had an address in Washington to which she could write. He almost added "or visit," but his New England sense of delicacy told him not to rush matters or he might upset the whole structure. For the first time in many months he began to have pleasant dreams instead of nightmares, and he even found himself humming snatches of tunes as he went about preparing to move. He saw Ann as a herald of the new life that was about to begin for him and vowed that, if possible, he would make her a part of it.

He and Eckman moved in the early spring, before the roads had dried out, and they arrived in Washington looking like refugees from the Great Dismal Swamp. Amidst all the other construction there were the incompleted houses he and Morris had begun, bleakly reminding him of his dreams of glory, and he promised himself that as soon as he was able he would see to it that they were finished. He no longer knew who owned them, but imagined it might be Thomas Law, who had bought up a good deal of the syndicate property. At the moment, however, there was nothing James could do; simple survival was the best he could hope for. His first move, as he had written Daniel, was to try to re-establish his good name and then to start making restitution to those who had been most grievously hurt on his behalf. Daniel had been forced to move to Quincy, where he was once more setting up as a druggist, and for him there could be no restitution commensurate with his loss, but any sign of good faith would be welcome. He had heard that Daniel and Dawes and Newman were constantly being brought into court and sued for various notes of his they had cosigned, and he could only hope that somewhere, in the not too distant future, he could find the money with which to reimburse them. But until then, there was no point worrying about them; his first duty lay to himself.

There were perhaps two thousand residents of Washington when James and Eckman arrived, and the city consisted of one hundred square miles of reddish mud, dotted here and there with houses and liberally sprinkled with tree stumps. Only the most wild-eyed optimist could visualize it as the nation's capital, but James found comfort in the fact that he and the city could grow together, and with luck both would prosper equally.

His first hint that the past was still dogging him occurred one night in December 1798. Eckman came back to the rooming house, put down his bag of medicines, and shook the snow from his coat, then in an offhand way said, "What do you know about a Captain Duncanson?"

"Duncanson?" James replied. "What's his full name?"

"William Mayne Duncanson. He is apparently a friend of Thomas Law's."

"I've never heard of him. Why?"

"He lost all the money he invested in the city, and he is now blaming you."

"Blaming *me*? For what?"

Eckman shrugged. "I know only what I hear."

"Is he saying this in public?"

"He must be. I heard it from a man who heard it from someone who said he heard Duncanson denouncing you."

"What was he saying?"

Eckman hesitated. "Nobody is very clear. It seems rather generalized."

James felt his face beginning to burn. "I am accustomed to abuse," he said, "but if he so much as questions my integrity—does anyone know his exact words?"

"Not that I have heard. I think it could best be characterized as random vilification."

"I'll have him in court!" James said. "I'll retain Billy Cranch, and I'll strip him of every farthing—"

"I don't believe he has many farthings to be stripped of," Eckman cut in. "That is one of the reasons for his denunciation. But it might be wise to see Cranch and see what he advises."

When James arrived at the door, Cranch thought at first it was a social call, and he beamed and called over his shoulder to Nancy. James held up a hand as he stepped inside.

"I had rather my sister didn't hear this," he said in a low voice. "I shall be delighted to see her later, but for the moment you are the one I wish to consult." Cranch nodded, called to Nancy to wait, and then escorted James into his study.

It turned out he had already heard of Duncanson's tirades,

and his advice was to forget them. "Unless Captain Duncanson has openly, either in print or at a public meeting, accused you of either thievery, falsifying the records, or knowingly and wantonly causing his properties to lose their value, you have no case. The fact that he is upset is understandable, but unless he accuses you of deliberate malfeasance, knowing the inevitable results of such malfeasance, and thereby intending him direct personal harm, he has accused you of nothing more than ineptitude, which is not a crime. Believe me, dear brother, I have heard many accusations against you more vituperative than those of Duncanson, and while I have challenged some, I have not felt others worthy of reply. Most people, in trying to make someone out a villain, end by making themselves into one instead. It is far better to let them rant on than to call attention to them with a rebuttal."

"I admit my mistakes, but no man may question my motives." James's rage had made him pompous, because he could find no other way to express it.

"An honorable sentiment," Cranch replied. "But take my advice and do not let it goad you into making one more mistake."

"Then I shall challenge him to a duel."

"Dear God in heaven, not that."

"I had rather die on the field of honor, than live with a soiled name."

Cranch started to say something, then out of kindness stopped. "In that case, there is no way I can help you," he said. "The choice must be yours."

Eckman's reaction was somewhat the same. "Do you mean you are actually going to commit suicide?" he asked.

"Certainly not," James replied. "I am going to challenge him to a duel."

"It comes to the same thing. Have you held a pistol since we were in Moodus?"

"I don't believe so, but that's not the point. The point is—"

"The point is you are challenging an Army officer to a duel, using a weapon more dangerous to you than to him. You might as well pick up an adder and try to throw it at him."

"Then I shall call for swords."

"Worse. He will vivisect you on the spot. He will make hemstitching of your *ductus deferens*. Besides, I believe the challenged has the choice of weapons. Unless you are, as I said, intent on committing suicide, do not challenge this man to a duel."

James took a deep breath. "Will you be my second?"

"No."

"Then I'll get someone else." He sat at the table that served as a writing desk, and picked up a quill and paper.

"What are you doing?"

"Writing the challenge. Will you deliver it for me?"

"No."

"Then I'll do it myself." James began to write, and for a while there was silence, broken only by the staccato scratching of the quill. Finally Eckman sighed.

"Very well," he said. "Since you are determined to kill yourself, the least I can do is pick up the remains."

James nodded, and when he finished writing he sanded the letter, folded it and handed it to Eckman. "I shall await his pleasure," he said. "But the sooner the better."

In the icy predawn darkness of January 6, 1799, James and Eckman huddled under a bearskin robe in the cab that took them from their rooming house over the frozen ruts of Pennsylvania Avenue, past the Capitol construction on Jenkins Hill, then northeastward to the Bladensburg Road and the Maryland line. Neither of them spoke; James's tongue and mouth seemed made of wood and his head ached from the sleepless night behind him, while Eckman was absorbed in thoughts of his own so deep that he seemed unaware of anything at hand. The sky had begun to turn gray as their cab crossed the creek known as Blood Run, their horse's hoofs making a hollow clop on the bridge, and then they saw dim lights in the windows of the Bladensburg Tavern. The adjoining field, which was the dueling ground, was still dark, with darker patches indicating stands of trees. A carriage stood in front of the tavern, and when James and Eckman went inside they saw two men sitting in the far corner. The men didn't look at them, but James knew immediately which one was Duncanson and which his second. Even sitting down Duncanson looked tall, and his face had the impassive look of a man shopping for a new hat. His second was smaller but equally at ease, and James wondered how many times the two had been through this same thing. He also wondered why there weren't more peo-

ple present; he'd always heard there were several witnesses to a
duel, as well as a doctor to care for any wounds that might result. Duncanson, he thought, must be extremely sure of himself
not to have brought a doctor.

"Shouldn't there be a doctor here?" he asked Eckman, mois-
tening his lips. "I mean, just in case of—"

Eckman looked at him oddly. "It may have escaped your
memory," he said, "but I am a doctor."

"Of course, but—I mean, would you tend to *him?*"

For a moment, it looked as though Eckman were smiling. "A
doctor takes no sides," he replied. "Where a wound appears, he
treats it."

"I imagine that's right."

James lapsed into silence, and Eckman said, "Would you care
for a tot of rum, for warmth?"

"If you please. I don't seem to have any blood today." As he
said it, James visualized blood spurting from his bullet-punc-
tured heart and quickly added, "That is—my circulation isn't all
it might be."

They had two rums, and just as James was beginning to feel
better he heard the scrape of chairs and saw Duncanson and his
second rising from their table. He realized that daylight was tint-
ing the room, and when he looked out a window he saw the
sharp outline of the trees against the overcast sky. Duncanson
went past without looking at him, but his second nodded to Eckman, who rose.

"Very well, then," Eckman said to James. "Let us proceed."

James felt stunned as he pushed himself up from the table. He
was bereft of thought and his muscles felt like melting wax, and
his instinct was to remain seated at the table and plead a sudden
illness. But he knew this had been his idea and there was no escaping it, so with as great an outward show of calm as he could
muster, he followed Eckman out into the cold, where his breath
made clouds of steam and his ears felt as though they'd been
shaved by knives. The walk to the dueling ground was short;
Eckman went ahead and conferred with Duncanson's second,
and after what seemed to James like a long time he turned, with
the pistol case under his arm, and paced off a measured distance. Then he indicated where James should stand, and held out
the pistol case to him. One pistol lay there, its silver chasings

glinting dully and its flinted hammer already cocked. It looked alive, like the adder Eckman had mentioned earlier. James picked it up, hoping his hand wouldn't tremble too violently.

Then Eckman backed away, and James was looking at Duncanson, who seemed much too close. At this range Duncanson couldn't miss, whereas only by the wildest luck could James's bullet hope to find the target. He was about to protest and ask for a greater distance where neither one could be sure of hitting, when Duncanson's second began the count. At the command James squinted his eyes and pulled the trigger; he saw the puff of smoke and flame from the pan, and that was all. There was no report and no kick, and what was more important, there was nothing from Duncanson's pistol. He stared in disbelief as Duncanson donned his cape and walked off the field, and then he felt Eckman take his pistol from him and give it to Duncanson's second.

"What happened?" James asked, his voice rising. "Why didn't he shoot?"

"Don't excite yourself," Eckman said, putting James's cape around his shoulders. "It's all turned out for the best."

"I demand to know what happened!" James shouted. "If you won't tell me, I'll find someone who will!" By now Duncanson and his second were entering their carriage, and James could see nobody but Eckman.

"I'll tell you on the way back," Eckman said. "Would you like a rum, for your circulation?"

"I shall not budge from this spot until you explain! That is final!"

"There's no mystery. You had a blank load, and Duncanson had none. The code duello says—"

"But why? Whose idea was that?"

Eckman cleared his throat. "The code duello says that when there is an obvious mismatch—"

"Was it yours?"

". . . the challenger's honor may be satisfied by—"

"I repeat, was this your idea?"

"Not exactly. We all agreed it was more sensible this way. The challenger's honor may—"

"You arranged this entire farce without consulting me. I am the one whose honor was at stake!"

"Your honor has been vindicated. The code—"

"I care not one damn for the code. I have been cheated!"

Eckman's tone, which had been placating, hardened. "You are at least alive," he said. "Would you rather be alive and, as you so self-pityingly put it, cheated, or would you rather have your precious honor and at this very moment be a drooling corpse or, worse, thrashing on the ground in your final agony? Those were your only choices, and you know it. You can credit your life with the fact that Captain Duncanson felt it beneath his dignity to shoot you."

James whirled around and stamped off to the cab, got inside, and ordered the driver to start off. As they clattered away from the tavern and crossed Blood Run, he could see Duncanson's carriage far ahead down the road, and his first thought was to tell the driver to overtake it and force it to stop, so he could confront Duncanson then and there, but after a few minutes, when his pulse had stopped racing, a cool breeze of sanity wafted through his head, and he began to relax. Finally, as they were nearing the District line, he told the driver to turn around and return to the tavern.

Eckman was in the taproom, and neither one said a word as James took off his cape and sat down at the table. Eckman had a rum in front of him, and James motioned to the tavern keeper for the same, and when it arrived he bobbed it in salute and took a sip. It felt warm and sweet as it went down, and for several minutes James stared into his mug, trying to frame his thoughts in the proper words. Finally, after several false starts, he spoke.

"I think one trouble," he said, slowly, "is that so many people misunderstand me."

"Including you," said Eckman.

There was a pause of several seconds, then James said, "Possibly. But I'd just as soon you didn't bruit it about."

EPILOGUE

James was alone in his Washington house on Wheat Row when the messenger arrived with the word of Nancy's illness. His wife, Ann, was visiting relatives in Allentown, and he was left in a house that was too big for him but one he couldn't sell, because of liens against any large amounts of cash that might come his way. He was intestate because there was nothing to leave in any will he might make; his only holdings were in unimproved or unproductive real estate, and the suits that had dragged on through the years had consumed virtually every negotiable bit of property, not only his but that of many of his friends and relatives as well. He still remembered a letter Daniel had written him a few years before, which had burned itself into his mind until he could repeat every word. It wasn't the anguish of the letter that hurt him so much as it was the fact that it came from Daniel, who had been his main support during the days of the disaster, defending him against the sniping and caterwauling of ex-friends, creditors, and other enemies. This letter had dealt with the ordinary run of business, of trying to find something of value with which to placate the creditors who continued to press for satisfaction on their notes, and then Daniel had written:

I can truly say that from the first moment I knew those lots were conveyed to Mr. D., I gave up all expectation of a single cent benefit from them; and I wish not to play the dog in the manger and deprive another of a blessing because I may not partake in it. On the other hand, I am unwilling to put my name to any paper which may deprive a single individual of your creditors of a chance for *remuneration* tho' ever so small (for myself, I have long since given up all expectations of that sort). Nearly 15 years have elapsed since I became responsible on your account! it is almost 13 years since I was driven from my business! my home! my native town! in consequence of that responsibility; and yet the business (to my view) is as far from being bro't to a close as it was ten years ago.—But I mean not to complain; I know from past experience that complaining availeth nothing . . .

James had wept when he received the letter, then had composed himself and written a cool and impersonal reply, instructing Daniel to do as he saw fit with the lots in question. By now he was inured to the liquidation or collapse of his various holdings; as far back as 1803 he had found out that the large tract of land in Vermont on which he was counting had been obtained by a so-called snatched judgment, that is, in actions against defendants some of whom were dead, and the subsequent appeals and writs of error nullified the land as a tangible asset. That was only a part of the pattern, but it was typical of the way in which things could fly apart at the most inconvenient times.

Now, as he dressed to go to the Cranch residence, he worried about Nancy because he knew Cranch wouldn't have sent for him unless she were desperately ill. She had been in precarious health all the previous winter, and the damp cold that hung over the Potomac had filled her lungs with rheum and made her eyes bright with fever. At seventy-one she no longer had the stamina to fight off a fever, and Eckman, although not the Cranch family physician, had told James he thought she should be moved to a different climate if she were to survive. James, seven years her senior, had replied that if he could stand the climate there was no reason she couldn't, and besides, it was not up to him to tell his brother-in-law what to do. But he was nevertheless concerned, because she and Becca were his only two surviving sisters, and with himself, Daniel, and John, they were the last of the fifteen children of William and Mary Greenleaf.

As he stepped out of the cab at Nancy's house, he knew he was too late. The house looked as it always had, but there was something empty about it, and when the door was opened by a weeping maid his instinct was confirmed. He went in and up to Nancy's room and then wished he hadn't, because instead of his sister on the bed there was a little old lady made of wax, whose jaw was bound to keep it from sagging open. He kissed her cold forehead, then went downstairs to find her husband. Cranch was in the library, staring out the window, and the two men embraced and said small and meaningless things. James stayed with him until other members of the family began to arrive, and then he quietly got his cape and started home. He found he was uneasy with the others; their affluence reproached him, and those who were cordial to him were trying just a shade too hard. (With those who looked straight through him, he at least knew where he stood.) The thing he hated most was the faint air of condescension he caught in passing.

And it was the condescension, if he were really to be honest about it, that had increasingly come between Ann and himself. It had been her dowry that kept them going during the first years of their marriage, while James still had hopes that his investments might pay off, and then, as one plan after another fell through and the creditors remained strident, it was she who had gone to her family for money, so that her and James's daughters, Mary and Margaret, could be brought up in proper Washington society. James had tried to maintain the fiction that it was his money and for a while Ann played along, but more and more often he found her looking at him when he mentioned money matters, and the look she gave him was one of weary impatience. When, two weeks ago, she left to go to Allentown, her parting remark was, "Do you think you can survive until I get back?"

"I believe so," James replied. "I survived very nicely the first thirty-five years of my life."

"Yes, dear," she said, and she got in the carriage and drove off.

As he neared home, James thought back on his sister Nancy, lying silent in her bed beyond care or worry or grief, totally and irrevocably at peace, and suddenly he envied her. It was the peace he envied most, and he thought if he could have that peace, and still be alive, he would have achieved the best that any man could hope for. The trick would be to gain it without dying, and that was . . . He stopped, as an idea began to take form, and then walked on more slowly, pondering the different angles. Instead of going home he went to Eckman's office, where he found his friend puttering among some bottles of what looked like urine.

"I have a theory," Eckman said, without waiting for James to speak. "I think the stone is formed in the water, not the kidney. It's something in the water that turns solid."

"Could you get me a cadaver?" James asked.

Eckman stopped, and looked at him. "I beg your pardon?"

"I said, could you get me a cadaver. An anonymous corpse, in a plain coffin, to be delivered to my house."

"May I ask why?"

"I'll explain when you tell me if you can do it."

"I suppose I can. But not this afternoon—it may take a while."

"Tomorrow?"

"Perhaps. Does it matter which gender?"

"Male, if possible."

"I can do no more than try. Now, may I be let in on the secret?"

"When you bring it to my house, I'll tell you."

With that James left the office and walked on home, where he went upstairs to make notes for his obituary.

BIBLIOGRAPHY

Alexander, John. *Ghosts*. Washington, D.C.: Washingtonian Books, 1975.

American Guide Series. *Washington: City and Capital*. Washington, D.C.: Federal Writers' Project, 1937.

Bryan, W. B. *History of the National Capital*. Vol. 1. New York: Macmillan, 1914.

Clark, Allen C. *Greenleaf and Law in the Federal City*. Washington, D.C.: Columbia Historical Society, n.d.

Coffin, Margaret M. *Death in Early America*. New York: Thomas Nelson, 1976.

Davidson, Marshall B. *Life in America*. Vol. 1. Boston: Houghton Mifflin, 1951.

Flexner, James Thomas. *George Washington*. Vols. 3, 4. Boston: Little, Brown, 1969, 1972.

Green, Constance. *Washington: Village and Capital*. Princeton University Press, 1962.

Greenleaf, James Edward. *Genealogy of the Greenleaf Family 1574–1896*. Boston: Frank Wood, 1896.

Greenleaf, Jonathan. *A Genealogy of the Greenleaf Family*. New York: Edward O. Jenkins, 1854.

Greenleaf, Lewis Stone, III. Collection of letters from and about James Greenleaf, also balance sheets, deeds of property, receipts, etc., involved in various Greenleaf transactions.

Jones, Howard Mumford, and Bessie Zaban. *The Many Voices of Boston*. Boston: Little, Brown, 1975.

Laing, Alexander. *Seafaring America*. New York: American Heritage Press, 1974.

Langer, William L., ed. *An Encyclopedia of World History*. Boston: Houghton Mifflin, 1968.

Miller, Nathan. *The Founding Finaglers*. New York: David McKay, 1976.

Morison, Samuel Eliot. *The Oxford History of the American People*. New York: Oxford University Press, 1965.

Netherlands Bicentennial Committee. *The Dutch Republic in the Days of John Adams*. Amsterdam: 1976.

Raubenheimer, H. C. *Pharmacy and Pharmacists in Colonial Boston.* Massachusetts Historical Society, n.d.

Russell, Francis. *Adams: An American Dynasty.* New York: American Heritage Press, 1976.

Wagner, Frederick. *Robert Morris: Audacious Patriot.* New York: Dodd, Mead, 1976.